ACCEPTABLE LOSSES

Acceptable Losses

IRWIN SHAW

BOOK CLUB ASSOCIATES LONDON

This edition published 1983 by
Book Club Associates
by arrangement with New English Library

© 1982 by Irwin Shaw

Printed in Great Britain by
Richard Clay (The Chaucer Press) Ltd.
Bungay, Suffolk

To Charles Tucker

'Sir,' the Aide said to the Commanding Officer, 'G1, G2, G3, and G4 concur in the opinion that the proposed plan for the operation has an 85 percent chance of success, with acceptable losses.'

From this and other missions forty-four of our aircraft are missing.

The National Safety Council predicted yesterday that there would be five hundred and fifty-eight fatal traffic accidents over this forthcoming holiday weekend.

CHAPTER
ONE

HE WAS having a pleasant dream when the bedroom telephone extension awoke him. In the dream he was a little boy, holding his father's hand, walking on a sunny autumn day toward the Yale Bowl in New Haven to watch his first football game.

'Sheila,' he mumbled, 'get it, will you . . .' The telephone was on the table next to his wife's side of the bed. Then he remembered his wife wasn't there. He groaned and pushed himself stiffly across the bed. The glow of the arrows on the small clock on the table pointed toward three-thirty. He groaned again as he fumbled for the phone and picked it up.

'Damon,' the voice said. It was a voice he did not recognize, rough and hoarse.

'Yes?'

'Mr Damon,' the voice said, 'I heard the good news and I wanted to be one of the first to congratulate you.'

'What?' Damon said, dazed, his speech thick. 'Who's this? What good news?'

'All in due time, Roger,' the voice said. 'I read the papers like everybody else. And I decided from what I know about you you're one of those nice people who like to share their good fortune – spread it around, so to speak.'

'It's past three in the morning – what in the name of God do you think . . . ?'

'It's Saturday night. I thought you might be home celebrating with friends. Saturday night and all, maybe you would invite me up for a drink . . .'

'Oh, quit, Mister,' Damon said wearily, 'and let me sleep.'

9

'Plenty of time for sleep. Roger, you've been a bad boy and you're going to have to do something about it.' The tone was heavily playful.

'What?' Damon shook his head confusedly, wondered if this was another dream. 'What the hell are you talking about?'

'You know what I'm talking about, Roger.' Now the tone was not playful, but menacing. 'This is Zalovsky. From Chicago.'

'I don't know any Zalovskies. And I haven't been in Chicago in years.' Damon allowed his wakening anger to sharpen his voice. 'What the hell do you mean by calling me up in the middle of the night? I'm going to hang up and . . .'

'My advice is not to hang up, Roger,' the man said. 'I have to talk to you.'

'I don't have to talk to *you*. Good night, Sir. I'm hanging up right now . . .'

'I'd hate to see you do something you'd only be sorry for – very sorry, Roger – something like hanging up on Zalovsky. I want to talk to you, I said. And I want to talk to you tonight.'

'I'm not in Chicago. Or didn't you notice that when you dialed my number?' Thoroughly awake now, he wanted to strike back at the man, even if it was only over the telephone. 'What are you, man – one of those telephone nuts?' Then it occurred to him that perhaps it was one of his friends, drunk at an all-night party or in a bar, playing a practical joke on him. In his business he had accumulated some strange friends. 'Okay, okay,' he said, more calmly. 'What have you got to say for yourself?'

'Not for me to say anything for myself,' the man said. 'I'm the boss here, Mister. And I'm not in Chicago; I'm just a couple of blocks away from you. On Eighth Street. Why don't you get out of your woolies and put some clothes on and meet me at your corner in say, let's say ten minutes, give you time to brush your teeth and comb your hair . . .' The man laughed, a brief tuneless bark.

'I don't know what you think you're doing, Mr Zalovsky,' Damon said, 'but if you have any business with somebody called Damon, you've got the wrong Damon. You might make sure you're not making a mistake calling up a man in the middle of the night and . . .'

'Zalovsky isn't in the habit of making mistakes. I have the right Roger Damon and you know it. You better meet me in ten minutes. If not . . .' The man cleared his throat. 'If not, there will be consequences, Roger, consequences that you won't like, not like at all . . .'

'Fuck you,' Damon said.

'Without the bad language and before you hang up, Roger,' Zalovsky said, 'one last warning. It's a matter of life and death. *Your* life and *your* death.'

'Fuck you again,' Damon said. 'You've been seeing too many gangster movies.'

'You've been warned, Roger. I may not call you again.'

Damon banged the phone down, cutting off the hateful thick voice.

He had been lying stretched across the bed to reach the telephone, but now he swung around and sat up. He knew there was no use in trying to get back to sleep. He ran his hand through his hair, then pushed at his eyes. His hands were trembling and he was angry with himself because of it. It was a good thing his wife wasn't home this weekend, but visiting her mother in Vermont. The call would have frightened her, then angered her, then made her suspicious and she'd have quizzed him for hours about just what he had done to get a threatening telephone call at three-thirty in the morning. It would have turned into one of their infrequent arguments in which she would use the phrase 'your well-known proclivities' and 'with your past . . .' By nature she was a calm woman, but she didn't like mysteries. When she worried about him or when she felt he was perversely keeping some pain or a problem from her, she became abusive. He wondered if it would be wiser not to tell her about the call. Before she came home he'd think up some excuse for changing sides of the bed with her so that he would be the one who would answer the telephone. She would be suspicious about that, too, because she knew he hated to speak on the phone. She was his second wife. He had lived with his first wife for less than a year and was divorced by the time he was twenty-four. He had married for the second time at the age of forty, and during the more than twenty years of their marriage Sheila had invented – or, to be honest, not completely invented –

II

a lurid notion of his history before they had met. She was fifteen years younger than he and if anybody was to be jealous, it should have been himself. No logic in marriage.

Ah, he thought, it was probably one of those tricks kids indulged in to amuse themselves – picking a number at random out of the telephone book and calling to make obscene suggestions or outlandish threats, with their friends giggling in the background. But the voice hadn't been a kid's and there had been no giggling in the background. Still, he wouldn't say anything about it to Sheila. The man had said he might not call again. Until he did he might as well have peace in the family. He hoped Sheila was enjoying her visit in Vermont and would be in a good mood when she got back.

In the meantime . . . In the meantime, what?

He sighed, turned on the light. It was cold in the apartment and he put on a warm robe, remembering the taunting voice saying, 'woolies.' He went into the living room. It was dark. He had come into some money recently but the frugal habits of a lifetime persisted. He turned on all the lights. The room was comfortable, a little battered, overflowing with books. The apartment was a top floor through in a converted rent-controlled brownstone and none of the rooms was large. His wife was constantly after him to get rid of some of the books and he kept promising to do so. But somehow the books piled up.

Robe or no robe, he was still cold, shivering a little. He walked stiffly. He was in the middle sixties, solidly built, with a ruddy outdoorsman's face that was the result of his walking bare-headed the two miles to the office and back each day, no matter what the weather was, and long, solitary hikes during his vacations. Still, it took a half-hour after getting out of bed for his legs to warm up.

He picked the Manhattan telephone directory off the bottom shelf of one of the bookcases and put it on a table under the light of a lamp. He was proud of the fact that although he wore reading glasses, when necessary, if the light was good, he could read the names and numbers in the telephone book without their aid.

He turned to the D's. He saw his name, Damon, Roger, and the address on West Tenth Street. It was the only Roger Damon listed in Manhattan. Although his name was also in the book under G's. There was Gray, Damon and Gabrielsen, literary agency. Gray had started the firm and taken Damon on as a partner when Damon was under thirty. Gray had been dead for years but out of loyalty to the old man Damon had not changed the name of the agency. Loyalty had its virtues, especially at times like this. Gabrielsen was a recent addition, under different circumstances.

He closed the book and put it neatly on its shelf. No clues for Sheila when she came home. He would wait for the appropriate moment to tell her what had happened. If any moment could be considered appropriate.

He poured himself a stiff whiskey and soda from the table against the wall and drank it slowly, deep in his favorite armchair. The drink didn't help him make any sense of what had happened at three-thirty that morning. New York is full of madmen, he thought. Not only New York. America. The world. Random assassins prowling the streets. Presidents, popes, people waiting in railroad stations, coming out of churches or department stores. Life and death, the man had said. *Your* life, *your* death.

Unless it was all a grotesque prank, somewhere a stranger or somebody who knew him and wished him ill was waiting for him. He was too tired now to try to figure out who that might be and why he was waiting or had waited until now.

Night thoughts.

He shivered. When he went into the bedroom to try to sleep, he left all the lights in the living room on.

CHAPTER
TWO

HE WAS awakened by the sound of bells. He had been dreaming. Once again it was his father in the dream, but alone, in a bright light that glowed off his smiling and loving face. He looked young, as he had when Damon was about ten, not like the gaunt, exhausted man he became toward the end. He was leaning over what seemed like a carved marble balustrade, beckoning with one hand. In the other hand he held a small piebald hobby horse. His father had been a maker of children's toys, a manufacturer of gewgaws and trinkets. He had been dead twenty years.

The ringing this time was not the telephone. Church bells. Sunday morning. Calling New York to worship. Come, all ye faithful of the Imperial City – come, ye adulterers, ye blackmailers, stock-riggers, jury-fixers, drunkards, drug addicts, muggers, murderers, perjurers, bag ladies, disco freaks, joggers, marathon runners, prison guards, shooters-up and shooters-down, come you believers and preachers of false doctrine, come and worship the God that may or may not have made you in His image.

Damon stirred in the bed. Not having Sheila beside him made him feel strange. Then he remembered the call during the night. He looked at his watch. Nine o'clock. Usually he was up by seven. Nature had been kind to him, it had allowed him to sleep from four to nine. Five hours of forgetfulness. Sunday's gift.

He pushed himself out of bed and instead of going into the bathroom and brushing his teeth and showering, padded barefoot into the living room. All the lights were still on. He went to the front door, looked to see if there was an envelope, a message lying on the floor there. Nothing.

He examined the lock. It was flimsy, simple. A child could have picked it open with a pen-knife. In all the years he had lived in New York he had never been robbed, had never thought about locks. The door was wooden, old, had been installed when the building was put up. When? 1900? 1890? He would have it changed, get one with a steel sheath, an unpickable lock, a peep-hole, a chain. There was no doorman below and all the tenants of the building, including Sheila and himself, were careless about pushing the button that opened the front door when the buzzer went off in their apartments. The speaking apparatus by which you were supposed to inquire who was below before pressing the button had been broken for years. As far as Damon knew neither he nor his neighbors had ever complained to the landlord and demanded that it be put in order. Innocents, falsely secure. Tomorrow.

He made himself breakfast. When Sheila was home on Sunday she fed him freshly squeezed orange juice, pancakes and bacon with maple syrup. Today he drank a cup of coffee and made do with a slice of yesterday's bread.

His ordinary Sunday ritual was different. While Sheila was preparing breakfast he went and bought two copies of the Sunday *Times*, because both he and Sheila liked doing the big Sunday crossword puzzle without interference by the other, and they spent the mornings in amicable silence at opposite ends of the kitchen table scratching away. It was a point of honor with them to do the puzzles in ink. The two huge bundles of news, opinion, results, advertisements, praise and condemnation represented something of an extravagance, but it was a weekend treat and the quiet pleasure of the hour or so after breakfast was worth it.

He dressed and went down the dimly lit and silent stairs. His neighbors all seemed to be sleeping late. He wondered if any of them had a telephone call in the middle of the night. There were no notes in his mailbox, either.

He touched his pocket to make sure he had his keys, that he could get back into the house and went out onto the small stoop that led down to the street. It was a raw, gray day, with gusts of cold wind. Spring was late this year. He looked up and down the street. A fat woman with two small dogs on a leash and a young man pushing a baby carriage made up the Sunday morning traffic. No ambushes there, at least as far as he could tell. For all he knew, to a trained eye the street might have been full of ominous signs. He grimaced, displeased with his nervousness.

At the kiosk he hesitated briefly, trying to decide whether to buy one or two copies of the paper. He picked up two of them, annoyed, as always, with the senseless bulk and weight. He doubted that Sheila would have gotten the Sunday *Times* in Vermont and she would be grateful if she saw that he had been thinking of her in her absence and had saved a copy of the puzzle for her when she got home, even if she didn't have time to do it. He glanced at the first page. The name *Zalovsky* was not on it. Perhaps that wasn't his real name. Maybe his name was actually Smith or Brown and Zalovsky was his *nom de guerre* and on the inside pages there would be a story describing the many crimes he had committed, for which the police of ten states were now searching for him. Although adopting a name like Zalovsky, for whatever vengeance or misdeed the man contemplated, seemed, Damon had to admit, needlessly elaborate. The notion made him smile. As he made his way home he glanced at the passersby without suspicion. The morning had fallen into its ordinary Sunday pattern and when the clouds parted for a few moments and the street reflected the rays of the sun, he found himself humming comfortably as he approached his door. But when he sat down to do the crossword puzzle it was with difficulty that he managed just a few lines. Either the puzzle was harder than usual or his mind wasn't on it. He tossed the magazine section aside and opened the book review section to the bestseller list. *Threnody*, by Genevieve Dolger, was still on it. Number four. Despite the title it had been on for twelve weeks now. Damon shook his head ruefully, remembering that it was only because of Oliver Gabrielsen's insistence that he had agreed to work on it with the author and try to sell it and that they had nearly parted company because of it.

Oliver Gabrielsen was his assistant and had been with him nearly fifteen years. He was an omnivorous reader, with a remarkable memory and a shrewd if somewhat eccentric eye for unusual material. Oliver had met Mrs Dolger at a party outside of Roslyn, Long Island, not the kind of place in which best-sellers ordinarily were found. The author was a woman in her fifties, whose husband was the vice-president of a small bank. She had four children and had never written anything before and had begun the novel, it seemed to Damon, mostly out of boredom with her life as a suburban matron. It was a simple-minded fantasy about a poor girl who made her way up in the world by using her beauty, her body and her appetite for men and who finally came to a tragic end. It was the oldest of stories and Damon couldn't understand why Oliver was so keen on it. Most of the time their tastes were similar, but when Oliver said, 'Money. This book has money written all over it. For once, let's get a piece of the big pie for ourselves,' Damon had shaken his head skeptically. 'Oliver, my poor boy,' he had said, 'I'm afraid you're working too hard or going to too many parties.'

Still, to keep peace in the office and because it was a slack time when everybody was out of New York for the summer, he had worked with the woman, who was a placid and undemand-ing soul, on making the book at least presentable, toning down the more explicit love scenes and the surprisingly rough lan-guage and correcting the grammar. She had been easy to convince about everything except the title. Although he had warned her that *Threnody* was the sort of title that emptied book stores, she had been obdurate and deaf to all argument. He had sighed and given in. To her credit, after the book's success she had never taunted him about his doleful prediction. Unprofes-sional in everything she did, she had insisted upon his taking 20 percent of all her earnings on the book instead of the usual agent's 10 percent. Half-jokingly he had warned her to keep this act of wanton generosity absolutely secret, since if the news got out, she risked being boycotted for the rest of her life by every writers' organization in the country.

It was not the sort of book that either he or his old partner Gray had ever bothered with before. For the most part they had devoted themselves to discovering young writers and nursing them along to good reviews and modest sales, often keeping the writers alive out of their own pockets while they were finishing their books or plays. Neither of them had ever made a great deal of money, and a disappointing percentage of the young men and women they had helped had turned out to be one-book writers or had taken to dope or drink or had disappeared in Hollywood.

He had had small hope for Mrs Dolger's book and was almost relieved when a half-dozen houses had turned down the novel in quick succession. He had been ready to call the lady in Roslyn and tell her, with polite regret, that the book was unsaleable when a small publishing house took it, paying an infinitesimal advance for a small first printing. It had risen quickly to the top of the bestseller list, had sold to the paperbacks for a million dollars and had been bought for Hollywood.

His commissions were, for him, astronomical. For the first time, his name had been mentioned in the newspapers and his office was being flooded with manuscripts by well-known and highly paid writers who were dissatisfied with their current agents for one reason or another and most of whom he had never even met in his long career in the business.

'The roll of the dice,' Oliver had said complacently. 'Finally we had to come up with a seven.' He had demanded that his salary be doubled and that his name be put on the door as a partner. Damon was pleased to be able to accede to both requests, had changed the name of the firm to Gray, Damon and Gabrielsen and had merely asked Oliver to attend fewer parties. But he had firmly refused to move out of what Oliver described as their sorry two-room excuse for an office to more splendid and what Oliver considered in their new affluence, would be more appropriate quarters. 'Face it, Roger,' Oliver had said, 'when anybody walks in here, they think we've furnished this place as a set for *Bleak House* and they look to see if we're still using quill pens.'

'Oliver,' Damon had said, 'let me explain myself, although by now you've been with me for so long I shouldn't have to. I've put in almost my whole working life in what you call this sorry excuse for an office and I've been lucky here and loved coming to work here in the morning. I have no wish to become a tycoon and I've made a decent living, although perhaps not by what modern young people think are proper standards. I have no wish to look out over a sea of desks and know the people at them

18

are working for me and demanding that I hire them, fire them, judge them and pay their social security and pension plans and God knows what else. The case of *Threnody* is a freak, lightning striking once. To tell the truth I hope nothing like it ever happens again. I cringe when I pass it in a book store window and my weekends have been ruined by seeing it on the list every Sunday in the *Times*. I have gotten infinitely more pleasure out of ten brilliant lines in a manuscript by an unknown young writer than I ever will out of the royalty statements on *Threnody*. As for you, my old friend, you are young and as is the custom these days, rapacious.' This was a bit unfair and Damon knew it, but he wanted to make his point. Oliver Gabrielsen was not as young as all that – he was approaching forty – and was as devoted to the service of decent writing as Damon himself and when he had asked for raises, he had done so almost apologetically, and Damon knew that if it weren't for his wife's salary Oliver would be living close to the poverty line. He also knew that Oliver had often received offers to work as an editor in publishing houses at much higher wages than he received from Damon and had turned them down because of what he considered the unbridled commercialism of the big houses which could afford what must have seemed like princely wages to him after the iron rations he received from Damon. But the unexpected tide of money that was rolling through the office seemed to have temporarily unhinged him and the percentage of the commissions which he now received as a partner had noticeably changed the fashion in which he dressed and the restaurants in which he lunched, and he had moved from a dingy apartment on the West Side to a smart address in the East Sixties. Damon, as was to be expected, blamed Oliver's wife, Doris, who had given up her job and now appeared from time to time in the office in a mink coat.

'You may be too young, Oliver,' Damon continued, enjoying the opportunity of lecturing on a subject on which his old employer, Mr Gray, had often expanded, 'to know the comfort of modesty; the arrogance, even, of rejoicing in moderate aims and even more moderate worldly achievements, to know that the things that other men are pressuring themselves into the grave to reach are of no consequence to you. I have never had a sick day in my life and I've never had an ulcer or high blood pressure or visited a psychiatrist. The only time I've been in a hospital it was because I was hit by an automobile while crossing the street and was laid up with a bad leg.'

'Knock wood,' Oliver had said. 'Better knock wood.'

Damon could see he was not taking the lecture graciously.

'I'm not suggesting we rent the Taj Mahal, for Christ's sake,' Oliver went on. 'It wouldn't kill us if we each had a room for ourselves and a decent place where we could put another secretary to help with all the damned mail. And with all the calls we're getting these days it's pretentious to have only one telephone line. Just last week a guy at Random House told me he dialed our number for two days before he could get through. The next time he wants to communicate with us he said he was going to use tom-toms. Putting in a switchboard wouldn't mean that everybody thought you were surrendering your soul to the Philistines. And it wouldn't be sinful luxury if we had windows that were washed once every six months. Here, if I want to know what the weather is outside I have to listen to the radio.'

'When I'm gone,' Damon said, purposely sonorous, 'you can hire a floor at Rockefeller Center and have the winner of the Miss America contest for your receptionist. But while I'm still here, we'll conduct our business as usual.'

Oliver sniffed. He was a diminutive blond man, almost an albino, and to make up for it he carried himself very erectly, with his shoulders militarily squared. Sniffing was uncharacteristic for him. 'When you're gone,' he said. 'You won't be gone for a thousand years.' They were good friends, as they had to be, working in their shirt-sleeves so close to each other day after day, and there was no ceremony between them.

'As I've told you repeatedly,' Damon said, 'I intend to retire as soon as possible and catch up on reading all the books I haven't had time to read keeping this office going.'

'I'll believe it when I see it,' Oliver said. But he smiled as he said it.

'I promise never even to visit you in your palatial new quarters,' Damon said. 'I'll be satisfied merely to collect the quarterly checks you're bound by our contract to send me and

20

trust that you haven't found yourself a thieving accountant to doctor the books.'

'I'll cheat you out of your back teeth,' Oliver said. 'I promise.'

'So be it,' Damon said, patting him on the shoulder. 'And now let's leave it at that. As a concession to your sensibilities I'll pay a man myself to wash the windows tomorrow.'

They both laughed then went back to their work.

Sitting in the cluttered living room, with the Sunday bells still ringing and the book review open before him to the bestseller list, he recalled the conversation with Oliver and Oliver's words – 'Money. Money is written all over this book.'

Oliver had been right. Regrettably right.

Damon also remembered what Zalovsky had said – 'I read the papers like everybody else.' What Zalovsky didn't know was that a good part of the commissions had gone to pay off long-standing debts and to make the necessary repairs on the small house on Long Island Sound in Old Lyme, Connecticut, that a doting and childless uncle of Sheila's had left her in his will. They spent their summer vacations there and an occasional weekend, when they could manage it, trying to ignore its ramshackle condition. Now it would have a new roof, new plumbing and a new paint job. It would be ready for him when Damon found it was time to retire.

A simple case of attempted blackmail or extortion, Damon thought, the price of a few lines in some newspaperman's column on a slow day. Or was it as simple as that?

Still, it was a clue. He dialed the number in Roslyn. 'Genevieve,' he said when the lady herself answered the phone, 'have you seen the *Times* this morning?'

'Isn't it marvelous?' Genevieve said. She had a small defensive voice, as though she was used to being contradicted by her husband and children on all occasions. 'Week after week. It's like a fairy tale.'

More than you'll ever know, sweetheart, Damon thought. But, he said, 'You've touched the marrow of readers everywhere.' Before the sale to the paperbacks he would have

21

blushed to hear himself utter the words. 'I wanted to ask you – by any chance did you get a telephone call from a man called Zalovsky?'

'Zalovsky, Zalovsky?' Genevieve sounded uncertain. 'I don't remember. So many people keep calling these days. Television, radio, interviews . . . My husband says he's going to ask for an unlisted number . . .'

Another unlisted number, Damon thought. Succeed and hide. The American Way.

'Zalovsky . . .' Genevieve went on. 'Why do you ask?'

'I got a telephone call. About the book. He was quite vague. He said he might call again and I thought that perhaps he preferred dealing directly with you. As you know, there's only Oliver and myself and the secretary in the office, and since you hit it so big we find it hard to keep up with all the requests . . . It's not like in some of the big offices, with dozens of people and departments and all . . .'

'I know. They all turned my book down before I came to you.' The voice was not defensive now, but bitter and cold. 'And not with ordinary civility, either. You and Oliver were the first two true gentlemen I met since I wrote the book.'

'We try to keep in mind the old maxim, which my former partner Mr Gray liked to repeat – publishing is a gentleman's business. Of course that was a long time ago and times have changed. Still, it's nice to know that one's manners are appreciated in some quarters.' He was always uncomfortable when talking to Genevieve Dolger. His speech sounded in his ears as though it had been starched and ironed. He was disturbed that he could not speak normally to this woman whom circumstance had thrown into his life. He was not a man who dissembled. It was his policy, of which he was proud, that he said exactly what he thought to his clients, whether in praise or admonition. If they bridled at his criticism or became angry or overly defensive, he would tell them frankly that they would be happier with another office. That was the only way he could work, he explained to them. Now this woman, who had enriched him, made him speak as though he had a mouth full of marshmallows.

'Don't think that I'll ever forget your help or what I owe you,'

Genevieve was saying, her voice quivering. 'I'll be grateful to you two all my life for what you've done for me.'

'I'm sure you will,' Damon said, remembering all the authors who had at one time or another said much the same thing and then gone on, sometimes shamefacedly, sometimes in anger, to the large agencies which could introduce them to movie stars, send limousines to meet them at the airport, secure tickets at the last moment for Broadway hits that had been sold out for months, arrange television publicity campaigns throughout the country and business lunches in the best restaurants in town. 'Be sure to let me know when you get your unlisted number.'

'You'll be the first one I'll call, Roger,' she said, her voice, to Damon's sorrow, filled with genuine emotion.

'Oh,' he said, asking the question he knew she was waiting to be asked, 'how's the new book going?'

Genevieve sighed, a soft, sad sound over the wire. 'Oh, it's just terrible,' she said, 'I can't seem to get really going. I write a page and reread it and I know it's perfectly awful and I tear it up and then go bake a pie to keep from crying.'

'Don't worry about it,' Damon said, much relieved by her news. 'The beginnings're always the hardest. And don't press yourself. There's no hurry, you know.'

'You'll have to learn to be patient with me,' she said.

'I'm used to writers' blocks,' Damon said, knowing that he ought to cross his fingers as he pretended to accept the woman as a practitioner of that austere and terrifying profession. 'They come and go. Well, congratulations again and don't forget – if you need me just call.'

He hung up. If he was lucky, he thought, she would bake a hundred pies before she finished the new book, and he would have long since left the office and retired to the little house in Old Lyme on the shores of the Sound. At least, he thought, as he put down the telephone, Zalovsky hadn't gotten to her. If he had, she'd certainly have remembered the name.

He moved restlessly around the apartment. He had brought a long manuscript home with him to read during the weekend and picked it up and tried to read a few pages, but they made no sense to him and he tossed it aside. He went into the bedroom and carefully made the bed, something he hadn't done since the

23

day he was married. Genevieve Dolger with her pies, he with his bed. He looked at his watch. Sheila wouldn't be home for another six hours. Sundays without her were pointless. He decided to go out and take a walk until it was time to eat lunch. But just as he was putting on his coat the phone rang. He let it ring six times without moving toward the instrument, staring at it, hoping that whoever it was would get tired of waiting and stop. But the phone rang a seventh time. He picked it up, expecting to hear the heavy, hoarse voice. But it was the woman whose manuscript he had brought home with him and which he couldn't read for the moment.

'I just wanted to know if you'd finished reading my book,' the woman said. Her voice was the best thing about her – deep and musical. He had had a brief affair with her two years before. Sheila had said, when she was informed of it by a friend, that the woman had flung herself at his head. Sheila's phrases. For once the phrase had been accurate. After their second meeting the woman had said, 'I must tell you. You have the sexiest face of any man I've ever met. When you come into a room it's like a bull coming into the arena.' She had spent a year in Spain and she had read too much Hemingway and her speech was sprinkled with Iberian images. If she had used the word *cojones* he would not have touched either her or her manuscript. But she refrained and he had succumbed, even though he had never thought of himself in the terms in which she described him. Actually, he thought that when he came into a room he shambled. And he had never seen a bull with pale gray eyes like this. Look into the mirror and see an alien face.

The woman was fairly pretty and fairly intelligent and not a bad writer and kept her body in trim by going to a gym class daily. He had been flattered that such a woman would go to such lengths to get him into her bed. At his age. Well, sixty something was not the edge of the grave. In one of her rare bitter moments, Sheila had said to him, 'You *squander* yourself on women.' Marriage had not cured him of that particular weakness. The liaison had been agreeable, no more than that.

'I like what I've read so far,' he said. He had an image of her lying naked on the bed, the breasts taut, the gym legs muscled. He nearly invited her to have lunch with him, then decided

24

against it. Do not add to whatever testimony anyone is amassing against you. 'I'll try to finish it by tonight. I'll call you,' he said.

Then he went out and walked aimlessly around the streets of Greenwich Village. Nobody seemed to be following him. Usually, on Sundays, he and Sheila had late lunch at a small Italian restaurant which they both liked. *Buon giorno, Signor, Signora, va bene?* A gangster had been shot there several years before. Spaghetti with clam sauce. Cozy Sunday afternoons when they could unwind together and forget the stresses of the week behind them and the week ahead over a bottle of Chianti.

The restaurant was crowded and he had to wait for a table and the owner had asked after the health of the missing signora. The noisy people at the other tables made him feel lonelier than ever and the half-bottle of wine did not improve matters. As he ate, he wondered what it was like to be shot in a small Italian restaurant.

CHAPTER
THREE

WHEN HE got back after lunch there was a sheet of paper half-stuffed into the slot of his mailbox. He looked at it apprehensively, hesitated before he touched it, then pulled it out. The piece of paper had been torn from a sketch block and the message on it, scrawled in heavy black pencil, was from Gregor. 'We were passing by,' the message read, 'and rang your bell. We are rebuffed. Do you hide from us? Friends should be home on Sunday. We are celebrating. I will tell you about it when I see you. We wish to share our joy with our comrades. If you read this before midnight come to us. It will be a festa Hungarian style. There will be wine and women and hard sausage. At least *one* woman and *one* sausage. Avanti.'

Damon smiled as he read the note, then, as he climbed the stairs to the apartment, looked at his watch. It was not yet three o'clock and Sheila wasn't due home until six. He always enjoyed seeing Gregor Khodar and his hospitable and talented wife. Besides, Damon represented a playwright whose play was to go into rehearsal in September and he hoped Gregor could do the sets. Gregor, in his account of the process of his Americaniza-tion, had told him that he had started walking west when the Russians came into Budapest in 1956 and hadn't stopped until he reached New York. 'Whatever happened,' Gregor had once confided to Damon, 'I knew it would be bad for human beings. So I asked myself question – am I, Gregor Khodar, human being? I examined pros and cons. I decided, yes, maybe not highest class human being, but still in category.'

He had been twenty then, a penniless art student, and there

had been some dreadful times, of which he never spoke, before he established himself in New York. And he never disclosed whether or not he had left any family behind him.

Although he was proud of being Hungarian (a civilized people always caught in the wrong century was his way of describing his compatriots) he was not sentimental about it. 'Middle Europa,' he said, 'is like those coral atolls in the Pacific. The tide comes in – you don't see it. The tide goes out – it is there. The best that you can say for it is that it is peril to navigation. When I drink Tokay wine and I am little drunk I think there is after-taste of blood and sea water.'

With his high brow and receding sparse black hair, bland, archaic smile and round, comfortable middle-aged paunch, he looked, Damon had once told him, like a Buddha, contemplating mischief.

He spoke with a soft, peculiar accent, his dark Magyar face lit by deep, mocking eyes, his lips, with an extra little upturned curl like an ornamental bow which was meant to be hung on a wall but not for killing, making it seem that nothing he said was to be taken seriously. However, he was a dedicated and gifted artist and aside from his paintings, which had been exhibited in galleries all over the country, had done the scenery for many Broadway plays. He painted slowly and painstakingly and turned down commissions for plays by the dozen because they did not please him, so he could not afford to live like a rich man but made a jest of his poverty as compared to the affluence of his more accommodating colleagues.

His wife, Ebba, a large, lanky, sweet woman with a frontierswoman's worn face, came from Swedish stock in Minnesota and was a theatrical costume designer. Between them, aside from forming a devoted and socially most rewarding couple, they combined to make an extremely useful working team.

Damon had no idea what Gregor was celebrating, but a few hours of noise and conversation in their big loft near the Hudson River which the Khodars had converted into a studio in which they could both work and live would certainly be better than brooding through the long Sunday afternoon by himself.

Just in case Sheila arrived ahead of schedule he left a note saying that he was at Gregor's and for her to call. Sheila liked the couple and had even for once sat still enough for Gregor to paint her portrait the previous summer when the Khodars had visited them in Connecticut. Gregor had not been satisfied with his work and kept it on an easel in his studio so that he could keep dabbing at it from time to time. 'The problem, Sheila,' he had told her, 'is that you are noble, face, figure, character, everything, and they don't make paints anymore in the modern age to express nobility. At least not in human beings. People just don't look noble anymore. Only certain dogs, Newfoundlands, golden retrievers, Irish setters. Give me time, give me time. I must go back to the fifteenth century. It is not a short subway ride.'

Gregor greeted Damon with a hug and Ebba with a shy kiss on the cheek. Gregor, who had his own ideas about how an artist should dress, was wearing a checked flannel shirt with a large bright orange wool necktie and baggy corduroy pants. He had on a thick chocolate brown tweed jacket, which he wore in even the hottest weather. It was as though at one time in his life he had been so chilled that he would never be warm enough again.

Unlike other artists' studios there were no examples of Gregor's work on exhibition. Sheila's portrait on the easel was covered with a cloth and all his other canvases were stacked faces to the wall. 'I am afraid,' Gregor had explained, 'to look at what I have already done when I am doing something else. If I am tired or in rough passage, there would be great temptation to take easy way out – plagiarize myself. When I am drunk, late at night, all work done for the day, I look at them. I laugh or I cry, then I hide them again.'

Damon was relieved to see that it was not a large party, just a Mr and Mrs James Franklin, whom he had met several times before with Gregor. They were owners of a gallery they ran together on Madison Avenue. Both the Franklins were wearing No Nuke buttons and Damon remembered reading that there had been a demonstration that day against nuclear weapons.

There was also a pleasant, handsome lady by the name of Bettina Lacey of about sixty who had a divorced husband in her past and ran an antique store. They were all drinking wine, as Gregor had promised, and there were slim slices of hard Hungarian sausage arranged on a large platter, garnished with radishes.

After the greetings, and they had seated themselves, European fashion, around a large, scrubbed wood circular table, Damon asked, 'What's this about a celebration?'

'In good time, my friend,' Gregor said. 'First your drink.' He poured some wine into a glass for Damon. Damon saw the label. It was Tokay. When he sipped it he tasted neither blood nor sea water.

'Next,' Gregor said, 'Bettina must tell her story. Celebration after that. Bettina . . .' He made a sweeping gesture, spilling a little of his wine, in the direction of the lady who ran the antique store.

'Gregor,' Mrs Lacey protested, 'you've all just heard it.'

'Not Roger,' Gregor said. 'I want to see what he makes out of it. He is a hard-headed and honest man and I value his opinion on anything I do not understand myself. Commence.'

'Well,' the woman said, not completely reluctant, 'it's about my daughter. I think I told you, she's studying in Rome . . .'

'Yes,' Damon said.

'Aside from that, she tries to keep an eye out for any antiques – furniture, old silver, stuff like that that might turn up in Italy that I might be interested in. Last Sunday there was a great antique fair just outside Rome and she told me that she would be going and would write me about what she saw and what was available. I just got a letter from her two days ago explaining why she didn't go, even though she'd hired a car to drive out to it.' The lady sipped at her wine, as though the story she had to tell was a painful one and she had to reinforce herself to tell it. 'When she awoke Sunday morning, even before she got out of bed, she wrote, she had a feeling that she'd never had before – terrible apprehension, fear. In a vacuum, she said, without reason. She found she could hardly get herself together enough to make her breakfast and at the thought that she was going to have to drive a car out of the city, she broke into tears. She was all alone and she felt foolish, but she couldn't stop crying. And she's not a girl who cries easily. Even when she was an infant. She was shaking and it took her over an hour to get dressed. The feeling didn't leave her all that morning, in fact not all day, and she never even picked up the car. She just sat in the sun in the Borghese Gardens, not looking or speaking to anyone until it

29

got dark and then went back to her place and got into bed and fell dead asleep and didn't wake up until nine o'clock the next morning.' Mrs Lacey sighed, her face marked by sorrow, as though she felt guilty of not having been able to comfort her daughter on a day like that. She tried to smile and went on. 'Whatever it was that she'd been suffering from the day before had passed and she felt fine and rested and went down to get the morning newspaper on the way to the library where she was working. Then she saw the headlines. There had been a dreadful fire in the old wooden building where the fair was being held and all the doors had been locked and thirty people died.' She exhaled a long breath as though the telling of the story had exhausted her.

There was silence in the room for several moments.

'Do you believe in precognition, Mr Damon?' Franklin asked. He was a proper, businesslike man, who dealt in known quantities. From his tone Damon could tell he did not wish to make too much of the story of the daughter.

'Well,' Damon said, shaken more than he wished to show by the woman's recital, 'of course Jung and then Arthur Koestler . . .'

'Still, they never proved anything,' Franklin said. 'How about you, Gregor?'

'I believe in anything that can't be proven,' Gregor said. 'I think we all need another drink.'

As he went into the kitchen to get another cold bottle of wine, Mrs Lacey said, 'I'm sorry. I didn't want to spoil Gregor's party. Naturally, whatever it was, I'll raise my thanks to God for it the rest of my days.'

There was a small uncomfortable silence after she had spoken, the holiday mood broken for a moment. 'What's this about a celebration?' Damon asked, as much to keep himself from speculating about the troubling meaning of Mrs Lacey's daughter's behavior as to lighten the level of conversation.

'We've got joint foundation grant,' Gregor said, 'Ebba and me. For year in Europe. Generous. To refresh our talents at fountain of culture.' He grinned. 'Museums, opera, churches, rich dinners, French wines. It is better than food stamps.

America is bountiful place. Oil companies, Congress, the new Medicis. Except no strings attached. I do not have to paint pictures of oil derricks or portraits of corporation presidents or their wives. And Ebba does not have to design costumes for debutante daughters. I assure you, we will be good capitalists, we will not give them money's worth. We leave in a week. What's matter, Roger, you don't look happy.'

'Of course I'm happy,' Damon said. 'For you. But I hoped you'd look at a script I'm representing. The play's due to be put on in the fall and I'd hoped you might be interested.'

'Play is one set, two characters, am I right?' Gregor asked.

Damon laughed. 'Three,' he said.

Gregor nodded. 'Shakespeare had maybe thirty, forty characters, twenty different scenes.'

'Shakespeare didn't have to deal with the Shuberts, the banks, the unions.'

Gregor nodded again. 'Poor Shakespeare. Denied valuable experience. Showed in his work, didn't it? Roger, my dear friends, the theatre in New York has shrunk to size dehydrated walnut. Sidewalk tie salesman. Get yourself a carpenter or interior decorator. Describe to me the set when play opens. I'll be at La Scala watching *The Magic Flute*. Bedrooms, streets, cast of hundred, statues, hell-fire. When you find play with trains pulling into stations, cathedrals, palaces, forests, armies marching, mob scenes, two hundred costumes, all different, call us. America, richest country in the world, one-set plays, psychiatrist's couch, doctor there and patient. Act One, I am in trouble. Doctor. Act Two, I am still in trouble. Doctor. Finish.'

Damon laughed. 'You're a little hard on your contemporaries, Gregor,' he said. 'There're still good plays.'

'Narrow, narrow,' Gregor said morosely.

'I'll find a musical for you.'

'Yes,' Gregor said. 'Work year, two year, thousand sketches, hysteria, cost enough to feed all Cambodia for six months, close in one night. *Après moi, le deluge*. The guillotine next week. I am not man who can stand waste. I never throw anything away, not *anything*, not a piece of string, not a tube of paint that has one more dot of color in it.'

'As usual, Gregor,' Damon said good-naturedly, 'there's no arguing with you.'

Gregor beamed. 'If only everybody was as wise as you, my friend. I will send you postcard from Florence. Meanwhile, if you can find artist who want nice big studio cheap for one year, send him to me. But he must be worse painter than me. I won't enjoy Europe if I know man is using my place to produce masterpieces. But not one of those people my friend Jim Franklin shows in gallery – two lines on canvas eighty by eighty, background sprayed on acrylic. I can stand mediocrity here, but not desecration.' He glowered at Franklin.

'Come now,' Franklin said, not offended. 'I showed *you*, too.'

'How many canvases sold?'

'One.'

'Hah!' Gregor snorted. 'You have made them worship geometry. Roundness, passion, delight, admiration for the human face and figure – *kaput*. I am stray dog in your gallery.' This was obviously a sore point with Gregor and the good humor had gone out of his voice.

'Gregor, please,' Ebba said. 'Jim isn't responsible for the last fifty years of modern art all by himself.'

'He compounds felony,' Gregor said darkly. 'Fifteen shows a year. Look at them with their buttons.'

Franklin touched the button on his lapel self-consciously. 'What's wrong with being against nuclear war?' he asked defensively.

'I do not complain your being against nuclear war,' Gregor said loudly. 'But I'm against buttons. What do they announce? I am in a strict category, defined by somebody else, I listen, I do as I am told, the button says. I make myself fit, even if it means cutting out one-half of brain, that's what they announce.' He was in full flight now, not joking anymore. 'Marching down the avenues of America.'

'I invite you to march with us the next time there's a demonstration. See for yourself,' Franklin said, still calm, although Damon could see he was annoyed by the painter's attack.

'When you get equal number Russians, Czechs, Hungarians,

East Germans, Poles, Estonians, Latvians, Cubans to march with same buttons,' Gregor said, almost out of breath by the effort of getting out the list of names, 'I march with you. Meanwhile, in the Kremlin, they see pictures in papers of Americans, British, Frenchmen marching and they roar with laughter and send another hundred thousand troops to Afghanistan and they pick out best houses in America, Park Avenue, the Hamptons, Beverly Hills, on secret maps, where the commissars will live when they get here.'

'Gregor,' Ebba said sharply, 'stop being so Hungarian. This isn't Budapest.'

'Nobody ever stops being Hungarian,' Gregor said. 'And certainly not after seeing the Russian tanks on boulevards.'

'So what?' Franklin said, nettled. 'Do we start dropping bombs immediately?'

Gregor put his hand up to his head, scowled thoughtfully. 'I need drink before answer. Serious question.' He poured himself a full glass of wine, took a long swallow, put down his glass. 'I am against nuclear war we are going to have, no matter who marches. I am resigned. One way or another, human race can't wait for it to happen. I see one way out. Certain type nuclear weapon. Some time ago people make big fuss about it. Why, I don't know. Neutron bomb. Thirty-five thousand, forty thousand nuclear warheads, end the world in thirty seconds, men, women, children, birds in the air, fish in the sea, no cities left, nothing left. But neutron bomb invented by poet, philosopher, art-lover. Sure, he say, after he finishes calculations, world going to be blown up. But neutron bomb leaves something. Sure, kills all people, but leaves buildings standing, churches, museums, libraries, still-lifes, statues, books, leave something for two or three hundred people left over, Indians on the Amazon, Eskimos on North Pole, to start over again. Big stink. Everybody want total – we go, buildings go too, books, paintings go too. You start my type parade I march with you.'

'Gregor,' Mrs Franklin said, speaking for the first time, 'you have no children, you can talk like that.'

'True,' Gregor said in a low voice, 'we have no children, Ebba and me. Not our fault. God's fault.' He leaned over to Ebba, who always sat as close to him as she could and kissed her cheek.

Damon stood up. The conversation had disturbed him more than he wanted to show. He couldn't help but wonder if in the final explosion he could be sure that Mr Zalovsky were certain to be extinguished, he would not cheer it on. 'I'd better be getting back. Sheila should be getting in any time now and she doesn't like to come into an empty house.'

As he walked toward home he was not sure that it had been a good idea to go over to Gregor's that afternoon. For one thing he envied the year in Europe that lay ahead of the Khodars. How delicious it would be, he thought, just to be able to buy tickets for himself and Sheila and fly tomorrow to Paris or Rome leaving all responsibilities, contracts, business, threats, behind them, knowing that for twelve carefree months he could forget them all. The advantage of being an artist.

And the atmosphere in the studio had not been conducive to gaiety. Bettina Lacey's report about her daughter's experience was disturbing, to say the least, with its shadow of hideous death, even though the daughter had been spared. And Gregor's dark humor about the neutron bomb, if it could be called humor, had aroused fears that, like all the men and women of his time, Damon tried to suppress as much as he could.

He'd have been better off, Damon thought, if he had not come home after lunch and found Gregor's note, but had just gone into a bar, had a couple of drinks and watched a baseball game on television.

CHAPTER
FOUR

WHEN SHEILA hadn't gotten home by seven o'clock, he began to worry. She had said she'd be back by six and she was admirably prompt in her habits. He regretted that he hadn't phoned her in the morning at her mother's house and told her to get back before sunset, that he didn't want her walking alone in the twilight the five blocks from the garage where she was to leave the car a friend of hers had loaned her for the trip. He could have said that there had been a wave of muggings in the Village the last few days, which wouldn't have been that far from the truth anyway.

By eight o'clock he was almost ready to call the police and was pacing the floor nervously when he heard the key in the lock. He hurried to the door and embraced her, holding her tight against him as she entered the small foyer. Usually their greeting was a brief peck on the cheek and she stepped back from his arms in surprise. 'My,' she said, 'what's *that* all about?'

'You're late.' He picked up her small bag. 'That's all.'

'In that case,' she said, smiling, 'I'll be late more often.'

Her whole face changed when she smiled and even after the long years of marriage, he adored it. In repose her face was grave and dark, and made her look like the sober photographs of peasant women you were likely to see in picture books about Italy. He had once told her her smile brought her back to America. 'How was it in Vermont?' he asked.

'It's lucky I have only one mother,' she said. 'How was it here?'

'Lonely. I kept a copy of the crossword puzzle for you.'

'Dear man,' she said. She threw off her coat. 'I'll save it for later. Now I just want to freshen up and comb my hair and then you're going to make me a drink and take me out to a nice restaurant where we can have a decent meal. My mother's gone vegetarian since the last time I was there. Menopause in the kitchen.' She squinted at the ceiling light, which they rarely turned on, but which was blazing now, along with every other lamp in the room. At her age, she said, she reserved overhead lighting for her enemies. 'What've you been doing here – having a photographic session for a *Playboy* Bunny-of-the-Year?'

'I was looking up a telephone number,' he lied. He switched off the ceiling light. 'The drinks're a good idea, but I thought we'd have something here – eggs, whatever we have in a can. I had a late lunch and a big one and I'm not hungry.' The explanations were beginning already, but it was too soon to explain why he preferred his own home to what might be waiting for him at the corner of the block on their way to the restaurant.

'Oh, come on now, Roger,' Sheila said. 'Sunday night.'

He hesitated, almost asked her to sit down so that he could tell her the whole story. But he didn't want to spoil her home-coming. If he could avoid it, he didn't *ever* want to tell her the whole story. 'A restaurant it is,' he said. 'I'll have your drink ready.'

She peered at him intently. He recognized the look. He called it her hospital look. He had met her when he was lying in bed with his leg in traction after being hit by a taxicab. He was in a semiprivate room, sharing it with a man whose name was Biancella, who also had been run over and who was Sheila's unmarried uncle. They were very close, largely because they shared the same despairing opinion of Sheila's mother, who was Biancella's sister.

The two men had become friends in shared misery. Damon had found out that Biancella, a small, dark, handsome man with grizzled graying hair, ran a garage in Old Lyme, Connecticut, and came to New York only once a year, to see his niece. 'This would never have happened in Old Lyme,' Biancella had said tapping the hip-high cast ruefully. 'My mother warned me to stay out of big cities.'

'I've lived in New York for years,' Damon said, 'and I stepped off the curb just like you.'

They laughed at their mutual carelessness. They were both mending and they could afford to laugh.

Sheila came to visit her uncle every day after her work in the nursery school was over and it was in the semiprivate room that Damon had discovered her hospital look. Biancella always tried to put on a cheerful and uncomplaining face when his niece came into the room, no matter how bad the day had been for him up until then. And he had had some very bad days indeed, lying in the bed across from Damon's. But with one glance, as she came into the room, Sheila would say, 'Now, don't try to fool me, Uncle Federico, what's wrong today? A nurse is bothering you, a doctor is hurting you, what?'

Invariably, she was right. In the three weeks that she had been coming into the room, she had more or less adopted Damon, too, and his attempts at stoicism were swept aside by the dark, handsome young woman with the grave eyes, and again and again she had made him confess that all was not well with him, that they were not sedating him enough so that he could sleep, that his complaints to the doctors that his cast was too tight were being ignored. She made herself unpopular with the doctors and some of the nurses with her demands for immediate treatment, but as Damon watched her arranging her uncle's pillows, coaxing him to eat the delicacies she had brought him, which she insisted Damon share, speaking soothingly in a low, rich voice to her uncle about news of the family, entertaining him with bitterly comic anecdotes about her mother, telling him of plays she had gone to see, the performances of the children in her classes, Damon began to look forward to her afternoon visits as the climax of each day.

She made it her job to find vases for the flood of flowers that Damon's friends sent him and was coolly correct, although not cordial, when her visits happened to coincide with those of some of the ladies of Damon's acquaintance. She was sedate and proper and Damon could understand when Biancella, who was a bony and pain-wracked old man, said of his niece, 'When she puts her hand on my forehead to see if I have fever, I feel that she is healing me more than all the doctors and nurses and injections combined.'

By the time Damon had been in the hospital for two weeks he had decided that his divorced wife and most of the girls and women he had known were unbearably frivolous and unstable when compared to Sheila Branch, which was her maiden name, and that despite the difference in their ages (he was over forty and she twenty-five) he would marry her if she would have him.

But her sensitivity, while fine for a hospital, was sometimes difficult to bear in a prolonged marriage and now, in the first moments after her arrival, as she peeled off the gloves she had worn for driving, she said, 'You look awful. What is it?'

'Nothing,' he said brusquely, sounding irritated, which sometimes stopped her questioning. 'I've been reading all day and trying to make up my mind what's wrong with the manuscript and how it can be fixed.'

'It's more than that,' she said, peasant stubborn. He had said that to her more than once. 'You had lunch with your ex-wife,' she said accusingly. 'That's what it is. You always come back from seeing her as though it's thundering inside your head. What is it – she want more money again?'

'For your information, I had lunch alone and I haven't seen my ex-wife in more than a month.' He was glad of the opportunity to sound innocent and honestly aggrieved.

'Well,' Sheila said, 'look better – or at least different when we go out to dinner.' She smiled, ending the argument, at least for the moment. 'I'm the one who should be looking like thunder after two days with Madonna.'

'You look beautiful,' he said, and meant it. Although she never would have been chosen by the model agencies to be photographed for the fashion magazines, the stern, prominent lines of her face, the great dark eyes, the coarse, thick black hair, cut shoulder length, the strong, generous, olive-skinned body, had over the years become the standard against which he judged the worthiness and character of women.

Despite that, he had been attracted briefly but irresistibly to many women, and as he had with his Iberian beauty, taken his pleasure with a number of them. The long years of joyous bachelorhood after the break-up of his marriage had been given

38

over to two things – work and appetite, and his second marriage had not changed him in those respects. He was not a religious man, although when forced to think about religion, he opted for agnosticism. Still, he had a sense of sin, if appetite itself was sin. He did not blaspheme or bear false witness or steal or kill, although from time to time he did covet his neighbor's wife. His appetite was strong and natural and he made very little effort to curb it, although when possible he tried to do no harm either to himself or his partners in satisfying it. New York during those years was not a center of abstinence. He had been handsome when young and as people who have been good-looking in their youth are likely to do, conducted himself with ease and assurance even when age had left its grim traces on his appearance. He had not tried to hide this side of his character from Sheila. In any event, it would not have been possible – she had seen the parade of women who had come to visit him in his hospital room and arranged the flowers they had sent him. The lady from Spain had angered Sheila because of her indiscretion. To tell the truth, it had annoyed him, too, and he had given the lady up with something like relief and there hadn't been anyone else in the two years since they had parted.

He had never asked Sheila about her affairs before their wedding day or after or pleaded for forgiveness. By and large, although they had had their stormy periods, they had been happy together and, as he had done tonight, he always felt a lifting of the heart when she came through the door. Selfishly, he was glad that he was so much older than she and that he would die before her.

Now, with Sheila standing before him, safely home, he took her in his arms once more and kissed her on the lips, the familiar soft lips, which could on occasion set into stubborn harshness, sweet against his own. 'Sheil,' he murmured, still holding her, but whispering in her ear, 'I'm so glad you're back. The two days felt like centuries.'

She smiled again, touched his mouth with the tip of her finger as though to hush him and went into the bedroom. The way she walked, erect, not swaying, her head high and motionless as the rest of her moved, reminded him, not for the first time, of a girl he had liked and had an affair with just after he arrived in New

York. She was a young actress, dark and, like Sheila, had an Italian mother. Somewhere in her genes, as in Sheila's, there must have been a racial memory of women with heavy jars on their heads striding down the sun-struck paths of Calabria. Her name was Antoinetta Bradley and he was in love with her for the best part of a year, and he thought she was in love with him and they even had talked about getting married. But it turned out that she was in love with one of his best friends, Maurice Fitzgerald, with whom he shared an apartment in Manhattan. They tossed to see who would keep the apartment and Damon lost.

'The luck of the draw,' Fitzgerald said as Damon started packing.

Antoinetta Bradley and Maurice Fitzgerald left for London some time later and Damon heard that they had been married there and become British residents. He hadn't seen either of them in thirty years, but he still remembered how Antoinetta walked and the way Fitzgerald had said, 'The luck of the draw.'

In the kitchen, getting the ice out for the drinks, the memory made him sigh and brought back the early days before the war and just after when he had worked as an actor and still hoped for the break that would make him a star. He didn't do too badly and he was given enough small parts to keep him living fairly comfortably, and it had never occurred to him that he would at one time in the future try anything else but the theatre and perhaps the movies.

It was during the rehearsals of one of the plays in the late 1940s that his life had been changed. Mr Gray, who represented the playwright, came to the rehearsals from time to time and Damon and he had fallen into the habit of carrying on whispered conversations in the back of the darkened theatre in the long periods when Damon was not needed onstage. Mr Gray had asked him his opinion of the play and Damon had told him frankly that he thought it was going to fail and why. Gray had been impressed and had told him he was in the wrong end of the business and had said that if he ever needed a job, there would be one open for him in the Gray office. 'You've been honest with me about the play,' he said, 'and you're obviously an intelligent and well-educated young man and I can use you. Onstage it's a

40

different matter – you don't convince me and I'm almost certain you'll never convince an audience. If you try to continue in your career as an actor, it's my opinion that you're going to end up as a failed and disappointed man.'

Two weeks after the play closed Damon was working in Mr Gray's office.

Carrying the ice out of the kitchen and pouring the two drinks, Damon grimaced a little as he remembered Mr Gray's words. Tonight, in a manner of speaking, he would be onstage once more, with an audience of one. He would give the best performance he could, but the years had not improved his acting and he was almost sure that now as then he would not be convincing. There would be a long night ahead.

'Oliver,' Sheila was saying to Oliver Gabrielsen after they had given their luncheon order to the waiter in the restaurant downtown, where Sheila knew there was no chance of bumping into her husband, 'the reason I called you at home so early in the morning yesterday, just after Roger had left for the office, was that I didn't want him to know why I had to see you.' She had asked Oliver to have lunch with her that noon, but he had an appointment he couldn't break and now it was Tuesday.

'My wife was suspicious,' Oliver said. 'She isn't used to ladies calling me at breakfast to make a date with me. She says you're devastatingly beautiful. In an old-fashioned way.' He smiled and touched Sheila's hand across the table. 'The most danger-ous kind, she says. And that I'm always looking for a mother to get into bed with. She envies you and tries to copy you. Did you notice that since last year she's had her hair done the way you wear yours?'

'I noticed. If you must know the truth, I thought it was a little severe for that youngish face,' Sheila said. She did not add the word *empty* to the description although it would have made the image more accurate. She was not too fond of Doris Gabrielsen and thought that she was not worthy of Oliver.

'And once I caught her practicing walking like you in front of a mirror,' Oliver said.

'She'll never manage it,' Sheila said, briefly annoyed with this vision of another marriage. 'She's got a built-in sashay. Forgive me for being bitchy. She reminds me of how old I am.'

'Don't worry about it,' Oliver said. 'She's sometimes bitchy about you. This morning she said it was damned odd your wanting to see me alone. She was quite cross when I told her I had no idea what it was about, and she said she knew I was lying. She says that you and Roger and herself and me are not a quartet – we're a trio and a half and she's the half.'

'I'm sorry,' Sheila said.

Oliver shrugged. 'Do her good. Helps keep the necessary tension in the marriage.'

'Well, make up some story but don't tell her the truth because it's about Roger,' Sheila said.

'I guessed that.'

'And it's strictly between you and me. I was away two days and something must have happened while I was gone. He acted most peculiarly – for him. You know how he likes to walk everywhere . . .'

Oliver nodded. 'I suffer from it. When we have an appointment outside the office, even if it's halfway across town, he refuses to take a taxi and he despises buses. I told him I'm buying a pair of hiking boots to wear in the office, and he walks so fast I arrive everywhere panting and covered with sweat. It keeps him fit, but it just reminds me that all the males in my family died early of heart trouble.'

'Well,' Sheila said, 'fit or not, on Sunday night when we went out to dinner, he insisted on taking a taxi, even though the restaurant was only a ten-minute walk away and then a taxi back. He said the streets have become too dangerous to walk around these nights. Then when we got home, he began talking about the landlord's not having the buzzer fixed and anybody being able to get into the house at all hours of the day and night. And he said he was going to have a new door to the apartment put in, a steel door with a chain and real locks and a peep-hole. And changing our phone to an unlisted number. You know, he's not a fearful man – I've seen him break up fights on the street between two huge ruffians – and I couldn't get out of him what he was so suddenly worried about. He even said he thought we ought to move – to one of those big new dreadful apartment houses with what they call a security system – you know, television in the elevators and two men at the door and a switchboard where everybody has to give his name and be announced.' She shook her head distractedly. 'It's so unlike him. He loves the apartment and ordinarily he hates to change anything. I've been after him for years to have the walls done over – the paint's peeling all over the place – and he's refused to hear of it or even get rid of some of the books that're swamping us.'

Oliver nodded. 'When I suggested that it might be time for us to move into a larger office, he growled like bear and gave me a long lecture about the beauties of modest behavior.'

'To tell the truth,' Sheila said, 'I was stunned. Two short days and I come back to a different man.' She shook her head again. 'I tried to get an explanation out of him, but all he said was that it was the climate of the times and we were living in a fool's paradise and he'd suddenly realized it. I told him it was nonsense and I didn't believe him, and of course we had an argument and then in the middle of the night I heard him pacing the floor in the living room and I saw that he'd put on all the lights. Usually he sleeps as though someone had hit him on the head with a hammer. Frankly, I'm worried. He's a rational man and all this is so irrational . . . The reason I wanted to see you was to ask if you'd noticed anything . . .'

Oliver waited in silence while the waiter put their plates down in front of them. He fidgeted a little with his hands and stared soberly across the table at Sheila, his pale eyes grave. 'Yes,' he said when the waiter had gone, 'there *is* something. Yesterday morning when he came into the office, he prowled around and kept fiddling with the lock on the front door, you know we always keep it open, what's anybody going to steal from us, a thousand rejected manuscripts? And he told Miss Walton, our secretary, to have it changed and have one of those small windows of bullet-proof glass that they have in banks, with a speaker system that you can talk through. And he said we were to stop picking up the phone when it rang – only Miss Walton was going to answer it from now on and find out who was calling and what his business was before buzzing either of us. I asked him if he thought we were going into the diamond business, and

43

he said, "It's no joking matter." He said offices all over town were being broken into and he knew a secretary who was raped at her desk when she was alone during lunch hour. You know Miss Walton – she's nearly sixty and she weighs about two hundred pounds, and I said she'd probably adore it. "Oliver," he said, "there's a frivolous side to your character that I've noticed for a long time and haven't said anything about. I tell you now I don't approve of it." So I shut up.'

'What do you make of it?'

Oliver shrugged again. 'I don't know. Money, perhaps. He's not used to it. Neither am I, for that matter, but I'm not about to buy a piece of bullet-proof glass just because we happened on one book in twenty years that's a blockbuster. Old age?'

'A man doesn't get old in two days,' Sheila said impatiently. 'Does he have any enemies?'

'Who doesn't have enemies? Why do you ask that?'

'I have a feeling somehow that he was threatened while I was away and he's reacting.'

'Whatever else you can say about our profession,' Oliver said, 'it's a pacific one. Writers don't go around killing people unless they're Hemingway, and unfortunately we don't have any Hemingways on our list. Of course, Mailer stabbed one of his wives with a pocket-knife, but we don't have Mailer either.' He tried to smile comfortingly and patted Sheila's hand again. 'Maybe it's just a passing mood. Maybe he was melancholy because you were away and this is the way he's showing it.'

'I've been away longer than two days before this,' Sheila said, 'and he hasn't proposed living in a fortress because of it.'

'Maybe he's hidden it up to now and the two days were the drop that made the cup brimmeth over.'

'Literary allusions don't answer this particular problem,' Sheila said curtly. 'Is there anything else you could tell me?'

Oliver hesitated, played with the food on his plate. 'One thing. Two things, to be exact.'

'What?' Sheila's voice was harsh. 'Don't hide anything, Oliver. Not from me.'

'Well,' he said, speaking reluctantly, 'he was supposed to read a manuscript over the weekend – it's by a woman we've had some luck with up to now – and he's always so punctilious about getting things read quickly – but on Monday morning he threw the manuscript on my desk and said he couldn't make anything out of it and asked me to read it and tell him if it was any damn good or not. It turned out that it was perfectly acceptable and he said, Okay, you handle the deal, even though he'd made the contracts for that particular writer every time. Oh, I forgot, I didn't order anything to drink. Would you like a glass of wine?'

'Forget the wine. You said two things. What was the second thing?'

Oliver looked uncomfortable. 'I don't know whether you want to hear this, Sheila,' he said.

'I've got to help Roger,' Sheila said, 'and so do you. And we won't be able to do it if we keep things from each other. What's the second thing?'

'Roger once told me that sometimes you reminded him of Medea,' Oliver said, postponing. 'Now I see what he meant.'

'I'd kill anybody who tried to harm my husband,' Sheila said evenly. 'And it has nothing to do with a young man showing off that he read enough Greek literature to know who Medea was.'

'I'm your friend, Sheila,' Oliver said, hurt. 'And Roger's. You know that.'

'Prove it.' She spoke without pity. 'What's the second thing?'

Oliver coughed as though he had caught something in his throat and drank half a glass of water. 'The second thing,' he said as he put the glass down, 'is that he asked Miss Walton to call City Hall and find out how he could get a permit to carry a pistol.'

Sheila closed her eyes. 'Oh, Christ,' she said softly.

'Oh, Christ it is,' Oliver said. 'What are you going to say to Roger?'

'I'm going to repeat every word of our conversation to him,' Sheila said.

'He'll never forgive me.'

'That will be just too bad,' Sheila said.

CHAPTER
FIVE

DAMON LOOKED at his watch impatiently. He had called his ex-wife, Elaine, and told her to meet him in the restaurant at one o'clock. It was now one-twenty. She had always been late for everything, which was one of the many reasons for their divorce, and she had not changed. She had not changed in other of her habits, either. She still smoked three packs of cigarettes a day and drank from morning to night and gambled away whatever money she could lay her hands on. The mixed odors of cigarette smoke and alcohol that had enveloped her still made the routine kiss of greeting on her cheek a trial for him. She had always dressed sloppily, like a girl going to class in the rain on a weekday morning in Northampton and now, a woman of sixty gone to fat, she still might appear in a restaurant in jeans and a sweater two sizes too large for her. What had seemed a charming lack of vanity in a girl when he had first met her in the book store where she worked was now a studied affectation of youthfulness in the woman.

She had been a pretty girl when he married her, with a pert, mischievous small face and long red hair, and she had been smart and witty and had a generous and compassionate heart, but her airy way with money and her indolent neglect of herself and him and their apartment, plus her three addictions, had destroyed the marriage. They had married in haste, ten days after their first meeting, and they had not slept with each other before their wedding. Their discovery that they did not satisfy each other sexually had started the marriage off as an unex-

46

pected and puzzling calamity from which finally there was no recovery.

Despite all this, the divorce had been amicable. Freed of the bonds of physical obligations, they remained friends. Her taste in literature was eclectic and dependable, and he sometimes gave her manuscripts to read to get her reaction to them, and her advice was usually helpful. It was only in the last three years, after her second husband died, that she had taken to asking him for money. Her husband had been a professional gambler, and together with him she had spent most of her time at Las Vegas and at racetracks around the country, sometimes, varying with the speed of horses or the turn of a wheel, living in high style and sometimes forced to pawn the jewelry her husband showered on her during lucky streaks.

Damon was not a miserly man and even with his limited means before *Threnody* he would not have begrudged her the comparatively small sums she asked of him if he hadn't known that the money would end up in the hands of clerks in liquor stores and of bookies and players who were more expert than she at the backgammon board. It was at those times that he returned home grim-faced and out of sorts and to endure Sheila's disapproval.

Still, through it all Elaine had retained her ability to amuse him. Today, though, he thought glumly, looking at his watch again, the conversation would not be amusing.

He saw her coming into the restaurant and looking around near-sightedly for him. Her hair was now cut short and dyed a violent magenta to hide the gray streaks. Gratefully, he saw that she had on a decent dark blue dress and was wearing high-heeled shoes instead of her usual scuffed moccasins. The fumes as he kissed her cheek, however, were still the same.

Her face was surprisingly young and unlined and her green eyes, against all odds, were clear.

'You look very well,' he said, as they seated themselves side by side on the banquette. 'Very chic, if you don't mind my saying so.'

'I've had a nice run with the horses,' she said. 'It improves the health. And I've got a new boy friend who insisted I burn all my old clothes.'

47

'Good for him,' Damon said, thinking, at the age of eighty she'll still be having new boy friends.

She turned on the banquette so that she could look at him. '*You* don't look all that well. What is it – doesn't good luck agree with you?'

'I didn't ask you to come here to talk about my health,' Damon said. 'It's something else.'

'If it's about the money I owe you' – she had always pretended that what he gave her were not gifts but loans – 'I probably could squeeze most of it out of my boy friend. He's a distributor.'

'Distributor of what? Clothes to undeserving ladies?'

Elaine smiled calmly, undisturbed by the jibe. She had never had a bad temper, except when drunk, when she insulted everyone in sight. 'Slot machines. It's a nice income, even though it means having business dinners with some very peculiar gentlemen.'

'It's just because of that,' Damon said, 'that I asked you to have lunch with me. As long as I've known you, with your penchant for gambling, you've mingled with peculiar gentlemen, at least in my view of things. Jockeys, horse-trainers, gamblers, bookies, touts, and God knows what else.'

'A girl has a right to choose her friends,' Elaine said with dignity. 'They're a lot more fun than those dreary writers always talking about Henry James you used to bring home. If you intend to lecture me I might as well leave right now.' She started to get up, but he waved her down.

'Sit down, sit down.' He looked up at the waiter who was standing in front of their table. 'What do you want to eat?'

'Aren't you going to offer me a drink? Or are you still crusading to keep me sober?'

'I forgot. What do you want?'

'What's that you're drinking?' She gestured toward the small glass beside his plate.

'Sherry.'

She made a face. 'Dreadful stuff. Hell on the liver. Vodka on the rocks is nice at this time of day. Or don't you remember?'

'All too well.' Damon looked up at the waiter. 'One vodka on the rocks.'

'Another sherry, Sir?' the waiter asked.

Damon shook his head. 'I'll make do with this. Take the rest of our order, please.'

The restaurant was well known for its French cuisine, but Elaine didn't even look at the menu and ordered a hamburger with fried onions.

'Still on junk food, I see,' Damon said.

'The all-American girl,' Elaine said, laughing. 'Or all-American lady, considering my age. Now – why are you so interested all of a sudden in my disreputable friends?'

Damon took a long breath, then speaking slowly and clearly to make sure Elaine understood every word, repeated the conversation over the telephone with Zalovsky, verbatim, stopping only for a moment when the waiter returned with the vodka. It was a conversation that was not difficult to remember.

Elaine's face turned grave as she listened, and she didn't touch her drink until he had finished. Then she drank off half of it in one gulp. 'What a sonofabitch of a night that must have been. No wonder you look the way you do. *Do* you know anybody called Zalovsky?'

'No. Do you?'

'No. I'll ask Freddie, that's my boy friend, if he does, but it's an outside chance.'

'Does your Freddie indulge in a little blackmail when he's not distributing slot machines?'

Elaine looked uncomfortable. 'It's possible. But only in the line of business.' She finished her glass and tapped it to indicate to the waiter, who was passing the table, that she wanted another one. 'He knows about you, of course, but as far as he's concerned, it could all have happened during the Civil War. The only agents he knows are from the FBI and the only thing he reads is the *Racing Form*.'

'Are you ever in Chicago?'

'Oh, once in a while, when there's a big race at Arlington or when Freddie asks me to go along on a business trip and we stop off on the way to Vegas.'

'Of course,' Damon said, 'it might have been somebody's idea of a nasty practical joke.'

Elaine shook her head. 'It doesn't sound like a joke to me. I don't want to frighten you any more than necessary, but my guess is it's a serious business. Dead serious. What do you plan to do when he calls you again?'

'I'm not sure. I thought you might have some ideas.'

'Let me think.' She sipped at her second vodka, lit a cigarette and tried to blow the smoke away with a gesture of her hand. 'Well, I know a detective on the homicide squad. Do you want me to talk to him and find out what he thinks you ought to do?'

'I don't like the word,' Damon said. 'Homicide.'

'I'm sorry,' she said, 'it's the only detective I know.'

'Talk to him and thank you.'

'I'll call you and let you know what he says.'

'Call me at the office. I don't want my wife picking up the phone when Zalovsky calls again.'

'You mean to tell me you haven't told her you're being threatened?' He could see Elaine meant it as an accusation.

'I don't want to alarm her unnecessarily.'

'Unnecessarily, for God's sake. If you're in danger, so is she. Couldn't you figure that out? If, for some reason whoever is after you can't get hold of you, what do you think they'll do – join the Boy Scouts? They'll grab her.'

'I haven't had as much experience in these matters as you have.' He knew that she was right, but even so he knew he sounded sulky at her rebuke.

'Just because I go to Vegas a few times a year, don't talk as though I was the queen gun moll of the Mafia.' Her voice was tinged with anger. 'It's just common sense, for God's sake.'

'I suppose you're right,' he said reluctantly. 'I'll tell her.' Another great night ahead at the Damon residence, he thought, as he watched the waiter put Elaine's hamburger down and his own filet of sole.

'Are you going to order some wine?' Elaine asked.

'Of course. What do you want?'

'What do *you* want? The host usually orders the wine and I gather that this is your lunch.'

'I don't like to drink in the middle of the day,' he said. It had always been difficult not to sound sanctimonious around Elaine.

'A half-bottle of Beaujolais,' she said to the waiter. In the old days she would have ordered a full bottle. Perhaps, he thought, she's tapering off.

'Zalovsky, from Chicago,' she said, almost to herself as she slathered the hamburger with ketchup. 'Have you any idea what he might look like?'

'I only talked to him on the phone for a couple of minutes,' Damon said, 'but actually, from his voice I made a mental picture of him. Forty-five, fifty, perhaps, a heavy man, flashy clothes, no evidence of any education.'

'What've you done about it so far?' Elaine asked.

'There's nothing much I can do about it – yet. Oh, I'm applying for a permit to carry a gun.'

Elaine scowled. 'I don't think that's such a good idea. You know what I'd do if I were you, Roger,' she said, 'I'd start making lists.'

'What kind of lists?'

'People who for one reason or other had a grudge against you, nuts who've come into your office and been turned away, people who think you've cheated them somehow, ladies you've discarded or husbands or boy friends of ladies you haven't discarded soon enough . . .' She grinned and her face was momentarily pert, ageless, again. 'Boy, that would be a list. And go way back. People let things fester for years, turn neurotic as they get older – have a run of bad luck and look for someone to blame, or see a movie about revenge or about a woman scorned or God knows what else. Some crazy writer may have offered you a script that you didn't even read and sent back with a one-line refusal and then read *Threnody* and seen it on the bestseller lists and think he'd been plagiarized. God, I haven't been close to you for donkey's years and even *I* could make a good-sized list without half-trying. And don't just look for clues under Z's. The name might mean nothing. And when you talk to the detective, his name is Lieutenant Schulter by the way, don't be shy about your exploits. He might just catch something, a hint, that you never thought of. And . . .' She hesitated, fork in air. 'And you might ask your wife to take a good look at her past. She's a beautiful woman I've heard, or at least *was* a beautiful woman, and I've never known a beautiful woman who hasn't had a pot full of grief in her life or who hasn't at least once

51

picked a real wrong man. And she's half-Italian and you never know what sort of connections Italians have that they don't care to advertise.'

'Oh, leave the Italian thing out of it, please. Her uncle owned a garage in Connecticut.' This was an old battle between them. Elaine came from strict Wisconsin German stock, which explained their chastity before their wedding day, if not after, and had strong opinions about the unworthy characteristics of Italians, Greeks, Jews, airline stewardesses, the Irish and Scotch. If she had ever met a Bulgarian or an Outer Mongolian, she would probably have discovered that one couldn't trust them, either.

Elaine watched the waiter pour the wine, her face stubborn. The waiter was dark and Mediterranean-looking. Damon hoped the waiter hadn't caught the end of Elaine's diatribe.

'So he had a garage in Connecticut,' Elaine said when the waiter left and she had swigged down half a glass of wine. 'I bet there's about eight other uncles who never saw a garage, but saw plenty of other things that might have interested the police from time to time.'

'I said leave the Italian thing out of this.'

'You asked me to help.' Now she was affronted. 'If you won't listen to me, what's the sense in my telling you what I think?'

'Okay, okay,' he said wearily, 'I'll make those lists.'

'And take a good look at your wife's lists, too, while you're at it,' Elaine said. 'And I hope you're still married at the end of it. Please' – her voice softened – 'please be careful. Don't let anything happen to you. I have to know that you're all right and still around. Today, as always, I'm glad to see you, no matter what the reason. Let's pretend for the rest of the bottle that this is a romantic, nostalgic lunch, and that you're my glorious old lover whose heart has been broken for thirty years because we parted.'

She poured herself another glass of wine, lifted it in a toast toward him. 'Now, let's forget it for the rest of the meal and try to get some pleasure out of being together again and still able to eat and drink without wanting to kill each other. Now tell me, honestly, do you think I ought to have my face lifted?'

CHAPTER
SIX

HE WALKED slowly on his way back to the office after lunch, going over in his mind what Elaine had said to him while slugging away at the drink, hardly noticing the people around him, the names of men and women he had known in his long life not arranging themselves in his brain in orderly and manageable lists as suggested by Elaine, but swirling around in a mist and confusion of identities. Then, suddenly, he saw a slightly stooped, small old man with thick glasses, dressed in a black coat with a fur collar approaching him. There was only one man he had ever known who had a coat like that – Harrison Gray.

'Harrison!' he said and hurried to meet him and put out his hand.

The man stopped and looked at him puzzledly, half-frightened by the greeting. He put his hands behind his back. 'There must be some mistake, Sir,' the old man said. 'My name is George.'

Damon stepped back, blinked, shook his head to clear it. 'I'm sorry,' he said, almost stammering. 'You look so much like one of my best friends. I don't know what I was thinking of. He's dead, you know . . .' The man stared at him suspiciously, sniffed as though to detect prelunch martinis on Damon's breath. 'I'm not dead,' he said, offended. 'As I hope you can see.'

'Forgive me, Sir,' Damon said lamely. 'I must have been daydreaming . . .'

'At the very least,' the man said crisply. 'And now if you'll permit me . . .'

'Of course.' Damon stepped aside to let the old man pass him. Then, when the man had gone, he shook his head violently again and, feeling the cold sweat break out all over his body, continued on toward his office, watching his every step and being meticulously careful when crossing a street to watch out for speeding cars. But when he came to the entrance to his building on Forty-third Street, he stopped, stared dully at the people going in and out and knew that he was not going to be able to enter and take the elevator and face Miss Walton and Oliver Gabrielsen at their desks and pretend that it was an ordinary afternoon and that they could depend upon him to go through an ordinary afternoon's routine of work.

Stopping dead men in the street. He shivered, thinking of it. Often, at this hour, he would have just had lunch with Mr Gray at the Algonquin on the next block uptown and more often than not would move from the dining room to the bar, to which Mr Gray was attached, by many years of quiet tippling, for an after-lunch brandy, Mr Gray's preferred drink.

Almost automatically, Damon walked toward Sixth Avenue, now called the Avenue of Americas (Oh, amigo, what is America?) and turned into Forty-fourth Street and went into the Algonquin bar, which he had patronized rarely since Mr Gray's death. He liked the bar and had not permitted himself to delve into the reasons why the death of his friend and partner had been the signal somehow to avoid it.

The dead have their claims, he thought as he sat himself down at the small familiar bar; the places in which our conversations have taken place in the lull of an afternoon are reserved for them. The bar was empty except for himself and he didn't recognize the barman. He ordered a Cognac, not his usual Scotch, remembering that Mr Gray (strangely, after their long friendship, he thought of him as Mr Gray instead of by his Christian name) had liked Bisquit Dubouchet. The fumes assailed his memory and for a moment Mr Gray was a living presence at his side. The presence was not macabre, the memory not sorrowful, but warm and comforting.

The last time he had seen Mr Gray had been on the occasion of the Damons' tenth wedding anniversary. There had been a small party at the Damons' apartment, with a few of the agency's clients of whom they were particularly fond and an old friend of Damon's, Martin Crewes, who had been a client and had gone to Hollywood, where he was now a highly paid screenwriter and had a business manager who made his deals for him. He was in New York for conferences with a director, and Damon had been pleased to hear his voice on the phone the day before. They had been good friends, and he had been an honest and gifted man and had always been good company. He had written two fine novels about the small town in which he had grown up in Ohio, but they had hardly sold at all and Crewes had told Damon and Mr Gray as he was leaving for the West Coast, 'The hell with it. I surrender. I'm tired of starving. There has to be a limit to the number of times you hit your head against the stone wall. The only thing I know how to do is write, and if somebody wants to pay me for it, God be with him. I'll try not to write shit, but if that's what they want, that's what I'll give them.' He had been a humorous and zestful man when Damon had known him, but after a few minutes over the drinks before dinner, Damon was saddened to see that his friend had turned into a solemn and pompous windbag who told dreary anecdotes about producers and directors and movie stars, punctuating his conversation with a high, nervous giggle that put Damon's nerves on edge.

He had been a solidly built, slightly fat young man but now was trimmed down to the bone and Damon guessed that he did calisthenics at least two hours a day and ate only fruits and nuts to maintain that tense, ballet dancer's figure. His hair glistened, an unnatural ebony, and was cut in a kind of pageboy bob that completely covered his ears. He wore a black turtleneck sweater, with a thick gold chain hanging on his chest and black pants and a fawn-colored cashmere jacket. The boy from the little town in Ohio about whom he had once written had successfully disappeared.

In his first ten minutes in the room he had already told the assembled guests that the picture he had just completed had cost a cool seven and the next one was going to be epical in scope and they'd be lucky to get in under ten. It took a few moments for Damon to realize that the seven was seven million and the ten ten million.

When Mr Gray came in, later than the other guests, he made his disapproval of Crewes plain with his first words to the man – 'Ah, Stonewall Crewes has finally returned to take the salute of his ragged but loyal troops' – and Damon knew that it had been a mistake to invite the screenwriter to the party. And when Mr Gray stepped back to survey Crewes, as though to get a better look at a painting in a museum and said, in tones of mock wonder, 'Is that the Paramount uniform?' Damon knew that Crewes would never call him again, no matter how many times he came to New York.

Still, the party was agreeable; Crewes left early, after drinking only soda water with a slice of lemon in it and merely nibbling at some salad and around the edges of the slice of baked ham that Sheila had put on his plate.

The Damons were leaving the next day for a month tour of Europe and the friends who had been to Europe advised them of places they couldn't afford to miss, and the friends who had not been to Europe told them how much they envied the travelers and Mr Gray, in a ceremonious speech, presented Damon with a leather-bound diary in which to put down his impressions of the trip and gave Sheila a slide rule in a suede leather case with which you could figure out how to change meters and centimeters into yards and inches and foreign currencies into their value in American dollars.

The party ended late, but Damon could see that Mr Gray was loath to leave and poured him his third brandy of the night and whispered, 'Stay a while,' before saying good-bye to his other guests. Sheila went into the bedroom to do some last-minute packing, and Damon fixed himself a drink and sat down in the chair near the end of the couch on which Mr Gray was sitting.

'I have to apologize, Roger,' Mr Gray said, 'for what I did to Crewes. After all, he was one of your guests.'

'Nonsense,' Damon said. 'Anybody who comes to a party in New York dressed like that deserves what he gets.'

'I just couldn't hold myself back,' Mr Gray said. 'You know, I have nothing against the movies, *per se*. In fact, I love them. And I have nothing against the people who make them. But when I see a man who had the talent Crewes had let himself go like that and never write a decent word in ten years, I mourn.

The waste, man, the waste. There're writers who've gone through our office I've counseled to go out there and stay there because I knew they'd be happier adapting other people's material and relieved of the heavy burden of creation. They'd be paid besides and I don't underestimate the love for money some men have, and anyway the language wouldn't be a phrase the loser by their spending their lives writing to order. And there are other men I've counseled to go and do one picture, for the experience, for the money, because I knew they'd come back and do the work they were born to do.' He sipped sadly at his brandy. 'And in Crewes's case it was a personal disappointment. I thought I was molding him. I saw a one-act play of his in one of those Equity Library presentations, and I sought him out and told him he was a novelist, not a playwright, and I financed him for a full year while he was working on his first book and he was one of the most promising young men ever to come into the office. Now, what is he? A sun-tanned cockerel, crowing in the barnyard.' His mouth twisted in distaste. 'Ah, why go on about it? In our profession disappointment is the one commodity we can be sure will arrive with every morning's mail.' He sipped his drink in silence for a few moments, staring thoughtfully into the embers of the dying fire. 'Not only in our profession,' he said bitterly. 'My son, for example.'

'What?' Damon said, surprised. He knew that Mr Gray had been married and had been a widower when they had first met, but the son had never been mentioned before.

'My son,' Mr Gray repeated. 'He's a grain merchant, dealing in futures, things like that. He made a fortune during the war. And after. Waiting till the market went up before selling wheat to the starving millions of Europe and Asia. He was a brilliant boy, he was close to being a genius. His field was mathematics, physics. He could have been the shining star of any faculty at any university in the country. He was the one golden gift of an otherwise dreadful marriage. He used his talent all right – to wheel, to deal, to take advantage of every trick and turn of the law and the marketplace. I read not long ago that he was the youngest multimillionaire in the United States who had made all his money by his own efforts. With the cold heart of a guard in a concentration camp. It was in *Time* magazine.'

'I never happened to read it,' Damon said.

'I didn't carry it in my pocket to show to my friends.' Mr Gray smiled faintly.

'I never knew you had a son,' Damon said.

'It pains me to talk about him.'

'You didn't talk much about your wife, either. I gathered it was a painful subject.'

'My wife died young.' Mr Gray shrugged. 'No great loss, either. I was shy and she was meek and she was the first girl who let me kiss her. She died, I think, of embarrassment, embarrassment at being alive and taking up space on the planet. There wasn't a flicker of real life in her from the day she was born, she had the spirit of a slave. My son, I believe, turned out to be what he is because he looked at his mother and told himself that in every possible way he would be different from her. And he despised me. The last time we talked he told me – I can still hear the contempt in his voice as he said it – he told me I was content to live in a corner on crusts all my life, but he wasn't.' Mr Gray gave a short laugh. 'Well, I'm still in my corner and he's the youngest self-made multimillionaire in America.' He sighed, finished his brandy, looked questioningly at Damon. 'Do you think I might have just one more?'

'Of course,' Damon said and refilled his glass.

Mr Gray bowed his head to sniff the Cognac. Damon had the impression that he was crying and trying to hide it. 'Ah,' he said finally, his head still down, 'I didn't keep you up to wail about my private life. An old man, late at night, under the influence of just a little too much brandy . . .' His voice trailed off. 'If you don't mind, Roger, I left my briefcase in the hall, would you kindly get it for me?'

Damon took his time getting the briefcase, so that Mr Gray could dry his tears. He heard him blowing his nose loudly. The briefcase was heavy and Damon wondered what Mr Gray could have in it or why he would carry a briefcase to a party.

'Ah, there we are,' Mr Gray said brightly as Damon came into the room. 'You found it.' He put his brandy down and placed the briefcase on his knees. The briefcase was usually filled with manuscripts that he took home to read after office hours and on weekends. He caressed the worn leather and the battered brass lock, then opened the case and took out a small bottle of pills. He shook out a pill and placed it under his tongue. Damon noticed that the veined, liver-spotted hand was shaking. 'Brandy makes the heart race,' Mr Gray said, almost apologetically, as though as a guest it was discourteous to his host to provide his own nourishment. 'The doctors warn me, but one can't live completely without vices.' His voice suddenly became stronger and his hands stopped shaking. 'What a nice party this was. And Sheila always looks so splendid in her own home. Ten years, is it? My, where do the years fly?' He had been a witness at the wedding in the judge's chambers. 'You've been good for each other. If I were younger, I'd be jealous of your marriage. And if I were you, I'd be most careful not to do anything to disturb it.'

'I know what you mean,' Damon said uncomfortably.

'Those little absences from the office in the afternoons, the telephone calls . . .'

'We have an understanding, Sheila and I,' Damon said. 'A tacit understanding. Sort of.'

'I'm not rebuking you, Roger. In fact, I took a vicarious pleasure in your mid-afternoon excursions. I had fantasies of what it would be like to be handsome like you, lusty, pursued by women . . . It brightened many a dull day. But you're no longer young, the fires should be banked by now, you have something precious to preserve . . .'

'As you just said, one can't live completely without vices.' Damon laughed, to put the conversation on a lighter plane. 'And I very seldom drink brandy.'

Mr Gray laughed then, too, an old friend sharing masculine rascality in a locker room. 'Well,' he said, 'at least manage to get away with it.' Then his face grew serious again. Once more he opened the flap of the briefcase which he had been cradling on his lap. He took out a thickly stuffed large manila envelope. 'Roger,' he said, speaking softly, 'I'm going to ask you to do me a great favor. There are years of work in this envelope and a lifetime of hope. It's a manuscript.' He laughed uneasily. 'It's a book I've just finished writing. The only book I ever wrote or probably ever will write. When I was a young man, I wanted to be a writer. I tried, but it was no use. I had read too much to believe what I put down was of any worth. So I did the next best thing, I thought. I would be the vessel, the means, the conduit, if you will, for the work of good writers. Here and there you might say I've succeeded, but that's not the point. With age, with the immersion in words, so to speak, with the years of observation, criticism, editing, I thought perhaps I had accumulated enough wisdom so that I could create something that would salvage what was left of my life. Now you're going on a voyage, there will be days of rain when you can't leave your hotel, perhaps long train trips, nights when you're tired of listening to a foreign language. When you get back, I hope you will have read it. No one but me, not even a typist, has glanced at it until now.' He took a deep breath, put his hand to his throat as though to relieve some hidden strain there. 'If you tell me it's good, I'll show it around. If you tell me it's no good, I shall burn it.'

Damon took the envelope. On it, in Mr Gray's neat round script was written *Solo Voyage*, by Harrison Gray. 'I can't wait to read it,' he said.

'Please,' said Mr Gray, 'be at least three thousand miles away before you look at the first line.'

The trip was everything they could have hoped for – and better. They wandered without a schedule, as the mood seized them, footloose and free, finding new joy in being together twenty-fours hours a day, walking hand-in-hand like young lovers along the Seine, on the banks of the Tiber, through the Uffizi Palace, on a mountain path in the Swiss Alps, over the bridges of the canals near the Great Lagoon. They stood silent before the Cathedral of Chartres and climbed on the top of Mont St Michel. Together, they read Henry James on Paris, Ruskin's *The Stones of Venice* and Stendhal on Rome, dined off bouillabaisse in spring sunlight at restaurants overlooking the port of Antibes and *fettuccine al pesto* at tables facing the Ligurian Sea. If it hadn't been for Mr Gray's manuscript, Damon could not have imagined a more perfect holiday. When Sheila asked him what the book was like, Damon said it was fine. But he was lying. The book lay dead in his hands. Harrison Gray, as a young man, had traveled for a few months on a tramp steamer around the islands of the South Pacific, and the book was a recollection, in the form of a novel, of that voyage. In the writing it seemed like a dull parody of Conrad's *Youth*.

Mr Gray, that delicate and fastidious man, so tuned to the turn of a phrase, so acute in pointing out a wrong note in an imaginary character, so sharp in detecting falsity or rhetoric, so steeped in and devoted to the glory of great literature, had written a book so stale, trite, clumsy, that Damon wept inwardly as he went through the pages on which there were no two sentences that followed each other with any of the music or savor of the English language. As the month drew to its close, Damon dreaded the idea of the trip home and the moment when he would arrive at the office and have to confront his old and beloved friend.

But Mr Gray, gentlemanly and considerate to the end, spared Damon the confrontation. When he went to the office carrying the manuscript on his first day back, Damon was greeted at the door by a weeping Miss Walton, at that time thinner, with coquettish bangs of mousy hair, who told him that she had not known where to reach him in Europe to tell him that Mr Gray had died the week before.

That night, although it was warm and New York was already seized by summer, Damon lit a fire in his living room and fed *Solo Voyage* page by page into the flames. It was the least he could do in honor of his friend's memory.

Remembering all this, Damon stared down at the glass of brandy on the bar, sighed, picked up the glass and finished the drink, paid the barman and went out of the hotel.

For once he did not walk the two miles to home. Facing the long night that lay ahead of him with his wife, with its explanations, confessions, fears and alarms, he was in no mood to meet any others of his familiar dead on the streets of the city.

Hailing a taxi, he drove downtown in silence.

CHAPTER
SEVEN

WHEN HE kissed Sheila good-bye the next morning on his way to work, she looked sober and drawn. It had been an exhausting night, which had begun as he came through the door, with the question, 'What's all this about a pistol?'

'Where did you hear anything about a pistol?' he had asked, already sorry that even for a day he had left her in ignorance of what was happening.

'I had lunch with Oliver,' she said. 'He's as worried about you as I am.'

'All right,' he said. 'Sit down. We have some talking to do. Quite a lot of talking.'

Then, in the same words he had used at lunch to Elaine, he told her about the midnight telephone call. He also told her most, but not all, of what Elaine had said about making lists of people who might wish him harm. Out of fear of wounding her and making her feel he mistrusted her, he omitted Elaine's advice to get Sheila to make her own private list. For other reasons he also omitted the name of one woman he had been involved with long ago, who had called him from Chicago recently and whose family or who herself might be tempted by the idea of revenge, either by violence or in cold cash.

'I hate to ask this question, Sheil,' he had said after hours of discussion and speculation that went round and round and ended, as far as he could tell, in no decisions, 'but is it possible that somebody has something against you and is getting at you through me?'

'Did Elaine suggest that?' Sheila asked suspiciously.

'Something of the kind.'

'She would,' Sheila said bitterly. 'Did she ask for money again?'

'No. She has a rich boy friend now.'

'Thank heaven for small mercies,' Sheila said ironically. 'Let me see if I can count my enemies. Yes, there's a five-year-old boy in one of my classes who said he hated me because I stood him in the corner for ten minutes for making a little girl cry.' She smiled. 'Ah, my head is weary and it's late. Let's go to bed and maybe things will look clearer in the morning.'

But it was morning now, an ordinary working day and she was saying good-bye looking careworn and distressed, and he could tell that she had not slept well because of the lines under her eyes. He himself had not slept all that well either, and once more he had had the dream about his father standing at the marble balustrade holding the toy horse and smiling and waving invitingly to him.

They kissed again, lingeringly, at the door and she said, 'Take care,' and he said, 'Of course,' and went down the stairs and out of the house into a howling cold spring wind. At other times he would have thought it bracing weather for the long walk uptown, but today he huddled into his raincoat, with the collar up around his ears and walked as fast as he could to try to keep warm. The faces of the people he passed looked pinched and hostile and if *en masse* the faces represented anything, it was a generalized and all-encompassing hatred and an inner certainty that all men, or at least all New Yorkers, were their enemies.

In the office it wasn't much better. When Oliver came in, Damon shut the door that separated the room in which they worked from the outer room to keep Miss Walton from hearing what he had to say. Then, harshly, he said, speaking too loudly, 'What kind of old lady have you become? Blabbing all over town. I thought we had an agreement that what goes on in this office remains in the office.'

'Oh,' Oliver said, 'Sheila told you we had lunch.'

'She certainly did.'

'Listen, Roger,' Oliver said, speaking calmly, although Damon could see he was hurt, 'Sheila's been mystified by the way you've been behaving since she came back from Vermont and so have I. A pistol, for God's sake. You've been yelling for years about a gun control law, I've seen your name on dozens of petitions to congressmen.'

'So – I happen to have changed my mind,' Roger said, his voice still too loud. 'That's no excuse for blabbing behind my back.'

'Roger, talking to your wife about a problem that has nothing to do with the office isn't blabbing all over town,' Oliver said.

'Why're you so sure it has nothing to do with the office? Maybe it damn well does.' Even as he spoke Damon knew that he was being unfair, but he couldn't stop himself. 'And from now on keep your goddamn mouth shut.'

As Oliver turned and went silently across the room to his desk, Damon thought, One more mark against me.

They didn't say a word to each other all morning and Damon could only make a pretense of working, shuffling papers irritably around on his desk. It was nearly eleven o'clock when his buzzer sounded.

'Mrs Damon on the phone,' Miss Walton said.

Damon was surprised. Sheila made a point of never calling him at work. When she did call the office, it was around five o'clock, when she knew that he was getting ready to leave the office and she wanted him to pick up something on the way home or was uptown herself and thought it would be nice to meet for a drink near the office and have dinner and go to a movie.

'Put her through,' he said.

'Roger,' Sheila said, without preliminaries, 'I've been thinking about what you said about my perhaps having enemies.'

'Is it about the little boy you stood in the corner?' Damon said. 'Has he turned vicious?' It was a bad joke and he knew it as he said it.

'I'm glad you're in such a good humor,' Sheila said crossly. 'I'm not.'

'Sorry.'

'Something happened last term that I should have remembered. There was a man who took to hanging around the school and offering the kids candy and asking them could he take them with him for an ice cream soda. And you know, sometimes the

64

mothers're late to pick their children up, and the other teachers and myself are too busy to go out in the street and wait for the dear ladies to show up, and we give them strict instructions not to budge from the front gate, but there's never any telling with four- and five-year-olds. It began to worry me and I went down one afternoon and told him I didn't like him loitering in front of the school and talking to the kids. He was about fifty years old and well-enough dressed, but I didn't trust him on sight. He pretended to be insulted and said he was a lonely, retired old man and liked children, and he was offended that I thought there was anything wrong in giving an infant a piece of candy. After that, he didn't come around as often, but from time to time I would see him pretending to be just walking by when the classes were let out, and I told a policeman about it and the policeman found him and told him if he caught him hanging around the school again, he'd run him in on suspicion. I saw him only once more, by accident, on our street just in front of our house, and he glared at me and said, "Lesbian bitch. Now go tell the police *that*."' She sighed. 'I laughed at him and he walked away and I never thought of it again until this morning. But I was going through my desk just now and I found the piece of paper on which I'd written down the name the police gave me. Do you want it? Maybe it's nothing, but who knows?'

'What's the name?'

'McVane. I don't have his first name. It happened so many months ago and it doesn't seem possible . . .' Her voice trailed off.

'Anything's possible. Thanks, Sheil.'

'I'm sorry to have interrupted your work, but I thought you'd like to know.'

'I do.'

'How's it going in the office this morning?'

'Swimmingly.'

'You didn't bawl Oliver out, I hope.' She sounded anxious.

'There was a brief discussion.' He saw Oliver's back, which was turned to him, stiffen, and was sure Oliver knew to whom he was talking and what the conversation was about.

'Oh, dear,' Sheila said. 'What a mess.'

Miss Walton broke in then, 'Mr Damon,' she said, 'there's

another call waiting for you, a gentleman who says his name is Schulter. It's important, he says, and he's calling from a phone booth and can't wait.'

'I have to hang up now, Sheila,' Damon said. 'If I'm a little late getting home, don't worry.'

'Last bulletin to brighten your day,' Sheila said. 'This morning the little boy said he loved me.'

'As does all the world,' Damon said, then heard the click as she hung up.

There was a moment of telephone noise as Miss Walton fiddled with the old-fashioned little telephone console in the outer office. Then a man's voice said, 'Detective Schulter.' The voice was gruff, reminding Damon of the noise a callused hand makes running over a rough piece of bark.

'Yes, Sir,' Damon said.

'Mrs Sparman asked me to call.'

'Who?'

'Elaine Sparman.'

'Oh, yes.' He had forgotten that Sparman was the name of her second husband. When he thought of her, it was as Mrs Damon.

'I'm near you. I'll be at the big sandwich bar near you on Sixth Avenue. Could you come around?'

'When?'

'Right now. I've got some other individuals to talk to in the neighborhood and I've got to get to them before lunch.'

'I'll be there in ten minutes. How will I recognize you?'

Schulter laughed. 'I'll be the only detective in the place and it sticks out all over me. Anyway, I'm wearing a gray overcoat and I'm carrying a copy of the *Wall Street Journal*.'

'Got it. And thanks.'

'Don't thank me yet. I ain't done anything for you yet. See you in ten minutes.'

Damon sat for a moment staring down at his desk, trying to imagine what sinister business Mr Schulter of homicide was engaged in with the other individuals in the neighborhood, as he called them, and if his acquaintance with Elaine had come about in the exercise of his profession. He also wondered just what kind of detective it would be who read the *Wall Street*

Journal. Then he got up and without saying anything to Oliver went into the anteroom to get his coat, told Miss Walton to take any messages for him, he didn't know when he'd be back, and went out. The elevator took a long time coming and he pushed impatiently at the button again and again. Mr Schulter sounded like the kind of man who meant it when he said ten minutes. If he arrived at the eleventh minute, Damon had a feeling Mr Schulter would be gone.

But he wasn't late and when he went into the bar, he saw a burly man in a gray coat reading the *Wall Street Journal*, sitting alone and drinking a cup of coffee.

'Mr Schulter?' Damon said, standing at the table.

Schulter looked up. He had a square, monumental jaw, a bluish-black stubble of beard that looked as though it would destroy razors and small, mineral-blue eyes set in heavy pouches, the eyes permanently devoid of affection or confidence in the human race. When he looked up, Damon thought of the guns of battleships moving in their turrets, preparing a broadside. All this man understands, Damon thought, is duplicity and firing for effect.

'Sit down.' The detective folded the newspaper carefully and put it down on the table beside him. He did not ask Damon if he wanted anything to eat or drink. He wasted no time on amenities. 'Mrs Sparman says you've been threatened on the telephone,' he said. He sounded bored, as though Damon should have known long ago that everyone was threatened in one way or another, that it was a fact of life, like the weather, and that there was little, if anything, to be done about it. 'She told me the gist of what the individual said on the phone. It isn't much to go on, unless you have some idea of who it was and why he called you at this particular time.'

'Well,' Damon said, 'I'm a literary agent and . . .'

Schulter nodded, the guns elevating slightly. 'Mrs Sparman explained about your work.'

'I made an especially profitable deal for an unknown author and it caused quite a stir in publishing circles and I've been interviewed and my name and photograph have been in the papers.'

Schulter nodded again. 'The goddamn newspapers,' he said.

'Troublemakers. I've lost some open-and-shut convictions because they spilled the beans on cases before I could make my
evidence hold up in court. So – this individual thinks he has
something on you that you'll pay him for to keep his trap shut.
Does that sound reasonable to you, Mr Damon?'

'Yes.'

'Have you any idea why the individual called you a bad boy?'
Schulter stared coldly at Damon and Damon knew that he was
looking for something in his face, a twitch, a change of expression that would reveal to the detective whether Damon was going
to lie or not.

'I haven't the faintest idea,' Damon said. There was no
indication in the glacial blue eyes that the detective either
believed or disbelieved him.

'The individual, this Mr Zalovsky, didn't mention any sum
of money?'

'No.'

'But he said that you'd have to pay for being a bad boy.'

'Yes.'

'Payment doesn't always have to mean money. Revenge
comes to mind.'

'I thought of that.'

'Have you any idea?'

'Not really,' Damon said.

'What does that mean?'

Damon had the feeling, from the harsh, demanding tone of
Schulter's voice, that when the detective finished quizzing him,
he would take out a pair of manacles and march him off to the
police station. 'It means,' Damon said, 'that just about everybody has known people who think you've injured or insulted
them in some way.'

'Would you give me an example, please? From your own
life.'

'Well, not exactly from my own,' Damon said. 'My wife
remembered something this morning and spoke to me about it
on the phone just before you called.'

'Your wife,' the detective said. 'Mrs Sparman mentioned
her. What did she remember?'

Schulter was looking at his watch and Damon told him as

briefly as possible about the man hanging around the school and Sheila's going to the police and the encounter in front of their house and the man calling her a lesbian bitch. 'She found his name on a scrap of paper in the drawer of her desk,' Damon said. 'McVane. No first name.'

Schulter snorted, sounding disgusted with the criminal carelessness of the people with whom he was forced to deal. 'Does she know the name of the police officer she complained to and who allegedly warned the individual?'

'I'm pretty sure she doesn't,' Damon said apologetically.

'The badge number?'

'I'll ask her, but I'm just about certain she doesn't have it.'

Schulter shook his head irritably. 'If only people would learn that they have to help the police if they want them to protect them . . .'

'Neither my wife nor myself,' said Damon, showing irritation himself, 'have had anything to do with the police before this. We're complete amateurs in crime.'

'There's always a first time,' Schulter said. He said it as though from now on Damon and his wife could expect a series of events that would force them into a more professional approach to criminal behavior. 'Anyway, I'll put McVane's name through the computer and see what comes up. Probably nothing.' He gazed reproachfully at Damon. 'Anything else?'

Damon hesitated, took a long breath. 'I got a call from Gary, Indiana, about two months ago,' he said. 'From a lady. In my office. I haven't said a word about it to anyone and I don't want my wife to know about it. I'd like you to promise me you won't say anything about it that might get back to her . . .'

'You're the one who's being threatened, Mr Damon,' Schulter said coldly. 'Nobody's threatening *me*. I'll do my best, but I can't promise anything. But if you want protection, you'd better tell me.'

It was warm in the restaurant and Damon took out his handkerchief and wiped off the sweat on his forehead. The detective had not taken off his heavy coat, but there were no signs that the heat was bothering him or that any extremity of climate would ever make the slightest difference to him. Damon looked around to see if there was anyone near enough at any of the tables to overhear what he was going to say. 'It was a girl,' he said, dropping his voice so that he was almost whispering, making Schulter lean toward him to hear what he was saying. For the first time, there was a look of interest, almost of pleasure, on the detective's face. 'A girl,' Damon went on, 'a young woman really, married. I had an affair with her. Her husband was the coach of a high school football team in Gary, Indiana. She was in New York to see her parents and I met her. She – well, she became pregnant. By me. They hadn't been able to have any children. They tried, she told me, but nothing worked. She wouldn't have an abortion. She was going to keep the child, she said, and let her husband believe it was his.'

'Ah,' Schulter said, with satisfaction, 'you *have* been a bad boy.'

'I don't feel guilty,' Damon said. 'She used me instead of artificial insemination, that's all.'

'It wasn't as artificial as all that.' For once, there was a glint of amusement in the detective's eyes. 'Do you want to tell me her name?'

'I suppose I should. Mrs Julia Larch.'

'There might be a connection there,' Schulter said thoughtfully.

'She lives in Gary. The caller said he was from Chicago.'

'Gary isn't far from Chicago. Let's go on a little. How do you know the child was born?'

'She wrote me a letter to my office.' Damon closed his eyes, seeing the letter once more, the backward slanting handwriting on scented blue paper. *Congratulations*, he had read, wrinkling his nose a little because of the scent of the heavy paper, *you are now the father of an eight-pound boy*. He remembered the mixture of shame and elation as he had torn up the letter and the envelope and dropped the scraps into the wastebasket. He and Elaine, sensing from the beginning that their marriage would not last, had been careful to avoid pregnancy. Sheila had wanted children but their efforts had been without result. They had spared themselves the pain of discovering whose fault it was. Now he knew that he, at least, was fertile. An only child himself, ever since his older brother, Davey, had died of leukemia at the age of ten, he finally had a son, even if he didn't know his name and probably would never see him. His blood would be carried on.

Schulter was asking him a question and he opened his eyes. 'How is it,' Schulter was saying, 'that suddenly, so many years later, out of the blue, you might say, she happened to call you?'

'About a year ago she wrote me again. She was coming to New York with the kid and she wanted me to meet her and him. She gave me the address of a friend of hers where I could write her safely.'

'*Did* you see the kid?'

'No. I wrote her that it was long in the past and that I thought it would be better if we didn't complicate things,' Damon said. 'Actually, it's occurred to me through the years that I didn't really know anything about the woman, that she might have been sleeping with a dozen men around New York while she was here, that it might have been anybody's son. Well, when she called, she said she'd kept the letter, hidden away, and the husband found it.'

Schulter nodded. 'The lesson is – never put anything in writing. Go on. What else did the lady have to say on the phone?'

'She was crying, so that it was hard for her to talk and she was not very coherent, but I managed to piece out that the husband began beating her until she told him the whole story. True or not. She told me he swore he'd grind me to a pulp if he ever ran across me. And he said I'd better pay for the support of the boy and his education if I knew what was good for me.'

'Have you been paying?'

'I sent her a thousand-dollar check.'

'That was a mistake,' Schulter said. 'Your name on it and all.'

'I didn't know what else to do,' Damon said wearily. Truth and consequences, he thought, was not a game, but a blood sport.

'Do you have her address?'

'Yes.' Damon took a small notebook out of his pocket and wrote the address down and tore the page out of the notebook and handed it to Schulter.

'I'll call a police captain I know in Gary,' Schulter said, 'and ask him to check the guy out.'

'Tell him to be discreet, for God's sake.'

'Discreet' – Schulter's upper lip curled. 'That's a word police captains have to look up in the dictionary. The next time that individual, Zalovsky, calls you, what're you going to do?'

'I thought maybe you could tell me what I ought to do.'

Schulter thought for a moment, took a sip of his cold coffee. 'Well, the first thing I suggest is that you attach a recording machine to your phone. Then when he calls, try to make an appointment to meet him the next day. Then let me know where and when the meeting's going to take place and I'll try to be there or somewhere around there, hoping he won't notice me.'

'The time he called,' Damon said, 'he said he wanted to see me in ten minutes. On the corner. I imagine his next call will be like that, too. There won't be any time to call you.'

Schulter blew his breath out through his teeth, making a whistling sound. 'You could buy some equipment to wire yourself up so that you can tape what he says to you. You can get the stuff in any of the electronic equipment stores.' He looked at his watch, pushed the cup and saucer away from him. 'I got to be going. If you have any more nice little stories in your past like Mrs Larch's, you might try to remember them and put them down on paper, with names and dates, for the next time I see you.' He stood up, stolid, bulky, not sweating in his heavy overcoat, and put on a narrow-brimmed dark brown felt hat that looked ridiculously small on his massive head. 'One last thing,' he said as Damon rose, 'Mrs Sparman said that you were considering asking for a permit for a pistol.'

'That's right.'

'How old are you, Mr Damon?'

'Sixty-five.'

'You ever handle a small arm before?'

'No. I never touched a gun in my life.'

'Where were you during the war?'

'I was in the Merchant Marine. They didn't issue guns.'

Schulter nodded. 'A gun'll do you more harm than good,' he said. 'Anyway, there're too goddamn many guns on the street as it is. Merchant Marine, eh?' There was no mistaking the contempt in his voice. 'Overtime pay for days spent in combat zones. Rough duty, we used to call it.'

'Were *you* in the war?'

'First Marines,' Schulter said. 'No overtime pay.'

'Weren't you awfully young? What are you now – fifty?'

'Fifty-seven,' Schulter said. 'I joined up when I was seventeen. Balmy days in the romantic South Pacific. I still turn yellow a couple of times a year. Well, I'm on my way. I ain't got the time to tell you the story of my life. Those crazy Jews in the diamond district – they walk around with two hundred thousand bucks' worth of stones in those attaché cases – they might as well put a sign on their backs – Come and get me. Then they're surprised they're murdered. If I was them, I'd hire a platoon of infantrymen from the Israeli army to patrol Forty-seventh Street. I got a heavy afternoon ahead of me – I got to check on two dead men's dearest friends.' He settled the absurd little hat more securely on his balding head. 'Stay here for a minute or two after I leave. I don't want us to go out on the street together. And hope for the best.'

There was no handshake and the old Marine strode toward the bar, rolling like a sailor in a storm as he went through the doorway.

CHAPTER
EIGHT

HE WALKED slowly up Sixth Avenue, remembering that there was a big store that sold electronic equipment near Fiftieth Street. He felt physically bruised after his session with Lieutenant Schulter. It was as though he had just gone through an excessively rough massage. Schulter hadn't been of much help, had, in fact, raised more questions than given answers. And it had been painful to have to tell him about Julia. After all these years to come weeping out of the past to bedevil him with a problem not of his own making. He remembered the evening they met. He and Sheila had gone to a small party at which the talk had been mostly about books. Someone had brought Julia to the party. In talking to her, Damon learned she had been a librarian before her marriage and regretted having left New York. She only joined in the general conversation at intervals, although the few things she said made it plain that she had read a great many of the contemporary writers, knew about all the books that came up in the course of the evening and kept up with literary gossip, even in Gary, by reading a lot of magazines and by correspondence with friends she had left behind in New York who were on the fringes of the publishing and theatrical worlds. She was a pretty little thing, in a pale, washed-out, shy way and she made no distinct impression on Damon, either good or bad.

He was going through a rough period with Sheila. He was drinking heavily because his business was going badly and several of his more successful clients had drifted away. Three or four nights a week he stayed out until two or three o'clock in the morning with friends of his who could be counted on to drink themselves into a stupor by midnight. He, himself, more often than not, reached his apartment walking unsteadily and fumbling as he put the key into the lock of the front door. His excuses were lame and Sheila listened to them in icy silence. They hadn't made love for weeks before the night of the party. When they got home after it, they barely said good night to each other before Sheila turned off the light on her bedside table.

He was feeling lustful and had a huge erection and reached out to caress her. She pushed his hand away angrily. 'You're drunk again,' she said. 'I don't make love to drunks.'

He lay back, wallowing in self-pity. Nothing is right, he thought, everything is sliding downhill, this marriage won't last much longer.

In the morning, he didn't wait for Sheila to make his breakfast, but had it in a cafeteria on the way to work. Miraculously, he had no hangover. Clear-headed, he decided that his behavior of the last few months had been Sheila's fault as well as his. The deterioration of the marriage had started with a quarrel about money. He was bringing very little in and Sheila never made much, and the bills were piling up. Then a publisher with an unsavory reputation who had become rich by publishing sensational semi-pornographic books had made him an offer of a job in his office to start a more respectable line. The money he promised was very good, but the man was a vulgarian and Damon felt it would take ten Damons ever to make him respectable. He had turned the offer down and had made the mistake of telling Sheila about it. She had been furious and let him know it.

'You've had it too soft up to now, my dear husband,' she had said. 'Integrity is all very well, but it doesn't pay any bills. If you'd ever had to deal with abused, bewildered, violent children, like me, you'd know what it's like to have to do the meanest and ugliest of jobs to keep from starving.'

'Don't be melodramatic.'

'You're the one who's being melodramatic. Sacrificing everything to keep the holy flame of literature alive. Okay, remain pure and three cheers for Roger Damon's precious integrity. I know you too well to think for a minute that you'd change anything just to please me. Go back to that seedy shrine of an office of yours and smoke your pipe and wait for the next T. S. Eliot to come through the door and anoint you with a signed contract.'

'Sheila,' he had said sadly, disturbed by this echo of what Mr Gray had told him of his last conversation with his son and the son's contempt when he said that his father was content to live in a corner on crusts all his life. 'Sheila, you're not talking like yourself.'

'There's one thing I can guarantee you, my dear husband,' Sheila said harshly, 'and that is that poverty is one sure way of changing the tone of a lady's voice.'

It was after that he took to drink and late nights with the boys, as Sheila sardonically called them. Any excuse in a storm, he thought, too honest with himself to be able to shift all the blame.

Remembering all this and the stubborn resentment on Sheila's face that had persisted now for months, he thought, She looks like a peasant and she's acting like a peasant. It was ugly and he didn't like it and although he wasn't sure how it would turn out in the end he was certain he wasn't going to endure it any longer.

He had been sitting at his desk, unhappily going over his accounts and thinking resentfully of how Sheila had pushed his hand away in bed the night before when the phone rang and he picked it up. It was Julia Larch. He had tried to keep the surprise out of his voice when she announced her name. 'I've been thinking how nice it was to meet you last night,' she said, 'and how much nicer it would be to meet you again.'

'That's very kind of you, Mrs . . . uh . . . Mrs Larch,' Damon said.

'I dreamed about you just before I woke up this morning.' She laughed softly. 'That's just about ten minutes ago.'

'I hope the dream was a pleasant one,' Damon said, beginning to feel embarrassed and hoping that Oliver at his desk couldn't guess what was being said at the other end of the telephone line.

She laughed again. 'It was very sexy,' she said.

'That's good news.'

'And I thought, Wouldn't it be a good way to end my holiday in New York if you'd come up to my room right away, before I could forget the dream, and make love to me.'

'Well, I, . . . I,' Damon stuttered. 'It's very tempt . . .'

'I'm at the Hotel Borden. It's on East Thirty-ninth Street. The room number is 426. The door will be open.' And she hung up.

Damon put the phone down slowly, painfully aware, after weeks of abstinence, of how much the low voice over the phone had aroused him.

'Anything important?' Oliver asked.

'Just somebody saying good-bye.' He sat for five minutes more looking at the dire figures listed on the page before him, then stood up and went out of the office and walked across town to East Thirty-ninth Street and the hotel door that would be open for him.

He was still thinking about that call almost eleven years ago and the day that had followed it as he made his way through the heavy noontime pedestrian traffic of Sixth Avenue. In bed, Julia Larch had proved to be neither pale nor washed out or shy and by the time night fell he had had more orgasms than he had ever had in one day or one night, even when he was a youth of eighteen.

Whether it was a coincidence or not, after that his fortunes improved abruptly. A client whose previous two books had been badly received and had not sold came out with a novel that stayed somewhere in the middle of the bestseller lists for two months; Damon swung a contract for a newspaperman to co-write an autobiography with a movie star and arranged for a whopping advance; an aunt in Worcester died and left him ten thousand dollars in her will. He no longer felt the need to drink and Sheila, at first suspicious that this was only a passing phase, finally became the old Sheila again and apologized for being a shrew. It was no longer necessary to reach out for her in bed because she now reached out for him.

Looking back at it now, he could date his happiness for the last decade from the day he went up to Julia Larch's room. But now, remembering the events of the past few days, he felt that a new era, dark and cold, one of wire-taps and warnings, of men who dealt in murder, an era of shameful memories, ushered in by the continuing presence of the dead, was beginning for him. He knew he was going to get drunk that afternoon. He also knew that Sheila, her faith in him as a dependable provider now restored, would forgive him for it.

He had reached the store that sold electronic equipment and gazed into the window, marveling at the limitless ingenuity of mankind which had so cleverly solved the most abstruse of problems which nature had set before the race to produce the tiny computers, the radios and cassette players and minute television sets. Before he went in, he decided he'd buy a message-taking machine for his home telephone, but not the gadget with which he could turn himself into a peripatetic recording studio. I am not built for spying, he told himself righteously. But without really confessing it to himself, he knew he was being superstitious. If he wired himself for sound, when Zalovsky called next, he would feel compelled to see him. Unwired, there would be no good reason, he told himself, to confront the man.

He went in and crossed to a counter where a clerk was waiting on a customer. 'I want one that's small and light enough so that I can throw it into my bag when I travel,' the customer was saying.

Damon started as he heard the voice. It was the voice of the man who been in acting classes with him before the war and had been a shipmate and close friend of his in the Merchant Marine and shared an apartment with him for several years, Maurice Fitzgerald. At the time that Damon was deciding to give up acting, Fitzgerald was already doing very well on the stage and in constant demand. They had remained good friends, even though Damon had left the theatre, but had parted coolly. Their friendship had been irreparably damaged and Damon had not gone to the farewell party for Fitzgerald and Damon's recent lover, Antoinetta Bradley, on the eve of their departure for London. But now, seeing the familiar jaunty face, under the Irish tweed hacking cap, the coolness was gone and replaced by the old comradely warmth of the days on the ship and of the

78

bachelor apartment. In London, with his sonorous Irish voice and his ability to play any sort of part, Fitzgerald had made a solid career for himself as a dependable second lead. Despite his talents, he had known he never would be a star. He was short and his face, elastic and sly, would have been useful to a comedian in burlesque. He could never have been called handsome, even by his mother, as he used to say with a rueful smile.

Damon was tempted to go up to the man, whose back was now turned to him, and tap him on the shoulder and say, 'On deck, mate.' But, feeling a strange, disturbing tingling all over his body and remembering his encounter with the man he had thought was Mr Gray, he waited until he could get another good look before saying anything. One encounter in a week like the one with the false Mr Gray was enough for anyone.

But when the man turned around, Damon saw that it *was* Fitzgerald: not the young man he had known, with black hair and an unlined face, but a man of about the same age as himself, with gray sideburns under the cap.

'Well, I'll be damned,' Fitzgerald said. 'Roger Damon!'

Even as they shook hands, Damon knew that no matter what, out of fear of ghosts, he would not have been the first to speak. 'What're you doing back in the old country?' Damon asked.

'I'm in a play that's starting rehearsals tomorrow. I didn't realize I'd get such a kick in being back in New York. Is there a man with soul so dead, who etcetera, etcetera . . . And bumping into you the second day back is just the icing on the cake.' He gazed fondly at Damon. 'You look well, Roger.'

'As do you.'

'A little ragged around the edges.' He took off his cap and touched his head. 'Gray hair. Worry lines around the eyes. The eyes no longer shining and innocent. Well, I'm glad to see you still have your hair, too.' He grinned. 'Two old cocks. Bare, ruined choirs, where late the sweet birds sang and all that.'

'You don't look old at all.' Damon said. He was speaking the truth. At the worst, Fitzgerald looked no more than fifty, although he was several months older than Damon.

'Being in the public eye. Does wonders, in a desperate sort of way, towards keeping up the illusion of youth.'

'Sir,' the clerk, who had been standing patiently watching the two men, now asked, 'Sir, are you taking this set with you?'

'Yes, thank you.' Fitzgerald tossed a credit card down on the counter. 'What're you buying here in this house of magic?'

'I'm just looking, not buying.' Damon didn't want to have to explain to Fitzgerald why he needed a machine that took messages over the phone and excused you for not taking the calls in person. 'I think this reunion calls for a drink. Don't you?'

Fitzgerald shook his head regretfully. 'Damn it, I've got a lunch with the producer of the show. Mustn't stand up the brass, you know. I'm late as it is.'

'How about tomorrow night? Have dinner at our place. I'd like you to meet my wife.' Fitzgerald had known Elaine and had congratulated Damon on getting rid of her, but he had gone to London long before Damon married for the second time.

'That sounds smashing,' Fitzgerald said. 'What time and where?'

'Eight P.M. Here, I'll give you my address.' He took out the notebook from which he had torn a page to write Julia Larch's address for Schulter and wrote his own address for Fitzgerald. The local habitations and names of friends and enemies, torn out of a twenty-cent notebook. Poet's work, as Shakespeare had noted.

'Before you go,' Damon said, hesitating before asking the question, 'is Antoinetta here with you?'

Fitzgerald looked at him queerly. 'She died in an airplane accident,' he said, his voice flat. 'Ten years ago. The plane went down in the Irish Sea. All hands lost.'

'I'm sorry,' Damon said lamely. 'Very sorry.'

Fitzgerald shrugged. 'The luck of the draw,' he said. 'Ah, I try to be offhand about it, and I thought I'd get over it, but I never have.' He tried a smile. 'No sense thinking about.' He made a little ambiguous gesture, dismissive, warding off pity? Damon couldn't tell.

They walked out onto the avenue together.

'See you tomorrow night at eight,' Fitzgerald said. 'Tell your wife I eat anything at all.' He jumped spryly into a taxi. Damon watched as the taxi drove off, then went back into the shop and up to the same counter and bought the instrument for taking messages off the phone.

Then, carrying the machine in a wrapped box, he went into the nearest bar and ordered the first drink of the afternoon and thought of the good times and bad times he and Fitzgerald had had together.

Among them were the long nights in Downey's Restaurant or Harold's Bar, where actors gathered after their shows were out, and he and Fitzgerald would argue with anyone who came along about the different talents of O'Neill, Odets, Saroyan, Williams, Miller, and George Bernard Shaw. Fitzgerald, who had a prodigious memory, would quote from all of them or anybody else, to prove a point. Styles of acting were examined and Fitzgerald dubbed The Method, as exemplified by the Group Theatre, 'The New York School of Mumble.' His father was Irish and had gone to Trinity in Dublin and had bequeathed his son a clear and pleasing musical speech, which could rise to Shakespearean heights or drop into a lilting Irish accent when he quoted passages from Joyce.

Despite his stature and the comedian's face, he always attracted girls and there were always two or three of them around, asking him to recite favorite poems of theirs or one of the great soliloquies, which Fitzgerald delivered with quiet passion and admirable clarity, no matter how drunk he happened to be at the time.

He also had a great talent for picking up girls who could cook and would bring them to the apartment triumphantly to prepare feasts of *boeuf bourgignon* and *fritto misto* and *duck à l'orange*. When he found a girl who could cook better than the current candidate for the title, he ruthlessly cut her off and dubbed the new one *la Maîtresse de la Maison*. Damon couldn't count the names of *Maîtresses de la Maison* they went through while they had the apartment together.

The first time Damon had brought Antoinetta to the apartment, Fitzgerald had immediately asked, 'Can you cook?'

Antoinetta had looked questioningly at Damon. 'Who is this peculiar fellow?' she asked.

81

'Humor him,' Damon had said. 'He has this thing about cooking.'

'Do I look like a cook?' Antoinetta had asked.

'You look like the goddess rising from the foam,' Fitzgerald had said, 'and the foam is made of chocolate mousse.'

Antoinetta had laughed at that. 'The answer is no. I definitely cannot cook. What can *you* do?'

'I can tell a hawk from a handsaw and a flat soufflé from a sirloin steak.' He turned to Damon. 'What else can I do?'

'Argue,' Damon said, 'sleep late in the morning and make the rafters ring when you recite Yeats.'

'Do you know "In Flanders Fields"?' Antoinetta asked. 'I recited it once in the school auditorium when I was ten. They cheered when I finished.'

'I bet,' Fitzgerald said nastily. Damon knew Antoinetta well enough to know that she was joking, getting even for being asked if she were a cook. You couldn't joke about poetry with Fitzgerald. He turned to Damon. 'Don't marry the lady, good friend,' he said. He never told Damon if he had said it because Antoinetta couldn't cook or because he didn't approve of 'In Flanders Fields.'

In the end, Damon thought, ordering a second drink from the barman, he had taken Fitzgerald's advice. He had not married Antoinetta.

He should have warned Antoinetta before bringing her home that Fitzgerald was at his best with the Irish poets. If he had, she might have saved herself the snub and Fitzgerald would have been interested in her from the beginning and saved all three of them a great deal of trouble.

Fitzgerald's greatest admiration for poetry was reserved for that of William Butler Yeats, and during the slow voyage across the Atlantic in convoy, he and Damon would stand at the bow of the Liberty ship as it pushed across the long swells of the North Atlantic and he would intone the haunted verses of the poet. He recited 'Sailing to Byzantium' as a special treat on nights when it seemed they were out of danger and the sea was calm. Damon had heard it so often that even now, standing at a bar on Sixth Avenue, he could whisper it in Fitzgerald's Irish accent.

He whispered because he didn't want the other people in the bar to think that he was a madman, talking to himself.

> That is no country for old men.
> The young in one another's arms,
> Birds in the trees – those salmon-falls,
> The mackerel-crowded seas. Fish, flesh,
> Or fowl, commend all summer long
> Whatever is begotten, born, and dies.
> Caught in that sensual music all neglect
> Monuments of unaging intellect.

Fitzgerald would be weeping softly as he came to the end of the first verse, and Damon could feel the tears come to his own eyes as he remembered those moments.

Fitzgerald seemed to know practically all of Shakespeare by heart, and on nights of the full moon, when the convoy was outlined as perfect targets against the horizon for the wolfpacks of submarines, he would recite, with sardonic courage, Hamlet's soliloquy after Fortinbras's first exit –

> Examples gross as earth exhort me:
> Witness this army of such mass and charge
> Led by a delicate and tender prince,
> Whose spirit with divine ambition puff'd
> Makes mouths at the invisible event
> Exposing what is mortal and unsure
> To all that fortune, death and danger dare,
> Even for an egg-shell. Rightly to be great
> Is not to stir without great argument,
> But greatly to find quarrel in a straw
> And let all sleep, while, to my shame, I see
> The imminent death of twenty thousand men,
> That for a fantasy and trick of fame,
> Go to their graves like beds, fight for a plot
> Whereon the numbers cannot try the cause,

Which is not tomb enough and continent
To hide the slain? O! from this time forth
My thoughts be bloody, or be nothing worth.

One night just after he had recited the soliloquy, a ship in their convoy had been torpedoed. The ship had blown up, and they had watched the flames and the sinister column of brilliant smoke in despair as the ship went down. It was the first time they had seen one of their ships destroyed and Fitzgerald sobbed dryly, once, then said, in a soft voice, 'Good friend, we're the eggshell and all thoughts on the sea and deep in it tonight are bloody.'

Then, recovering, he had quoted from *The Tempest*, with an ironic lilt,

> Full fathom five thy father lies
> Of his bones is coral made.
> Those are pearls that were his eyes:
> Nothing of him that doth fade,
> But doth suffer a sea change
> Into something rich and strange,
> Sea nymphs hourly hourly ring his knell:
> Ding-dong.
> Hark! Now I hear them – ding-dong bell.

Fitzgerald had been silent for a moment after that, then said, 'Shakespeare, the speech for all occasions. I'll never live to play Hamlet. Ah, I'm going below. If we get hit by a torpedo, don't tell me.'

They were lucky and were never hit by a torpedo, and they came back to New York joyous, young and eager to resume the work they were born to do, as Mr Gray had said on another occasion. It was then that they decided to share an apartment. They found one near the Hudson River, in a district where the streets were mostly given over to used-car dealers and ware-houses. It was a rambling, ramshackle flat that they furnished with odds and ends of furniture, quickly cluttered with books and theatrical posters, which the girls who kept drifting in and out kept trying to put in order.

Like Damon, he had been married before the war but had received a Dear John letter from his wife in which she admitted being in love with another man whom she wanted to marry. 'It was a cold divorce,' he said. 'The legal ties were broken in Reno while I was just below Iceland in the North Atlantic.'

He swore he would never marry again and when one woman who had endured three months in the apartment made it plain she wanted him to marry her, he had declaimed to her, in Damon's presence, a mock-heroic from a play he had acted in, 'I've been swindled by women, mulcted by women, rebuffed by women, divorced by women, jilted, mocked, teased by women, laid, belayed and betrayed by women. It would take the power of Shakespeare to describe my relations with women. I was the Moor unmoored, the Dane disdained, Troilus tripped, Lear delirious, Falstaff falsified, Prospero plucked, Mercutio with a hole in him twice as deep as a well and five times as wide as a church door – and all by women.'

Then he gave the lady a chaste kiss on the forehead. 'Does that give you a faint idea of my feelings on the subject?'

The lady had laughed as he expected and had not brought the subject up again. Placidly, she had kept frequenting the apartment along with the successive bevies of other girls.

To maintain their friendship, Fitzgerald and Damon had an unspoken agreement that each would keep his hands off the girls the other had brought home, and it worked, even through the wildest of parties, until Damon appeared with Antoinetta, who soon became a fixture in their lives, sleeping over with Damon three or four times a week and even stabbing at preparing a meal for them during those infrequent intervals when Fitzgerald had run out of cooks.

In the mid-afternoon silence of the New York bar, free of submarines, a prey to other dangers, Damon ordered another drink. 'Make it a double this round,' he said to the barman. Even though he had had nothing to eat since breakfast and was drinking on an empty stomach, the whiskey was having no effect on him. He felt sober and melancholy, reflecting on the lost, exuberant years, and then the one really bad time with Fitzgerald.

Damon knew that there was something wrong when he came back to the apartment after work. It was a polar New York winter evening. The walk over from Mr Gray's office had left him chilled to the bone, and he was looking forward to drink and the warmth of the fire that he hoped Fitzgerald had started.

But there was no fire and Fitzgerald was red-eyed, still in a dressing gown, which meant that he hadn't gone out all day. He was pacing up and down unsteadily in the living room with a drink in his hand, and Damon could tell with one glance that he had been drinking all afternoon, something he never did before going onstage, which he would have to do that night.

Fitzgerald looked startled when Damon came into the room. 'Oh,' he said, raising his glass, 'you caught me in the act. An actor's unforgivable crime. Reporting for duty while under the influence.'

'What's wrong, Maurice?'

'What's wrong,' Fitzgerald said, 'is that I'm a shit, if that can be considered wrong in this day and age. Join me in a drink. We're both going to need it tonight.'

'Curtain time is in less than three hours, Maurice.'

'I can go through that piece of money-grabbing Broadway junk in my sleep,' Fitzgerald said contemptuously. 'I can also let the curtain go up without me and let the audience guess who's missing.'

'Cut it out, Maurice. What is it?'

'All right, nursey-nurse.' Fitzgerald went over to the table where they kept the bottles and the ice and glasses. 'Here, let me fix you a drink. The maids have all fled. And about time, too.' His hands shook as he made a drink for Damon and freshened his own. The lip of the bottle clinked against the rim of the glasses. Spilling whiskey from both glasses, he crossed the room to where Damon was standing. Damon took a glass, sipped at it and sat down.

'That's it, good friend, sit down. It might be a long chat.'

'Okay, Maurice,' Damon said, 'what is it?'

'It,' Fitzgerald said, 'is Antoinetta. Or to be more accurate, it is Antoinetta and your good friend, Maurice Fitzgerald, aptly named. Bastard son of Gerald.'

'You don't have to spell it out,' Damon said quietly, although he had to fight back the impulse to strangle the man at whose side he had survived the war and had celebrated hundreds of hilarious nights.

'You didn't guess?' Fitzgerald, Damon could see, was trying to look contrite, but with all he had drunk, the expression on the loose comedian's face was a leer.

'No,' Damon said, 'I didn't guess.'

'Bless the innocents of this black world.' Suddenly, Fitzgerald hurled his glass into the empty fireplace. The whiskey made a trail across the floor and the glass shattered against the back wall of the fireplace.

'How long has it been going on between you two?' Damon still managed to keep his voice down. He didn't want details or explanations; all he wanted was to rid himself of the flushed, leering face hanging over him. But the words came out automatically.

'A month. Just enough time for a lady to make up her mind.'

'Christ,' Damon said, 'she slept with me all this weekend, and last night, for God's sake, with you in the next room.'

'*Amor omnia vincit*,' Fitzgerald said. 'Or perhaps the other way around. *Omnia amor vincit*. Men and women, good friend, men and women. Beasts of the jungle.'

'*Are* you going to marry her?'

'Probably in due time,' Fitzgerald said. 'There are decks to be cleared, regrets to be expressed.' He had been having a long affair with one of the cooks he had brought home. She was cloyingly devoted to him and Damon guessed that was one of the decks to be cleared.

'There's no rush to the church,' Fitzgerald said. 'I'll make an honest woman of Antoinetta in the end.'

'You *are* a shit,' Damon said bitterly.

'I said it first,' Fitzgerald said, 'but I don't mind being quoted. Where the hell is my drink?'

'You threw it in the fireplace.'

'Oh, the lost and wind-grieved ghost of a bottle of Scotch. From the works of Thomas Wolfe, a famous American author. A stone, a leaf, an unfound door. More from the famous author. God, I never can forget anything. What a burden. I won't forget you, good friend.'

'Thanks,' Damon said. He stood up. 'I'm going to pack and get out of here.'

Fitzgerald put out his hand to stop him. 'You can't. I'm the one who has to go.'

'I'm not wild about living in a whorehouse,' Damon said. 'Especially after I find out what the red light in the window means.'

'One of us has to stay,' Fitzgerald said. 'Our lease still has a year to run.'

Damon hesitated. He couldn't pay for another place to live and pay half the rent for the apartment at the same time.

'I have a prop-proposition to make,' Fitzgerald said. 'Let's toss for it. The loser stays and pays the full rent.'

Damon sighed. 'Okay,' he said.

'You got a coin?' Fitzgerald asked. 'All my change is on the table in my room, and I hate the thought of your being alone for a minute, good friend.'

'Just shut your mouth, Maurice,' Damon said, reaching into his pocket for a coin. He pulled out a quarter. 'And if you call me good friend once more, I'll break your jaw. I'll toss. You call.'

'Tails,' Fitzgerald said.

Damon tossed the coin, caught it in the palm of his hand and covered it for a long ten seconds with his other hand. Then he lifted the hand. Fitzgerald was bending over to see the coin. He let out his breath in a low hiss of sound.

'Heads it is. I lost. I stay,' he said. 'The luck of the draw. Acceptable losses, as the military so delicately put it when drawing up plans for the next invasion which would cost only eighteen thousand lives. I'm sorry, Roger.'

Damon flipped the coin at Fitzgerald, who made no move to catch it and let it hit him in the forehead before dropping to the floor.

Then Damon went in to pack. It didn't take long, and when

88

he came out of his room, he heard Fitzgerald singing in the shower, preparing for his evening performance.

Full fathom five Antoinetta lies, Damon thought, and moved with his glass down toward the end of the bar because a group of men had come in and were arguing loudly next to him about a television show, for which one of the men was the sponsor's representative and the other men were advertising executives and people connected with the program in one way or another.

Full fathom five, Damon thought. Is there coral in the Irish Sea? He had never seen Antoinetta again, and the wound had long since healed, and her double defection had left him free to marry Sheila, blessed woman, lover, stalwart companion, many years later. Fitzgerald had done him a service, even though neither he nor Damon had known it at the time. Before the farewell party for Fitzgerald and Antoinetta Bradley, to which Damon had been invited and had not gone, he had received a letter from Fitzgerald, in which his erstwhile friend had written, 'Forgive me. I love you like a brother and I am not one to use the word *brother* loosely. But brothers are fated to screw each other. Consider Cain. Be happy. And the next time we meet I hope we can embrace.'

Well, this afternoon had been the next time they had met, and if Damon had been a man used to such gestures between men, he would have embraced his old deceitful friend. When Maurice came to dinner the following night, he would remind him of his letter and he would embrace him.

By this time the whiskey had taken effect and the world was misting over, and for no reason that he could explain to himself he tried to repeat the first verse of 'Sailing to Byzantium,' but stumbled over the words and didn't remember the middle lines and giggled foolishly as he said, with great dignity, to the barman, 'The check, please.'

Under the influence, as Fitzgerald had put it, he left the message-taking machine on the bar. He was not thinking of Zalovsky or Lieutenant Schulter at the moment.

He never got the chance to embrace Fitzgerald. When he opened the *New York Times* the next morning, there was Fitzgerald's photograph on the front page and beside it the story. 'Maurice Fitzgerald, the noted actor, whose career spanned more than forty years on the American and late the English stage, suffered a heart attack and collapsed in the restaurant in which he was lunching with the theatrical producer, Mr Nathan Brown. He was taken to the Lenox Hill Hospital in an ambulance but was pronounced dead on arrival.'

Damon put the paper down on the table beside his coffee cup and stared vacantly out the window at the house across the street. Then he bowed his head and put his hand over his eyes.

Sheila, who was sitting across from Damon at the breakfast table, saw by the expression on his face that something was seriously amiss. 'What's the matter, Roger?' she asked anxiously. 'Are you all right? You've suddenly gone dead pale.'

'Maurice died just after I saw him yesterday afternoon.'

'Oh, the poor man,' Sheila said. She reached over and took the newspaper from his side of the table. She glanced at the small headline at the bottom of page one, then read the short article. 'He was only sixty-five,' she said.

'My age,' Damon said. 'Time to go.'

'Don't say that,' Sheila said sharply.

Damon felt that he was going to break into uncontrollable sobs. To stem them, he made a hideous joke. 'Well,' he said, 'he's missed a good meal tonight.'

CHAPTER
NINE

WHEN HE got to the office, the first thing he did was apologize to Oliver for his outburst the day before.

'Oh, everybody has the right to show a bit of annoyance once in a while,' Oliver said, embarrassed by the apology. 'Sheila seemed so worried, and to tell you the truth, so was I.' He smiled childishly at Damon. 'A little temper clears the air.'

'Well,' Damon said. 'Sheila knows everything by now – or at least everything *I* know, so there's no need for her to get daily bulletins from the office anymore.' He said it without anger but Oliver understood it.

'Whatever you say, boss,' he said. '*Omerta*, as they say in Sicily. The code of silence. But if you ever need my help . . .'

'Thanks,' Damon said, 'I'll be all right.'

Damon looked up the number of Nathan Brown, the producer, and called him. He had to wait a long time. 'I'm terribly sorry to have kept you waiting, Mr Damon,' the operator said, when he had given his name. She sounded flustered and was close to tears. 'This morning here . . . Everybody in the whole world is calling. You can imagine what it's like in the office. I'll give you Mr Brown.'

There were some clicks on the wire, then Brown was on. 'The last words he spoke were of you,' Brown said. 'He told me, "I met a wonderful old friend just before I came to lunch. It's a lucky omen. Roger Damon, do you know . . . ?' And before I could answer, he began to sway in his chair in the most frightening way, and before I could reach over to help him, he toppled to the floor. The restaurant suddenly became still as the grave and I guess a waiter called for an ambulance, because I heard the siren in what seemed just a few seconds later, although at that moment, it's curious, I had no sense of time. The ambulance men did what they could, but it was no use and they carried him off. It's a terrible loss to all of us . . . Such a fine and talented man . . .'

'Who's making the funeral arrangements?' On the walk uptown from the office Damon had been able to gain control of his nerves and he spoke unemotionally.

'When I got back to the office after the hospital, when it was all over,' Brown said, 'I took a chance and called his number in London. A woman answered. I didn't know who it was, if it was his wife or whatever and I asked and she said she was a friend, a very close friend and that she knew Maurice had wanted to be buried in England. I wrote down her name. I'll give it to you and the telephone number. You might want to call her.'

'I do,' Damon said. 'Who's making the arrangements?'

'I am,' Brown said. 'Or at least trying to. It's so complicated.' He sounded weary and uncertain of himself. He had expected the beginning of rehearsals and he had come in as the curtain descended on the last act of closing night. 'Would you like to view the body? It's at the . . .'

'No,' said Damon, 'I would not like to see the body, thank you.' The knowledge that Maurice was dead was as much as he could bear; he did not want to be confronted with the cold mortal fact. His friend was now just a memory in a long box; he would not mind traveling alone to the lady who answered the phone of his place in London when he was out of town and who now would take full possession of the man, who while he had been living with her had been possessed by the memory of a woman drowned in the Irish Sea a long time ago. It would be cruel to encumber her with an old American friend who might break down and inadvertently blurt out stories of the dead man's past that she did not want to hear.

'Do you know what his religion was?' Mr Brown was asking.

'Catholic,' Damon said. 'Not much of one. I doubt that he believed in the Virgin Birth.'

'These days.' Brown sighed, sad at the decline of faith since

Moses and Jesus Christ. 'Still, I asked the priest at the hospital to administer Extreme Unction. Just in case, you know.'

'It didn't do any harm.' Damon didn't remember Fitzgerald ever having gone to Mass.

'I thought that it might be fitting if we arranged a kind of memorial service for him in a week or two. In a small theatre. Nonsectarian. He was very popular among his fellow actors, even though most of his career was in England. He did some recordings of Shakespeare for the BBC. Play one of those, have people give small eulogies. As his oldest friend, would you . . . ?'

'Sorry, no,' Damon said. He remembered Fitzgerald's speeches the evening when they had tossed for the apartment, but doubted that even the nonsectarian audience assembled in Fitzgerald's memory would be pleased to hear them.

'Did he have a favorite hymn? Or poem?'

'When I knew him, it was "Sailing to Byzantium." His taste may have changed since that time.'

'Would you consider reading it, Mr Damon?'

'No, get an actor. If I read it, he'd turn in his grave.'

Mr Brown gave a short, sad laugh. 'We're not used to such modesty in the theatre,' he said. 'By the way, do you happen to have a brilliant young playwright among your clients who is just waiting to break upon the scene and needs a producer?'

Business as usual, even as dead friends are being loaded on planes to fly across an ocean. The show must go on. Scratch entry, prepare for the next race. 'Alas, no,' Damon said.

Mr Brown sighed. 'I'll have to cancel the production of the play we were just starting to rehearse. There's nobody I can think of who could replace him.'

Good for his tombstone, Damon thought. Here lies Maurice Fitzgerald, Irreplaceable. 'Have you got the number of the lady in London handy?'

'Right here.' Brown gave it to Damon and Damon wrote it on a scratch pad. 'There's a six-hour time difference, you know. I woke her. She sounded amazingly calm when I called her. English phlegm. My wife would be tearing her garments and rending her flesh in similar circumstance. Different customs, racial characteristics. Equal grief, though, I imagine.'

Damon had only known the man casually and had seen good plays and bad plays he had put on, but now he knew he liked him. He had been faced with unpleasant responsibilities and he had met them. 'Let me know,' Damon said, 'when the memorial is to take place. I'd like to be there.'

'Of course,' Brown said. 'Well, thank you. It's a sad day for all of us.'

Damon felt a wave of fatigue overcome him and he was narcotically drowsy. He looked longingly at the cracked leather couch along one wall of the office, which had been there since the first days of Mr Gray's tenure and was used only when there were two or more people in the office for conferences. What hopes had been voiced there, what failures confirmed.

'Oliver,' he said, 'would you please tell Miss Walton not to buzz us? I have to lie down and try to drop off for a few minutes.'

'Of course,' Oliver said. He looked concerned. Neither of them had ever slept on the couch. 'You okay, Roger?'

'Just a little sleepy. I had a bad night.'

Oliver gave the message to Miss Walton and Damon stretched out on the couch. He dozed off immediately, but the sleep was not restful. He had a jumbled and terrifyingly erotic dream. In it he was in a large bed he had never lain on before, with Antoinetta Bradley, young and voluptuous, and Julia Larch, muttering obscenities, both of them making love to him with wicked abandon. Maurice Fitzgerald, clothed and looking as he had looked in the electronic supply shop the day before, stood, glass in hand, leering down at the spectacle before him, and somehow, Damon's father, smiling and waving invitingly, was on his balustrade, bathed in his golden light.

When he opened his eyes, Damon was more tired than when he had lain down, shaken by the vision of lust, betrayal and accusation, of the concupiscent interweaving of the dead and the living his subconscious had conjured up in a few seconds of slumber.

Oliver was looking over worriedly at him from his desk. 'That wasn't much of a sleep,' he said. 'You were making the most awful noises.'

'I was dreaming.' Damon sat up and rubbed his eyes. 'I'll read Freud again tonight.'

'It sounded as though you were crying . . .'

'I wasn't crying,' Damon said. 'Quite the opposite.' He went over to his desk. His legs felt leaden. He pushed the button on his phone as he picked it up and told Miss Walton he was taking calls again.

'A Mr Schulter phoned a little while ago,' Miss Walton said. 'I told him you were occupied. He left a number.' She gave him the number and he wrote it down. At least, he thought, Schulter wasn't in the dream. He had been spared that. He didn't ask Miss Walton to call the number, but dialed it himself. He didn't want Miss Walton speculating on why he had business to discuss with a detective on the New York City police force. When a man's voice said, 'Homicide' over the phone, he knew he had been right to put the call through himself.

'Lieutenant Schulter,' he said to the man. 'Mr Damon returning the lieutenant's call.'

'Hello, Mr Damon,' Schulter said. His voice on the phone sounded to Damon's ear very much like Zalovsky's. 'I have some news for you. We ran your Mr McVane through the computer and found a McVane who lives near you on West Broadway. It's probably the same one. He was arrested on the complaint of a kindergarten teacher at a public school in lower Manhattan who didn't like the way he was always hanging around the kids. When he was searched, a large hunting knife was found strapped to the calf of his leg.'

'Did he go to jail?'

'Six months suspended sentence for carrying a concealed weapon,' Schulter said. 'We'll check him out. If we find the knife on him, he'll serve the time.'

'Thanks, Lieutenant,' Damon said.

'Now,' said Schulter, 'have you got any news for me? Any more calls?'

'No. I'm still waiting.'

'Have you made out those lists I asked you to make yet?'

'I'm working on it,' Damon said.

'If I was you,' said Schulter, 'I wouldn't take too long about it.'

'I'll have them for you in a day or two.'

Schulter grunted, as though he didn't believe Damon would have them in a day or two. 'I talked to my friend in Gary. He'll do some . . . uh . . . checking. What was the word you used?'

'Discreet.'

'That's it. I just told him to ask around quiet like, not to make a federal case out of it. He says he's seen the man, Larch, his being a football coach and all. He says he's well-liked, he's had three winning seasons in a row.'

'That makes me feel a lot better,' Damon said, then knew it was a mistake, because Schulter grunted again, more loudly than before. He was not a man, Damon realized, to be amused by irony when it came to the exercise of his profession.

'By the way,' Schulter said, 'did you get that electronic stuff I told you to buy?'

For the first time, Damon remembered that he had left the package on the bar the afternoon before. 'Yes,' he said, 'I bought an answering machine.' He didn't think it advisable to tell the detective that a few hours after he had bought it he had forgotten it in a crowded saloon.

'What the hell good is that?' Schulter said disgustedly. 'You think Mr Zalovsky is going to leave a message that he intends to blackmail you or shoot you through the head?'

'The clerk said the only machines he had to tape conversations off a phone give off a beeping tone to warn anybody calling that they're being taped. What's the good of that?'

'One thing I'm glad of, Mr Damon,' Schulter said, 'is that you're not serving under me in homicide. All right, attach the goddamn machine and we'll see what happens. When you got those lists, call me.'

There was an extra-loud click on the phone, as though Schulter had slammed down the phone. Damon looked thoughtfully at the couch, then stood up. 'I've got to go out for a few minutes,' he said to Oliver. 'I forgot something in a bar yesterday and I just remembered it.'

Once in the open air he was glad the errand was taking him out of the office, away from the morbid temptation of the couch and from the curious, wondering glances Oliver kept sneaking at him when he thought Damon wasn't noticing.

It was only eleven o'clock, but the bar already had a morning population of the devoted drinkers of the neighborhood. The barman was the same one who had served him the day before. When Damon asked him if anybody had turned in a package he had forgotten and left on the bar the day before, the barman looked blank. 'Hey, Eddie,' he called to the barman who was taking care of the clients at the front end of the saloon, 'we find a package yesterday? This gentleman says he left it here – What time about, Mister?'

'Four, five, something like that,' Damon said.

'Four, five o'clock, he thinks, Eddie.'

The second barman shook his head. 'Not that I heard,' he said.

'Not that he heard,' the barman said, as though he thought Damon was deaf. 'Sorry. You drinking today?'

'It sounds like a reasonable idea,' Damon said.

'What's your pleasure, Sir?' Now that he saw that Damon had turned into a customer, he became professionally courteous.

His pleasure, Damon thought, would be to leave this bar, leave this city, go to a distant foreign land where the people who died were all unknown to him, and lie on a beach and listen to the waves whisper in from thousands of miles of untraveled ocean. 'A Scotch and soda,' he said.

The dead arranged themselves beside him at the quiet morning bar. *What is your pleasure, ladies and gentlemen?* A slug of Jack Daniel's with a touch of water from the fountain at Lourdes? Antoinetta, a beaker of sea water, flavored with rue? Maurice, old Shakespeare spouter, some cakes and ale? Mr Gray, another Cognac spiked with nepenthe to forget your merchant son? Mrs Larch, although alive and kicking in Gary, Indiana, trespassing in dreams among the tombs, how about a goblet of nectar for a carnal morning on East Thirty-ninth Street or a glass of champagne on Sixth Avenue to celebrate a birthday?

Damon shook his head, annoyed at the fantasy. Back to the land of the living; McVane with his knife; Sheila pouring coffee at the breakfast table; Elaine, her face lifted, her hair dyed magenta, with her new boy friend; Mrs Dolger, the royalties

97

coming in, standing over her oven baking pies; Lieutenant Schulter among the murdered Jews, demanding lists of men or women in this real and corporeal world who might conceivably walk into the bar, gun in hand, at any moment, intent on murder.

Mr Damon, another Scotch?

A reasonable idea, Mr Damon, at this time and place and under these circumstances. Another Scotch, please.

Just five short days before, he had been a reasonably happy man, in robust health, content in his marriage, comfortable in his home, respected in his profession, fearlessly walking the streets of New York in all weathers and at all times of the day and night, never having spoken to a policeman for anything more than to ask directions, the memory of his dead mellowed by time and the realization that the generations followed each other in inevitable and eternal rhythms. Then a man whom as far as he knew he had never met put a dime in a slot and dialed a number and graves opened. Now he accosted phantoms in broad daylight, learned that a woman he had loved had lain at the bottom of the sea for ten years, her fate unknown to him. He had met a friend who once called him brother, had been reminded of one of the most painful moments of his life, had shaken the friend's hand in grateful reconciliation, had invited him to a dinner which was never served because the friend had fallen dead between one course and another in a fashionable restaurant minutes after the handshake.

'Miss Otis Regrets.' Popular song. *She cannot come to tea*. Did he dare shake any man's hand again? Could he demand that all slots be abolished, all dimes taken out of circulation? Could he walk the streets blindfolded so that he would not recognize in the flesh men who had long since turned into bare bones? Could he command himself to censor his dreams? Was he not only an agent for books, plays, stories, mild and harmless fictions, in which when one mourned as characters died all that was necessary was to turn the page, or was he a secret and dreadful agent of some unknown client, a go-between who dealt in death and whose touch, either real or imaginary, made him the prophet and unconscious recorder of dissolution, past and in the future?

He had become a psychic sonar, plumbing the depths of dreams for deadly prowlers, finding the shapes of old ship-wrecks, listening to derisive and delusive echoes that might be whales, schools of minnows, the songs of dolphins, the voices of mermaids, speaking in an unlearned language, but all saying, 'Beware.'

He was not Hamlet; the ghost of his father did not rebuke him or spur him on to revenge from the gray battlements of sleep, but stood silent in that midsummer noon sunlight, a childhood toy in his hand, beckoning him. He was not an antique Greek, he had not sailed with Ulysses; the shades of comrades-in-arms and parents who had been deprived of their proper funeral games had no claims on him from their last home in the underworld.

He was a man of today, rational, convinced he was, like his contemporaries who had probed the utmost limits of the universe, a descendant of lizards and apes, a man not favored or disfavored by primitive gods or goddesses, a scientific explainer of phenomena, a man who believed in what he could touch, see, smell or deduce from known quantities, and he felt himself drifting into an Arctic, fog-shrouded sea of necromancy.

He remembered the conversation in Gregor's studio. 'Do you believe in precognition?'

'I believe in anything that cannot be proven.'

Was he merely a signpost on the road to some supernatural Auschwitz where a final solution was being carried out for people whom he had loved or who had loved him or whose lives had barely touched his in their separate passages or was he being punished or the instrument of punishment? And if he was either or both, for what reason? Breach of trust, a few hours of casual fornication, the begetting of bastards? Self-satisfaction, the egoistic neglect of the suffering of humanity across every continent on the planet? As the twentieth century after the death of Christ drew to its close, who made the rules and what were they?

What was the message for him in all this? Who could tell him, what wife or comrade or priest or rabbi or gypsy could reveal it to him? Was there a detective in homicide who could decode it for him into rough, everyday English to tell him what it was?

Did he really want to know? Did he, like the dead Jewish diamond merchants, carry on his back the sign, *Come and get me?*

CHAPTER
TEN

THE BARTENDER put another glass down on the bar in front of
him. He did not remember ordering it, but was pleased with the
man's solicitude. He sipped at the drink, thinking, I must have
a list of some kind for Lieutenant Schulter. Where to begin? It
was necessary to be orderly. He took out his notebook, wrote on
the left page *Possible enemies – professional*, then on the facing
right page, *Possible enemies – personal*. Now, he thought with
satisfaction, I am advancing, organization is all, I have made
categories, as Gregor would put it.

He took another sip at his drink. Who had ever overtly
threatened him? Step number one. He congratulated himself on
the clarity and logic of his thinking. Candidate number one.
Damon closed his eyes, remembering a courtroom. He had
been summoned to testify as a witness in a libel case. The truth,
the whole truth and nothing but the truth, so help me God.
God, Himself had been libeled for millenia. The name of the
man was Machendorf. He had been a client, a moody, gaunt
dark youngish man, his face set against the world.

Damon had handled Machendorf's first two novels and they
had been published. They had been crude and full of violence,
but the writing had a certain rough honesty that was not to be
ignored, and Damon felt that Machendorf's report on the
hateful underside of American life had the right to be heard.
The man had acted correctly, although without gratitude, and
Damon could not bring himself to like him. But if he represented only people he liked, he would have had to close the
office in six months.

Now the manuscript of Machendorf's third novel, which Damon had finished reading the night before, was on his desk like a barrier between him and his client, with Machendorf staring at it gloomily.

While Machendorf had still been working on his book he told Damon, 'Now the bastards are going to have to sit up and take notice. If the critics have the sense they were born with, they'll recognize that they have an American Celine on their hands.'

But Damon knew as he came to the last lines of the book that nobody in his right mind would hail Machendorf as the American Celine or the American anything.

Damon had given the man good advice. He told him not to try to have it published.

Fiction or not, the protagonist was in the public eye, his habits were well known. Machendorf had caught him perfectly. The character would be recognized from the first page by almost anybody who read the New York City newspapers. The man's name was John Berkely and Machendorf had recklessly dubbed him James Berkin. Berkely was a daring real estate operator and had put up three or four of the most prestigious office buildings in midtown Manhattan. He owned a stable of thoroughbreds and was married to a beautiful woman who had been a movie star. He dabbled as an angel backing plays and was often photographed with his wife on his arm at the more spectacular openings and in the winner's circle at various racetracks, smiling widely and gingerly patting the neck of victors in highly publicized stake races.

Machendorf, senselessly, as though driven to his own destruction by some malevolent demon, had given the character in the book his profession, his stable, his movie star wife and his penchant for investing in the theatre. In the book Machendorf had made him a figure of evil, unsavory and hateful. Berkin and the other characters, also drawn from life and moving in the same circles as Berkely-Berkin, were described in lurid prose, scatological and profane, of the kind found in graffiti in public lavatories.

Before the publication of his first book Machendorf had worked for Berkely as a clerk in his office and had been fired and his animus pulsed in every line. Perhaps the man *was* evil, perhaps not. Damon had met him several times at opening night parties, but they had barely said hello to each other and Damon didn't know the man well enough to judge. But while the description of the character and his various interests was close to reality, some of the acts Machendorf had the man perform were clearly inventions and savagely presented and there was no doubt in Damon's mind that any jury would find against the writer.

Machendorf had listened in smouldering silence while Damon explained to him as gently as possible that he would be in for trouble, big trouble, if he published the book or even showed it around to editors.

'So,' Machendorf said, 'what you're trying to say is that you won't send it out with the name of the agency on it.'

'I won't send it out, period.'

'You've made a lot of money out of me.'

'Not a lot. Some.' The two books Machendorf had written before this had both been moderately successful.

'So,' Machendorf said, 'you refuse to represent me.'

'Yes,' Damon said. 'Not on this book. I'm not partial to being sued for millions of dollars.'

'You're a piss-poor yellow bastard,' Machendorf said bitterly. 'You'll never get a look at anything else I write, contract or no contract. Why don't you just handle children's books – *Bobby and Joan at Summer Camp Playing Doctor*, crap like that. That's about your speed. And the same goes for that albino fag you got working for you and licking your ass, too.'

'If I were a younger man,' Damon said, 'I'd knock you down for that. Now I'm going to show you what I think of your contract.'

The man glowered silently at Damon while he got up and went to a filing cabinet, opened it, riffled through the folders and took out some legal-looking papers, clipped together. 'This is your contract, Mr Machendorf,' he said, then began tearing up the pages. Machendorf watched him, smiling sardonically. Damon's hands were trembling and he had trouble tearing more than one page at a time of the stiff paper. 'The hell with it,' he said. 'You get the idea, I hope.' Then he threw the sheaf of papers to the floor at Machendorf's feet. 'Now, get out of the office,' he said.

'I want my manuscript,' Machendorf said.

'Here it is.' Damon pushed the thick, neatly bound pile of paper to the edge of his desk. 'It pollutes the room.'

Machendorf picked up his manuscript, ran his hand caressingly over its cover. 'Fucking flesh peddler,' he said. 'Ten percent. That's a good number for you. Ten percent of nothing. I'll be laughing at you when this book comes out and I'm sitting on my yacht reading the reviews.'

'If I were your friend,' Damon said, 'and wished you well I would hope that no one else in the whole world ever even read it, much less publish it. But I'm not your friend and I hope that the first house you show it to takes it and gives it the greatest publicity possible, because it'll be the end of you. Now, if you'll pardon me I have to go to the men's room. I believe I have to vomit.'

He left the man in the office, but pushed the door as he went out so that it remained open and both Miss Walton and Oliver Gabrielsen could see if Machendorf took it into his head to vandalize the desk or the shelves lined with books as his final revenge.

Oliver looked at him questioningly. It was the first time Damon had ever asked him to leave the room while he talked to a client. 'What's hap . . . ?' Gabrielsen started to ask.

Damon waved away the beginning of the question. He really did have to vomit; it had not been a figurative declaration of disgust. He hurried out of the office and down the corridor to the men's room and reached the toilet booth just in time, the vomit mounting in his throat.

He retched until his body was shaken with dry convulsions, washed his hands and face and rinsed out his mouth.

When he got back to the office Machendorf had gone and Gabrielsen was at his desk. 'What was that all about?' Gabrielsen asked. 'Machendorf looked as though he had just swallowed a keg of nails when he came out of there.'

'I would like to have fed them to him one by one,' Damon said. 'Sing Hallelujah and cross off one client.'

Damon's wish had been fulfilled. The book had been published, although not by the first house to which Machendorf had submitted it. The senior editor of the firm, which had published Machendorf's other two books, had called Damon two weeks after the scene in the office and told Damon that Machendorf's manuscript was on his desk. 'What's the story?' the editor asked. 'How come we didn't get the manuscript through you as usual?'

'Why don't you ask the author?'

'I did.'

'What did he say?'

'That you were an old fart, that you were out of touch and that he'd fired you.'

Damon laughed. 'Have you read the manuscript?'

'Enough of it,' the editor said, 'to know that we won't touch it. Our insurance would never cover anywhere the amount Mr Berkely could get if we went to court. Besides, it's a crude piece of junk.'

'Those are two of the reasons I told Machendorf I wouldn't handle him anymore,' Damon said. 'Another reason is that he's a most unpleasant man.'

'I figured it out by myself, Roger,' the editor said, 'but I wanted to hear it from you. Thanks. Mr Machendorf's manuscript will be in the mail this evening.'

The book came out six months later, published by the pornographer who had tried to lure Damon to work for him. They deserve each other, Damon thought with satisfaction when he saw the announcement of its publication. It was hardly reviewed by the regular critics, but it got widespread and malicious attention in the gossip columns. One month after publication, Mr Berkely's lawyers sued Machendorf and his publisher jointly for the sum of ten million dollars. Damon and Oliver Gabrielsen had a quiet celebratory lunch at the Algonquin on the day the story came out in the *Times*.

Damon was not surprised when he was asked by Berkely's lawyers to testify on their client's behalf and he said he would be glad to do so. He was not a vindictive man but he felt that

Machendorf's behavior called for reprisal and he did not mind having to wait in the courthouse while the case dragged on, with the testimony of other witnesses who were called before him prominently displayed daily in the newspapers. The lawyers, for their own reasons, were saving him to testify last.

When he was finally called to the witness stand and was sworn in, the trial was winding down to its close. He purposely avoided looking over to the table where Machendorf and his publisher were sitting with their lawyers. He did not want to see the writer before he testified. He wanted to speak calmly and fairly, without malice, and he was afraid that if he saw that hateful face he would be unable to keep it out of the tone of his voice as he spoke.

After preliminary questions meant to establish his credentials before the court, Berkely's lawyer asked, 'Mr Damon, you were Mr Machendorf's agent for how many years?'

'Six,' Damon said.

'You represented him in the sale of his other two books?'

'I did.'

'You no longer represent him. Is that true?'

'Yes.'

'May I ask you to tell the court under what circumstances you parted company?'

'I didn't like the book. It was distasteful to me.'

'Was there any other reason?'

'I didn't want to be in this court as one of the defendants instead of as a witness.'

Laughter broke out in the courtroom and the judge rapped his gavel once.

'Why would you think that there was any reason to suppose that if you continued your association with Mr Machendorf you might be named as one of the defendants?'

Damon thought for a moment. The last conversation he had with Mr Gray before he died came back to him. 'I would be the vessel, the means, the conduit, if you will, for the libelous work of a writer and also responsible,' he said, using Mr Gray's word.

'Thank you, Sir,' the lawyer said. 'Your witness,' he said to the opposing lawyer.

Machendorf's lawyer shook his head wearily and Damon

stepped down. As he passed the table where Machendorf was sitting jotting down notes, Machendorf looked up at him, his face contorted by hatred, and whispered, 'Motherfucker, you put the last nail in the coffin. I'll get you for this.'

'I tremble,' Damon said, smiling.

He ordered a third drink at the bar. It had happened more than three years before and the court had awarded damages of four million dollars to Berkely, two to be paid by the author, two by the publisher. The court had attached all of Machendorf's assets and the pornographer had declared bankruptcy and gone out of business and gotten himself a job as a space salesman of advertising on one of the more reprehensible of the girlie magazines. Machendorf had dropped out of sight, although Damon had heard some time before that he had made the rounds with a new novel, which no one would touch.

Three years was a long time but a man who in court said to him, 'Motherfucker. I'll get you for this,' and who after that had good reason to suppose he had been driven out of his profession by a man who had testified against him was a fair candidate for being included in the list of professional enemies.

Damon wrote Machendorf's name on the left-hand page of the notebook.

CHAPTER
ELEVEN

DAMON STARED thoughtfully across the bar. Along the wall behind the bar there was a long mirror that reflected his image. The mirror was old and cracked and dark, almost iron-colored. To Damon his face looked distant and insubstantial, as though it wavered in a shifting somber mist. If I must drink, he thought, I should go to a more congenial saloon. But he had barely touched his last drink. I must not waste the money, he thought, I may have need of every cent I have soon.

The notebook was still open before him and he looked down and saw the right-hand page, blank except for the heading at the top of the page – *Possible enemies – personal*.

It had never occurred to him that he had personal enemies. Machendorf was a different matter, but even so, Damon hadn't even thought of him in over a year. Memory was a tricky thing and forgetting often was the means by which the mind defended itself against past pain and regret for lost opportunities.

Personal enemies. Now that he was forcing himself to remember he put down two names – Frank Eisner and in parentheses Melanie Deal.

He had met Melanie Deal about a year and a half before. She was a secretary for a theatrical producer by the name of Proctor and she had come to the office with some contracts that the producer had had drawn up by his lawyer for a play entitled *An Apple for Helen*, written by one of Damon's clients. It was late in the afternoon and Oliver Gabrielsen and Miss Walton had left for the day. Damon himself was just putting on his coat to leave when the girl came in. She was young and pretty, twenty-two, -three, Damon guessed, with thick brown hair streaked blond in front, as though she spent long hours lying on a beach in the sun. Her eyes were brown, too, but with a glint of some other color that made her seem a little strange, out of the ordinary, ready to laugh inwardly at some continuing joke that only she would understand. Damon had seen her once before, when he and Oliver had gone to Proctor's office to discuss the terms of the contract for the play. When the two men had gone out together, Oliver had said, 'Whew! Did you see that girl? There's trouble there.'

'She seemed to be okay to me. And her boss told me she's very efficient.'

Oliver laughed. 'Roger,' he said, 'you're getting old. Her boss couldn't take his eyes off her all the time she was in the room and when she stood up and went back to her own office his look practically undressed her right there and then. His tongue was almost literally hanging out of his mouth and he looked like a terminal case of frustration. Miss Deal may be efficient in the office, but I'll bet she's a lot more efficient in bed. If you want to know the truth, after about five minutes I was pretty frustrated myself.'

'I must really be getting old, as you say.' Damon smiled. 'I didn't notice anything in particular about her.'

That was the girl who came into the office while Damon was putting on his coat to leave. Because of what Oliver had said about her and out of old habit, which he had thought he had broken since the Iberian lady, after whom he had subsided into uncomplicated monogamy, Damon looked at her with more interest than he had shown the first time he had seen her and decided Oliver had been right in being so disturbed by her. Lusts of the mind as well as those of the flesh. Nymph, in thy orisons be all my sins remembered.

They went down in the elevator together after Damon had locked the office and Damon said, 'I usually stop for a drink on my way home in the evening. Would you like to join me?'

She looked at him with a glint of knowing amusement in her eyes, no stranger to men's overtures. 'That would be very nice,

Mr Damon,' she said, demurely. 'I was hoping you'd ask me.' Her voice was a little husky and fitted her appearance and Damon guessed that she had worked at it, either in acting school or with a singing teacher.

In the lounge of the Algonquin, where he had taken her, although that was not the place he usually patronized for his post-workday first drink, it turned out he had been correct in his guess.

'The reason I hoped you'd ask me for a drink,' she said, sipping at her glass of white wine, 'is I wanted to talk to you about *Apple*.'

He smiled a little at her quick assumption that they were professionals together, with theatre people's universal trick of abbreviating the titles of plays. 'I'm not really a secretary,' she said. 'I work with Mr Proctor only when I'm between plays.' She spoke in small, rapid bursts, as though the words were bubbling up irresistibly in her throat.

'Have you been in any?'

'A few. Off-Broadway. Off-off-Broadway. Equity Library. Summer theatre. Drama school productions. Podunk.' Her voice mocked herself. 'The usual rocky road to stardom. Have you ever seen me?'

'I don't think so,' Damon said. 'In fact, I'm sure. If I'd seen you on the stage I'm certain I'd have remembered you.' He was too gallant a man to say otherwise.

'They ought to put up a monument outside Sardi's. With an eternal flame. To the unknown actress.' She laughed, without bitterness. 'The last play I was in was downtown. *Man Plus Man*.'

'I saw the play,' Damon said, 'but I walked out after the first ten minutes.' He remembered it well. It had opened and closed just after the opening which was the night he and Sheila had gone to see it. He did not tell the girl why he had walked out. 'You must have come on after that.'

'Second act,' she said. 'You didn't miss anything. I had a big scene in the second act. No reviews, though. The critics all left at intermission.' She laughed gaily. 'So did my mother and father. I would have, too, if I hadn't signed a contract.'

'I remember the evening,' Damon said. He had been invited by the producer, a man named Guilder, whom he didn't know, except by reputation, which was not good. He was a very rich young man from a family which owned mines in Colorado and had backed a few shows, all failures. His reputation came neither from his wealth or his career in the theatre. He had been arrested for felonious assault, with intent to kill, after he had picked up a young man in a bar and then had beaten him terribly when they got to his apartment. His plea was that the young man had made homosexual advances to him and in a rage he had struck the fellow. He had adroit and highly paid lawyers and although just about everyone in the courtroom knew that Guilder had homosexual leanings himself, to say the least, with a taste for rough trade, he was acquitted.

In an interview for the newspapers Guilder had berated the producers of the New York theatre indiscriminately for their timidity and their choice of material and its staging, and announced that from now on he would produce plays himself, without partners. *Man Plus Man* was his first independent production, off-Broadway in a theatre near the Damons' apartment, and having nothing else much to do on the evening of the opening they used their gift tickets at the last minute, more out of curiosity than any hope that the production would yield them much pleasure.

But they were not prepared for what they saw. The play was about a transvestite and his friends and while Damon, in the fashion of the time, was neutral on the subject of homosexuals and often invited clients of his who were gay to his house for dinner, the scatological language and the snickering display of nudity were too much for him. He stood up in the middle of the first scene and said to Sheila, knowing what he was doing, 'Come on, let's go. I've had enough. It's pure filth.'

They had been sitting up front of the theatre and Damon spoke loudly and clearly and strode up the aisle with Sheila behind him. Before he and Sheila had reached the exit, other couples followed their example, some of them shouting at the stage.

Guilder was standing at the back of the theatre as the Damons passed him. Damon recognized the man from photographs in the newspapers and in a poetic pose on the cover of the program, but went by without saying anything.

The play closed that night, having given only the one performance.

'I never saw a man so furious,' Melanie Deal was saying. 'He told the cast you had deliberately wrecked the play, knowing that everybody or practically everybody in the opening night audience knew who you were and the influence you had. There wasn't even a critic left for the second act. The reason you'd done it, he said, was that you were a closet queen and that you couldn't stand to see the truth on the stage and he promised the cast he was going to ruin you in the theatre and send you back to digging ditches where you belonged.' She giggled. '*Has* he ruined you?'

'As you see,' Damon said, smiling, 'I can still afford to buy drinks for a pretty young lady in the Algonquin. Although I did hear some rumors that he was bad-mouthing me all over town and twice he outbid producers who wanted to do plays I represented and then never put them on.' Damon shrugged. 'You've got to expect spoiled rich kids in the theatre. Nobody takes him seriously and if I *really* was responsible for closing the play I ought to get a medal for public service for it. Mr Guilder doesn't interest me. He's of no consequence. Let's change the subject, shall we, to something more pertinent? What did you want to talk to me about *Apple*?'

'When you were talking about casting in the office . . . You described what Helen should look like. How she should do the part . . .' She spoke in short gasps. 'Well, I thought, That nice man is describing me.'

Damon smiled again. 'Perhaps I was . . . ah . . . subconsciously influenced.' He was enjoying the small flirtation. 'Have you talked to Mr Proctor about a test for the part?'

She shook her head vigorously, her thick, gleaming hair whipping around her face. 'Mr Proctor regards me in only two ways – as a secretary and sex object.' There was malicious glee reflected in her small, fine face. 'He can only imagine me at the typewriter or in bed.' She laughed coarsely, her laughter a little out of control. 'No hope, New Jersey. Tell him, if he happens to ask.'

'What does that mean?'

'I played in summer stock at New Hope, New Jersey,' she said. 'Everything went wrong. Every time we started rehearsals on a new play somebody would say, No hope, New Jersey. It became our way of saying not a chance in a million.'

Damon began to feel the first electric tingle of desire and he wished he had left the office earlier and told Oliver to close up. Tomorrow he had to tell Oliver that his boss was not as old as he seemed.

'Mr Proctor,' the girl went on, 'thinks highly of your taste and experience. Whenever you send in a play he reads it right away, no matter what else is on his desk. If you put in a word for me, he'd listen.' The words kept tumbling out breathlessly and she was leaning forward so that he couldn't help but notice the enticing shape of her breasts under the tight cashmere sweater she was wearing, with no brassiere underneath. Generous offerings, he thought sadly, remembering his young manhood, on a ritual platter. He now understood Proctor's rapt gaze while he tried to talk contracts with Melanie Deal in view.

Troubled, he ordered another drink, to keep the evening from getting out of hand. The girl gulped her wine down and he ordered another glass for her. She was flushed with the wine and the speed and vehemence with which she had been talking. 'Well,' he said, looking around the hotel lounge to see if there was anybody there who knew him who would spread the word that old Roger Damon was now robbing cradles. There was no one he recognized and he relaxed a little. 'Well,' he said, 'the casting is a long way in the future. And there's no director yet. And the author has to rewrite the whole first act.'

'I know all that,' she said impatiently. 'But if you put the bug in Mr Proctor's ear, I'd wait.'

'I'd advise you, Miss Deal, to . . .'

'Melanie.'

'I'd advise you, Melanie,' he said, trying to sound paternal, 'not to give up any parts that you're likely to be offered while we're waiting to get into production.'

'All I want is a chance to try out.' She was speaking earnestly now, leaning across and gripping his forearm, her hands surprisingly strong. 'All you'd have to do is suggest.' She swept her hair back from her pale, high white forehead. 'Look,' she said challengingly, throwing her head back, her eyes glittering, 'am I or am I not the girl you described in the office.'

'You're beautiful,' he said softly, then tried to recover himself and make the compliment sound banal with a fatherly, 'my dear.' He heard a clock chime somewhere. 'Oh, it's getting late. My wife will be worried.' Sheila never worried about what time he came home from the office as long as it was before eight o'clock or he had called her if he was going to be delayed for an hour or two, but he wanted to sound uxorious before this tempting girl, who was young enough to be his daughter. And then some.

'I live near you,' she said. 'I looked you up in the telephone book after you came into the office the other day.' She laughed. Again there was something wild and out of control in her laughter. 'We can go together. I live on West Twenty-third Street.'

'Well,' he said, not knowing by now whether he was glad or sorry he had invited her to join him in a drink, 'I usually walk.'

'I'm a great walker,' she said, grinning, pinning him down. 'I'm one of the most notorious walkers in New York. And I don't wear high heels to work.'

'All right,' he said. He felt the need for fresh air. And he doubted that she would try anything outlandish on a public thoroughfare at six-thirty in the evening.

'If that's what you want,' he said, 'we'll go downtown together.'

'That's what I want. I'm a persistent cuss, aren't I?' she said triumphantly. She grinned, her perfect teeth gleaming in the youghtful face.

'You'll go a long way, Melanie,' he said as he paid the waiter. 'In the theatre and out of it.'

'You bet your ass,' she said. She helped him on with his coat, patting his shoulder as she did so and they went out of the hotel, she with her hand possessively on his elbow.

The evening had turned nasty and a fine drizzle was coming down. Damon thought it would be the act of a sadist to make a girl like that, with her lovely hair uncovered, and the pretty moccasins and the sheer stockings on the beautiful long legs to walk more than a mile in the rain. He waited for a moment at the entrance to the hotel and said, 'This is no night for walking.'

'I don't mind,' she said. 'Let the north wind blow, let the heavens come down.'

'Do you have a scarf or anything?'

She shook her head. 'It was sunny when I went to work this morning.'

'We'll take a taxi,' he said. 'If we can ever find one.'

Just then a taxi drove up and stopped in front of the hotel and a couple stepped out. Melanie let go of Damon's arm and dashed across the sidewalk and held the door open defiantly before the man who had just gotten out could close it and before a woman who had seen the taxi as it turned the corner onto Forty-fourth Street and had run after it waving and shouting, 'Taxi! Taxi!' could reach it. 'Tough shit, Lady,' Melanie said, grimly victorious, as the woman came panting up. Melanie gestured impatiently at Damon to get moving. He shambled across the sidewalk and said, shamefacedly, to the woman as he climbed into the taxi, 'I'm sorry, Ma'am.'

'Young people these days,' the woman said, gasping. 'Barbarians. The language.'

Melanie got into the taxi and gave her address to the driver. She settled cozily next to Damon and put her hand on his thigh. 'It's an omen,' she said.

'What's an omen?'

'Our getting this taxi on a rainy night,' she said. 'With one million people running after them on the streets of New York.'

'A good omen or a bad one?'

'Good, silly.'

'Not so good for that poor woman.'

'Old fat bag,' Melanie said coldly, disregarding the fact that the man at her side had at least twenty years of age on the old bag. 'Wherever she's going, nobody's waiting for her. Are you superstitious? About omens and things like that?'

'Yes. I always put my left shoe on first when I get dressed in the morning and get out of the left side of the bed.' He laughed. 'At my age.'

'You're not so old.'

'My dear young lady,' Damon said, 'if you woke up just one

morning and felt your bones creaking like mine, you wouldn't say that.'

'I'll tell you something, Mr Damon,' she said, stroking his thigh. 'You're one of the most attractive men in New York, whatever your age is.'

'Good God!'

'Would you like to hear what several other ladies you've known told me about you?'

'Absolutely not.' The tingle he had felt in the office when he really had looked at her for the first time had now grown to an alarming voltage.

'I'm going to tell you just the same.' She laughed with evil, gleeful mischief. 'Ladies in my acting class. Mature ladies. Been around. Know what they're talking about. Three of them. Well preserved. We were having coffee together during a recess from class. The talk turned to sex. Ladies' locker room talk.' She laughed that slightly wild laugh again.

'I'd prefer it if you stopped right now, Melanie,' Damon said with all the dignity he could muster.

'Don't pretend to be a prude.' She lifted her hand from his thigh, then jabbed at his leg sharply with one finger. 'After what I heard about you the performance doesn't wash. It so happens that all three ladies had affairs with you.'

'You're impossible, my dear girl,' he said flustered. 'I don't want to know what they said or who they are.' He was lying. From the way she was speaking he knew that what she was going to tell him would be flattering and would remind him of agreeable moments in the past.

'All the girls,' Melanie said, 'were rating their various lovers. Who was the best, who was the worst. That sort of thing. If I told you the names of the ladies you'd know they had plenty of comparisons to go by. The vote was unanimous for the top of list. You turned out to be the best lay in town by a landslide.' She laughed again. 'The worst lays they'd encountered were their own husbands.'

He couldn't help joining in her laughter. When he stopped laughing he said, 'That was long ago.' He guessed who the ladies were. 'I was younger and more active then.'

'Not so long ago,' she said. 'And stop talking about age. My present lover is fifty years old. He's a broker down in Wall Street and he has a platinum plate in his head. They knocked the top off his head in Korea. He was a big hero there. He's got a chest full of medals and he's got guns all over the house he brought back with him. Well, he's not a big hero anymore and nobody would pin a medal on him now for anything and every once in a while he thinks he's in a foxhole or whatever he had in Korea and he thinks I'm a Chinaman creeping in on him and he's grayer than you are and we have great times together.'

'He sounds like a young girl's dream,' Damon said dryly.

'I have a father fixation,' Melanie said, 'and I love it.'

'Well,' said Damon, 'I don't have a daughter and I haven't a daughter fixation and I love it.' He tried, without success, to sound irritated. 'I haven't touched anybody but my wife in God knows how long.'

The girl ignored what he had said and ran her hand under his coat high up his leg. 'I'm making a pass at you, Mr Damon,' she said flatly, without emotion.

He put his own hand out and clasped her arm firmly so that she couldn't go all the way up. He was both charmed and annoyed by her brusque directness, annoyed because there was a chance, more than a chance, that she was offering herself to him not for his reputation with the ladies in the acting class but as a lever to move him to suggest her for the part in the play to Proctor.

'In my day,' he said, 'ladies waited to be asked.'

She didn't try to move her hand any further but said, 'This isn't your day anymore, Mr Damon,' she said, 'and I'm not a lady. I like to choose, not be chosen. What I would like would be for us to have a long languorous, romantic affair, starting tonight. Sneaky afternoons, slipping off to country inns on weekends . . .'

'That's quite romantic – sneaky afternoons,' he said ironically.

She ignored the irony. 'Climate of the times. You can be pragmatic and romantic at the same time,' she said calmly. 'Don't fight it. And don't tell me you haven't been chosen before.'

He remembered Julia Larch. 'Maybe,' he said, but did not

volunteer any information about the hotel on Thirty-ninth Street. 'But the ladies kept it to themselves. Rules of the game. They had the grace to allow me to make the first move. And the second and the third.'

'Different times, different customs. Haven't you heard about the Sexual Revolution?' A street lamp threw a hard light on her face, but she looked young and lovely and vulnerable in it.

'Let the old man go in peace,' he said gently.

'I will give you no peace.' Once more she laughed, refusing sentimentality. She looked out of the window. 'Oh, God, I'm nearly home.' As if this were a signal she threw herself across his legs and pulled his head down and kissed him. Her lips were soft and active and she smelled marvelous. It was a long kiss and she only released him when the taxi stopped in front of the house in which she lived. She sat up and straightened her coat, looked at him, her face full of the mischief that lay just under the surface at all times. 'Last chance,' she said. 'Want to come up?'

He shook his head sadly.

'You'll regret it,' she said.

'I'm sure I will.'

She shrugged. 'Have a merry domestic evening with your wife,' she said. 'You don't have to tell her you're a good man. I'm sure she knows it.' She jumped out of the cab and ran up the outside steps of the house, lithe, graceful, swift, product of the private climate of her times. His own climate was a different one.

Damon watched her go, a wave of sadness coming over him, then gave his address to the driver and lay back against the imitation leather seat reeking of years of cigarette smoke and closed his eyes, trying to remember the names of the three ladies he had guessed had shared the recess coffee with Melanie Deal.

The next time he saw her, she was standing in the lobby of his office building when he came down after work. It was a week later.

She had a scarf over her head and her face looked drawn and worried. This time, he thought, if Oliver were to see her he wouldn't be tempted to exclaim, 'God, did you see that girl?'

'I have to talk to you, Mr Damon,' she said, without preliminaries. 'Alone. You're in trouble. Can I walk a way with you?'

'Of course.' He took her arm and they went out into the street. Automatically he started toward Fifth Avenue. It was a fine spring evening, with the last glow of the sun in the western sky and the people around them, released from the day's labors, seemed all to be bubbling with some secret joy as they savored their freedom and the prospect of the evening ahead of them.

They walked in silence awhile, the girl withdrawn, gnawing at her lips. 'Why am I in trouble?' Damon asked quietly.

'I did an awful thing. Unforgivable, but I hope you'll forgive me.' She sounded like a frightened child.

'What awful thing?'

'I told you about my lover, the fifty-year-old one . . . the stockbroker. In Wall Street.'

'Yes.'

'His name is Eisner.'

'I don't know the man,' Damon said sharply. 'What has he got to do with me?'

'He says he's going to kill you,' she said. 'That's what he's got to do with you.'

Damon stopped walking and faced the girl. 'You're joking, aren't you?'

She shook her head. 'Not on your life,' she said.

'Why does a man I've never seen want to kill me?' Damon asked incredulously.

'He's crazy jealous. That platinum plate he got in his head in Korea, maybe.'

'I never . . . I mean with you . . .' Damon stuttered.

'I told him you did. I told him I was wild about you and you were wild about me.'

'What in God's name did you do that for?' Damon was icily angry and was pleased to see that his voice and the look on his face made the girl try to cringe away from him. He pulled her to him roughly.

'He slapped my face at a party.' She was weeping now. 'He

thought I was flirting with somebody. In front of more than twenty people.' Then her voice turned defiant and hard. 'I don't let people get away with things like that. Not anybody. I wanted to hurt him and I did. You were the first one who came to my mind, and he knows who you are and that you're a lot older than he is. That turned the knife.'

'Well done,' Damon said sardonically. 'Well, what you're going to do is go back to that idiot and explain everything, that you were lying, that we've had nothing to do with each other and that I for one am damn sure we're never going to. He can put away his goddamn gun and go back to Wall Street and stop being a damn fool.'

'It won't do any good,' she said, snuffing back her tears, looking more like a distraught little girl than ever. 'I told him all that last night, that I was lying. He didn't believe me. He just sat there in his living room oiling the automatic he brought back from Korea.'

Damon took a deep breath. 'All right,' he said grimly, 'if he's so goddamn set on it, you tell him tonight that I'll be walking north on Fifth Avenue on the block in front of Saks, unarmed, at exactly noon tomorrow. Let the soldiers shoot and be done with it. And now,' he said with frozen fury, 'leave me alone and never come near me again.' He let go of her arm and strode down the avenue in the direction of home.

He had arrived at the corner of Fifth Avenue and Forty-ninth Street promptly at noon the next day. The weather was mild and sunny and the girls from the neighboring office buildings out on their lunch hour and the women going in and out of the glittering stores seemed all to have put on bright colors to confirm the advent of spring. It was not the place or the hour for a man to be waiting with a gun or for another man to await execution.

Damon squared his shoulders and slowly and deliberately walked the one block. It took him four minutes. No one accosted him. There were no shots. Melodrama, he thought contemptuously. Play-acting. Fantasy love games. The crazy ambitious little young girl pretending to be so modern and

120

grownup. The poor sonofabitch with the plate in his head, ostentatiously oiling his gun for her benefit.

He knew a good restaurant on Sixty-third Street and he walked toward it, enjoying the spring sunshine and the store windows and the bright colors on the women he passed as he made his way at a sauntering pace to the restaurant, where he treated himself to an exquisite and expensive lunch, with a full bottle of wine.

He saw that his glass was empty and he thought, what the hell, and ordered another whiskey. He knew he wasn't going to work any more that day and if he wanted to get through until evening, the whiskey would help him manage to do it.

He hadn't seen or heard from Melanie Deal ever since the conversation on Fifth Avenue, and that was more than a year ago. He had never run into Mr Eisner, the Wall Street broker with the platinum plate, the guns and the chestful of medals. The production of *An Apple for Helen* had fallen through and the author was still trying to rewrite the first act.

Still, if a man had declared he was going to kill him, even if he hadn't shown up in front of Saks to carry out his threat, that was no lifetime guarantee of immunity. The stupid, Boy Scout act of bravado had seemed like a victory at the time and Damon had enjoyed his lunch, but an armed man might think twice about gunning down a rival in the noonday sun among the crowd on the main avenue of the city of New York and decide to bide his time, wait for a less public opportunity, lie and wait, nursing his dream of revenge for months, years. Jealousy was the most permanent of emotions and did not flare up and die down in twenty-four hours. Damon was sure Lieutenant Schulter would like to know about him. The broker had earned his place, Damon thought, on the list of personal enemies and maybe Melanie Deal, as flighty and unpredictable as she was, belonged there with him. At any rate, she was worth a telephone call.

He searched in his pocket for change for the telephone, then stopped. Mr Eisner wasn't the only man she had mentioned who had threatened him. Damon remembered what Melanie Deal had told him about Guilder's peroration to the cast at the close of the opening night performance of *Man Plus Man*. Guilder had promised to ruin him and had done as much harm as money and whispered defamation of character would do toward that end. He had not succeeded and his failure might well have eaten at his soul enough since that time to have driven him into more direct action. Damon had dismissed him as of no consequence. He had been wrong to do so. At the place where he stood now no leads, no matter how flimsy they might seem, were to be ruled out. And the power of a frustrated demented rich young man who had narrowly escaped a long prison term for felonious assault with intent to commit murder and with the wealth to hire paid assassins was not to be ignored.

There was no doubt about it, Damon thought, as he found two dimes in his pocket, Melanie Deal was worth a telephone call.

He left his glass of whiskey on the bar and went to the back of the saloon where there was a telephone booth. He looked up her number in the Manhattan directory, remembering that she lived on Twenty-third Street and also remembering the soft touch of her lips on his in the taxi and her saying. 'I have a father fixation and I love it.'

He dialed the number, but a mechanical voice came over the phone, saying 'The number you have called is no longer in service.' He retrieved his dime, thought for a moment. He knew he could call Proctor's office and find out how to reach the girl, but remembering what Oliver had said about Proctor's practically undressing her in the office with a look, he felt it would be embarrassing to inquire about her in that quarter. God knew what had gone on between them, even though she had said, 'No hope, New Jersey,' about the producer's chances with her.

He thought for a moment, then looked up the number of Equity, the actor's union. She would be listed with them and when he gave them his name they'd know he was connected with the theatre and that his call was legitimate and give him her number. As he dialed he thought, Well, it's not as legitimate as all that.

It took some time to get the person who could give him the information he wanted, but finally a woman came on the phone whom he knew. 'Sophie,' he said, after the exchange of greetings, 'I'd like to get in touch with an actress by the name of Melanie Deal. An author of mine thinks he could use her for a play he's writing,' he lied.

'Oh . . .' There was a long pause. 'She died three months ago. In Chicago. She was touring with a revival and she was in an automobile accident. A drunken actor at the wheel and the roads were icy. I'm sorry. A pity. She was a bright young thing and she had a future. I'm terribly sorry. Was she a friend of yours?'

'Not really,' Damon said. Chicago, he thought. Add one to my dreams. Then he hung up.

CHAPTER
TWELVE

HE CAME to on the floor. There was the smell of spilled beer and cigar and cigarette butts and a babbling of voices and faces staring down anxiously at him and somebody saying, 'Don't move him, his neck might be broken.' For a moment he thought he had fainted and tried to apologize to the faces above him, but he couldn't get the words out. Then he remembered. When he had come back from the telephone booth to where he had left his drink and the open notebook, two men were shouting at each other next to him. Something about money, he remembered. Then one of the men, the smaller of the two, with a face like a wizened monkey, grabbed a bottle of beer from the bar and swung it at the other man, who ducked and retreated past Damon shouting, 'Thieving bastard,' and covering his head.

'Here, here,' Damon said, grabbing instinctively for the arm of the man with the beer bottle, to stop the fight. He missed and the man swung crazily and the beer bottle crashed into Damon's forehead. He had slumped onto the bar, stunned. Then he must have gone under and slipped to the floor.

A liquid, warm and sticky, was dripping into his eyes and mouth. He tasted salt. He sat up. The faces above him wavered against the battered tin ceiling. 'I'm all right,' he said thickly, wiping at his eyes and mouth, then looking at his hand. Seeing the blood on it, he said senselessly, 'The blood of the lamb. If you don't mind . . .' He was embarrassed at being the center of attention of all these strange people who had just come into the bar for a peaceful drink before lunch. A man who detested scenes, he was the protagonist or victim of one. Hands helped him to his feet. He gripped the bar to keep from slipping down again. The notebook, he noticed, was blotched a wet, rusty red. The blood of the lamb, staining paper, the essential stuff of his life, now the altar of sacrifice. The ram in the thicket.

'Friend,' the bartender said, 'the first lesson is, Don't be a referee when the punching begins in a saloon.'

Damon smiled wanly. 'I'll remember that. Where's the man who did it?'

'Both long gone,' the barman said. 'Honorable gentlemen.' The tone was resigned. 'The guy who hit you left a tenspot before he ran.' The barman held up a bill. 'He said he was sorry, what he really wanted to do was kill the other feller. They were both very well dressed. These days you can't tell anything.'

A woman came running out of the kitchen with a first aid kit. 'You better sit down, Mister,'she said. 'Let me clean that cut.'

Before she led him to a chair he took one look at himself in the mirror behind the bar. The same ghost stared back at him. The mirror was too dark to reflect blood.

He slumped into a chair, and the woman began swabbing at his forehead with a wet cloth that made the cut sting as the babble of voices diminished and the drinkers went back to their glasses. 'It don't look too bad,' the woman said. She was fat and black and smelled of frying oil, but her hands were sure and delicate as they ministered to him. Sheila's hands in the hospital, he thought.

'Thank the Lord the bottle didn't break,' the woman said. 'How do you feel?'

'Fine,' Damon said. He didn't feel anything much, except that the room kept swimming in waves around him and somehow the word *Chicago* kept repeating itself, breaking through the low humming in his ears. He had never been knocked out before. He decided it was not an unpleasant sensation. Now he remembered falling, as though from a great height. That, too, had not been unpleasant, but rather euphoric. A first time for everything, he thought, grateful for the soft hands and the wet cloth clearing his forehead and his eyes and mouth.

'You're going to be fine, honey,' the woman was saying,

taping on a small bandage with adhesive tape. 'I'm afraid I can't do nothing about your clothes, though. Just telephone your wife before you go home to warn her that you won't look exactly the same as you did when you left the house this morning.'

'I love you, Lady,' Damon said. 'I would like to take you home with me.'

The woman laughed, a rich, rolling sound. 'I ain't heard that for a long time, and I been around some dudes who was hurt lots worse than you. Now, you want to sit here awhile and wait to see if you can voyage a little.'

Damon stood up. He had the anxious feeling that if he remained on the chair, he would never get up again. By an act of will he kept himself from tottering. 'I'll just finish my drink,' he said, making sure he was speaking clearly.

The woman looked at him compassionately. 'At your age, honey,' she said, 'I'd let the young folks settle their disputes by theirselves.' She put the roll of bandage and the adhesive tape back into the first aid kit. 'If you need help, I'm in the kitchen. My name is Valeska.'

'Valeska,' he said, delighted with the name, wondering what its origin might be, 'you're my angel, my dark angel. My wife has hands like yours. Permit me.' He leaned over and kissed the broad, unlined forehead under the graying hair.

She laughed, the same deep rolling sound. 'I don't know about the hands or the angel part, but I know about the dark,' she said, and went back into the kitchen.

Damon looked around him sternly, forbidding the other patrons of the bar to help him. Uneasily, the men nearest him looked away from him, made a point of attending to their drinks. Above all, he thought, glaring threateningly at the men who had now turned their backs to him, no pity and no jokes about the old man who had broken the New York code of not interfering in what the black lady had called the disputes of the young. He saw that almost by a reflex action the space next to where he had been standing had been cleared of other drinkers. He walked, almost steadily, from where he had been sitting to the bar, where his drink stood, with the notebook, still open and stained with his blood, at its side. He saw that his glass had not been touched in the fracas, but the ice in it had melted and the first taste was almost pure ice water. 'Barman,' he said, his voice firm, 'another drink, please.'

The bartender looked worried. 'You sure, Mister?' he asked. 'Maybe you got a concussion and it'll hit you hard.'

'One Black and White,' Damon said. 'If you please.'

The barman shrugged. 'It's your head, Mister,' he said, and poured the whiskey into a jigger and gave him a fresh glass with ice and a small bottle of soda.

Damon drank it slowly, felt it restoring his strength. A transfusion of Scotch, that supporter of life. Perhaps, he thought, glass in hand, from now on I shall become a daily drunk. With his handkerchief he wiped at the stained pages of the notebook, the names of Machendorf and Melanie Deal and Mr Eisner blurred by caked blood. When he called for his check, the barman said, 'It's on the house, Mister.'

'As you wish, Sir,' Damon said. 'I thank you.' He walked steadily out the door, conscious of the rust-colored blots on his collar and jacket and the sidelong glances of the men at the bar.

It was a long time before he could hail an empty taxi and while he stood at the curb, vainly waving, he saw a young boy who looked about twelve run across the street, dodging the speeding cars. For a moment he blinked. The boy was carrying a fielder's glove. Damon remembered a snapshot his father had taken when he had been just the boy's age and had just come back from playing a baseball game. He smelled the freshly mown grass of the outfield turf. The boy was capless and smiling recklessly at the oncoming taxi and was dark and built exactly as Damon had been when he was the boy's age, lanky and strong. For a moment Damon thought that his own photograph had come alive, and he almost made a move to save the boy from a taxi roaring down on him. Just in time the boy made the sidewalk safely, then turned round and thumbed his nose at the driver. I could have been killed, Damon thought, confused. He shook his head, turned to shut out the sight of that grinning, familiar, impudent young face that might have been his own when he was that age.

When he arrived home, he was relieved to see that Sheila wasn't there. Sometimes she walked over from the day nursery to make lunch for herself. He would have time to change his clothes before she saw him.

He went into the bathroom and stared at his face. Under the weathered ruddiness of his skin he thought he detected a greenish tinge, and there were curious patches of almost dead white under his eyes.

Then he remembered the boy with the fielder's glove dodging the taxi. He went back into the living room and began searching for an old photographic album that he hadn't looked at in years. He and Sheila didn't even own a camera and when friends of theirs took pictures of him, he was dismayed by the signs of age in his face. If he was given one of those photographs, he said, 'Thank you,' and immediately tore it up. Getting old was a sad enough decline, without keeping an accurate year-by-year record of the process.

He found the album under a pile of old *New Yorkers*. All those Notes and Comments, all that elegant prose, crisp, muted fiction, polite biographies, clever cartoons, reviews of books and plays that were long forgotten. He had never gone back and reread the magazines and doubted that he would ever do so, but still he kept them, neatly ranged in stacks on the bottom shelf of the long, stuffed bookcase. Perhaps he was afraid to reread even his favorite essays and stories. Doing so would remind him of more joyous times, old friends who had disappeared, editors on the magazine to whom he had submitted the work of some of his clients and who had been the most intelligent and courteous of men and who had somehow vanished from his life.

He ran his hand lovingly, regretfully, along the ten-inch pile of magazines, then lifted the album of photographs from its resting place under that impressive paper monument to years of intensive labor, success and failures, that subdued transitory thin clamor for immortality.

'I'm married to a hoarder of paper,' Sheila had said. 'One day I'm going to sneak in here when you're off to work and clear out all the junk you've accumulated before we're buried under a mountain of print.'

He dusted off the album and sat down at the desk in front of the window, where the light was good, and opened the album. He had trouble finding the snapshot of himself at the age of twelve. He had put the pictures in haphazardly, emptying the large envelopes in which they had been stored at random. He had been confined to the house with his leg in a cast after getting out of the hospital and had not yet married Sheila and was trying to get the apartment in order before the wedding. That had been more than twenty years ago and he didn't remember having looked at the album since then.

He riffled through the brittle, cracked pages. There were pictures of his father, looking boyish and muscular, his mother with short, bobbed hair, in the style of the twenties. Maurice Fitzgerald and himself leaning against the rail aboard ship, Fitzgerald smiling widely and looking dashing, even in sailor's dungarees and a pea coat. *Full fathom five*. Damon remembered the sound of Fitzgerald's voice as he said it and his bitterness as he told Damon, as the next ship in the convoy sank, 'We're the egg-shell. Don't tell me if we're hit by a torpedo.'

Damon turned some pages, stopped at a photograph of Sheila taken just before their marriage at Jones Beach on a summer day, Sheila looking superb in a tight one-piece black bathing suit. Damon sighed and lingered over the page. Then he turned it and there was the photograph of himself he was looking for.

He studied the snapshot carefully. The fielder's glove he was wearing was small, not like the big webbed mitts in use now, but otherwise the boy in the photograph and the boy he had seen on Sixth Avenue might have been twins.

He stared thoughtfully out the window, wondering if he had really seen the boy or if it was a mirage, a trick of memory, after the blow to his head. The bartender had warned him that the last drink might hit him, and the man could have been right. He closed the album and stood up and took it back and put it under the pile of old magazines, the past, for the moment at least, well buried under print.

Then he went into the bedroom and changed his clothes. After that he went downstairs and stuffed the bloodstained shirt and tie he had been wearing into the trash bin and took the pants and jacket to the tailor's to be dry-cleaned. He decided not to tell Sheila about the fight in the bar. The bandage on his forehead was a small one, and he could say that while rising from his chair he had hit his head on his desk lamp at the office and that Miss Walton had repaired the damage.

When he got back from the cleaners, he realized he was hungry and looked in the refrigerator to see what there might be for his lunch, then decided that it would be unwise if he left evidence that he had come home at midday, something he never did during the working week. He didn't want to have to do any more explaining to Sheila than was absolutely necessary.

Just as he was about to go out there was a knock on the door. At this hour of the day there would be no reason for people who knew his and Sheila's schedules to suppose that anyone would be in the apartment. He froze for an instant, then on tiptoe went over to the fireplace and picked up a poker from the stand for the utensils there. There was another series of knocks on the door, then the doorbell began ringing and kept on ringing as though whoever was outside the door was leaning against the button.

Holding the poker, letting it dangle casually from his hand, as though he had been cleaning out the fireplace and had absent-mindedly forgotten to leave the poker behind, he called, 'Coming,' and went over and opened the door. A large man in workman's coveralls was standing there. 'I'm sorry to bother you, Mr Damon,' the man said, 'but the landlord says your wife called him and said your intercom to the front door isn't working.'

'Oh, yes,' Damon said, but still kept a firm grip on the poker.

'We been working on it, my partner and me,' the man said, 'and I just wanted to test to see if it's okay. Can I come in?'

'Yes, of course.' Damon stepped back, blocking the entrance to the living room. 'The buzzer and intercom are right next to the door.'

The man nodded and pushed the buzzer button, then turned on the switch for the intercom. 'Yeah?' A man's voice came through the intercom, sounding hollow and mechanical, like the ghostly voices in echo chambers in horror movies.

'Buddy, I'm in the Damon apartment,' the electrician said. 'You hear me all right?'

'Roger,' the voice said. Damon was surprised, for the first

time, that his name was used by whole sectors of modern society to indicate that communication was loud and clear.

'Okay,' the electrician said, 'I'll be right down and we can go to lunch.' He turned to Damon. 'There we are. Now if you can get everybody in the building to use the machine, you won't be surprised by unwelcome visitors.'

'Thank you very much,' Damon said. He fumbled in his pocket, took out two dollar bills and gave them to the workman. 'Here, get yourselves a couple of drinks.'

The man grinned as he took the money. 'We was supposed to come this morning because your wife said the cleaning woman would be in the apartment. I'm glad we was held up, because you don't get drinking money from cleaning women. Here . . .' He took out his wallet and selected a soiled card. 'If you ever need any electrical work, just call us and we'll come right over.'

'Thank you,' Damon said. 'Have a good lunch.'

The man left and Damon looked down at the card in his hand. 'Acme Electrical Appliances,' he read. 'P. Danusa.' Nice man, Damon thought, I should have made it five dollars. The next time P. Danusa came to the door he wouldn't be in danger of being hit over the head with an iron poker. Damon put the poker back in its stand and then started out, but stopped because he remembered that when he had changed his clothes, he had emptied his pockets and had left the telltale notebook on the top of the dresser in the bedroom. He got it, saw that it was now dry and put it in his pocket. He had not finished his list. Besides, he couldn't leave it lying around for Sheila to discover.

When he went out of the apartment, he locked the door with two keys, one for the old lock and the second for the new supposedly burglar-proof lock that Sheila had had installed right after her lunch with Oliver Gabrielsen. She had done it reluctantly, but she had done it. She had balked at the steel door and the lock bar, though. 'I refuse to live as though we're at war,' she had said, 'just because of one crazy telephone call. If anyone gets this far,' she added, her Sicilian heritage inflaming her, 'I'll figure out a way to take care of him.'

Damon grinned as he remembered this. It was lucky for Mr P. Danusa that it hadn't been Sheila who had answered the knock on the door, poker in hand. Otherwise Mr P. Danusa might very well be lying on the floor of the foyer at this moment with a broken skull.

Damon walked uptown, keeping his eyes on the pavement so that he wouldn't recognize anybody, living or dead, young or old, in the passing crowd. He didn't go directly to his office, but had a hasty lunch and then went on to the electronic equipment store near Fiftieth Street. The clerk recognized him and looked surprised when he asked for a telephone answering machine.

'Didn't you buy one yesterday?' the clerk asked.

'I did.'

'Is there anything wrong with it? You can bring it back if it's defective.'

'It's not defective,' Damon said. 'I forgot it in a bar.'

'A pity.' The clerk looked for a long moment at the strip of bandage and adhesive tape on Damon's forehead, then brought out another machine. 'That will be ninety-six dollars and eighty cents,' the clerk said.

Damon gave him a credit card and signed the slip. Danger, he thought as the clerk wrapped the box, is an expensive luxury.

This time he did not go to a bar. He was off bars and drinking, at least for the day. He went back to the office and made no explanations of his long absence to Miss Walton or Oliver, although they both looked at him questioningly.

'What's that, Roger?' Oliver asked, tapping his own forehead.

'The bump of wisdom,' Damon said curtly, and sat down at his desk and began going through two contracts that Miss Walton had put there for him to read.

Before dinner that night he and Sheila disconnected the extension telephone in the bedroom and attached the answering machine to the telephone in the living room and Sheila recorded the necessary formula – 'Mr and Mrs Damon are not at home at the moment. If you wish to leave a message, please wait for the beeping sound and leave your name and telephone number. You will have thirty seconds to record the message. Thank you.'

They looked at each other uneasily as Sheila pushed the

button so that they could be sure the recording could be understood. Without saying so, they both knew that the machine was a further intrusion into their lives, a capitulation to reality, to the idea that a Mr Zalovsky existed and had to be warded off.

'The wonders of the modern age,' Sheila said ironically as she ran the tape back. 'How did we ever live without it? Now, let's have dinner.'

She had prepared the meal and the table was set, but Damon said, 'I feel like having dinner out. Leave the stuff for tomorrow.' What he didn't say was that if they remained at home, they ran the chance of just sitting there staring fearfully at the answering machine most of the night.

'You're sure you're up to it?' Sheila asked. She had accepted his explanation of the bandage on his forehead, but had noticed that he had taken two aspirin when he arrived home. 'No more headache?'

'All gone,' Damon said. He never took drugs at any time and they had to search all over the apartment for an old bottle of aspirin that the cleaning woman had put behind some bottles in the kitchen cabinet. 'Also,' he said, 'I'd like to take in a movie after dinner. I hear *Breaker Morant* is playing in the neighborhood, and everybody who's seen it gives it the highest marks.' With the dinner, the movies, and a couple of drinks in a bar after it, they could stay out until nearly one A.M. Six or seven hours of respite, engaged in the problems of creatures of fiction, not in their own.

They had a good dinner and Sheila, as always when she dined out alone with Damon, was at her best, vivacious and full of bright anecdotes about the children and their mothers at the nursery school. They were in a good mood as they settled themselves in their seats just in time for the beginning of the picture.

The movie was all that he had been told about it and more, and they both watched it fascinated, like two privileged and awed children. Damon believed that they were seeing a masterpiece. It was a word he almost never spoke and rarely thought, but he could tell by the tense silence in the crowded theatre that his opinion was being shared by the rest of the audience, which broke into applause as the picture came to an end, something he had never seen or heard in the routine running of a movie in a neighborhood theatre. Sheila, whom he didn't remember ever weeping in a theatre, was crying at the end, when the two soldiers, sitting in chairs on a wide field, outlined against the rising sun, were executed by the firing squad.

God, Damon thought, brushing at his own tears, what a glorious thing talent is and how often it is misused. Even though the movie was about the corrupt processes, the callous political purpose and the blind, omniprevalent malevolence of the race of man, which led to the inevitable deaths of the two officers, he could feel the surge of elation and gratitude in the people around him. Catharsis through pity and terror, he thought, even though perhaps only a handful of spectators in the theatre had ever heard or read the phrase.

But after the showing was over and they had gone to their local bar and were sipping their first drinks, Damon began to reflect somberly about the movie. Magnificent as it had been, he thought, it was not the night on which to see it, at least not for him. Of course the two actors who had gone calmly and courageously with disciplined soldierly dignity to their deaths must have stood up from where they were lying after the *coups de grace* and the director had called, 'Cut.' They would have been laughing, joking at something someone had said, had undoubtedly gone off in high spirits to have a celebratory beer, since it was an Australian production, and prepared to learn their lines for the next day's shooting.

What jokes was he ready to make, what were the lines he might prepare for tomorrow, what director was on hand to shout, 'Cut' and stop the action?

In the past few days, he felt, he had been steeped in death and thoughts of death. Zalovsky, with his warning, Harrison Gray, whose name turned out to be George, Antoinetta and Maurice Fitzgerald, Gregor with his neutron bomb, Melanie Deal, victim of a drunken driver. Masterpiece or no, he would have been better off if he had bought tickets for some inane musical comedy in which nobody died and which ended happily in a blare of sound as the curtain came down.

He felt the bloodstained notebook in his pocket. That was

134

reality, not the formula for pre-Christian Greek playwrights; there was terror there in his pocket, but no pity and no catharsis.

Sheila, too, was subdued and he guessed that her thoughts were very much like his. Sensing this, he put out his hand and took hers. She squeezed his hand hard and tried to smile, and he saw that she was near tears.

When they got home, it was past one o'clock. As if by magnetic attraction, their eyes were drawn to the answering machine. 'Let's go to bed,' Sheila said. 'Leave the damned thing alone until morning.'

It had been a long and tiring day, and Damon fell asleep almost immediately, cradling Sheila's warm, naked body against his own. Sheila, shield, he murmured just before sleep overtook him.

His dreams tormented him and he struggled to awake. When he did, he was trembling. Carefully he moved away from Sheila, who was sleeping peacefully, and got out of bed. He put on a woolen robe and went barefooted into the living room. He didn't switch on the lights, but sat himself at the desk in front of the window and looked down on the empty street below. The clock on the desk stood at four o'clock.

The dreams came back to him. He was dressing for a funeral and was putting on his dark blue serge suit for it. There was a button loose at the end of the sleeve, and he tugged at it to take it off so that he wouldn't lose it. The button didn't come off, but the whole sleeve came away in his hands from the middle of the forearm down. In the dream, he remembered being slightly amused at it, but waking he was not amused. Rending garments, he remembered the producer, Nathan Brown, saying over the phone when they were talking about Maurice Fitzgerald and the reaction of the woman who had answered the phone in his flat in London.

Damon shivered. Sleep was not as Shakespeare had described it, knitting the raveled sleeve of care.

Another dream, which had come to him immediately after that one, like a quick dissolve in a film, had been more puzzling. It had started, he remembered, ordinarily enough – he had lost his wallet and had searched all over for it in a large house he did not recognize. He had met his father coming down the stairs. His father was a young, hearty man and he, himself, was his present age, but that had seemed of no moment in the dream. With his father, there had been his dead brother, Davey, but not as he was, aged ten at the time of his death, but a grown man who unaccountably had turned into Lieutenant Schulter, overcoat, blue jaw, ridiculous small hat and all.

He had explained that he had lost his wallet and that there were some things he had to buy and he needed some money. His father had laughed and had continued walking down the stairs, carelessly saying, over his shoulder to Lieutenant Schulter, 'Davey, give the kid some dough.' Schulter had taken a little plastic gadget out of his pocket and handed it to Damon. 'There's some change in there,' he said and followed the father. Damon looked down at the peculiar change dispenser, but could find no slot or lever to get whatever coins out that were in it. He had run after his father and Schulter, crying that there couldn't be enough money in the machine for him to do the shopping he needed to do and anyway, there was no way to reach and get it. His father and Schulter were climbing up a snowbank piled up to the side of a road and neither of them looked back as Damon tried to get to them, as he kept slipping back off the icy embankment, his voice ringing desperately in his own ears.

He had almost awakened then, but sleep had seized him again, just as he had felt he was swimming up from the depths of some element with which he was not familiar to a light far above him on the surface, and he sank once more.

He must have slept calmly for quite some time after that, because the dream that followed was not linked as the other two had been. He couldn't remember how the dream had begun but suddenly he was conscious that he was bleeding, not from any one wound but from almost every pore of his body, his forehead, chest, belly, penis, his knees, ankles and the soles of his feet. The dream had been so vivid that when he awoke, he immediately ran his hands all over his head and body to stem the wild flow of blood. His hands had come away dry. He had lain stiffly in bed for a few moments, listening to the sound of Sheila's placid breathing, wondering how with the turmoil taking place so close to her she could still continue to sleep.

Do you believe in precognition? Precognition of what?

Then he had gotten silently out of bed because he knew there was no more sleep for him that night.

He was still sitting like that at seven in the morning when the alarm went off on the table next to Sheila's side of the bed and he had heard her go to the bathroom and the sound of running water. Then Sheila had appeared, yawning, in her blue bathrobe, and had come over to him, kissed the top of his head and said, 'Good morning. Have you been up long?'

'Just a few minutes,' he lied.

'Did you sleep well?'

'Like a top,' he said.

They both looked at the answering machine attached to the phone on the desk. 'Well,' Sheila said, 'we might as well find out if anybody called.' She looked at him anxiously, and he knew that she wanted him to say it could wait until later.

'Might as well,' he said as casually as he could.

Sheila switched on the machine. It played back her voice, then they heard the beep and after that a man's voice, one that Damon had only heard once but knew that he would always be able to recognize, came on. 'This is Zalovsky, Mrs Damon,' the voice said. 'The message is, tell your husband I am on his tail.'

Sheila turned the machine off. 'Marvelous invention,' she said, 'isn't it? Bacon and eggs?'

'Bacon and eggs it is,' Damon said.

CHAPTER
THIRTEEN

'I'M CALLING you early so I could reach you before you left for the office,' Sheila said on the phone to Oliver Gabrielsen. It was more than a week since they had had lunch together. 'Is your wife there?'

'She went out to get some fresh rolls for breakfast,' Oliver said, 'thank God. I have to talk to you, too. I was going to call you at the school.'

'Can we have lunch?'

'Whatever you say.'

'Same place. One o'clock.'

'I'll be there,' Oliver said.

Oliver was waiting for her in the restaurant just a few blocks from the school when Sheila arrived. He rose from his chair and kissed her cheek and then stepped back and looked hard at her.

'I know, I know,' she said. 'I look awful.'

'Let's not say awful,' Oliver said, as they sat down facing each other across the small table. 'Let's say, just not up to your usual level.'

'It's been a rough week,' Sheila said.

'I can imagine,' said Oliver. 'I get some of the flak in the office, too.'

'Like what?' Sheila asked.

The waitress came over and took their orders. When she went off, Sheila asked again, 'Like what?'

'Well, he sits at his desk like a zombie. He hardly says hello in the morning,' Oliver said. 'He brought what looks like a photographic album into the office, and he takes it out again and again and opens it and keeps looking at one page for what seems like hours. Once I had to go over to his desk with a memo, and he covered the page with his hands as though I was trying to steal a military secret from him. Do you have any idea what he's looking at?'

'I haven't seen any photographic albums around the house for ages,' Sheila said.

'When he's not doing that,' Oliver went on, 'he puts the album away in the bottom drawer of his desk, the only one he keeps locked with a key, and takes a letter, a statement, any piece of paper, and stares at that. Usually he and I have lunch together two or three times a week. Since Monday a week ago, he just stands up around one o'clock and goes out and that's it. The same thing for drinks after work. We're lucky if he says good night before he's out the door. And during the day if you ask him a question, he doesn't answer for the longest time or he doesn't seem to hear, and you have to ask him again before he sort of shakes himself and looks at you as though he's waking up from a dream.'

Sheila nodded. 'It's the same at home with me. Have you any idea of what it's all about?'

'No.'

'He didn't say anything about a telephone call?'

'No.'

'Does the name Zalovsky mean anything to you?'

'Never heard it.'

'Well, if you're going to be able to help, it's time you knew what it's all about,' Sheila said. 'It all began ten nights ago, when I was away for the weekend. At about four in the morning, while he was sleeping, he told me, the telephone rang. Somebody who said his name was Zalovsky threatened him, said he was from Chicago, that he'd been a bad boy, that was what the man said, bad boy, and now he had to pay for it. He said he was waiting for him on the corner of our street. He said it was a matter of life and death.'

'Jesus,' Oliver said, his pale face grave. 'Did Roger go?'

'No. He hung up. I told you when we had lunch how weirdly he behaved after that, and you told me about the gun.'

'Well, at least he hasn't gotten a gun yet, as far as I know. The form's still on his desk. Did this man, this Zalovsky, call again?'

'Once,' Sheila said. 'Four nights ago. He left a message on our answering machine.'

'I didn't know that you had an answering machine,' Oliver said, surprised.

'Well, we have one now.' She told Oliver what the message was.

They remained silent while the waitress served them with the food they had ordered. When she left the table, Oliver said, 'I sure as hell would act peculiarly too if I got calls like that in the middle of the night. Do you have any clue who it might be? And why he might be calling?'

'Not the slightest,' Sheila said. 'And if Roger suspects, he's not telling me. That's why I wanted to talk to you. There must be some secret there that never shows in public.' She picked at a roll, puzzled and unhappy. 'He's such a likeable man. Wherever he goes, people always seem so glad to see him when he comes into a room. Of course, it might be some woman I've never heard of. Even now, when he's a pretty old man. He doesn't ever show that he's conscious of it, but he seems to *exude* sex and that's one sure way of starting trouble. From the first time I saw him, even all trussed up in a hospital bed, I felt it. Wherever he goes, the ladies still congregate around him. And conscious or not, he wasn't above taking advantage of it from time to time. I've known all along, of course, and I'm sure you did, too . . .'

Oliver tried to smile, but it was a sickly grimace that he produced. 'Well,' he said, 'from what I've seen, he's refused more offers than he's accepted.'

'Faint praise,' Sheila said. 'Anyway, I've made my peace with it. And for the last few years there's been none of *that*, at least. I've tried to convince him that the calls didn't mean anything, some crank who picked his name out of the telephone book and called as a diseased joke. But I can't make him believe that. Somewhere in his past there's something that happened, somebody who wants him to suffer, and he knows it and that's why he's acting the way he is . . .' She stabbed at her food without appetite. 'I thought maybe you'd know something that I didn't know, enemies I've never met or ever thought about.'

Oliver squirmed uncomfortably. 'Well,' he said, 'he came into the office after lunch – late – he'd been out most of the morning – he was pale and had a bandage on his forehead, and when I asked about it, he cut me off and naturally I suspected somebody had hit him, but it was none of my business . . .'

Sheila nodded. 'He lied to me about it. He said he'd bumped his head on his desk lamp and Miss Walton had put the bandage on.'

'We don't even have a Band-Aid in the office,' Oliver said. 'And when he came back that afternoon late, long after lunchtime, he had on different clothes from the ones he was wearing in the morning.'

'I just got them yesterday,' Sheila said. 'When I went to the cleaners to get back a sweater of mine, they said they had a jacket and a pair of pants my husband had left there last week. He always leaves things like that up to me. I didn't even know he knew where the cleaners were.' She looked sharply at Oliver. 'Anything else?'

Oliver hesitated. 'I don't want to be disloyal to Roger,' he said. 'If he doesn't choose to tell you what's on his mind, I don't want to be the one to break the news.'

'What is it?' Sheila said sternly. 'If he can't help himself, we're the only ones who *can* help him.'

Oliver sighed. 'I suppose you're right,' he said. 'Well, two days ago, when he went out to lunch, I had to get a letter we received from a client out West that he told me he wanted me to answer. It wasn't like him. When a letter is addressed to him, he usually answers it himself immediately, but for the last few days . . .' Oliver left the sentence unfinished. 'And ordinarily he keeps his desk as orderly as an accountant's statement. But it was all messed up, papers everywhere, scraps of addresses, authorizations unsigned, one thing piled any which way one on top of the other. I had to hunt to find the letter and finally I found it and picked it up and there was an open notebook under it. I'd noticed that he'd been staring at it all morning, then pushed it away as though he was irritated with it.' He stopped uncomfortably. 'Really, Sheila, if he thought it was something you ought to know, he'd tell you himself.'

'You've been married more than ten years, Oliver,' she said, 'and you still don't know fuck-all about marriage. What sort of notebook?'

'The one he always carries around in his pocket,' Oliver said reluctantly, 'things to remember, ideas for magazine pieces, addresses, things like that. Well, it was open. There were no addresses or notes on the pages.' He took a deep breath as though to fortify himself for what he was going to say. 'On one page he'd written, *Possible enemies – professional*. On the other page there was, *Possible enemies – personal*. And then some names under each of the entries.'

'What were the names?'

'I could only read one of them,' Oliver said. 'On the professional side. Machendorf. You remember – Roger testified against him in that libel case.'

'Roger would testify against his own mother if he thought it had to be done,' Sheila said. 'What about the others?'

'I couldn't make them out.'

'Why not?'

'They were caked with blood,' Oliver said.

The reverberations of Oliver's last words seemed to echo between them, troubling them both and reducing them for several moments to silence.

Then Sheila spoke. 'There's either nothing more to be said or there's a great deal more to be said. What do you think?'

'A great deal more,' Oliver said.

Sheila nodded, then put up her hand to stop him from talking because she saw a woman, holding the hand of a little girl, approaching their table, smiling.

'Mrs Damon,' the woman said, 'I see you know the same restaurants I do. I'm delighted to see you. Phyllis' – she tugged at her daughter's hand – 'say hello to Mrs Damon.'

'I saw her all morning,' the little girl said. 'I said hello already.'

Sheila laughed and said to Oliver, who was standing, waiting to be introduced, 'Phyllis is one of the pupils in the school. One of the best pupils, aren't you, Phyllis?'

'Mummy doesn't think so,' Phyllis said, glaring up at her mother.

'Phyllis,' the woman said, 'I don't know where you ever got that idea.'

'From you,' Phyllis said.

Sheila laughed again, then introduced Oliver to the woman, whose name was Gaines. When the introductions were over, Mrs Gaines, tugging at her daughter's hand, started away, then turned back. 'Oh, I'm sorry I missed you the other night. I would have liked you to meet my husband.'

'Where was that?' Sheila asked.

'At the concert. I saw Mr Damon there during the intermission, and I suppose you went to powder your nose or something.'

'What night was that?' Sheila asked.

'Friday. When they played Mozart's *Requiem*. Wasn't it marvelous?'

'Marvelous,' Sheila said.

'Say good-bye nicely to Mrs Damon, Phyllis.'

'I'm going to see her tomorrow morning,' the little girl said.

'Phyllis,' Sheila said, smiling, 'isn't one for excessive formality. I've noticed before.'

Mrs Gaines shrugged helplessly. 'The logic of children. It's been a pleasure meeting you, Mr Gabrielsen.' Then she led the little girl to a table at the other end of the restaurant.

'Smart little girl,' Sheila said. 'I hope she turns out not to look like her mother.'

After a pause, Oliver said, 'The way you said "marvelous" to that lady was funny.'

'Was it? It may have been. Because I wasn't at the concert on Friday night. And Roger didn't tell me he was going, either. He called and said he had to have dinner and go see a rehearsal with one of your clients.'

'Now,' said Oliver, 'why would he do anything like that, do you think?'

'It might be because of Mozart,' Sheila said.

'What would that have to do with his making up a story to tell you? A concert isn't like having an assignation with another woman.'

'This particular concert,' Sheila said, speaking slowly, 'might be like having an assignation. Mozart's last work, the *Requiem*, contracted for by Count von Walsegg-Stupach to be sung for a Mass for his dead wife.' Sheila's voice sank to a whisper. '*Dies Irae. Lacrimosa.* Another kind of assignation. Remember, Roger was born a Catholic, even if he hasn't done much about it since.'

Oliver ran his hand over his face, covering the almost invisible white eyebrows, the pale troubled eyes. 'What bad luck,' he said, 'running into that woman here.'

Sheila shrugged. 'She lives in the neighborhood and the school is nearby, and she was probably too lazy to make lunch. Anyway, assignations are usually discovered finally, one way or another. I could use a drink.' She waved to the waitress. 'I'm going to have a Calvados,' she said to Oliver. 'I had a lover who fought in Normandy during the war, and he introduced me to Calvados. He said he used to fill his canteen with it, it made the war bearable. It rained most of the time and there was plenty of water. What will you have?'

'The same,' Oliver said.

'Two Calvados,' Sheila said to the waitress. They finished their coffee while waiting until the waitress came back with the two glasses. 'Salut,' Sheila said, raising her glass, as the waitress went off. 'If Roger is making lists of his enemies, maybe it would be a good idea if we made one of our own. Bloodstained or not.' She smiled wanly. 'I have one candidate. In my own family. A nephew, a son of my sister's. His name is Gian-Luca Sciacca. He had a bad time in Viet Nam and was badly wounded. When he came back, he was on heroin. His father threw him out of the house, and he went to a clinic to break the habit. He was in for more than a year. Then one day he showed up at our door. He swore he was off the stuff, but he needed a place to stay while he was looking for a job and he was broke. I talked it over with Roger, but we were having that bad time financially, and we couldn't afford to give him the money to pay for a hotel, and Roger suggested that we let him stay with us until he found a job. It was a nuisance, because our spare room doesn't have a real bed in it. Just a couch. Damon uses it when he has work to do at home or he has letters to write. Gian-Luca had to sleep on the couch. He was all right for a couple of weeks, although he was never pleasant to have around the house all the time. He's a sulky, messy young man with a huge chip on his shoulder and an enormous grudge against the world. He got a job as a shipping clerk, but he was fired when he got into an argument with the foreman and hit him with a monkey wrench.' Sheila shook her head sadly, as she remembered the strain that Gian-Luca's presence had put on her marriage. 'After that, he stopped looking for jobs and I suppose began hustling on the streets. I suspected that he was shooting heroin again and I imagine Roger suspected it too. Then things began disappearing from the apartment – a silver coffee pot, some old china, a silver platter that Mr Gray gave us as a wedding present, a long carving knife with a bone handle . . . other things.' She sighed. 'For a while Roger didn't notice that things were missing. Things were bad enough as it was, and I didn't have the courage to tell Roger that my nephew was stealing us blind for his daily fix.'

'Poor Sheila,' Oliver said softly.

'Poor everybody,' Sheila said, 'including Gian-Luca.'

'What did Roger do when he found out?'

'It was quite an evening,' Sheila said, trying to keep her tone light but not succeeding. 'There was a terrible argument, with Gian-Luca swearing on his mother's head that he wasn't on drugs anymore and that he'd never stolen anything in his life. Roger told him to get out that minute and that if he didn't, he'd go to the police. Gian-Luca refused to go. He just lay down on the living room couch and folded his arms and said he wasn't going to move. Roger didn't say anything. He just went over to the couch and grabbed Gian-Luca and picked him up bodily. The boy was so thin and weak a baby could have carried him, and Roger is one of the strongest men I know, and he's awesome when he gets angry. "Open the door," he said to me, with the boy struggling in his arms. I opened the door and Roger carried him onto the landing and threw him down the stairs. He wasn't hurt, but he was raging. He went down about half a flight before he could get up. Then he shook his fist at Roger and yelled, 'I'll get you for this, you cold-ass WASP sonofabitch. And your fake guinea fat wife.'' The usual conversation around the family dinner table.' She smiled ruefully. 'Roger started down the stairs after him, with me hanging onto him to keep him from killing the boy, and the kid got scared and ran away. And that was it.'

'How did it end?' Oliver asked.

'Just like that. We never saw him again. But his mother called me a few months later, crying, to tell me that Gian-Luca had been arrested while he was threatening a lady in the Bronx with a large carving knife, while he was trying to grab her handbag. Only the lady turned out to be a female cop and he got a three-year jail sentence. I imagine the knife was the one he took from our kitchen. Anyway, the three years were up four months ago, and I guess he's on the loose again, bringing glory to the family name. I imagine he deserves to be on the personal list.'

'I would think so,' Oliver said. 'Did you ever tell Roger about his being arrested?'

'No. I suppose I was wrong, but I didn't want to stir up old nasty memories. I'll tell him tonight,' Sheila said. 'I'm also going to tell him to disconnect the answering machine and the next time Zalovsky calls to make a date to meet him. Roger's a brave man and if he knows exactly what he's confronted with, he'll handle it. This way he's in a void. Naturally he sees threats in every quarter, and he doesn't know which way to turn and it's grinding him down. I pretend I don't notice, but he thrashes around in his sleep as if he's fighting shadows in his dreams and he sits up almost half of every night . . .'

'It's beginning to show in the way he looks,' Oliver said. 'I've never seen him so strained and worn out. And the work is piling up and he's not touching it. I try to take up as much of the slack as I can, but I'm an enlisted man, not an officer, and when there's a real decision to make, he's the one who has to make it. Still . . .' He looked troubled. 'I don't like the idea of his taking the kind of risk you're talking about – meeting whoever it turns out to be alone, probably in the dark in some deserted place . . .'

'He won't be alone,' Sheila said flatly. 'I'll be with him.'

'Sheila,' Oliver protested, 'the guy might be a murderer.'

'Then we'll find that out,' she said. 'Now – who've *you* got to contribute to the rogues' gallery?'

146

'Nothing very useful, I'm afraid,' Oliver said. 'I'd have said Machendorf, too. He's rough and he was brought up like a mongrel dog, and if you can judge anything by the way a man writes, there's an awful lot of violence there. Otherwise . . .' He pursed his mouth, reflecting, looking like a thoughtful infant. 'Otherwise the only one I can think of is Gillespie.'

'That's a surprise,' Sheila said. 'Roger thinks highly of him.'

'*Thought* highly of him,' Oliver said. 'After his first book. That was a beauty. Then he went off his rocker. Manic-depressive, paranoid, schizophrenic, you name it, he was it. When he brought in his second book, Roger thought it was some kind of crazy put-on. He made me read it, too, before he talked to the guy. It was pure gibberish, three hundred pages of it. It didn't make any sense at all. When he came into the office to talk to us about it, *he* didn't make any sense at all. He was in one of his manic periods, I guess, he kept laughing and striding around the office waving his arms shouting that the book was the greatest thing since Joyce and that he was sure that he was going to win the Nobel Prize with it. Then, before we could get a word in, either of us, he began to tell us that he was being hunted by the FBI and the CIA and the Russians and the Jews because he had atomic secrets they wanted to torture out of him. People were giving information against him, he had many two-faced friends, they were involved in a giant plot against him. He knew who they were. Their Day of Judgment would come. But in the meanwhile they'd turned his wife against him and she'd tried to have him committed to an insane asylum, and when she couldn't, she'd run away from him, taking their two kids with her. That was some day . . . Whew!'

'What a world we live in,' Sheila said. 'What a race we are. We go through days like that, we live through scenes like Roger throwing a sick wasted boy down the stairs, then we bathe, go out to dinner, go to a concert, listen to Beethoven, enjoy a play, buy a newspaper on the way home, toss the paper aside to read at breakfast after glancing at the headlines that scream about a massacre in India, an air-raid in Lebanon, an air-crash with two hundred dead. We make love, snore, worry about our bank balances, forget to register to vote, prepare for a holiday . . .' She made a grimace, as though she was remembering all her holidays without pleasure. Then she shook her head and said, 'What did you do with that poor crazy man and his manuscript?'

'What would you have done?' Oliver asked.

'I suppose just what you and Roger did,' Sheila said wearily, 'whatever it was.'

'We tried to calm him down. We told him we'd read his book, but that it needed some work before showing it to the publisher, that there were some parts we hadn't understood.' Oliver held his glass of Calvados up to the light and squinted at it, as though, there in the pale golden essence of apple, the first fruit, he could find some solution to Gillespie's dilemma. 'Gillespie took what we said jovially. He called us his pitiful earthbound friends, naturally we couldn't understand his book, it was written for the finer, more sensitive souls who would inhabit the world in centuries to come. In fact, he said, he was delighted we couldn't understand the book, he would have known he'd failed with it if we had, we'd only understand it when we died many times and came back many times in new incarnations. All this interspersed with great brays of laughter. I am honoring you, he said. You are the messengers of my apotheosis. Deliver the manuscript to Charles Bernard at my publisher's, he has a touch of the divine afflatus, you will be remembered in the annals of literature for all posterity. Then he declaimed the whole sonnet – you know it, the one that has the line in it – not brass or stone shall outlive this powerful rhyme.'

'Roger didn't tell me one word of this,' Sheila said.

'He never said anything to anyone about it and he made me swear to absolute silence, also. He didn't want to add to the man's troubles by spreading the word that he had gone completely around the bend. And this is the first time I've mentioned it to anyone.'

'What did Roger say to Gillespie himself?'

'What could he say?' Oliver shrugged. 'He said he'd deliver the manuscript by hand himself the next morning. Then, as gently as possible, he suggested that it might be useful if Gillespie would have a little talk with a psychiatrist. Gillespie looked at him suspiciously. Psychiatrists were in league with *them*, he said, they excavated writers' brains and left only empty skulls. Then he looked at a watch on his left wrist, then one he was wearing on his right wrist, then took a third one out of a pocket and looked at *that*. He whispered, as though he was letting us in on a great secret. The time in Washington, the time in Moscow and the time in Jerusalem, he confided to us, with a wink. Time to go, he said and danced rather than walked out of the office.'

'*Did* Roger deliver the book to Mr Bernard the next morning?' Sheila asked.

'He did. He always keeps his promises, even to certifiable lunatics. Bernard asked him what he thought about the book and Roger said, "No opinion. You read it for yourself." Two days later Bernard called. He said the book was impenetrable, that was his word, impenetrable. He's a decent man and he could have said much worse. We got the manuscript back by special messenger the next morning. We had no idea where Gillespie was living, he had told us he had a series of safe houses and he never slept in the same bed two nights in a row. All we could do was wait. Finally, Gillespie came into the office. It was a rainy day and he was walking around without a hat or a coat and he looked as though he'd been dragged up from the bottom of the sea. He said he'd come for his advance. When Roger told him that there was no advance and that the manuscript had been returned, he first took it philosophically. They have eyes, he said, but they do not see. Then he turned suspicious. Bernard was a false-faced friend, he had misjudged him. He had misjudged Roger, too. The cabal, he said, had many evil roots, always spreading, but the Day of Judgment would see the tree hewn down. His vocabulary had suddenly turned quasi-biblical. He took the manuscript, in a torn cardboard box, and went out. It was raining even harder than when he'd come in, and if he walked two blocks in that downpour his manuscript would have been a sodden, illegible mess in that cardboard box.' Oliver finished his Calvados. 'Another one?' he asked.

'No, thank you,' Sheila said. 'Is that the end of the saga of Mr Gillespie?'

'Not quite,' Oliver said. 'About a week later he came back to the office to demand his advance again. He hadn't shaved since we'd seen him there and he must have been sleeping on park benches and flophouses, because his clothes were filthy and ragged. Luckily, Roger was out at the time and I said I didn't know anything about the advance. You just tell Roger Damon, Gillespie said to me, that the next time I come here he'd better damn well be here. I asked him when that would be. When the book commands me, he said and left. But he didn't go home, wherever that happened to be at the moment. He went to Bernard's office and asked *him* about the advance, and when Bernard told him there was to be no advance, he took out a pistol and began waving it about, threateningly, shouting tags of poetry of all kinds, Bernard told me, and quotations from his book. Luckily, a secretary saw what was going on and called the police. When they came, Gillespie laughed at them and tossed the pistol to them. It was a children's toy. They took him to Bellevue for psychiatric examination, but he put on his sanest, most convincing, modest act and they released him after a few days and we've never seen or heard from him again.'

Sheila closed her eyes in pain. 'I hate to think of where Mr Gillespie is at this moment and what he's doing.'

'So do I,' Oliver said sadly. 'But there's nothing we can do about it. Except' – he paused – 'except to consider that the next time he comes into the office it may not be a toy pistol he has in his pocket.'

CHAPTER
FOURTEEN

WHEN SHE got back to the school after lunch Sheila found a telegram waiting for her. It was from her mother's doctor in Vermont. Her mother was in serious condition. She had had a stroke and was in the hospital in Burlington.

Sheila called Damon's office, but Miss Walton said that Mr Damon hadn't come back from lunch yet, but Mr Gabrielsen was just coming through the door, did Mrs Damon want to talk to him.

'Yes,' Sheila said. Then when Oliver was on the line she explained about the telegram and asked Oliver to tell Roger to call her at the apartment, where she was going to pack a bag before leaving for Vermont on an Allegheny Airlines plane. If he didn't get in before going to the airport she would leave a note for him at home. 'Oliver,' she said, her voice troubled, 'I don't like to impose on you, but I hate to leave Roger alone at a time like this. I don't know how long I'll be away, but do you think you could take him in at your place for a few days? I don't want him alone in the apartment, especially at night, and I know he'll refuse to go to a hotel.'

'Of course, Sheila,' Oliver said. 'I'll try. But I can't guarantee anything. He doesn't seem even to hear what I'm saying these days. But I'll do my best. I'll ask him to stay with us or I'll offer to stay with him till you come back or anything you suggest.'

'You're a dear friend, Oliver,' Sheila said.

'I hope everything goes all right up in Vermont.'

'Thanks.' She hung up and took a taxi to the apartment and before doing anything else turned on the answering machine. There were no messages. She unplugged the machine and started throwing things into a suitcase. She waited as long as she could, then wrote a hasty note for Roger and left it on the little table opposite the front door in the foyer, ran down the steps and hailed a passing taxi to take her to the airport.

Damon had his lunch alone in a restaurant where he was not known. He didn't want to see anybody he would have to talk to this afternoon. He had had another puzzling dream the night before and he wanted to try to figure out what it meant undisturbed. In the dream he was at a big party with Sheila, surrounded by a great many people, none of whom he recognized. Dinner was served from a buffet and people were wandering around with plates of food. The food was elaborate and rich, but very good. Suddenly his father came in, but it was not the smiling, rosy man in Damon's recurrent dream, nor the young, careless man who had called to his brother Davey, who had somehow grown into Lieutenant Schulter, 'Give him some money, Davey.' Now his father was of an age somewhere between the young man of that dream and the older man of the other. He had thinned down and he had a sullen, sneering expression on his face and Damon was surprised to see him because his father was supposed to be in jail. Damon didn't know why he had been in jail or why he had been able to come out of it and asked, 'How is it you're out, Dad?'

'They let out one hundred and twenty of us yesterday,' his father said. He looked around at the other guests unpleasantly, then went up to Sheila and said, 'Are you still my wife or aren't you?'

'Of course,' Sheila said, 'I'm still your wife.'

'Then why are you eating all this fancy slop?' his father said, taking the plate from her hand and tipping it to pour most of the food, in a heavy sauce, onto the floor.

Perhaps the dream had gone on, but Damon didn't remember any more of it.

Sitting, solitary and disturbed in the noisy restaurant, Damon tried to figure out what the dream meant. His father had never committed a crime, had always been fond of his surviving son to the point of doting, had died before Damon had me

Sheila, had never tried to appropriate any of his son's girl friends, had been blessed with the gentlest and most courteous of manners. Was it possible that after death, with the corruption of the body there was an ongoing corruption of the soul? Or was he, Roger Damon, subconsciously, while he slept, rearranging his image of his father from the tender and loving man he had known, to a surly and distasteful figure in order to reject the temptation to join that once-smiling and gesturing ghost?

And what did the number one hundred and twenty mean?

He had closed his eyes and had put his hands over them as he bent over the table to shut out the other patrons of the restaurant. He was so deep in memory and conjecture that he was almost startled when he heard the waitress's voice saying, 'Is there anything more, Sir?'

'No, thank you,' he said. 'The check, please.'

He paid for his meal, left a tip, asked for change of a dollar because he had a telephone call to make, which he would not make in the office because he didn't want Oliver to overhear any part of the conversation. The call was to Lieutenant Schulter. He had tried to reach the lieutenant every day since he and Sheila had listened to Zalovsky's message that morning before breakfast, but each time he had called the man at homicide had said, 'Lieutenant Schulter is not available.'

'Do you know when he's going to be available?'

'No, Sir. Do you want to leave your name?'

'Thank you, no. I'll call again.'

He found a bar, went into it, ordered a whiskey to show his honorable intentions and left it on the bar as he went toward the rear, where there was a telephone booth.

This time he was lucky. He was put on immediately to the detective and Schulter's rasping voice grated in the receiver. 'Lieutenant Schulter here.'

'Lieutenant,' Damon said, 'I called a few days ago but . . .'

'I was out of town on a case. Anything new with you?'

Damon told him about the message.

'Uhuh. Four days ago, was it?'

'Yes.'

'Nothing since then?'

'No. Not a word.'

'He's probably getting tired playing the game,' Schulter said 'He's kept you awake enough nights, now he's probably calling five or six other people. I wouldn't worry too much.' Damon could tell that Schulter was becoming bored with the case. 'There's nothing much to go on so far. If you want, you could go to your local precinct and lodge a John Doe complaint claiming obscene and threatening telephone calls, although I doubt they could help you any more than I can. There must be ten thousand calls like that a night in New York. You finish making your list yet?'

'I'm working on it,' Damon said, feeling like a backward pupil who hasn't prepared his homework, caught out in class.

'If anything comes up, call me,' Schulter said. 'Oh, by the way, they checked out that feller, McVane. Nothing there. His neighbors say he hasn't gone out of the house at night for more than a year, and he didn't have a knife in the house you could cut even a steak with.'

'Thanks, Lieutenant,' Damon said, but the detective had already hung up.

He went back to the bar, drank half his whiskey, paid for it and left a large tip for the barman. Who knows, he thought sardonically, when a bartender might become your enemy?

Still, he didn't want to go back to the office. He knew he had been disagreeable the last few days, had been brusque with Miss Walton, had built an invisible wall of silence between his desk and Oliver Gabrielsen's, had scolded Miss Walton for putting a call through to him from a man she should have known he detested and tried to avoid, had told her at the end of the scolding that he would only take calls from his wife and a Mr Schulter.

The atmosphere in the office had reflected all this. When Oliver talked to Miss Walton, it was in hushed tones. And when he came through the door into the office, even if for the moment neither of them was talking, the hush, Damon felt, became more intense.

Standing there at the bar, staring down at the rest of the whiskey, which he would not drink, he felt ashamed of himself for loading his own troubles on the shoulders of his loyal and uncomprehending friends. An idea came to him and his spirits rose. He would go out and buy a present for both Miss Walton and Oliver and bear the presents to them as a peace offering, an acknowledgment of guilt and a promise of more comradely behavior in the future. Shopping for others, trying to find just the gift that would give pleasure to the faithful was an antidote to self-pity. Thinking of the faithful, he would also get something for Sheila.

The streets, after he had left the bar, seemed brighter than when he had entered it, and he felt better than at any moment since he had picked up the telephone on the bedside table on that Saturday night.

First, Miss Walton. Poor woman, she was too fat to find any frilly feminine thing that would make her more attractive, and the only piece of jewelry he had ever seen her wear was a small gold cross that she always carried on a thin chain around her throat. He imagined that Saks might have something that had a chance of pleasing her. He would have to find a sympathetic saleswoman. As he walked toward the store, he snapped his fingers. He knew what he would look for. Miss Walton was always cold in the office. Both he and Oliver liked as much fresh air as they could get, and when they worked, they kept the temperature as low as they could manage without actually freezing them out of the place. Miss Walton always wore a heavy sweater at work in mute complaint of her bosses' tastes in the New York climate. She wore it, too, in the summer with a second sweater under it when the air-conditioning was turned on. It had been the same sweater as long back as Damon could remember, a drab, dark maroon cardigan that she had knitted herself. Since during the years she had worked for the office she had grown fatter and fatter, she must have kept knitting new sweaters to accommodate her swelling bulk, but they were always the same style, the same heavy drab maroon. He decided he would get her a cardigan sweater, since that seemed to be her taste, but in a more cheerful color.

He quickened his step, pleased with himself. The old head was working, he thought. It was the first decision he had made in ten days that had not involved The Problem, as he now thought of it, with the capital letters.

There was a pleasant feminine hum in the store. Women shopped quietly. It was agreeably different from the high treble in restaurants where women congregated for lunch, restaurants he avoided as much as possible, himself.

He found the section where women's sweaters were sold. When the nice young black girl who was serving him asked, 'What size, Sir?' after he had described what he was looking for, he was stumped. He knew what size coats Sheila wore and Sheila was a big woman and wore a forty-two. As far as he could judge, Miss Walton was about twice as large as Sheila although not as tall. He didn't know much about womens' clothes, but he knew he couldn't ask for a size eighty-four.

'Well,' he said to the salesgirl, 'I'm not quite sure.' He put out his hands in front of his chest to make a semicircle that he guessed was about the amount of space Miss Walton's bosom took up. 'I would say she's about this big in this vicinity,' he said.

The salesgirl laughed, showing brilliant teeth and he laughed, too. Buying and selling was a humorous enterprise, a friendly bond between races. 'I'm afraid, Sir,' the girl said, 'that you won't find anything nearly like that here. I suggest that you try the men's department.'

'Thank you,' he said and started toward the elevators, thinking, Whoever hires people for the store should be congratulated.

He found a sweater in light blue cashmere that was too big for him when he tried it on but bought it when the salesman assured him that if it didn't fit the lady, she could bring it back and exchange it. He felt that the price was hideously expensive, but he was in no mood to worry about money. Anyway, he was paying with a Saks credit card and the bill would only come in at the end of the month and that postponed the pain.

While he was in the men's department, he thought he might as well look around for something for Oliver Gabrielsen. He knew Oliver's size because Sheila had bought a ski sweater for him at Christmas.

He browsed happily along the aisles and the racks of suits and jackets, enjoying the little shopping holiday, finally understanding how women could spend afternoons on end shopping and realizing at the same moment that it could become a deadly addiction.

He bought a blue flannel blazer with brass buttons for Oliver and asked that it be gift-wrapped, too.

'Would that be all, Sir?' the salesman asked. 'Not something for you?'

Damon hesitated for a moment. 'Why not?' he asked. Everybody was coming up with great ideas this afternoon. 'What do you suggest?'

'We have a new selection of corduroy jackets,' the man said. 'They're being featured in our windows this week. And they last almost forever. They're very useful if you spend any time in the country.'

'Yes, I can see that.' Another splendid idea. 'I expect to be living in the country full time shortly.' Suddenly the concept that he might retire and live overlooking the Sound in Connecticut, which had only been an idle fancy for the vague future up to then, became a reality.

'If you'll follow me, Sir,' the man said, leading him to a long rack where the jackets were ranged. 'What size would you say? Forty-six?'

'You flatter me,' Damon said. The afternoon was getting better and better. 'Fifty-four would be more like it.'

The salesman looked dubious, but took a natural-colored corduroy jacket down. 'We'll just try this on for size, shall we?'

It fit perfectly.

'You're much larger than one would think,' the salesman said.

'Alas,' said Damon. 'Will you send this, please.' He gave the man his address. 'And the delivery will have to be in the morning, when the maid is in the house. I'll tell her to expect you.'

Again he took the credit card out of his wallet. The jacket cost more than any entire suit he had ever bought, but he hadn't bought a new suit in six years. Inflation, he thought lightly. Grin and bear it. The wallet was old and cracked, he saw. He forgot how long he had had it. 'Where's the leather goods department, please?'

'Downstairs,' the man said.

Humming gently to himself, Damon went down to the leather goods department and bought a pigskin wallet. Inflation, he saw, had not spared the leather goods department, either. No matter.

'Shall I have it gift-wrapped?' the salesman asked.

'No. It's for myself. I'll just slip it in my pocket, if you don't mind.' He put his old wallet on the top of the glass case where the wallets were displayed and emptied it – credit cards, driver's license, social security card, bills, proof of his existence and evidence that he was a citizen in the country of his choice. He put them carefully into the new wallet, then put it into his inside breast pocket. As he turned to leave, the salesman said, 'Excuse me, Sir, what do you want done with this one?' He held up the cracked, worn old piece of leather as though it were staining his fingers.

'Throw it away,' Damon said grandly. Then he remembered Sheila. Mustn't forget the skipper in this fiesta of self-pampering. She would be angry if she knew that he sometimes thought of her as the skipper. She firmly believed that all decisions were made by equal consent in their household. This was not true. 'By the way,' he asked the salesman, 'can you tell me where the furs department is?'

The salesman told him and he took the elevator again, lightly carrying the boxes with Miss Walton's sweater and Oliver's blazer in them. Roger Damon, bringer of peace among the nations, dispenser of gold, goodwill and harmony, rising in the world of Saks.

The saleswoman who greeted him in the fur department was a handsome lady with beautifully coiffed gray hair who apologized that since it was spring the stocks were depleted, but she would be happy to show the gentleman what there was.

The season didn't matter to Damon. Sheila would be around for many winters. He had seen an advertisement in the Sunday *Times* magazine section for sports furs. Sheila could stand a little sport, he thought. 'Here is something in ranch mink,' the elegant lady said to him. It was a pale three-quarter length coat with a belt and a shawl collar. Damon couldn't imagine what sport any woman could play in the coat but didn't inquire. Nor did he inquire what sport the mink had indulged in at the ranch.

Not an endangered species. His ecological principles were not being violated. The elegant lady, he guessed, was just about Sheila's size, age and general shape. 'Would you mind trying it so I can see how it looks on you?' Damon asked. 'My wife is just about the same height as you and if I remember,' he tried to smile without making it a smirk, 'about the same . . . uh . . . formation.' Then, to gain goodwill in the fur department at Saks forever, he said. 'She's beautiful.' He did not add that while the saleslady had silvery-gray hair, his wife's hair was glittering black and would make a more striking contrast with the color of the coat.

The coat looked magnificent on the gray-haired lady as she walked back and forth modeling it, throwing the shawl collar up around her ears, plunging her hands in the deep pockets, opening it wide, like a butterfly's wings, to display the rippled silk lining.

'I'll take it,' Damon said.

The woman looked at him sharply. 'Don't you want to look at any other coats? And the price?'

'No,' Damon said, then added inanely, 'I'm in a hurry.'

'Very well, Sir.'

This was no afternoon for haggling. He had finally joined the most civic-minded tribe of Americans, the insatiable consumers. He was soaring. Buy, buy, buy and sing all your troubles away.

Carelessly, with a flourish, he signed the slip for his credit card, that totem of the tribe, without looking at the price and made sure the woman would have the coat delivered between nine and twelve the next morning.

As he walked out of the ground floor exit of the store he thought momentarily of going to the office and giving their gifts to Miss Walton and Oliver. But the ecstasy of spending which he had never experienced and never appreciated was on him now. The afternoon was young and the treasures of the Imperial City lay all around him, waiting for his credit card.

He hummed an air from the musical *Camelot*, remembering the words of the tune 'The Lusty Month of May' and singing the words in his head to himself . . . 'the time for every frivolous whim, proper or im . . .'

He chuckled aloud, making a passing couple look at him questioningly. It was only April. Not too far off, he thought. Because of matters beyond his control, he was just a little ahead of the season. Now, where to go, what kind of store to visit? A grave decision. The echo of the song within his head made the decision for him. He turned off Fifth Avenue and went down the street toward Madison Avenue and the big music shop on the corner. Music, soothing the savage breast, next on the agenda. He did not know how long he lingered in the store, going over the catalogue, the salesman who waited on him becoming more and more affable as he called out the names of the records he wanted – the last quartets; Beethoven my father, my brother; Chopin, ardent and light-fingered Pole, hater of Russia; Mozart, that dazzling fountain; Liszt, that dark rhetorician; Brahms, a deep, tremendous sigh from the middle of Europe; Mahler, Richard Strauss, the lost world of Vienna; Poulenc, light and bell-like and not given enough credit for what he'd written; *tant pis*; Elgar, Ives, come into the twentieth century, boys; Gershwin, the jangled, blue sounds of the streets of New York; Copland, Appalachian dances, Western rhythms, the frenzied Mayan rhythms of Mexico; Shostakovich, Stravinsky, was that the Russian soul? Call on Lenin or Tolstoy to answer. The list grew longer and longer, the salesman more and more genial. We must have a little of the great soloists, Artur Rubinstein for openers, Casals, Stern, Schnabel, even if it's an old recording, Horowitz, Segovia, for the flamenco, Rostropovich, to compare with Casals. Don't go away yet, young man, there's still the opera to consider. Verdi's *Falstaff* to begin with, *Così Fan Tutte* and naturally, *The Magic Flute*. I'll confer with my wife and drop in tomorrow for some others. Omit Wagner, if you don't mind. Well, perhaps *Die Meistersinger*. And we must not snub the conductors . . . Bernstein, Karajan, Toscanini. You seem to be one of those young people who are up on the new men, I'll trust you to give me some of their best.

I guess that's enough for one day, young man. But it would be blasphemy to submit all that glorious anthology of sound to the scratchy old phonograph in the living room. Let me hear one of the newer models. He listened to several radio-phonographs.

Those clever Japanese, every one of the records sounding as though the orchestra was in the room, pure, sonorous, non-Oriental. He imagined himself sitting on the porch of Uncle Biancella's little house in Connecticut, himself the country gentleman in a smart corduroy jacket that was guaranteed to last almost forever, looking out at the golden sheet of the Sound at sunset, growing older to the sound of angelic voices, a thousand glorious instruments addressing his ear only. The machine he chose was not the cheapest, nor the most expensive. He wrote a check, the figures of no importance; he told the salesman, who by now was dreaming of becoming at least a vice-president of the corporation that owned the store, to make sure everything was to be delivered in the morning, went out of the store immensely satisfied with himself.

He was surprised when he left the store. The sun was low in the sky, it was past six o'clock. New York was a hundred Grand Canyons, eroded by the flow of mankind, the sun a dying star descending on the Meadowlands of New Jersey. All the big stores were closed for the night. But as he had been choosing the music he wished to hear over and over again in his last year, he had decided that there were books that had vanished from his library that he would want with him in Connecticut and new ones that he never had time to read during his active life. Of course, he might change, he would be aghast at what he had spent this afternoon, revert to his usual parsimony, be caught, in his declining years, with only the memory of the books that had disappeared or those he had borrowed from friends or public libraries and returned. Luckily, he remembered that the big book shops on Fifth Avenue remained open all evening. When he had first come to New York, it had been a city for book-lovers, shops on almost every side street, great dusty stores where old, spectacled clerks would say, when asked for a particular volume, 'Ah, I do think I know where I could find that,' and would then leave among creaking shelves and reappear ten minutes later with some schoolboy's copy of Burke's *On Reconciliation with the Colonies* or a first edition of Kipling's *Barrack Room Ballads*. All the best things are swept away by the tide of time, he thought, ravaged by nostalgia. No more, no more, quoth the raven, Nevermore.

Do not look back. Think forward. Generations have their own demands. Space has become one of the dearest commodities on this crowded small outcropping of water-girt stone. 'Out of Print' could easily be the name of every publishing house he now dealt with. Tell me not in mournful numbers that when Scott Fitzgerald died, no book he had written could still be found except at exaggerated prices by rare-book dealers who advertised in small print in the back pages of *The Nation* and *The New Republic*. Do not linger over the fact that last year's huge bestseller has already been shredded into waste paper.

Still, here and there treasures could be found. He made up the list in his mind as he walked along Fifth Avenue. The list was enormous. Stopped at a traffic light, he finally reflected upon what he had been doing all afternoon, was still doing. He had been building a wall of *things*, permanent or semi-permanent, around himself and those he loved in their different ways – Sheila, with a coat to keep her out of the wind for many winters to come, Miss Walton, a hardy perennial flower at her desk, warmed now for many seasons after his eventual departure, Oliver chic in his blazer for future festivities on Long Island, he in his own corduroy jacket, guaranteed to last almost forever, the hundreds, thousands, of concerts that would take years to listen to and know completely and assimilate. The books he had just included in his mental list, with his own overflowing library, meant decades of quiet afternoons and evenings to go through. He was thumbing his nose at death, at Zalovsky, he had put his bet down on the future in the space of a few hours of an April afternoon, and he walked toward the book shop euphorically, even smiling to himself at the thought that even if Zalovsky somehow managed to put his hand on what money he had, the sum would be immensely diminished by the day's purchases.

Significantly, he had not bought a television set, although the one they had at home was small and emitted a wavery image and was broken more often that it worked. Television did not stretch into the future. It was of today, immediate, it left tomorrow up for grabs. When he moved to Connecticut, he would donate the set to the Red Cross.

In the book shop he ordered first the complete collection of the poetry of Yeats, in honor of the memory of Maurice Fitzgerald, for Oliver Gabrielsen to read when he was not at the modish parties in his blue blazer. He hesitated at what there was on the shelves that might be useful to Miss Walton. She could not wear the cashmere sweater twenty-four hours a day. He chose the poems of Emily Dickinson – dry, New England words of consolation across a century from one spinster to another, to make the lonely nights of New York endurable for the sweet and dutiful spirit locked in that mound of fat.

The first thing he ordered for himself was the great two-volume edition of the unabridged *Oxford English Dictionary* in micro-print, that came with a magnifying glass to enlarge the words. After all, he thought, excusing himself for the extravagance, words were his trade and if anything in this century could be considered permanent, it was the English language.

Then he ordered a handsome copy of the King James Bible in large, elegant print. His own was tattered and worn, and the pages were yellowing, and the print seemed to grow smaller and smaller with each year.

Then, in a disorderly spate, he ordered *Don Quixote*, the collected essays of Ralph Waldo Emerson, the *Goncourt Journals*, Milton's *Paradise Lost*, *Nicholas Nickleby*, *The Brothers Karamazov*, Ortega's *The Revolt of the Masses*, Auden, Lowell's *The Confederate Dead*, Freeman's immense biography of Robert E. Lee and for balance the memoirs of General Grant, whatever book Marlowe's *Tamburlaine* and *Dr Faustus* were in (*the topless towers of Ilium – sweet Helen make me immortal with a kiss*), thought sadly of how the word *topless* was used these days. After that, Hugo's and Rimbaud's poetry, in French. Long hours of venturing into a new language that he had not really spoken since his last year in college. Who knew – he and Sheila might want to travel in the wintertime, when the seaside climate was hard to bear. Boswell's *The London Diaries* would be another kind of traveling too.

Except for the Hugo and Rimbaud, he had bought most of the books before or had borrowed them from libraries or had loaned them to friends who had promised to bring them back and had forgotten to do so. One must collect the past – precious baggage.

The list he gave to the clerk who was waiting for him had finally grown to more than a hundred titles. A mere drop in the boundless sea of literature, spanning the ages between the Greek dramatists and Saul Bellow. He might drop in tomorrow, he told the clerk and order some more. Let the rapture continue. Dear Mrs Genevieve Dolger, with her *Threnody*, who had made this afternoon possible. Bless her sentimental housewifely heart, might all her pies come out crisp and delectable. Let Zalovsky curse as his visions of ill-gotten wealth, which he probably now regarded as his rightful heritage, dwindled. Let his voice whine in beggary instead of sneering in threat. Standing at the salesman's desk, going over the long list of books that would now be his, Damon resolved, almost joyously, that he would unplug the answering machine, take the telephone calls himself, coolly agree to meet Zalovsky the next time he called and go fearlessly and contemptuously to meet him, no matter what the hour or place. This afternoon he had purchased an amulet, a charm, that would protect him. It was unreasonable, he knew, but that was the way he felt and he was prepared to act on it.

He told the clerk to gift-wrap the books for Oliver and Miss Walton. The other books he would save in their cartons in the locked space in the cellar where they stored things. He would not open the cartons until they made the move to Connecticut. Otherwise Sheila would weep in despair at the enormous added clutter they would make in the apartment.

He walked out of the shop gloating at the prospect of all the reading he had ahead of him, was about to turn downtown toward home when it occurred to him that while during the afternoon he had provided for the spirit, he had neglected the flesh. There was a fine wine and liquor store on Madison Avenue that he patronized on special occasions because they had the widest choice of bottles in New York and he hurried to get there before the shop closed. Inside, he browsed among the shelves, reading the great names on the labels, Montrachet, Château Lafite, Château Mouton-Rothschild, La Tache, Corton Charlemagne, Mët-Chandon, Dom Perignon, Château Petrus, Château Margaux. The names chimed like wedding bells in his head.

Yes, young man you may take my order now. A case of this, a case of that, three cases of the Lafite. I know it won't be ready for drinking for at least eight years. I don't have a proper cellar to store it in the city, but you can keep it in your warehouse until I'm ready for it. I intend to move to my house in Connecticut shortly, there's an excellent cellar there. Oh, it is difficult, if not illegal, to transport wine or spirits across state borders? No matter. When the time comes, I'll hire a U-Haul truck to put the cases in, I'll be moving a great many books and pictures and things like that at the same time, I don't foresee any problems. And I imagine you have some champagne in the refrigerator, I'll take two bottles of Mumm's, please wrap them carefully, I'll take them with me now.

With a flourish he signed a check for twenty-six hundred and seventy-three dollars and forty cents and went out of the shop, the cold bottles of champagne added to the packages that contained the gifts for Oliver and Miss Walton, gifts he would have to wait until tomorrow to present because the office would be closed by now. Loaded down as he was, the walk downtown would be tiresome so he hailed a cab. The champagne would still be the right temperature when he opened the first bottle for Sheila and himself.

When he opened the door to the apartment, he shouted, 'Sheila,' but there was no response. The light in the foyer was on and as he put down the packages, he saw the note in Sheila's handwriting on the little table.

Dear Roger [he read], Mother's had a stroke and is in serious condition. I've gone up to Burlington, where she's in the hospital. I tried to call you at the office, but by four o'clock, when you still hadn't come back, I had to run to catch the plane. Oliver wants you to stay with them until I get back or if that doesn't suit you, he'll come and stay with you in the apartment. Please don't be stubborn about this. And please don't think of joining me. A hospital with a dying old lady who wouldn't want to see you at the best of times is no place for you to be now. Besides, I called my sister and she'll be there, too, with her dreary husband and I know how you feel about them. She told me Mother's sister, the aunt who is the mother of Gian-Luca, will also be there and that's a

165

meeting I would like to avoid and you certainly shouldn't be bothered with. Just call me at the Holiday Inn in Burlington, so that I know you're all right. And pray for Mother.

Love, Sheila

Slowly he put the note down, the elation he had felt all that afternoon drained away, replaced by a sense of guilt. While he had been spending money like a drunken Texas oil prospector whose gusher had just come in, Sheila had needed him and he had not been there. He did not like the old lady and she certainly had never liked him, but he didn't want her to die. He didn't want anyone to die. Or anyone, Sheila especially, to be confronted with death this week.

He went into the living room, turned on the light. He saw that the answering machine had been unplugged, remembered that he had decided to disconnect it himself as soon as he got home. Telepathy. He sat down heavily and started at the telephone. He dared it to ring. It did not ring.

He reached over and picked up the telephone, dialed the operator, got Information in Vermont to give him the number of the Holiday Inn in Burlington. It was the wrong name for a hotel in which you were staying waiting to find out whether your mother was going to live or die. In other days Americans had been more apt in naming places – Tombstone, Arizona; Death Valley; Laughing Water. The language, like so much else, was declining.

Sheila sounded calm when she came to the phone. She had already been to the hospital, she said, and had just come back to the hotel to check in and have a bite to eat. Her mother's condition was stable. 'Whatever that means,' Sheila said. 'Her left side is paralyzed and she can't talk and I don't know if she recognized me or not. You wouldn't think vegetarians would have strokes.' She laughed harshly. 'Eating all that grass for nothing.'

'Sheila, darling,' Damon said, 'are you sure you don't want me to come up there?'

'Absolutely sure,' Sheila said firmly. 'Have you called Oliver yet?'

'No. I just got into the apartment.'

'Will you call him?'

'Yes.'

'You won't stay alone in the apartment tonight?'

'No. I promise.'

'Roger . . .' She hesitated.

'What is it?'

'I had lunch with Oliver today . . .' She let the words trail off as though she wasn't quite sure how to continue.

'Yes?' Damon could tell that whatever else they had spoken about over lunch, she and Oliver had discussed him.

'He happened to see your notebook, Roger,' Sheila said. 'You left it open on your desk.'

'So?' He couldn't be angry. He and Oliver went casually back and forth to each other's desks all the time.

'It was open and he saw the beginning of your two lists – personal enemies and professional enemies. He could only make out one name. Machendorf. I can guess why you started that list, but . . .'

'I'll explain when I see you, dearest,' Damon said gently.

'What I want to tell you, what I must tell you, is that Oliver and I started a possible list of our own. I hate to do this over the phone, but who knows, one day later may be too late . . .'

'I think I covered the ground pretty completely,' Damon said, sorry he hadn't hung up earlier. 'I don't think either you or Oliver could . . .'

'Did you think of Gian-Luca?' Sheila asked, interrupting him. 'His mother's up here and I asked about him. He's dropped out of sight. For all anybody knows, he's dead. But all the same . . .'

'I'll be on the lookout for Gian-Luca if he ever shows up,' Damon said, wanting to end the conversation.

'One more,' Sheila said, persisting. 'Oliver told me about that Mr Gillespie, who went crazy . . .'

'He hasn't been back since,' Roger said impatiently. 'Actually, I have the feeling that nobody, not anybody that you and Oliver thought of or anybody I dragged up is of any importance. Maybe nobody is of any importance, or it's somebody out of the blue, somebody who's . . .' He stumbled a little. 'Well, it's hard to put into words – somebody who's unknown, a random evil spirit and we may find out tomorrow or we may never find out. Darling,' he said, 'you have enough to worry about. Forget about this for the time being. Please.'

'All right,' she said. 'Just promise me once more that you won't stay alone tonight.'

'Promise. One more thing . . .'

'What's that?' Sheila sounded fearful, as though the one more thing would turn out to be another blow.

'I love you,' Damon said.

'Oh, Roger,' Sheila said brokenly, 'I've sworn not to cry. Good night, my darling. Take care.'

Damon put the telephone down, closed his eyes, thought of the mean old vegetarian lady who had never liked him lying stricken, at last speechless, in the hospital bed. It wasn't a lucky month. Troubles arrived in bunches. He remembered the French saying – *jamais deux sans trois*. Well, Sheila and he had had their two. Be prepared for the third. And why only two without three? Why not three without four? Then without twenty?

He opened his eyes, shook his head to rid it of further dire speculation. He was grateful to Sheila for refusing to let him come to her side, sparing him from the swamp of her family's grief, the weeping aunt, the blowsy sister with the dreary husband, whose son he had thrown down the stairs.

He remembered his own father's death, just after the war, in the hospital in New Haven. The wasted hand searching for Roger's, the last bond of family dissolving. Well, if Sheila was on a family visit, he decided, it was a good time for himself to pay a visit, too.

He dialed Oliver Gabrielsen's number. 'God,' Oliver said worriedly, 'where the hell have you been?'

'Just around,' Damon said. 'I had some errands to run.'

'You know about Sheila's mother . . .'

'Yes. I just talked to Sheila. Her mother's in a stable condition.'

'Do you want to come up here?' Oliver said. 'Or do you want me to come down to your place?'

'Neither.'

'Roger,' Oliver said, pleading, 'you can't stay in your place alone tonight.'

'I won't be staying,' Damon said. 'I'm going out of town for a few days.'

'Do you want to tell me where you're going?'

'No,' Damon said. 'Keep the office going. I'll be in touch.' He hung up. Oliver would have to wait for his blue flannel blazer.

CHAPTER
FIFTEEN

HE ROSE early the next morning and went directly from the motel just outside Ford's Junction to the cemetery. The cemetery bordered the tracks of the New York, New Haven and Hartford railroad on one side and one of the two main streets on another. It was well-kept but because of its position between commerce and transportation was not an adornment to the town, although its inhabitants had not made any known complaints. Its population had grown considerably since the last time Damon had been there for the funeral of his father.

The Damon family plot had three stones on it, with a place for a fourth, himself. His father had been a thoughtful and family-loving man. Damon stared down at the three graves, that of his mother, his brother Davey and his father, green with the sprouting April grass. Damon had not been at his mother's funeral because she had died while he was at sea. He had been too young, his parents agreed, to assist at his brother's funeral.

There were no other Damons in the cemetery because his father had immigrated to Ford's Junction from Ohio as a young man.

If Damon had been asked why, after all the years since he had last visited the family graves, he had come this morning, he would have been hard put to phrase an answer. He knew it had something to do with the recurrent dreams he had been having lately in which his father figured, and at his age it was more or less natural to have thoughts about death and a last resting place, but his decision to rent a car and drive to Ford's Junction the night before after the telephone conversation with Sheila had been almost automatic, instinctive. Now that he was there, paying homage to people he had once loved, he felt an easing of tension, a melancholy but not sorrowful sense of peace, which was not disturbed by the clicking of a train going south to New Haven or the sounds of work and conversation from a nearby plot where two men were digging a new grave, the smell of the fresh earth a springlike loamy odor, defying death or at least making death bearable.

Three good people who belonged to him, his father gentle and honorable and hard-working, his mother a staff to lean on at all times, his brother too young to have sinned. Family, family . . . .

Yes, it had been a good idea to drive up from New York to his boyhood home to commune with his only family and to see for himself that their modest tombs had remained proper and fitting receptacles for those irreproachable and beloved souls.

The day after he had heard the Mozart *Requiem* he had looked up the words of the Mass. His memory was good and his schoolboy Latin served well enough so that he could remember the first section. He said it to himself above the tombstones.

> *Requiem aeternam dona eis, Domine, et lux*
> *perpetua luceat eis.*
> *Te decet hymnus, Deus, in Sion, et tibi reddetur*
> *votum in Jerusalem.*
> *Exaudi orationem meam, as te omnis caro veniet.*

He skipped the repetition of the first three lines of the Mass and whispered the last two somber resounding phrases – 'Kyrie eleison, Christe eleison.'

Honor thy father and thy mother, as the Lord God hath com-manded thee, that thy days may be prolonged and that it may go well with thee . . .

With a feeling of shame that he had left their care to others for so many years, he went out of the cemetery, found a florist's shop nearby, bought some branches of early-blooming white lilac and went back to the plot and carefully laid the fragrant fragile blossoms against the three stones. Repose, gentle souls, he thought, and intervene for me . . .

That it may go well with thee . . .

Impossible to prevent some form of selfishness to intrude in even the most devout of actions.

With a last look backward, he left the cemetery and slowly drove the rented car through the town.

Steeped now in the past, he resolved to visit the places of his joyous boyhood and youth, an old man feeding the springs of memory, remembering the times when he had been carefree and unwounded to balance, for a day, the blows and erosion of age. He would go to their old house, he decided, where he was born and in which he had lived for eighteen years before he went off to college and which he had never lived in since. He would stroll past the high school he had attended, remember the Latin classes, the verses of 'The Ancient Mariner' which the English teacher had read aloud, the prom where he had first danced with a girl, the football field where he had cheered the team on crisp October afternoons . . . Maybe, he thought, I will look into the telephone directory and see if any of the friends who I had thought would remain comrades for life and had soon forgotten, still remained in the town.

Now for the living, he thought, or the still living. He turned toward the hotel and, postponing breakfast, telephoned the Holiday Inn in Burlington.

Sheila's voice on the telephone was grave. 'She's still about the same. That's a good sign, the doctor says. Doctors . . .' She sighed. 'We hang on their words, try to interpret them in the best light possible, put our faith in them. It's not their fault, but there's no escaping it. How about you? How are *you*?'

'Fine,' he said.

'Is Oliver with you?'

'No. I drove to Ford's Junction last night. I'm in the motel there. I thought it might be useful to get out of New York for a couple of days.'

'Ford's Junction,' she said almost reproachfully. 'Don't you have enough to remember these days without that?'

'I've had a most rewarding morning,' he said. 'Believe me. It's turned out to be a very good idea.'

'I hope so.' She sounded doubtful. 'Look,' she said, 'I can't stay away from the school for more than a couple of days. Stay where you are or wander around anywhere you please. Just don't go back to New York until I can get there, too. I've been thinking – the Easter holidays start next week and we can go out to Old Lyme and camp out and relax together and not see a soul for ten days or so. We can both use the vacation and if there's anything drastic with mother, Burlington's not all that far away. Doesn't that sound like a good idea to you?'

'Well . . .' He started to say something about work, but Sheila interrupted him.

'Think about it,' Sheila said. 'You don't have to decide now. Call me tomorrow morning and we'll talk about it some more. I promised the doctor I'd be at the hospital before ten. Please, please take care of yourself, my darling. And leave your dead in peace.'

First he drove toward the house where he was born and where he had lived until he had gone off to college. As he turned into the familiar street, he slowed down as he passed the old Weinstein house. Like the other houses set behind their neat lawns, all of them clapboard or shingle, it was modest and old-fashioned, with a comfortable front porch and Victorian scrollwork for decoration. But it had special associations for Damon. Manfred Weinstein, who was the same age as himself, had been his closest friend from the age of ten until they had separated to go to different colleges. Manfred had been one of the best athletes in town, had been the star shortstop for the high school baseball team. He had been chubby and deceptively soft-looking, with tow hair and a snub nose and a pink, childish complexion that even the afternoons in the sun never turned tan. His voice had been deep and incongruously loud for his age and during the games you could hear him over all the noise of the crowd as he encouraged the pitcher. He was a fair enough student, with a taste for reading, mostly Dumas and Jack London, but fanatically devoted to improving himself as a baseball player. Like a good friend, Damon, who was not much of an athlete himself, spent long afternoons hitting grounders to him, which Weinstein gobbled up gracefully until they were the only figures moving on the deserted playground as dusk settled over the town. Among his friends it was confidently predicted that Weinstein would end up in the big leagues. Now Damon realized that he had never seen Weinstein's name in any newspaper's box score of a National or American League game and wondered what had gone wrong.

Weinstein had gone to Arnold College in New Haven, which prepared students for careers as teachers of physical training. Damon, already planning to assault Broadway as an actor, had gone to Carnegie Tech, which had a highly regarded dramatic school. In the summers, Manfred had played in the twilight league on Cape Cod, which drew its players from the New England colleges, while Damon had gotten jobs in various theatres on the straw-hat summer circuits.

When the war broke out, Manfred had joined the Marines and Damon had chosen the Merchant Marine because his family was already in financial straits and the money he could earn as a merchant seaman was necessary to keep his father and mother afloat. When he came back to Ford's Junction for his father's funeral, Damon heard that Manfred had been badly wounded on Okinawa and was still being treated in a naval hospital.

Looking at the Weinstein house as he slowly drove past, Damon felt a pang of regret that the close boyhood friendship had, because of the accidents of time and geography, been allowed to slip away. He didn't know what Manfred had done with his life or even whether he was alive or dead and he wondered if they would recognize each other if they crossed each other in the street.

The swift young shortstop was not the only inhabitant of the house he had been interested in. Manfred's sister Elsie, who was one year older than her brother, had been the first girl Damon had gone to bed with, when she was eighteen and Damon was seventeen. She had been a sweet-faced, blond, blue-eyed girl, a little chubby like her brother, but attractively so. She was a shy, romantic girl, even though her slightly curved, slender longish nose gave her an exotic, almost stern beauty, and she seemed older than she was. She was one of the best students in the school, a devourer of books, and helped her brother and Damon prepare for their exams in history, which was her strongest subject. She had confided to Damon that she wanted to study at the Sorbonne in Paris and travel through Europe to see the places she had read about – Agincourt, the Field of Gold, Napoleon's battlefields, the church in San Juan de Luz where Henri IV had married the princess of Spain and where Velázquez had died. Damon had had a crush on her since he was ten years old and was dazzled by his luck when she had kissed him for the first time and later on had allowed him to make love to her.

As was Damon, she had been a virgin and their affair had been clumsy and brief. It had been brief because after the second time they made love, hastily, because they were in his room and he didn't know when his parents would return, Damon, inexperienced and shy as he was, with only the haziest notions of what precautions Elsie was taking, had asked what she would do if she found she was pregnant.

'I'll kill myself,' she had said calmly.

Thinking back on that afternoon, Damon reflected about the drastic change in customs and standards of adolescent behavior that had swept America since his own high school days. He had no children of his own if you excepted Julia Larch's son, but among his friends with teenage children he had heard of how boys not yet old enough to vote had brought girls into the house for casual weekends with their parents present and of mothers who had put their daughters on the pill on their fifteenth birthday. He didn't know whether the change had been for the better or worse, whether love showed a profit or a loss in the long run because of it, but he doubted if any eighteen-year-old girl of today would announce her decision to kill herself because of a pregnancy.

At any rate, terrified by what she had said, he had never touched Elsie again, and after she had graduated from high school in the class ahead of his own and had left town for a summer job in Boston and then college, they had not seen each other again. Manfred had never indicated that he had known of the affair between his best friend and his sister and Damon wondered now, as he drove past the house which he had known

175

as well as his own, whether Manfred had kept quiet out of ignorance or tact.

Used as he was to the constantly altering of the landscapes and quality of the neighborhoods of New York City, since the war, Damon marveled at how this one street had remained the same, peaceful, with the air of having one hundred years before been exactly as it looked today and would probably look for a hundred years to come. The only difference was that the trees had grown enormously along the curbs since he had been there last, but as he approached his house, it was just about as he remembered it, except that the last time he had seen it, on the occasion of his father's funeral, it had been painted white and now it was dark brown with red shutters. His father had left it to him in his will, but the mortgages on it were so high that Damon, who at that time was still trying to gain a modest foothold in the theatre in New York, knew that even with the income he might have gotten if he managed to rent it out, he couldn't keep up the yearly payments. He had sold it and with the money from the sale, had been lucky to pay off his father's last debts.

The years before his father had died had not been prosperous ones for the sick old man and his attempts to keep his toy-manufacturing business alive in nearby New Haven, to which he had commuted daily for so many years, had drained whatever resources he had in reserve. When he died, he was penniless.

Damon stopped the car and got out and looked at the house. The lawn was well-kept and there was a baby carriage and a bicycle on the front porch.

Every two years he had helped his father whitewash the entire house and the shed in the back garden which his father used to fashion the toys he was designing, small models of horse-drawn carts, all the harness meticulously cut to scale in leather, with tiny brass buckles, spring-driven metal models of old-fashioned locomotives, with coal tenders and coaches, small hobby horses on rockers, tin soldiers in Revolutionary and Civil War uniforms, complete with rifles and horse-drawn artillery.

His father had been deft with his hands and modest in his ambitions and if at the end, he had told Damon on his deathbed

176

that he had wasted his life in footling tinkering, Damon remembered the hours he had spent, whistling contentedly in the shed, carving wood and delicately painting miniature uniforms.

The inside of the house had always been as geometrically neat as its exterior and the grounds about it. His mother had been a scrupulous housekeeper and even though she had spent three afternoons a week in the small office next to the workroom in New Haven going over the business's books, checking invoices and sending out letters, the house was always sweet-smelling and immaculate. Remembering the crisp New England order in which he had been reared, Damon smiled, despite himself, at the thought of the horror which his mother would have felt if she saw the dusty clutter of books and records into which her son had subsided in his later years.

He suppressed the desire to get out of the car and knock on the front door, introduce himself and see who lived there now and perhaps get a glimpse of the interior. Nostalgia could too easily dissolve into masochism and he was not a masochist. Just as he was about to start the car, the front door opened and a dark-haired boy came out. He was wearing corduroy pants and a sweatshirt and was carrying a baseball glove. Damon stared hard at him. It could have been the same boy he had seen darting among the taxis on Sixth Avenue, or the twin of the boy in the photographic album who had been himself. The boy wheeled the bicycle off the porch, swung himself onto it, glanced curiously at Damon, sitting in the parked car, and pedaled off.

Damon shook his head, impatient with himself and the tricks time and memory were playing on him. He started the motor and turned the car back in the direction from which he had come.

Thomas Wolfe had been inaccurate when he wrote that you can't go home again, Damon thought. Wolfe *had* gone home again, but after his death. You could go home again, but it was wiser not to.

As he drove slowly up the street, he saw a man of about his age spading a flower border in front of the Weinstein house. The man had thinning gray hair and the babyish chubbiness had become hard fat around the middle, but Damon recognized him, even at a distance of twenty yards. It was Manfred Weinstein.

Damon hesitated before putting on the brakes. After all the years what could they say to each other? Had the grown men betrayed the unspoken promises that had bound two boys together? Would they both be embarrassed, ashamed, disappointed with each other? They had parted casually the day after the graduation ceremonies at the high school. 'I'll be seeing you around. Keep in touch. Good luck.' 'Yep.' What had seemed on the surface to be a temporary summer parting had widened, deepened, had become a gulf, a geological fault, an abyss. There were some abysses that were perhaps better left unspanned.

Damon had his foot tentatively on the brake pedal. He took it off, started to accelerate. But it was too late.

'Holy man!' It was Manfred Weinstein striding toward him, still holding the spade. 'Roger Damon!'

Damon got out of the car and for a moment they stood motionless, staring at each other, grinning foolishly. Then they shook hands. Weinstein dropped the spade and they embraced, something they had never done as boys and young men.

'What the hell are you doing here?' Weinstein asked.

'I came to visit you,' Damon said.

'Still the same fucking old liar,' Weinstein said. His voice was still deep and loud and Damon hoped that there were no easily shocked neighbors who could hear how Weinstein greeted his boyhood companion. 'I got some coffee on the stove. Come on in. We have a lot of time to catch up on, you and me.'

They sat at the scrubbed wood table in the kitchen of the Weinstein house, where Weinstein's mother, a tall, plump woman, whom Damon remembered as always wearing a starched blue apron trimmed with white lace, had fed them milk and cookies when they came in after playing ball in the afternoon. Now they drank coffee out of mugs from a pot that Manfred Weinstein kept warm on the back of the stove. He lived alone. While Weinstein was in the hospital after the war, his father had sold the clothing store in which Manfred had worked after his graduation from college.

Damon interrupted the flow of reminiscence. 'What were

you doing selling neckties and tuxedos?' he asked. 'I thought you were going to be a ball player.'

'So did I,' Weinstein said ruefully. 'I was being scouted by the old Brooklyn Dodgers and the Red Sox. Then I did something foolish.'

'That wasn't like you.'

'That's what you think. I could build a skyscraper out of my mistakes. Like everybody else, I guess.'

'What did you do?'

'I was playing in my last season at Arnold. We were leading seven to three and the game was on ice and everybody was coasting except your gung-ho friend Manfred. There was a ball hit way off to my right but too far for the third baseman, and I dove for it and managed to grab it, but I was way off balance and it was a long hard throw to first. I should have just held the ball and let the guy have his puny infield hit, it didn't mean anything. Instead, like an idiot, I made the throw across my body and just as I let it go I felt and heard something snap in my shoulder. There went the career. In one second.' He sighed. 'Who needs a shortstop with a dead arm? Instead of playing in the World Series I wound up, as you said, selling neckties and tuxedos to snot-nosed Yalies. As my father put it, a man has to eat. He was full of wise sayings like that.' Weinstein grinned. 'Anyway, I'm glad he's alive, down in Miami, nearly ninety years old, a gay widower among the geriatric ladies, with my mother safely gone, still sending me homely nuggets of philosophy from the Sun Belt. I married after the war, a pretty good marriage as marriages go. My wife was a good housekeeper and she didn't nag, or I don't remember now if she did and she gave me two nice children, a boy and a girl, they're grown people now, working in California. Let's change the subject,' he said brusquely. 'I haven't even thought about that one second in New Haven for years. I know about you. I read that piece in the newspapers about you. You're riding high now, aren't you?'

'Medium high,' Damon said. 'A good wife. The second. One mistake and I was careful after that. No children.' Then, remembering Julia Larch, 'that I know of.'

'I should have come down and visited you after that piece,' Weinstein said.

'I wish you had. For old times' sake.'

'Old times. Over in a second.' Weinstein closed his eyes momentarily, then waved his hand as if to sweep away imaginary cobwebs. 'I heard that when you came to town for your father's funeral,' he said, 'you asked about me and I thought about writing you, but I was too busy trying to keep alive to do much of anything else.'

'How long were you in the hospital?'

'Two years.'

'Good God.'

'It wasn't so bad,' Weinstein said. 'Nobody was shooting at me and I educated myself. I had nothing else to do and I read everything I could get my hands on.'

Damon thought he looked old, the hard lines of his face sagging. The jaunty shortstop was long gone. 'The Marines . . .' Weinstein sounded rueful. 'I joined the first week after Pearl Harbor. I was selling suits in my father's shop in New Haven and I didn't think it was the place to be when Americans were going to be fighting the Nazis.' He smiled bitterly. 'I never saw a German. All I saw was a lot of little yellow faces. The Jewish thing . . .' He made a grimace. 'Showing the goyim that Jews have balls, even if it means getting them shot off. Maybe the Israelis have taken some of the heat off.' He shrugged. 'You never know whether you're doing the right thing or the wrong thing. I made gunnery sergeant. There's a bronze star around the house somewhere. I think I got it for being alive.' He laughed softly. 'When I finally got out of the hospital, being a clerk in somebody else's men's shop didn't have much attraction for me. A friend of mine from my outfit was a cop on the New Haven police force and he talked me into joining. It wasn't a bad life. It had a special meaning for me. I don't want to sound like George Washington or a retired admiral with blood in his eye, but you fight for your country in different ways. I may be sentimental, but when you put your life on the line, you accept certain responsibilities. If this country's going to fail, it'll be through lawlessness. Mugging in broad daylight, race riots, assassinations, politicians stealing left and right, whole neighborhoods going up in flames for the insurance, kids playing cowboys and Indians with Saturday night specials, buying dope by the pound, then screaming about the draft, the National Rifle Association making sure that every nervous idiot has an arsenal stashed away at home, people driving cars as though they're Apache Indians on the warpath.' He was growling now, the sound booming through the old house. 'I was on the traffic detail for a while and when I stopped people when they were going ninety miles an hour through town and reminded them that Connecticut had a fifty-five mile an hour speed limit, they looked at me as if I'd just told them their mother was a whore and they did everything but lynch the governor because they thought the speed limit was his idea and that he'd insulted the honor of the state because suddenly it had the lowest accident rate in America.' He laughed at himself. 'I sound like a preacher at a cotton-pickers' revival meeting. But if you don't believe in law, you don't believe in anything. I saw plenty of crooked cops, but that doesn't change the idea. Besides, the job appealed to me. Maybe I'd just gotten sort of used to being around guns and tough men . . .' He spoke almost apologetically. 'Anyway, I retired five years ago, not a bad pension, detective lieutenant, it's all over now, good, bad or indifferent. I work in the garden, play some golf, umpire Little League games, go over to the high school field to try to show their shortstops how to go into the hole for deep ground balls, once in a while I visit the kids in California. I rattle around in this old house, it's miles too big for me, but this is a nice town and it's the only home I've ever known and I hate the idea of giving it up . . .' He laughed softly again. 'Well, there it is, Roger, the two-minute life of Manfred Weinstein. Not much there for a book, is there?'

'Not the way you put it, no,' Damon said.

Manfred chuckled. 'One of the reasons I always liked you,' he said, 'is that you made sure I never got a swelled head, even the season when I hit .356 in my junior year. I'm glad to see you haven't changed.'

'I know another cop who was in the Marines,' Damon said. He realized that subconsciously he had been comparing the gentle old man across from him at the kitchen table who looked like everybody's benign grandfather and the rasping, stone-faced Lieutenant Schulter. 'Man by the name of Schulter.'

Weinstein looked surprised. 'I heard of him. We used to get fliers from him. Homicide, in New York.'

'That's the man.'

'What the hell are you doing with a dick from homicide?'

Damon sighed. 'It's a long story.'

'We got all day. At least I have.' Now there was a hard glint in Weinstein's eyes and for a moment Damon could see the gunnery sergeant, the big city detective, and guess that Manfred Weinstein had not been a pleasant man to deal with when he was on a case.

'Well,' Damon said, 'it started with a telephone call . . .' Then he went through the whole thing, Zalovsky's threat, the message on the answering machine, the conversations with Schulter, the lists, leaving out his dreams, the encounter on the street with a man who had been dead for years, the boy with the baseball glove on Sixth Avenue and only minutes before swinging onto a bicycle just three doors down from the house in which they were sitting. Weinstein listened intently, searching Damon's face as he spoke as if looking for clues, now giving a hint that although physically the two men were so different, psychically Weinstein and Schulter shared many characteristics. What the French called *la déformation de métier*. He remembered more French than he gave himself credit for.

'Actually,' Damon said, 'the people my wife and I have come up with as possibilities don't amount to much as threats. They may dislike me enough to want to annoy me a little, but that's all. I was just trying to dig up some names for Schulter. To tell the truth, Manfred, my feeling is that the whole thing is out of the blue,' he said, knowing that he was repeating himself. 'I might just as well use a Ouija board or pick a name at random out of the telephone book. If this wasn't the twentieth century, I'd try religion and ask for the Pope to exorcise the demon. Demon, Damon – that's pretty damn close, isn't it?'

'What's your gut feeling about it?' Weinstein asked. 'I'd go by that.'

Damon hesitated, thought of the dreams and apparitions of the days and nights since the first telephone call. 'I think there's somebody out there who wants to kill me,' he said.

'That's simple enough for me. How are you going to handle it when you get back to New York?' Weinstein asked.

'I decided. The next time he calls me, any time of the day or night, I'm going down and meeting him. Get it over with, once and for all.'

'Did you tell Schulter that?'

'Not yet.'

'Did you intend to tell him?'

'Yes.'

'Do you want to hear what he'll say when you tell him?' There was a harsh note in Weinstein's voice. 'He'll say just what I'm going to say right now – you're crazy. Whatever else the guy is, he'll be armed. And probably as nutty as they come, to boot. You'd be lucky if he just kidnapped you and stashed you away somewhere and waited for the ransom money, if it's money he's after. I don't know what you've been doing or what you've been reading lately, but don't you know that people are knifing and shooting each other all over America these days for a parking place, a dollar and some change, for a package of cigarettes, because somebody is white and somebody else is black . . . ?'

'I've got to get it over with one way or another, Manfred,' Damon said. 'It's driving me out of my mind. I have the feeling I'm living in a haunted house and somewhere somebody is sticking pins into a doll in a voodoo curse and the doll is me.'

Weinstein got up and poured some coffee into Damon's mug, then into his own. He put the pot back on the stove, stirred some sugar into the mug, the small clinking of the spoon against the cup the only sound in the empty house. He put his head back and squinted worriedly at the ceiling as if he were deep in thought, trying to solve some complicated problem, and rubbed the side of his face, the stubble of his day-old beard making a rasping sound against the palm of his hand.

Damon watched him in silence, half-sorry that he had gotten out of his car to burden this accidentally rediscovered old friend with his problem, but relieved at the same time that he was sharing it with a man who had his survival at heart and who had spent his career dealing with criminals and putting them behind bars.

Finally, Weinstein spoke, crisply and with authority. 'No

way,' he said. 'There's no way you can go meet whoever it is, alone. This is what we're going to do. We're going to New York together and I'm staying with you. Night and day . . .'

'But . . .' Damon began to protest.

'No buts.'

'It may take weeks, months before the man calls me. Maybe never. I can't take you away from your home, put you in danger . . .'

'I got nothing but time,' Weinstein said.

'It's a small apartment. Sheila and I have a double bed. The only place I could offer you to sleep is on the couch in the little room I use to work in . . .'

'I've slept on harder ground. Anyway, I owe you a favor after all those afternoons you wasted hitting grounders at me.'

'Some favor,' Damon said ironically. 'There wasn't any chance of your being killed if I hit the ball the wrong way.'

'Drink your coffee,' Weinstein said. 'It's getting cold.' He sipped at his own mug. 'I've got nothing to do here. And I like the idea of getting one more sonofabitch off the streets.' He smiled, looking like a pleased child. 'It'll be a pleasure. If he makes any trouble, I'll have my pistol on me.' He grinned evilly, as though he were promising himself a particular treat. 'It's about time I hauled my old ass off the shelf. I feel younger already. You better call your wife and tell her you have a house guest coming. It's also about time I met the lady.'

'Okay, okay,' Damon said. 'If you want to act like a damn fool, I'm grateful.'

'When do you want to go?' Weinstein asked. 'You got any more errands to do here in town?'

'Not really. I did what I came here to do,' Damon said, thinking of the lilac branches on the graves. 'I was really only sightseeing when I spotted you.'

'Thanks for nothing, old buddy.' Weinstein smiled. 'All I have to do is shave and dress like a gentleman and oil the pistol. You check out of your room yet?'

'No.'

'If you come back for me in an hour, I'll be ready. You sure you know the way back?'

'If I get lost, I'll ask directions, Manny,' Damon smiled.

Nobody, Weinstein had made clear, could call him Manny instead of Manfred and Damon had only done it two or three times when he had been exasperated with his friend or was teasing him. Then he spoke more gravely. 'Do you really think you'll need a gun?'

'This isn't England, Roger. In the U.S. of A. cops use guns. If they left them home for twenty-four hours, it would be St Bartholomew's Eve all over again in every city in the country.'

'Have you ever killed anybody?' As he said it, Damon regretted asking the question.

'I was in the Marines. We weren't there to play ping-pong.' Weinstein sounded amused.

'I mean in civilian life.'

'There's no such thing as civilian life for cops. Two. I killed two men in what you call civilian life. All I can say is they deserved it. And I got a medal for each of the bastards. Don't worry. I won't shoot if I don't have to. And I'll try to keep the damage down to the minimum.'

'One thing I'm glad of, old shortstop,' Damon said. 'That you're on my side.' He stood up and Weinstein stood, too. 'Listen, Manfred,' Damon said, 'there's something I should have asked you about before.'

'What's that?' Weinstein looked at him suspiciously.

'How's Elsie?'

'She's dead,' Weinstein said flatly. 'She changed religion and became a Christian Scientist, and she wouldn't go to a doctor and she died sixteen years ago. Any more questions?' His voice was harsh.

'No.' One more dream, Damon thought, another shade in the procession. 'Did she ever go to Europe?'

'No. She married a shit in Boston who never held a job more than two weeks, and she had to support him. He was a half-assed writer and made a lot of noise about being an atheist and making fun of the Jews, who, he said, had imposed the blight of Christianity on the world – his words – Elsie had to hold me back from belting the sonofabitch more than once. I think she became a Christian Scientist because of him. The fucker's still alive. Worse luck. Last I heard of him he was setting up those goddamn encounter groups, you know, where everybody gropes everybody else. The things people fall into once they stop believing in God. How about you, Roger?' he asked challengingly.

'Fifty-fifty,' Damon said.

'Better than zero-zero,' Weinstein said. 'If I changed my religion, it would be to become a Catholic. They forgive sinners. We can all use a little of that. I talked myself blue in the face trying to convince Elsie that if she didn't want to be a Jew anymore to go to the priests, it's got form and rituals and a bone-deep history and at least the music is better in the churches.' He laughed sourly. 'What made you and her break up?'

'I'd rather not say.' You couldn't tell a religious man that at the age of eighteen his sister had threatened to commit suicide because of the result of an affair with his best friend.

'Well, you saved yourself a lot of trouble. She was a damn fool. In more ways than one. Now get out of here. And drive carefully. I don't want you to break your neck and cheat me out of my fun. I'll walk you to your car.'

They came out onto the sunny street and Damon got into the car. Before starting the motor he looked thoughtfully at Weinstein, the lines of age, sorrow and violence etched deeply in his face, but the cold blue eyes youthfully clear. 'You were such a quiet, peaceful boy,' Damon said. 'I don't remember your ever even getting in a fight. Who would have thought you'd turn into such a tough old bird?'

Weinstein grinned. 'Me,' he said.

CHAPTER
SIXTEEN

BACK AT the motel Damon called his office and got Oliver on the phone.

'Where are you?' Oliver asked worriedly. When he was nervous, as he was now, Oliver's voice rose to a high squeak.

'Out of town,' Damon said. 'But not too far away. I'll be in after lunch.'

'How's Sheila's mother?'

'The same. Sheila has to stay in Burlington at least till Wednesday.'

'Will you stay with Doris and me tonight or do you want me to come to your place?'

'Neither.'

'Roger,' Oliver said reproachfully, 'Sheila's going to be sore at me. She'll think I've let both you and her down. If anything happens to you, she'll blame me.'

'She won't think anything and she won't blame anybody. I've arranged for a friend to come in and stay with me.'

'You're not making that up, are you?'

'Have I ever lied to you?'

'Only sometimes,' Oliver said.

Damon laughed. 'Not this time.'

'Proctor called. He wants you to phone him. He says it's important. He has to make a decision before the weekend.'

'Phone him and tell him I'll call this afternoon. And stop worrying.'

'I'll try,' Oliver said wanly.

Damon hung up, finished packing, paid his bill and drove to pick up Weinstein for the drive down to New York.

When they got to the apartment, Damon was surprised to see the foyer piled high with cartons of books and records and the packages containing the fur coat for Sheila, the gifts for Oliver and Miss Walton, the corduroy jacket he had bought for himself, the two bottles of champagne he had carried home, now no longer cold. He had forgotten his buying spree and had neglected to leave instructions for the cleaning woman about what to do with the stuff.

'Holy man,' Weinstein said, 'what is this – Christmas morning?'

'I bought a few things yesterday,' Damon said. Was it only yesterday? It seemed like months ago. 'A few necessities of life. Books, records, things like that.'

'What's in that one?' Weinstein pointed at a huge carton.

'That must be the phonograph I ordered.'

'What're you doing – preparing for a nuclear attack?'

Damon laughed. 'Not as grave as all that. I'll be taking it up to our place in Old Lyme.' He had told Weinstein about the house on the trip down, as well as the reason why he wouldn't be seeing Sheila that evening. 'It's for when I retire into the woods and I want to be reminded of what civilization was like back in the big city.'

'Civilization in the big city would be a lot more bearable,' Weinstein said dryly, 'if that's all it was like.'

They went through the living room, with Weinstein looking around appreciatively, and into the small room where Damon worked. 'That's where you'll have to bed down, I'm afraid.' Damon pointed to the short, narrow couch.

'It's a lucky thing I never grew to my rightful height,' Weinstein said. 'It'll do. I warn you, I snore.'

'I'll close my door.'

'My wife used to say that my snores could he heard in Poughkeepsie. A door is a mere trifle,' Weinstein said. 'By the way, I see you have two locks on your front door. The upper one is new. You just put it in?'

'Since the first call.'

'How many people have keys?'

'Just Sheila and me and the maid.'

'Maybe it would be a good idea if I talked to the maid.'

Damon laughed. 'She's a big fat black lady with a great contralto voice. She sings in her church choir up in Harlem. We've gone to hear her several times. She's worked for us fifteen years and we leave money around the house, Sheila's jewelry . . . nothing's ever been touched. The only wrong thing she may have done in her life is hit a flat note when she's had a cold.'

'Okay,' Weinstein said. 'Cross off one contralto. Still, don't depend too much on locks.'

'I don't. That's why I'm happy to have you here, even if I can't get any sleeping in.'

Just then the telephone began to ring on both lines, the one in the bedroom and the one in the living room. Weinstein looked at Damon questioningly. 'You going to answer it?'

'Of course. My friend from Ma Bell never calls in the afternoon.'

It was Sheila. 'I phoned the motel in Ford's Junction,' she said, 'and they told me you'd checked out. I guessed you'd be home by now. Is Oliver with you?'

'No.'

'You promised me you wouldn't stay in the flat alone,' she said, rebuking him.

'I'm not alone. I have an old friend with me. You remember Manfred Weinstein, from Ford's Junction. I told you about him. When we were kids together. It turns out he's a retired detective and he's kindly offered to cling to me like a leech, for old times' sake. And he's heavily armed.' Damon spoke lightly as though having a house guest who wore a shoulder holster with a snubnosed .38 caliber pistol in it was an amusing bit of whimsy.

'Are you making this up?' Sheila asked suspiciously. 'To keep me from worrying?'

'I'll let you talk to him. Manfred,' he said, 'come and talk to the lady of the house.'

'Ma'am,' Weinstein said into the phone, his voice booming as usual, 'please let me thank you for your hospitality.'

If volume was reassuring, Damon thought, Sheila must be

reassured. Weinstein sounded like a two-hundred-and-twenty-pound basso.

Weinstein listened for a moment and Damon, who was standing next to him, could hear the anxiety in Sheila's voice even though he couldn't make out the words.

'Don't you worry, Ma'am,' Weinstein said, 'he'll be as safe as a baby in its mother's arms. I hope I have the pleasure of meeting you real soon.' He handed the phone to Damon. 'She wants to talk to you.'

'Roger,' Sheila said, 'it's very nice of Mr Weinstein to offer to take care of you, but I wish I could come down right now and see for myself. But I can't. Mother's still the same. Comatose, the doctors say, whatever that really means. There's a big specialist coming up from Boston on Tuesday and I've just got to stay here at least until he examines her. I called the school and they say they're getting along fine without me. It's nice to know you're not indispensable.' She laughed ironically.

'You're indispensable to me.'

'What do you think you are to me?' Sheila's voice had sunk to a whisper. 'Mr Weinstein's not going to do anything reckless, is he?'

'All I can say is that he was very careful as a boy,' Damon said, trying to joke, 'and he's hardly aged at all. Don't rush back on my account. I'm all right. As Manfred said, like a baby in its mother's arms.'

'I wish I could believe that,' Sheila said distractedly. 'Anyway, don't get drunk with your detective friend.'

'He only drinks coffee.'

'Don't drink too much coffee.' It was a sad little joke.

'And don't you act like a Jewish mother,' Damon said, an even sadder joke. But Sheila laughed, not very convincingly.

'Stay well, dear,' she said. 'And call often. It's the only ray of light in the darkness here.'

'I hope the specialist from Boston helps.'

'Nobody's very optimistic. The worst thing would be if she were to just lie here the way she is now. For months, for years . . .' Sheila's voice broke. 'It's awful. I dread going into her room. I keep remembering her as a pretty young woman. And it's raining up here. How is it in New York?'

'Fair. A little smoggy.'

'Have a good time with your friend. I'm glad now you found him. Tell him I like the sound of his voice. Tell him I like a man who speaks out loud and clear. Also tell him I hope he doesn't have to use that gun.'

'I'll tell him.'

'I've got to say good-bye now. I'm calling from a phone booth at the hospital and there's a lady standing waiting to get in.' Childishly, she blew a kiss into the mouthpiece.

Damon hung up slowly.

'Things aren't going so good up in Burlington, are they?' Weinstein said. He had been watching the changing expressions on Damon's face as he spoke on the phone.

'Old age,' Damon said. Sheila's mother was only a few years older than he and the two mournful words were as much for himself as for her.

'What do you want to do now? I could help you put away all that stuff in the hall. And I could attach the radio-phonograph. I'm pretty good around the house for things like that, and I remember you were clumsy as hell when you were a boy.'

'I haven't changed,' Damon said. 'Sheila won't even let me put in a light bulb by myself. But I'm hungry and I'd like some lunch.' He had had an early breakfast and it was past one o'clock. 'And I have to drive the car uptown and hand it over to the Hertz people. Then I guess I better put in an appearance at the office. I've been goofing off for days and the work must be piled high on my desk.'

'Fine,' Weinstein said. 'I'm hungry myself and I'd like to see what your office is like, have a little chat with your partner.'

'Don't make too big a deal of it. I've made him jittery enough as it is.' Damon thought back with shame about his behavior in the past weeks. 'I've been a zombie around the office. And he's a timid, scholarly young man and he's very fond of me and I'm afraid he thinks I'm going around the bend as it is.'

'Don't worry,' Weinstein said. 'There won't be any third degree.' Then he added, 'Not yet anyway.'

When they got to the office after lunch, Damon introduced Weinstein as a gentleman who was going to do some supplementary reading for them because since the success of *Threnody*, the volume of incoming manuscripts had more than doubled. Mr Weinstein would do his reading in the office for a while to accustom himself to their routine. Damon knew it sounded peculiar, but it was better than telling his co-workers that they might at any moment expect to be caught in the line of fire of a gunfight.

Then he gave Miss Walton and Oliver their gifts. 'I know I've been just about impossible to live with for the last few days,' he said, 'and this is just a small way of making up for it.'

Miss Walton attempted to hold back tears, with moderate success, as she opened the box and saw the cashmere sweater. Her chin quivered as she shyly kissed Damon, something she had only done so far when he gave her her cash bonus at Christmas. She insisted upon putting the sweater on at once. 'What a sensitive way to let me know that this ratty old thing' – disdainfully she held up the bulky hand-knit dull red cardigan that she had worn daily for almost ten years – 'was an eyesore.' She stuffed it into the wastebasket, giggled and said, 'Good-bye forever, you miserable rag.'

Oliver tore the wrapping off the Yeats book before glancing at the larger box with the blazer that Damon had given him at the same time. As usual, Damon noted with amusement, books came before anything else with his albino partner. Oliver looked reproachfully at Damon when he saw the title. 'Roger,' he said, 'don't you think I have a copy of Yeats at home?'

'I'll bet you ten dollars that when you look for it, you'll find that somebody's nipped it and conveniently forgot to return it.'

Oliver laughed. 'Come to think of it,' he said, 'I haven't seen it for a long time.' Then he opened the big box and took out the blazer and put it on and modeled it. It fit him perfectly. He took it off and carefully hung it in the closet. 'It's too splendid for weekdays,' he said. 'It's much too extravagant, Roger, but I'm glad you splurged. It'll cost me money, though.' He smiled gratefully and Damon was afraid he was on the verge of tears, too. 'My wife'll be wild with envy and I'll have to get one like this for her.'

'It won't cost you a penny. I'll get one for her, too,' Damon said grandly. 'The way I've been treating you, you must have been a nuisance around the house recently. Tell her it's a peace offering from the boss. Now let's all get back to work.'

Then he sorted through the pile of manuscripts and picked out a twelve-hundred-page novel by someone he had never heard of and gave it to Weinstein, who had already ensconced himself on the couch, which faced the door. 'Here,' Damon said, 'this should keep you busy for the rest of the afternoon.' Then he took off his jacket, hung it up and sat down at his desk. He saw that Weinstein was keeping his jacket on and hoped Oliver wouldn't speculate on the reason for the man's formality. When Weinstein left the office for a few minutes to go to the men's room, Oliver came over to Damon's desk and said, in a low voice, so that Miss Walton couldn't hear him, 'Where did you pick up that fellow?'

'He's an old friend of mine,' Damon said. 'He majored in English literature. He's particularly good on crime fiction.'

'He doesn't look like a literary type.'

'Neither do you. Literary types come in all sizes these days.'

'How much are we paying him?' Every once in a while Oliver tried to sound like a partner.

'Nothing,' Damon said. 'We'll see how he works out. Until we make a final decision, I'll pay him out of my own pocket.'

Oliver started to protest, but Damon stopped him. 'It's only fair. The reason we're so overloaded is because I've neglected everything for so long. Ssh. Here he comes.'

Just before closing time, the phone rang. It was Schulter. 'I've got some news for you, Damon. Can you meet me in ten minutes? Same place as last time.'

Damon felt a shiver of apprehension at the tone of the detective's voice. 'I'll be there. I'll bring a friend if you have no objections.'

'Can he keep his mouth shut?'

'Guaranteed.'

'Ten minutes,' Schulter said, and hung up.

He was sitting in the bar, wearing the same coat, buttoned up, and the ridiculous tiny hat, looking ominous and threatening, when Damon and Weinstein came in. He didn't stand up to greet them or put out his hand when Damon introduced Weinstein, but merely grunted and sipped at his coffee. The waitress came right over and Weinstein ordered a coffee. Damon asked for a beer. Whenever he talked to Schulter, he realized, his throat went dry.

'Mr Weinstein knows who you are,' Damon said. 'On a professional basis.'

'What do you mean by that?' Schulter asked suspiciously. 'Professional?'

'He was a detective on the New Haven police force. Now he's retired. I've known him since we were boys. He's come to live with me – well, act as a kind of bodyguard – until our little problem is solved.'

Schulter looked with new interest at Weinstein, who was starting around the room, his eyes alert, taking everything in, the other customers, the movements of the waitresses and the bartender.

'You armed?' Schulter asked.

'I'm armed,' Weinstein said, now looking at Schulter and smiling thinly.

'You better be.'

'Courtesy of the New Haven police department.'

'You mind if I check on you in New Haven?'

'I don't mind,' Weinstein said. 'The first name is Manfred.'

'I never heard of a detective with the name of Manfred,' Schulter said.

'There's a first time for everything.' Weinstein smiled more widely.

'Now,' Damon said, 'what's *your* news, Lieutenant?'

Schulter waited while the waitress put down Weinstein's coffee and Damon's beer. When she had gone, Schulter said, 'It's about the Larches. Mrs Larch was committed to an insane asylum two days ago.'

'Oh, Christ,' Damon said. The feeling of apprehension he had had when talking on the phone to Schulter had been justified. Since Zalovsky's first call, disaster had spread around him like ever-widening ripples from a stone thrown into a pond. And he was the stone.

'They found her walking around naked in the street,' Schulter said. 'It turns out she was going to a psychiatrist for nearly a year. The psychiatrist says she's schizophrenic. I thought you ought to know.'

'Thanks,' Damon said dully.

'By the way,' Schulter said, 'her psychiatrist says she never told her husband about who was the kid's father. She made it all up. Mr Larch is still crazy about the kid according to all the neighbors.'

'Thanks again.'

Weinstein looked puzzled. 'Who's Mrs Larch, Roger? And what has she got to do with you and the lieutenant?'

'I'll explain later,' Damon said.

'Anything new with you, Damon?' Schulter asked. 'Any more calls?'

Damon shook his head. 'Nothing new. No calls.'

'I advise you to keep your wife out of the way for a while.' It was not advice, but a ukase.

'She's out of town for the moment.'

'Try to keep her there. Well' – Schulter stood up, pushed the absurd hat down heavily on his head – 'I'll be moving off. Detective,' he said to Weinstein, a touch of malice in his voice, 'don't shoot yourself in the leg when you pull out your popgun.'

'I'll try not to,' Weinstein said affably. 'I haven't made any mistakes so far.'

Schulter looked down bleakly. 'I hope you get lucky. Finish your drinks and call me if anything turns up.'

Damon and Weinstein watched the broad bullying back go through the door out into the street. 'Friendly little fellow, isn't he?' Weinstein said. 'Not a devoted admirer of the New Haven police department. Now tell me about Mrs Larch.'

Damon told him, Weinstein listening in silence. As he spoke, Damon could see the growing disapproval on his friend's face.

When Damon finished, Weinstein said, 'You sure acted like a damn fool for a grown man. Letting your cock do the thinking for the family. You're lucky she only told her psychiatrist. If she hadn't, I wouldn't blame the husband if he came gunning for you.'

'Don't be a goddamn rabbi,' Damon said, irritated. 'You

195

never have sneaked off for an afternoon with a girl? If you say no, I won't believe you.'

'At least I was careful. I don't have any illegitimate kids with another man's name running around.'

'Bully for you,' Damon said. 'Pray for the salvation for my soul the next time you happen to visit a synagogue.'

'Calm down, pal,' Weinstein said. 'What's done is done. What we have to do now is figure out what to do about it.'

'All right,' Damon said, slightly mollified.

'You think this might be the last straw for the husband?' Weinstein asked. 'His wife in the nut house and you getting your picture in the papers and stories saying what a great man you are and how much dough you're making.'

'Who knows? I suppose I ought to call him.'

'What for?' Weinstein looked surprised.

'To tell him the truth, for example. Certain men – like me for example – have a habit of examining their consciences.'

'Conscience-shomscience,' Weinstein said impatiently. 'What is this – Yom Kippur, the Day of Atonement for the goyim? If the guy ever had any reason for shooting you before, he'd be ten times more likely to do it if you called him. He's got enough troubles as it is. Just to satisfy some crazy, egotistic notion of how you think an upright seducer ought to behave, you'd put another monkey on his back. Anyway, from your account the lady was over twenty-one and knew just what she was doing. And how do you know there weren't eleven other guys in there at the same time?'

'Of course,' Damon said, 'that's a possibility.'

'A lot more than a possibility. She may be gaga now but she wasn't gaga eleven years ago. You told Schulter I was your bodyguard. I see I have to be your brain guard, too.'

Damon was shaken by Weinstein's vehemence, but hurt because of the jeering references to his conscience. The boyhood friend had become an accuser, and for a moment he regretted that Weinstein had recognized him as he drove past the lawn where Weinstein had been spading the flower bed. 'You talk like a cop,' he said. 'If the crime isn't actually on the statute books, even if what's happening is right under your nose, you turn and look the other way.'

'You're damn right I talk like a cop,' Weinstein said. 'And a cop doesn't go around *inventing* trouble. If your conscience is bothering you, give a donation to some orphan home. Or go to confession and admit you were a sinner and mean to sin no more and drop a ten-dollar bill in the poor box.' There was no adolescent friendship in his voice. 'And one more thing. What about your wife? What do you think she'll do – say, welcome home, I'm delighted you finally have a family? Grow up, Roger, grow up. You're in deep enough as it is. Don't dig the hole any deeper.'

'You're talking too loud,' Damon said. 'People're looking over here to see what the roaring is about. Maybe there'll come a time when she has to know and I'll speak then.'

'I hope you never have that conversation. And if you do, just make sure that I'm not there for it.'

They marched swiftly downtown through the deepening twilight, neither of them speaking. By the time they reached Fourteenth Street, Damon's temper had subsided. He glanced sideways at Weinstein. Weinstein's face was set in stubborn lines.

'Hey, shortstop,' Damon said. 'Truce?'

For a moment Weinstein's expression didn't change. Then he grinned. 'Of course, old buddy,' he said. He reached out and patted Damon's arm.

Before going out to dinner, he helped Damon put the books down in the cellar and arrange the records. Damon hung Sheila's coat in her closet, and Weinstein commenced putting the phonograph arm together and stringing a wire for the radio's antenna. It didn't take long, and Damon made himself a drink and sipped at it placidly after putting the first record, the Beethoven triple concerto, on the phonograph.

In the middle of the record, the telephone rang. Damon stiffened. 'Go ahead,' Weinstein said. 'Answer it.'

Damon put down his drink, went over to the telephone, hesitated, his hand in the air over the instrument, then picked it up. 'Hello,' he said.

'This is Oliver. I just called to let you know that if I'd bet you about the Yeats, you'd have won.' He laughed. 'I've looked all over. It's not in the house. You're a wise old librarian, partner.

197

See you on Monday. Have a nice weekend. We're going out to the Hamptons in the morning and I want you to know the blazer's going to get its first workout.'

Weinstein had been watching Damon intently. When Damon hung up, he said, 'Well . . . ?'

'It was Oliver Gabrielsen. About a book.'

'Listen, Roger,' Weinstein said. 'I'll never answer the phone. If the guy calls, I don't want him to know that there's another man in the house.'

'Right you are.'

'And I won't pick up the other phone,' Weinstein said. 'I don't want him hearing a second click.'

'I wouldn't have thought about that.'

Weinstein nodded. 'You're in another line of business.'

'I'm learning fast.'

'Too bad,' Weinstein said. 'I hope you don't go too far – suspicious of everybody and everything at all times, like me. Where's your kitchen? Do you want me to fix us dinner? I've gotten to be a pretty good cook since my wife died.'

'There's nothing in the house,' Damon said. 'And I want to honor you as a welcome guest with a fine non-detective-cooked French dinner.'

'I'll come quietly, officer,' Weinstein said. 'Bring on the dancing girls.'

There were no dancing girls, but Weinstein ploughed happily through a bowl of onion soup and a steak *marchand de vin*. The waiter looked at him disdainfully as he served the table because Weinstein had ordered a black coffee immediately after they sat down and ordered another cup to wash down the steak, while Damon treated himself with a half-bottle of California red wine.

Weinstein ate hugely, consuming a half-dozen slices of bread with his meal and piling the french-fries into his mouth. But at the end of the meal, which he had topped off with a large slice of apple tart with ice cream and still another cup of coffee, he leaned back, saying, 'Ah, I could have really done this stuff justice when I was young and still had a real appetite and never enough money to eat in anything but diners. Well,' he said, 'if this is what the job is going to be like, I won't mind if that guy doesn't show up before I'm ninety. Ah, Roger . . . ' his voice lowered into sentimentality . . . 'we were such good friends . . . all these years . . .' He made a large sweeping gesture with his hands as though to encompass the lost decades. 'Why did we have to wait for something lousy to happen before we saw each other again?'

'Because the human race never gets its values straight,' Damon said somberly.

That night, although Weinstein's snores lived up to his wife's description of them and the house resounded with the regular crescendo and diminuendo of Weinstein's breathing, Damon slept without dreams. With no alarm clock to wake him because it was Saturday and not a working day, he slept till nearly ten o'clock, later than any time since he had been in the Merchant Marine and was on leave after a voyage on which six ships of his convoy had been sunk.

CHAPTER
SEVENTEEN

THE WEEKEND passed pleasantly. It turned out that Weinstein was a movie buff, with a special taste for films about criminals and murders, laughing hilariously at the most serious moments of the entertainments, when detectives shot it out with suspects or infallibly unraveled plots that were so complicated that no one in the audience, and certainly not Weinstein, could follow them. In between he regaled Damon with tales of his own life on the force. New Haven, Damon learned in the two days, was not only the home of Yale University. Damon enjoyed the two days and now did not regret having been driving past the Weinstein house just as his old friend had started to prepare his garden for the spring planting.

On Sunday night Weinstein insisted upon making their dinner himself, a Yankee pot roast with mashed potatoes, green peas, a thick gravy, and for dessert an apple pie. With an apron around his copious middle, his sleeves rolled up to reveal his powerful hairy forearms and the pistol butt jutting out of the shoulder holster strapped across his chest, he was an incongruous sight in the small kitchen, bustling among the pots and pans and deftly cleaning up after himself like the most experienced of chefs. Damon found himself laughing at the sight as he came into the kitchen, attracted by the odors floating through the apartment. Weinstein looked at him dourly. 'What's so funny?' he asked.

'You.' Then, placatingly, 'It all smells delicious.'

'Iron rations,' Weinstein said. 'You ought to taste my meals when I have really *appreciative* eaters at the table.'

After dinner they went to a bar below Washington Square. It was dimly but cozily lit and while the other drinkers along the long mahogany bar almost disappeared in the distance, there was enough light so that you could see the faces near you. At the far end of the bar, high up on a shelf, there was a television set. It was lit, but the sound was mercifully off.

The owner, Tony Senagliago, believed in serious drinking. While he was willing to indulge his patrons' taste for the networks' offerings to the extent of providing them with silent images which threw a constantly flickering rainbow of colors down the room, he understood that his best customers liked to drink in silence or in quiet conversation with their friends. It was not a bar in which people cruised for girls or men. Women, alone or in pairs or threes were, as courteously as possible, offered tables of their own. When they insisted upon standing or sitting at the bar, Tony would say, regretfully, 'Well there's no law against it,' and make sure that they were served with the utmost lethargy by his barmen. He had no fear of being called a male chauvinist pig and Damon liked and admired him for it. He was a thoughtful reader and in the good old times of the Village, a great many writers had run up tabs at his joint, as he called it. When a particularly good book came into the office Damon always gave Tony a copy and after the man had read it, listened with respect to his opinions.

'Nice place,' said Weinstein, looking around as they settled themselves on high stools next to each other at the bar.

'Many a pleasant afternoon and evening,' Damon said. 'What's your pleasure?' he asked, remembering the barman in the bar on Sixth Avenue where he had lost the answering machine and been knocked down while trying to stop a fight. This was a better bar, he thought, and a happier time.

For once Weinstein ordered a beer. As Damon sipped his Scotch and soda and Weinstein the beer, Weinstein said, 'I guess one beer won't kill me. Although the doctors swear that a single teaspoon of the stuff'll make an alcoholic start sliding down into the pit again.'

'You?' Damon asked, surprised. 'Were you ever a drinker?'

'Let's say, I was *on* the drink,' Weinstein said gravely. 'I ran into a tree with my wife in the car and I swore off. That was eight years ago. Did you know that my mother had gin bottles stashed all over the house?'

'No.'

'Well, she did.'

Damon shook his head wonderingly. That perfect motherly lady, with the blue apron trimmed with lace who had served them milk and cookies in the afternoon. The street he had lived on as a boy had not been as innocent as he remembered it.

After the disagreement on Friday evening they had spoken no more about Julia Larch and her son. Damon had the feeling that Weinstein was convinced that he had won *that* argument and Damon had given up the idea of getting in touch with Julia's husband. Weinstein was clearly a man who was not used to losing arguments.

'Drinking,' Weinstein was saying, 'is like bicycle riding – no matter how long you lay off, you never forget how to do it.' He had finished his first beer and was calling for another. 'If I order a third,' he told Damon, 'you have my permission to break my arm.'

'It makes you more human,' Damon said. 'Finally, a weakness.'

'If weakness is human,' Weinstein said somberly, 'I'm as fucking human as they come.' Then he switched the subject abruptly. 'I don't think we're fooling your Oliver Gabrielsen.'

'What do you mean by that?'

'When you went out of the room to talk to Miss Walton for a minute, he asked me why I didn't take off my jacket. It was warm in the office, he said, and I'd be more comfortable. And while he was talking to me, he kept looking at the bulge under my shoulder. And he asked me where I got my degree in literature.'

'What did you tell him?'

'I invented a place in Oklahoma. I got to remember the name, in case he asks me again. Butnam Christian University. That was the name of my boss on the force.'

Damon laughed. 'If I know Oliver, he'll look it up. What if he tells you it doesn't exist?'

'I'll tell him it went out of business during the war.'

'Wouldn't it be easier just to tell him the truth right away? He's wise to most of what's happening, anyway. My wife briefed him.'

Weinstein looked irritated. 'What is this with you and the truth? Some sort of obsession? Ever hear the phrase – "need to know"?'

'Yes. They used it on the Manhattan Project when they were making the atomic bomb. Just tell people what's necessary to do their job and no more.'

'It's a good rule,' Weinstein said. 'Everywhere. In government, police work, marriage. Do you think your wife needs to know about you and that crazy woman out in Indiana?'

'Not right now, no,' Damon said.

'What do you mean, not right now? Not ever. You tell me you've got a good marriage. What the hell sense would there be in breaking it up?'

'Let's drop it for a while, eh?' Damon said. 'But speaking of marriage, how is it you never got married again?'

'I'd like to say I'm a one-woman man,' Weinstein said. 'But I'd be lying. Marriage . . .' He shrugged, then took a long draught of his second beer. 'Who'd marry me? A fat old cop with a face like the beach at Iwo Jima, on a pension that just keeps me in meat and potatoes. What do you think I'd get? A maiden school teacher who's been turned down by every man she's ever met, a widow with dyed hair and tits down to her waist who's being advertising in the personal columns for a gentleman companion with similar tastes, a divorced lady with five kids who's used to cops because her husband was a traffic policeman? Naa . . .' He finished his beer with another mighty gulp. 'I got a lot of respect for two things. Myself and sex. I'd lose them both just by saying two fucking words – "I do."' He stared darkly at the empty glass on the bar in front of him. 'In the Jewish religion it says that when a wife dies the husband should marry the wife's sister. I was passing fond of my wife and I wouldn't mind doing that.'

'Well, why don't you?'

'My wife didn't have a sister.' He laughed hoarsely, like a stand-up comedian enjoying his own joke.

When the last rattle of laughter subsided, Damon asked, 'Are you a practicing Jew?' He had never seen any particular signs of piety around the Weinstein house.

'Well,' Weinstein said, immediately serious, 'I eat pork and the only time I've ever been in a synagogue is when I've gone in to make an arrest, but there's no doubt about my being a Jew, whether I like it or not. I've read the Bible, but . . .' He shook his head. 'Practicing, no, I don't think anybody could call me that. Religion . . .' He frowned, as though it was difficult to put his feelings into words. 'It's like a huge round cloud with a mystery hidden inside it.' He held his hands apart, as though he were grasping a great invisible globe. 'As big as the planet, maybe as the solar system, maybe it's so big across it can only be measured in light-years. And every religion is creeping along on the outside of the cloud, one religion getting one quick look at part of what's inside, another one getting a look at another part in the flick of an eyelash and so on and so on, nobody getting to see what's at the heart of it. Or, like my fucking brother-in-law, the atheist, used to say, maybe the whole thing's just an invention to console the human race because everybody knows we're going to die and religion feeds you the Big Lie. What's the Big Lie, you ask. Immortality.' He made a grimace as though the beer he had drunk had just turned sour in his stomach. 'He was so damned sure of himself you wanted to kick him in the ass. One thing I can't stand is people being sure of something they can't prove with numbers or arithmetic or at least expert witnesses. Let's say that as far as I'm concerned the jury's still out.' He played absently with the empty glass on the bar. 'Consolation. It's not a bad word. But what I know for sure about myself is that I've turned into a sorry old man. Nothing consoles me. I'm not consoled about the fact that I'm going to die. Or that *you're* going to die. One thing I know I'll never be consoled about is my wife's dying. And if it really turns out that I've got an immortal soul, that'll be the worst punishment of all. I sure as hell don't want to have to stand up when the trumpet blows for the Last Judgment. As for forgiveness – like I was saying the other day – we can all use some of that – but I still haven't even forgiven myself for trying to make that damn fool throw from deep short, and that was almost fifty years ago. Ah . . .' He made an impatient gesture. 'Beery night-time talk.' He called to the bartender for another drink. 'Roger,' he said, 'I postpone permission to break my arm until after the next one.' He tried to smile. 'Maybe you ought to ask Schulter when you see him what consoles *him*. I'm sorry,' he said, 'talking so much. About things I know fuck-all about. I've been living alone so long that when I go out in company I run off at the mouth.'

'I'm married and I don't live alone,' Damon said, 'but I run off at the mouth pretty often myself. You ought to hear me when I get on the subject of Ronald Reagan or the Broadway theatre.' He had spoken lightly, in an attempt to lighten Weinstein's gloom, but he could see he had failed.

'The world . . .' Weinstein said morosely. He shook his head and didn't continue, as though for this evening at least, the enormity of the world's evil was beyond his powers of description. He turned away for a moment to stare at the action on the television screen. It was a commercial for a beer company. There were brilliantly photographed shots of husky men, some white, some black, working on an oil rig, sweating healthily in bright sunlight as they carried pipe, fitted joints, wrestled with giant valves. Then as the sun was setting in a golden glow, the men stopped work, dropped their tools, slung their denim jackets and windbreakers over their shoulders and strode off happily toward a bar where amid silent laughter and back-slapping, they were served foaming glasses of beer, which they were never seen drinking because of network rules.

'What horseshit,' Weinstein said, growling. 'The merry, interracial American working man. Who do they think they're kidding?' He finished his beer with one last powerful gulp. 'Let's get out of here.'

It was almost midnight by the time they got back to the apartment and Weinstein was yawning. Before he went into the little room where he slept, he said, 'I'm sorry about my blowing off back there. I'll be better company in the morning. Sleep well, kid.'

By the time Damon got into his own bed and put out the

light, Weinstein's snores were rumbling through the apartment.

The ringing of the telephone awoke him. He had been deep in sleep and he seemed to be swimming up through dark waters to reach the surface. He rolled over and picked up the telephone. He was conscious that the snoring from the other room had stopped. The illuminated dial of the bedside clock pointed to twenty past three.

'Damon?' He recognized the voice. 'Zalovsky. I've got to see you. You got ten minutes. I'm right near you . . .'

'Wait a minute,' Damon said. 'I'm still asleep.'

He saw the door to the bedroom open and there was Weinstein, in pyjamas, outlined against the light streaming in from the hallway.

'Listen good,' Zalovsky said. 'I'll be waiting for you in ten minutes, like I said. In the Washington Mews. You know where that is, I hope.'

'I know where it is.'

'It's a nice dark quiet place for a little serious conversation. If you know what's good for you you won't try any funny stuff. Consider yourself warned.'

'I'm warned.'

Zalovsky hung up.

'It's him,' Damon said, as he put the phone back in its cradle.

'I gathered,' Weinstein said.

'He's in Washington Mews. We passed it tonight on the way home from the bar. The entrance is off Fifth Avenue just before you get to the Square. There're pedestrian gates on the other end.'

'I'll trail you,' Weinstein said. 'Maybe seventy, eighty yards behind you.'

'Give me a little time to talk to him, find out what it is that he really wants,' Damon said as he began to dress.

'Don't worry. I'll be there when you need me. How do you feel, kid? Nervy?'

'Not particularly. Curious, mostly.'

'Good boy.' Weinstein went back to his room to dress.

They didn't leave the house together. Weinstein waited in the downstairs hall for almost a minute after Damon went out, then slipped out and started to follow Damon just as Damon turned the corner onto Fifth Avenue.

There was very little traffic on the avenue. Occasionally a car sped by and Damon overtook the only people in sight, two drunks with their arms around each other's shoulders, singing hoarsely as they wove their way unsteadily downtown. They were singing 'As the Caissons Go Rolling Along,' and Damon guessed that they had been together in the army.

Damon walked swiftly, feeling clear-headed and remarkably calm. He didn't look back to see if Weinstein was following him. When he got to the entrance to Washington Mews he stopped. The little street which was really more of an alley than a street was dark, except for a pale glow coming from a single lit window near the entrance to the Mews. There was no movement that he could see anywhere on the street, which was only about a hundred yards long. He walked down the center of it toward the gates at the other end.

The sound of the two drunks singing came closer as they neared the entrance to the Mews, and Damon was fearful that by some mischievous chance one or both of them lived in one of the pretty houses that lined the cobbled street. He was about twenty yards from the last house when a shadow that was only a slightly deeper shadow in the darkness detached itself from a shallow doorway. 'All right,' the remembered voice said, 'you can stop there.'

Damon could not see the man's face and could only guess at his size and shape.

'Now, finally,' Damon said coolly, 'what the hell is all this about?'

'I told you no funny business, didn't I?' The shadow moved closer to him.

'I'm here, aren't I? Alone.' Damon suppressed the almost irresistible urge to turn for a moment to see if Weinstein was visible.

'Those your friends?'

'Those who?'

'Those two guys singing.'

'I don't know who they are. Two drunks. I passed them on the way here.'

'You think you're pretty smart, don't you? Drunks. Where'd you learn *that* trick?'

The noise of the singing was louder now, echoing between the buildings. Damon turned. The two men had stopped at the entrance to the Mews, two dark shapes outlined against the faint lights of the street lamps of Fifth Avenue. The drunks seemed to be serenading the inhabitants of the Mews. Then a shadow moved from the wall of one of the buildings near the entrance and was caught in the glow from the one lit window on the street. It was Weinstein.

'Fuck it,' Zalovsky said. He pushed Damon violently and Damon half-fell against a doorway. There was an enormous noise as Zalovsky fired and Damon saw Weinstein go down. Damon threw himself at Zalovsky and spun him to one side. Another shot boomed. There was a cry of pain and Damon saw one of the singers crumple to the pavement. At the same moment light blazed in the front windows of the house across from where he and Zalovsky were struggling. Zalovsky was terribly strong and tore his arm away from Damon's grasp. The light was behind him and Damon couldn't see what the man looked like. Zalovsky was panting heavily. 'You fucker,' he said, 'you're not getting away with this.'

Damon started to run toward the entrance to the Mews. He had only gone about five feet when there was another shot. But this time it was in front of him. Weinstein, kneeling on the cobblestones, had fired. He heard a grunt from Zalovsky, then the noise of metal hitting the cobblestones. He stopped and turned. Zalovsky was running away from him toward the gates at the rear of the Mews. He ran holding his right arm, clumsy but swift. In two seconds he was through the gate and had disappeared.

Damon ran toward where Weinstein, no longer kneeling, lay stretched out on his back, with his blood dark on the cobblestones.

From far off there was the wail of the first police siren.

CHAPTER
EIGHTEEN

'YOU CAN go in now,' the doctor said. 'Mr Weinstein is conscious and he's asking for you. But only just a couple of minutes, please.'

Damon was sitting with Lieutenant Schulter in the little waiting room on the same floor as the Intensive Care Unit of the hospital to which Weinstein and the drunken singer who had been hit by Zalovsky's second bullet had been brought. The singer wasn't asking to see anyone. He had been pronounced dead on arrival.

It had been a long day. The shootings had taken place a little after three-thirty in the morning, and it was now seven P.M. First some other detectives had questioned Damon while Weinstein had been on the operating table and then Schulter had come down and taken over. Mercifully, the police had kept all newspapermen out of the hospital, but Damon could imagine what the front pages had been like. He hadn't been able to call Sheila until one o'clock, but she was on her way down from Vermont and was due to arrive any minute now.

Schulter had been surprisingly gentle and had insisted upon sending for some sandwiches and coffee for Damon as he asked him over and over again to describe every movement everybody involved in the shooting had made. There was a trail of blood, Schulter told Damon, from the spot where the gun that Zalovsky had used had been found to the gates and onto the curb on Waverly Place. A witness had seen a man throw himself into a car that had been parked there and drive off. Unfortunately, the witness had not noted the license number of the car. Even more unfortunately, Damon could give no description of the assailant, except that he seemed of medium height, was heavy set, very strong, and had staggered and nearly fallen when he had been shot, but had managed to recover and stumble off. The bullet must have gone into his right side or his right arm because he had been holding his gun in his right hand and had dropped it immediately after he had been hit.

'He won't get too very far with a big hole in him,' Schulter said. 'And sometime soon – very soon – he'll have to get hold of a doctor to patch him up, and we'll be right on his ass ten minutes after he leaves the doctor's office or the hospital.'

'I wish you the best of luck,' Damon said. 'And me, too.' He did not feel as confident as Schulter.

Weinstein had been hit in the knee, which had been shattered. He had quickly lost a great deal of blood, and Schulter marveled that even so, he had been able to get a shot off and hit his man in the wavering pale light. Schulter casually dismissed the death of the man who had been singing 'As the Caissons Go Rolling Along' at the Fifth Avenue entrance to Washington Mews. It was the sort of thing that happened every day in New York, Schulter said. 'The law of averages,' was the phrase he used. It was obvious that Schulter considered onlookers as a normally endangered species.

Damon didn't say so, but felt that the actuarial scales by which Schulter judged the chances of anybody's survival varied greatly from his own. In his case the law of averages for the past two weeks had been monstrously broken. It was true that the early-morning singer was the first person with whom he had had anything to do as he made his way to the rendezvous with Zalovsky, if passing a drunk on Fifth Avenue in the middle of the night could be described in those terms, but Schulter's statistics did not include those other victims on Damon's list, such as Maurice Fitzgerald, Melanie Deal, Elsie Weinstein, Julia Larch, and Sheila's mother, as well as Manfred Weinstein himself. Damon knew that he was being neurotic and morbid, but he couldn't help but feel that if you were in any way connected to Roger Damon, you could be a victim without actually being killed on the spot or in the past two weeks.

The man who had been shot had been identified. His name was Bryant and he had come to New York from Tulsa, Oklahoma, for a conference of insurance executives. Damon remembered Maurice Fitzgerald's speech about acceptable losses and wondered if Schulter would include the luckless Mr Bryant among them.

Weinstein lay pale and still on the hospital bed, drainage and transfusion tubes attached to him by intravenous needles. His cheeks were shrunken, and his inert figure under the sheet seemed also to have been diminished, but his eyes, now deep in their sockets, were alert. He was the only patient in the room.

'How goes it?' Damon asked him, keeping his voice low.

'I'm breathing,' Weinstein said faintly.

'The doctor tells me you're going to be all right.'

'I bet he tells that to all the girls.' Weinstein tried a small smile.

'Anyway, you're going to be able to walk in a couple of months,' Damon said.

'Where to?' Weinstein said. 'Now, how about you?'

'Fine,' Damon said. 'Untouched.'

'The luck of the Irish.' Weinstein put his hand to take Damon's. The pressure was feeble. 'I was worried about you. The sonofabitch got away, didn't he?'

'Yes. Not far, Schulter thinks. You hit him. He can't do much running.'

'I should've dropped him with the one shot. That goddamn third beer,' Weinstein said bitterly. 'And then you started running toward me, and you covered him and I never could get off a second one. Then I suppose I passed out. Some body-guard. Amateur night in Dixie.'

'Anyway,' Damon said, 'you saved my life. If that's any comfort to you.'

'Comfort.' Something that may have been a laugh issued from the pale lips. 'I heard one of those guys who were singing behind me yell. Was he hit, too?'

'He's dead . . .'

'Oh, Christ.' Weinstein groaned. 'Did you at least learn anything? Who the bastard is? What he wants?'

'Nothing,' Damon said. 'He was suspicious, he thought those two men who were singing were backing me up, and then he saw you . . .'

'It's always the things there's no way of figuring on . . .' Weinstein said, his voice croaking. 'Two guys coming home from a party just in the wrong place at the wrong time. Luck.' He withdrew his hand from Damon's. 'I'm sorry, I can't talk anymore. They got me full of stuff, I think they want me to drift for two weeks. Just take care of yourself. And don't worry about me. I'll be . . .' He closed his eyes and relapsed into drugged sleep.

Damon was relieved to get out of the Intensive Care Unit, with its hushed air of tension, its watchful nurses monitoring the screens on which electrical impulses made erratic bright lines which described the lives and deaths of the grotesquely bandaged bodies plastically linked to sighing machines which he glimpsed through the open doors of the other rooms. Mortality, he thought as he passed the rescued debris of humanity in the unit, is the trade here.

Sheila was waiting for him, with Oliver, now paler than ever. She had called Oliver from Vermont and he had gone to the airport to meet her. Her bag was on the floor at her feet and anxiety had bitten deep into her face. She put her arms around Damon when he came into the room and held on to him silently.

There was nothing more they could do for Weinstein that night, and Damon was stumbling from fatigue; so with a last word to the doctor that if there were any crises during the night to call them at Oliver's apartment where Oliver had persuaded Sheila they should stay, they followed Schulter through the maze of corridors to a small back door to avoid the reporters at the front entrance. Now that Schulter had the evidence of one murdered man and two badly wounded, his air of boredom with Damon's problem had been replaced by an almost paternal solicitousness, and there was no talk of cranks making ten thousand obscene telephone calls a night in New York. He insisted upon getting into the taxi with them for the drive uptown to Oliver's apartment and helped Damon get out as though Damon was an invalid. 'Don't worry,' he said as they parted at the front door of the building, 'that individual won't be in any condition to bother you anymore. If you need me for anything or there's something you think I ought to know, you have my number. There'll be some depositions to sign in the next few days, but that's all. Nobody's going to make a federal case out of it.' Then to Sheila, 'Mrs Damon,' he said, 'take good care of your husband. He's a pretty brave man and he's had a rough day.' He tipped his ridiculous hat, got back into the taxi and drove off.

Doris Gabrielsen was a small, plump, fair-haired woman with a lilting little inflection of speech that made all her sentences go up at the end. It was an affectation that at other times had annoyed Damon, but now her obvious concern about what had happened to him and the warmth of her welcome made Damon feel grateful. There were flowers arranged for them in the guest bedroom and all newspapers were tactfully hidden from view. She had laid out a spread of cold cuts and cheese and potato salad on a buffet and gave Damon a Scotch, with not much soda, before they sat down to eat. She served drinks to the others and took one herself, and before drinking she raised her glass and said, 'To better days. And to Mr Weinstein's health.'

'Amen,' Oliver said.

The whiskey burned as it went down Damon's throat but in a minute or two the effect hit him, a pleasant feeling of remoteness, dreaminess, a feeling that was comforting and relaxing, a sense that he was no longer responsible for himself, that he was in other, safe hands and that he was freed from the necessity of making decisions for himself.

He was not hungry, but he ate dutifully, like an obedient child, and drank the cold beer that Doris poured for him thirstily.

After the meal, Damon said, 'I hope you'll excuse me. I'm completely bushed. I have to lie down for a while.'

'Of course,' Doris said.

Sheila followed him into the guest room and knelt to take off his shoes as he sat on the edge of the bed. She had hardly spoken since she had embraced him in the hospital, as though afraid that a few words would unleash a dark torrent of emotion that until now she had locked inside her.

'Rest, dear,' she said after throwing a blanket over him. 'And don't think about anything. You've got loving friends. I'll go downtown with Oliver and pack a bag with the things you'll need.'

He reached out and took her hand and brought it to his mouth and kissed it. Her whole body seemed to shudder, as though she was torn by one bone-shaking sob, but there were no tears. She leaned over and kissed his forehead. 'Sleep well,' she said, and put out the lamp and left the room.

Damon closed his eyes and almost instantly fell into an exhausted, dreamless sleep.

When he awoke he did not know for a moment where he was, but he saw Sheila sitting beside the bed, staring down at him, lit by a thin stream of light that came in through the door, which was slightly ajar. There was no sound in the apartment. He felt sick. There was a burning sensation high up in the middle of his chest, and he knew he was about to throw up. He pushed himself up from the bed with difficulty. 'Excuse me,' he said thickly, his tongue still heavy with sleep, 'I'm going to be sick.'

Sheila helped him out of bed and started with him toward the guest bathroom, whose door was open and which was softly lit. He waved Sheila back and stumbled into the bathroom, closing the door behind him. He threw up his entire dinner, along with most of the sandwiches and coffee he had had throughout the day. He rinsed his mouth, brushed his teeth with the toothbrush and paste Sheila had arranged for him on the shelf above the basin, then washed his face with ice cold water. Feeling better, he went back into the bedroom.

'I guess potato salad doesn't agree with me,' he said to Sheila. She laughed dryly. 'How about murders?' she said.

Despite himself, he almost laughed, too. 'What time is it?' he asked.

'Two-thirty A.M.'

'Time to take off these clothes. For you, too.' As he took off his clothes, the smell of stale sweat, fear, the lingering medicinal odor of the hospital assailed his nostrils. He threw everything he had been wearing into a pile under the open window and got into bed naked. He noticed that the twin beds in the guest room had considerably been pulled together by Doris, who had visited the Damons often and had noticed that they slept together. Suddenly, unbelievably, he felt a great desire to make love, and when Sheila came out of the bathroom in a nightgown, he said, 'Take that thing off. And come close.'

They didn't need the second bed until late the next morning when they both awoke.

He did not leave the Gabrielsen apartment for a week. He felt he could not face a reporter, a stranger, answer a telephone call, read a contract, decide for himself what he wanted to eat in a restaurant. Sheila, who had to go back to work, also managed to visit Weinstein in the hospital every day and came back each evening with reassuring news of his recovery. Oliver took care of the office, but aside from telling Damon that everybody he had ever known kept calling the office daily to find out how he was and wishing him well, he said nothing about whatever business he was conducting. He also lied loyally when asked where Damon was staying and told one and all that he didn't know. 'It's surprising,' he said, 'how easy it is to drop out of sight in New York.' In Damon's eyes he seemed to have aged visibly in the past few days, and Damon thought he could detect some gray in Oliver's pale blond hair.

Nobody brought a newspaper into the apartment and Damon was grateful for that. He hoped his mood would eventually change but for the time being he had no interest in discovering how the world was faring, what the President had said in his most recent speech, in which country a new revolution had broken out, what new crime the CIA had been accused of, whose play had opened on or off Broadway, how the interest rate was climbing, or who had died the morning before.

Luckily, the baseball season had opened, and he watched the games by the hour, in a kind of bleacher trance, not rooting for any particular teams, satisfied to see such abundant evidence of quick, youthful skill and American vitality on the small screen. When the news came on, he turned the set off.

The others pretended they, too, had no interest in what was going on in the world and never turned the television set on casually. He accepted their solicitude numbly, like a sick child. When he was not looking at the ball games, he would sit for hours holding a book open in front of him and never turning a page. Doris, who at the beginning had tried to be bright and cheerful and talkative, soon accepted the fact that all Damon wanted was to be left alone and crept silently and unobtrusively around her own house. During the day, when the others were out, she served his meals to him on a tray so that he could eat alone. Quickly she learned that it was useless to ask what he wanted for lunch or dinner and made up the menus herself, putting a single rose in a small vase and a half-bottle of wine on the tray for him, along with the food. For the first two or three days he sipped at the wine, but the burning sensation in his stomach that accompanied the wine made him leave the bottle alone.

He said nothing about what he now considered a psychic ailment to Doris or Sheila, and although Oliver had stocked the small bar in the living room with Damon's favorite whiskey, never touched the ranged bottles. Sheila made no comment on his sudden abstinence.

If he dreamed at night or during the long naps he took each afternoon, he did not remember them when he awoke. He slept each night in the small bed with Sheila in his arms, like an animal seeking warmth in the body of its sibling in the depth of winter. After the first week, Sheila told him that it looked as though Weinstein would be able to leave the hospital, on crutches of course and in plaster, in about two months. She had become very fond of Weinstein, she said, in the long conversations she had with him daily, and couldn't bear the thought of his going home to live alone, with no one to take care of him in the big empty house. She had told him that when he was ready to leave the hospital she would drive him, with Damon, to the house in Old Lyme, where he could convalesce, and Damon wouldn't have to face the questions and sympathies of his friends and the demands of the office. At first, she told Damon, Weinstein had said he wouldn't hear of it; he'd been taking care of himself for years and he didn't want to be a burden on them just because he had flubbed the job of protecting Damon so badly. But Sheila had told him that the job was not yet over – Weinstein could bring along his gun, just in case Zalovsky had friends who might be anxious to avenge him, or even if Zalovsky himself might appear, despite Schulter's confidence that alive or dead Zalovsky would be in no condition to do any more damage.

Sheila did not ask Damon if he approved or disapproved of her plan, and Damon asked no questions and made no suggestions. Neither did he ask how Sheila's mother was. He was encased in a cocoon of invalid's selfishness, and although he knew eventually he would have to take up the reins of his life once more, the time was not yet.

Sensitively, Sheila did not try to rouse him from his hermetic lethargy or attempt to cheer him up. His nerves, he realized, and he supposed she did, too, were scraped ragged; and he could not escape his ghosts, in the silent days and dark nights, or his multiple dead and wounded. Although he tried to seem as serene and agreeable as possible, he alone knew the effort it cost him and how one wrong word would make him erupt in either tears or rage. He did not tell Sheila that he was haunted by a feeling that nothing had been concluded, by a foreboding of evil, a sense that everything that had happened up to then was an overture, a hint, enigmatic and sardonic, of catastrophe, doom, in the future.

Nor did he tell Sheila that more and more frequently now he found himself vomiting after the meager meals he managed to get down. He was sure that Doris, who kept out of his way religiously, did not suspect that her boarder was suffering from more than the effects of the shock he had experienced.

One thing at a time, Damon thought dully. When I get up the energy to leave this apartment, I'll go secretly to a doctor, tell him that my blood and bones are collapsing, that I am finally in need of the certitudes of science.

It happened sooner than he expected and there was no chance of silence.

On the morning of the eighth day after the shooting, he woke early, in the grip of a crippling pain in his stomach. Laboriously, trying not to wake Sheila, he crawled out of bed and, bent double, his knuckles touching the floor to keep himself from falling, he started toward the bathroom. Involuntarily, a groan escaped him. He wavered into the bathroom, but did not have the strength or the will to close the door behind him. He did not look up when he felt Sheila's hand on his forehead, supporting him and heard her say, 'It's all right, dear, I'm here.'

Soon after, Oliver was in the bathroom. Damon was ashamed of his own nakedness and couldn't look up to see if Sheila had a robe on or not. Oliver's voice was far away as though echoing in a bare corridor, as he asked, 'What's the number of your doctor?'

Sheila's voice, too, was almost unrecognizable as she said, 'He doesn't have one.' Damon recognized a twenty-year-old complaint in the tone of her voice. 'And my doctor is a gynecologist.'

This somehow struck Damon as comic, and bent over as he was above the toilet, he heard himself laugh.

'I'll call ours,' Oliver said. 'I hope he's not out of town.'

'No need.' Damon suddenly felt the pain drain away, his throat no longer in the grip of spasms. 'I'm all right.' He straightened up, with dignity put on his robe, which was hanging on the bathroom door. 'My stomach's a little upset. That's all.' He looked once at Sheila, was grateful that she had had time to put on a robe, then looked away because the set of her eyes and mouth frightened him. 'I'll just lie down and take a little nap.'

'Don't be so goddamn spartan,' Sheila said severely as she took his arm and led him back to the bed. Once in bed he felt his muscles relax, his stomach stop churning, the spike of pain disappear. He smiled encouragingly at Oliver and Sheila standing over him. 'I'm fine,' he said. 'The truth is I'm awfully hungry. Do you think I could have some orange juice and toast and coffee?'

The doctor was a tall, handsome old man by the name of Brecher, with gray hair and a brisk, no-nonsense manner that inspired confidence. He did not seem to think that the case was too serious. 'Just a little rest,' he said, 'and a bland diet for a few days, some Maalox before meals, and no worrying' – now he looked severe, as though worrying was one of the worst diseases he had encountered in many years of practicing in the city of New York – 'and you should be as good as new.'

Damon was glad that Oliver had had the good sense to patronize a sensible old-fashioned general practitioner instead of one of the new-fangled technicians who rushed their patients immediately into the hospital and subjected them to the complete gamut of medical torture, including the visits of specialists, each of whom discovered that the poor sufferer was the victim of just the disease which they had been expert at diagnosing since they emerged from medical school. Damon thanked the doctor profusely and assured him that at the moment he was feeling better than he had in months, as Sheila's face grew grimmer and grimmer, the disbelief in her eyes as plain as a flag snapping in the wind. Relieved by the doctor's assurance of the insignificance of his illness and the modesty of the treatment he had prescribed, the cloud that had been hovering over Damon's soul dissipated like a morning mist in sunshine, and he even felt that it was time to end what he now ashamedly thought he recognized as a hypochondriacal weakness and was impatient to be up and around and see to it that his business was not going to rack and ruin under Oliver's uncertain if devoted direction.

When the doctor had left, Sheila, who had gone to the door with him, returned, her face grimmer than ever. 'You act like a child,' she said to Damon, 'a macho little boy in a playground who gets punched in the nose and bleeds all over the place and says it doesn't hurt. What do you know about yourself – you never even look in the mirror except when you shave. You may be able to snow a doctor; you can't snow your wife. It hurts and the sooner you admit it the better. You're sick and all the acting in the world doesn't convince me. We'll talk about this when I get back from work this evening.'

Her deep dark eyes thunderous, she slammed the door as she went out.

Admirable woman, he thought as he lay back against the

pillows. Right or wrong, she doesn't hesitate to speak her mind.

But they didn't talk about his symptoms that afternoon when Sheila returned from work. Sheila came in with her eyes red and swollen, as though she had been crying for hours. Gregor Khodar had called the school after trying to call their apartment and getting no answer. Ebba Khodar had been killed that morning by a bomb hidden in a parked automobile while walking past a bank on a street in Rome. There wasn't anything identifiable, Gregor had told Sheila, that was worth burying.

That night, in bed, holding Sheila, mercifully unconscious after a dose of sleeping pills, Damon remembered Lieutenant Schulter's law of averages. The lieutenant had neglected to include the city of Rome in his statistics.

With Sheila sleeping in his arms in the darkened room, Damon finally permitted himself to weep. What warnings, Damon wondered in his anguish, anguish for his friend and for himself, had that sweet and simple woman ignored?

CHAPTER
NINETEEN

HE WAS trying to write a letter to Gregor and had already crumpled three sheets of paper and thrown them into the wastebasket and was on the fourth attempt. His brain was numb, all passages blocked, all perceptions fogged over. It was hopeless, he thought, staring down at the sheet of notepaper, to try to put into words what he felt about what had happened in Rome, and he was about to crumple the page when there was a timid knock on the guest room door.

'Come in,' he said.

'I hate to disturb you, Roger,' Doris said, 'but Dr Brecher's on the phone and he'd like to talk to you.'

'Thank you,' Damon said, and followed her out to the hallway, where the phone was on a table. As she went out of the hallway so that he could speak to the doctor without being overheard, he noticed that Doris was fully dressed, in a skirt and sweater, her hair neatly done and makeup in place, although it was only ten o'clock in the morning. Since he and Sheila had been in the Gabrielsens' apartment he had never seen her in a robe or with her hair ruffled and he realized that this early morning neatness was for his benefit, so that he wouldn't feel that he was interfering with what might have been a comfortable housewifely disorder. He would have to make it up to her for her tact, he thought. But some other time.

He picked up the phone. 'Dr Brecher,' he said.

'Mr Damon,' the doctor said, 'I've been thinking about you all night. I have the feeling that you didn't describe *all* the symptoms of whatever might be ailing you. For example, when you've vomited, has any of it been black?'

Damon hesitated for a moment. It was true, once or twice he had noticed specks of black, but he had been drinking coffee and attributed the color to that. 'Not really,' he said. After what had happened to Ebba Khodar, worrying about a dubious malfunctioning of his own body seemed like a callous frivolity.

'Please, Mr Damon,' the doctor said, 'this might be very important. I don't want to sound like a fussy old maid, but often a man like you, who has been in splendid health all his life, has a tendency to pooh-pooh the evidence, to dismiss what he thinks is just a moment of temporary discomfort.'

'Well, Doctor,' Damon said, 'now that you mention it, I have seen the kind of thing you mention. Yes, briefly, a few times, not too much. Actually, right now, I don't feel anything at all.' He was certain that Dr Brecher, no matter whatever his gifts might be, could not guess how accurate the phrase was.

'For everybody's sake,' Dr Brecher said, 'and most particularly for yours, you need a much more thorough examination than I can manage. I am going to make an appointment for you with a Dr Zinfandel, at the Boylston General Hospital. He is one of the most brilliant diagnosticians in the city and I won't feel safe until he's seen you.'

'It seems like such a fuss about . . .' Damon stopped. A sudden pain, a hot throbbing in his stomach, made talking difficult, then passed. 'Yes, Doctor,' he said, 'thank you for your trouble. I'll see him.'

'My secretary will call you and tell you when you're to see Zinfandel. If he finds out it's nothing, it will put my mind and yours and your wife's at rest. It will be worth your time.'

'Thank you, Doctor,' Damon said, and hung up. He went back into the guest room and sat at the small desk where he had been trying to write the letter to Gregor. He stared at the few words he had managed to get down on paper and was struck by how strange his handwriting seemed, shaky and almost illegible. With his elbows on the desk he cupped his head in his hands and shut his eyes.

The next morning he was in the Boylston General Hospital in the heart of Manhattan. The hospital spread over so much of the city and was so large that it looked as though, if every bed were filled within its towering stone walls, there should be nobody up and around and unafflicted by one disease or another in the streets of the city.

He was in Dr Zinfandel's office, feeling a little foolish because he had had no further attacks of anything for more than twenty-four hours. He had almost decided to cancel his appointment, but when he told that to Sheila, the grim look on her face had made him realize that he would have no peace with her as long as he insisted there was no reason to submit to examination. Oliver, too, had gotten into the act and had called his brother, who was a surgeon in the Cedars-Sinai Hospital in Los Angeles and had Dr Brecher's high estimate of Zinfandel confirmed.

Dr Zinfandel was a small, blondish, sharp-nosed, intense man, an implacable and tireless tracker among the jungles of hidden maladies. His questioning was thorough. At what intervals did the pain occur? Blood by oral passage? Bowel movements? Measles at what age? What did your mother die of? Your father? Have you ever had hepatitis? Are you allergic to penicillin? How many times during the night do you have to get out of bed to urinate? Have you ever had syphilis? Gonorrhea? Do you pant when you climb stairs? Have you lost or gained weight recently? How many times a week do you engage in sexual intercourse? A month? What operations have you had? Do you have a yearly medical checkup? When was the last time before this . . . ah . . . episode that you visited a doctor? Ah, twenty-five years or so ago? Eyebrows lifted in surprise, disapproval. The pen in Dr Zinfandel's hand scribbled swiftly on the chart he was filling out. Do you have Medicare or Medicaid? When did you first become aware of the pain? Describe it, please. What are your eating habits? Do you have a penchant for spicy foods – pickles, chili, pastrami? How would you describe your drinking habits?

'Moderate.'

Dr Zinfandel smiled wearily, showing that he had heard this description many times in his professional career, from sots, men who took a bracer of a full tumbler of gin upon rising in the morning, from patients who had been hospitalized for delirium tremens and others who had been discharged from responsible positions because of five-martini lunches followed by three snifters of brandy.

'What do you consider moderate, Mr Damon?'

'A couple of Scotches before dinner, a half-bottle of wine with dinner, an occasional party.'

The smile grew crooked, the hand scribbled faster. Later, Damon discovered that Dr Zinfandel, despite his name, which described the variety of grape from which a glorious wine was made, was a fanatic teetotaler, with all the loathing of alcohol of an only son who had seen his mother and father lying in the gutter sodden with drink.

'Let us go on. Have you been under any exceptional stress recently?'

Damon hesitated. He wondered if a great diagnostician of internal disorders would describe an attempt at murder, the bombing of one of his best friend's wife, which after all were external disorders, as worthy of mention as exceptional stress. 'Yes,' he said, hoping the good doctor would leave it at that.

'Physical? Mental?' The good doctor, Damon could see, was not in the habit of leaving anything at that.

'I suppose you could call it both,' Damon said. 'If you don't mind, I'd rather not talk about it.' He did not want to relive the moments when the shots boomed in the dark narrow street, when Weinstein fell and the drunk called in agony as he collapsed to the pavement. 'It was all in the papers.'

'I'm afraid I'm too busy to read the papers carefully.' Dr Zinfandel pursed his lips, pleased with his business.

'Let's say great stress,' Damon said.

Dr Zinfandel looked back over what he had written, scanning the chart swiftly. He seemed to have come to the end of his list of inquiries. There were still questions he might have asked, Damon thought. Such as, What is the state of your soul, Sir? Have you sinned? Was there at the time of your brother's death, mixed with your infantile grief, a sense of joy that now you were the only son and would receive the undivided love and attention of your mother and father? Do you believe in dreams, fate, the supernatural? Do you consider yourself a lucky or an unlucky man? At what age would you consider it fitting to die? Do you cheat on your income tax? Are you worried about money? Where would you prefer to be when a nuclear war is begun? You say you never have been wounded. Do you really believe that? Is there, in your opinion, a God? If you believe that, do you think that Ebba Khodar's death on a Roman street was part of God's plan for humanity? Do you believe that coming events cast their shadow before? Do you agree with the poet when he says, 'Not in utter nakedness, but trailing clouds of glory do we come'?

Damon watched the doctor closely as Zinfandel frowned, his nose twitching, while his eyes, like a radar scanner, ran over what he had written. He seemed displeased with what Damon's answers indicated to his trained professional mind.

'Actually,' Damon said, 'right now I feel perfectly healthy.'

The doctor nodded impatiently. He had heard that story before. 'I'm afraid,' he said, 'that it is not as trivial as you think. The only way we can be sure of anything is by putting you through a complete examination – X-rays, CAT scan, a cardio-gram, blood tests, gallbladder, liver, lungs, kidneys, urine and feces samples, etcetera, several days of close surveillance. I would like to show the X-rays and the results of the tests to a surgeon.'

'A surgeon?' Damon felt a sudden dryness in his mouth. 'What would I need a surgeon for?'

'It's always better to be on the safe side,' Zinfandel said smoothly. 'Cover all avenues, as it were. With all our machines, diagnostic techniques, sometimes the only way we can be sure is by going in.'

At least, Damon thought, he didn't say an ounce of preven-tion is worth a pound of cure.

'I don't want to alarm you,' Zinfandel said soothingly. 'The surgeon would only be held in reserve, as it were.'

If he says as it were once more, Damon thought, I'm getting up and leaving this office.

'Do you have a surgeon who is a specialist in internal medicine whom you have faith in?' Zinfandel asked, his pencil poised to put down a name.

'No.' Damon felt a little ashamed to have to admit that upwardly mobile as he had proved to be in his career he had neglected an important cultural accessory like a personal surgeon.

'I would suggest Dr Rogarth then,' Dr Zinfandel said. 'He is preeminent in his field and he operates here. Do you object if I call him in on your case?'

'I am in your hands, Doctor,' Damon said humbly, thinking, This place is overrun with preeminence.

'Good. Can you be prepared to come into the hospital tomorrow at noon?'

'Whenever you say.'

'Do you want a private room?'

'Yes.' Good old *Threnody*, Damon thought. Before its publication he would have asked for the cheapest bed in the hospital. Wealth had its advantages. You could suffer without witnesses and whatever groans you heard would be your own.

'Be prepared to stay a minimum of three days.' Dr Zinfandel stood up. The interview was over. He extended his hand as Damon stood, too. When they shook hands, Damon was surprised by the tension in the doctor's grasp, as though his hand were attached to his arm by live electric wires. When he got to know Dr Zinfandel better, Damon thought as he left the office, he would have a long list of questions of his own to ask the doctor about *his* health.

Five days later he was in the pleasant private room being prepared for an operation at seven o'clock the next morning on what the surgeon and Dr Zinfandel had agreed might very likely be a severe intestinal ulcer. The tests had been dismaying. Dr Zinfandel's hunch had been correct and his and the surgeon's warnings about the consequences of postponing the operation had been dire.

Oliver had called his brother again and his brother had said that the surgeon, Dr Rogarth, had an excellent reputation. When Oliver had told him this, Damon had smiled wryly and asked Oliver if he remembered his speech about never having had a sick day in his life. 'It taught me a lesson,' Damon said.

'The gods don't like boasting.' He tried to seem calm and take everything lightly, but he was panicky and he didn't like the feeling. Everything has been leading up to this, he thought, everything since the goddamn telephone call.

Dr Rogarth was not panicky. Corpulent, rosy-cheeked, dressed in pearly gray, he flowed into the room, a broad, slow moving Mississippi of a man, his gestures deliberate and papal, his speech unhurried and measured. He had soft, pudgy hands, not what one would expect in a preeminent surgeon. He sat himself down on a straight chair beside the bed. 'I have explained the procedure to Mrs Damon,' he said. 'I believe that she shares my confidence that all will go well. The anesthetist who examined you foresees no great difficulties. I expect you will be back in this room when you emerge from the recovery room after the operation, four or five hours after you have left it for the operating theatre.' He recited all this as though he had learned it in a manual and could repeat it a thousand times, on his own deathbed if necessary. 'If you have any questions, I would be pleased to answer them to the best of my ability.'

'Yes,' Damon said, 'I have a question. When will I be able to go home?'

A sad little smile fleetingly appeared on the full, girlishly curved lips, like a ripple sweeping placidly across the broad surface of the waters. People for whom the doctor wished well and to whose welfare he dedicated most of his life were always anxious to leave him at the first opportunity for flight, the smile said. 'It is impossible to be exact in these matters. I would guess twelve, fifteen days, depending on your powers of recovery. Do you have any other questions?'

'No.'

Dr Rogarth stood up, straightened the pearl-gray vest over his comfortable stomach. 'I suggest you eat nothing after five P.M. today. An orderly will be in to shave your chest and give you an enema this evening and you will be sedated for the night. In the morning the nurse will give you a shot before you leave this room and you'll probably be asleep before you're wheeled to the elevator. I trust you have a good night, Sir.'

As he left the room, Sheila was coming in. She had gone down to the cafeteria for a cup of coffee. Damon had kept count. It was the sixth cup of coffee of the afternoon for her. Ordinarily she had one cup of coffee at breakfast and that was it for the day. It was the one sign of strain that she permitted herself. Her face was calm and composed and her hair was carefully brushed. She smiled at Dr Rogarth, who made the slightest of corpulent bows.

'I just dropped in,' the doctor said, 'to assure myself of the state of your husband's morale, Madam. I'm happy to say I find it excellent.'

'He jests at scars who never felt a wound,' Damon said lightly. Empty bravado, he thought, for the gallery. Grand-standing, as Manfred Weinstein would have said in his baseball days. 'This is a first time for me.'

'You're a lucky man, Sir,' Dr Rogarth said. 'Myself, I've had three major operations in the last fifteen years.'

'Then you're a walking advertisement for them,' Damon said, a small blandishment for the knife wielder.

Dr Rogarth smiled bleakly. 'I'm too fat,' he said. 'I don't drink and I hardly eat and I'm too fat.' He left the room, majestically.

'That's the first thing he's said up to now,' Damon said, 'that sounded human. About being fat.'

'You all right?' Sheila stood over him, staring hard at him.

'Fine. I just feel foolish lying here in a bed in the middle of the afternoon.'

'This hospital's been here for over fifty years,' Sheila said. 'You're not going to change their routine in just five days. I called Manfred. He's chipper as a blue jay. He's hopping all over the hospital and he's already discovered a marijuana ring. He's also discovered a twenty-two-year-old nurse he's seriously thinking of marrying. He said he'd like to make a bet with you that he'd get out of the hospital before you did. He said he'd give you eight-to-five-odds.'

Damon grinned. 'Maybe we'll having a coming out party together.'

'I told him that no matter who gets out first he has to come and stay with us at least until he can throw away his crutches.'

'You're going to have two cranky old men on your hands. Why don't you arrange to hire a practical nurse to help out?'

'You two can be as cranky as you want,' Sheila said decisively. 'I don't need any help. You know me. I can match crank for crank with anybody.'

'That's no lie.' Damon reached out and took her hand. 'When I hold your hand like this,' he said softly, 'I feel that no harm can come to me.'

He felt a sudden spasm of pain in his stomach and involuntarily he gripped Sheila's hand.

'What is it?' she asked, alarmed.

'Nothing.' He tried to smile. 'The last flicker of Doris's potato salad.' He wished the hours would pass quickly and that the sedation he had been promised had already taken effect. For the first time in his life he longed for unconsciousness.

It was past noon and Sheila and Oliver were still sitting in the private hospital room. They had both been there when Damon had been wheeled out, with a last little sedated wave of the hand at seven that morning. By now they had exhausted all conversation and they tensed again and again when they heard footsteps approaching along the corridor. Sheila, who had given up smoking when she married Damon, had gone through a whole package of Marlboros and the room, even with the door open, was thick with smoke. Both Rogarth and Zinfandel had promised Sheila they would come down and talk to her as soon as the operation was over.

It was over five hours now and neither of them had appeared.

Then Dr Rogarth came into the room, still in his green operating smock and cap, with the gauze mask pushed up on his forehead. He looked tired and grave.

'Where is he?' Sheila demanded. 'How is he? What took so long?' Her voice was harsh, no trace of her usual melodic civility in it. 'You said he'd be here by now.'

'I'm sorry, Mrs Damon,' the doctor said. 'He's in the Intensive Care Unit. Your husband is a very sick man, very, very sick.'

'What does that mean?'

'The operation was much more extensive than we had hoped it would be,' Rogarth said wearily. 'Please try to be calm,

229

Madam. There were complications. The ulcer turned out to be perforated. There was an extensive infection of the tissues around the perforation that had to be excised. By all rights your husband should have been screaming in pain for days . . .'

'It's not his habit to scream.'

'By medical criteria,' Dr Rogarth said, 'stocism is by no means an advantage. These were complications that an earlier operation could have avoided. There was so much bleeding . . . so much.' His gaze wandered, his voice flattened. 'It was impossible to see exactly. We're doing everything we can. He's on all life support systems, respirator, transfusions . . . I have to go back now. I have to consult with Dr Zinfandel, the other doctors who were in attendance. It appears that some bleeding has started again. We have to hope that it will stop by itself.'

'And if it doesn't?' Sheila said, biting out the words.

'That is why we have to consult. We're not certain he could endure another session in the operating room. We have to discuss our options, hope the transfusions will be sufficient . . . They're continuing.'

'How many transfusions has he had so far?' Oliver asked.

'Twelve.'

'Good God,' Oliver said. 'And you're giving him more?'

'It's necessary. The blood pressure is down so drastically . . . You must understand – heroic measures.'

'I don't know much about medicine,' Oliver said, his voice as hostile as Sheila's, 'but my brother's a surgeon at Cedars-Sinai in Los Angeles and he once told me that multiple transfusions are terribly risky.'

Rogarth smiled wanly, all papal certainty gone. 'I agree with your brother,' he said. 'But if he were here today, I'm sure he would be forced into the same measures we're taking. I have to go now. They're waiting for me . . .' He started out the door.

'I want to see him.' Sheila put out her hand and gripped the doctor's arm.

'It's impossible just now, Mrs Damon,' Rogarth said gently. 'He's being worked on. Perhaps some time in the afternoon, if you come up to the Intensive Care Unit. I can't promise anything. I'm terribly sorry . . . It happens so many times . . .' He sounded vague. 'So many times. You go in looking for one thing . . . you find another. So much bleeding . . . Dr Zinfandel will try to come down and keep you abreast of developments.'

'Is he conscious?'

Rogarth shrugged. 'It's hard to be sure,' he said, and went out.

Oliver put his arms around Sheila. 'He'll pull through. I just know it. He's strong . . .'

'Your husband's a very sick man, very, very sick,' Sheila said in a monotone, like Rogarth's. 'Doctor's gobbledegook. Translation – prepare yourself for the minute that he's going to die. And soon.'

'Sssh, sssh.' Oliver pulled her closer, kissed her forehead. 'I'll call my brother. If anybody can tell us what has to be done, he can.'

'Three thousand miles away,' Sheila said, 'I feel as though *everything's* three thousand miles away.'

He awoke, or thought he awoke. He felt no pain. It's finished, he thought. I've pulled through. But he was not in bed. He was in what seemed like a small theatre. There was a white screen at the back of a raised stage. He was alone. At least, his was the only presence he felt in the room. He couldn't tell whether he was sitting or standing or lying down. The screen was lit by a white light, then an image appeared on it. A photograph of Dr Rogarth, in pearl gray, smiling. Under it the caption – 'Dr Alexander Rogarth Presents – The Death of Roger Damon.'

Damon was furious. 'That's a lousy idea of a joke,' he said or thought or might have said.

Then he was conscious that he was lying, slightly diagonally, on the floor of the apron of the small stage, as the light went off on the screen. Next to him Maurice Fitzgerald was lying, at the same angle. They were not their normal sizes, but elongated; they were both young men and they both were dressed in evening clothes.

'They're serious,' Damon whispered in the curious manner of talking and not talking at the same time that he seemed to have acquired. 'There're no drinks.'

Then he was conscious that the legs of a corpse jutted out from the wings of the stage on his left. The toes of the corpse were black and swollen, as though they had been bound tightly with wire at their base for a long time to cut off all circulation of the blood. One of the feet was pierced by a gaping dark hole at the instep. Damon knew it was Christ who was lying there, with the wound of the spike that had nailed his foot to the cross. He was Christ and Christ was him and being prepared for burial. He was swept by unutterable sorrow, but could not move.

Dr Rogarth, still in his pearl-gray suit, came out from the wings and touched the blackened foot, the congested toes. 'As I thought,' Rogarth said. 'The toes were frozen by pre-Flood water, which never freezes itself but turns everything it touches into ice.'

'I think he recognized me,' Sheila said to Oliver. They were in the little waiting room in the Intensive Care Unit. A small gray-haired woman in a pretty flannel suit was crying softly across from them. Sheila had been allowed in to see Damon for a few minutes toward eight o'clock in the evening. 'His eyes were open and I think he tried to wink at me. With all those tubes, especially the two going down his throat, he couldn't talk if he wanted to. They're still giving him blood. It's accumulating in his chest and abdominal cavity, and he's swelled there to twice its normal size and growing bigger by the minute. It's compressing the lungs, and he's having trouble breathing and they have him on oxygen.' She spoke flatly, as though giving a dry annual report to a PTA meeting. 'The circulation's stopped to his feet and they're as cold as marble. I got the nurse to wrap his feet in a warm blanket. You'd think they'd have thought of that themselves. There's no word of encouragement from anybody. Zinfandel just keeps repeating, "Your husband's a very sick man." He admitted that they now believe an artery has been cut. Until he told me that, all they kept saying was that there was excessive bleeding. Preeminent in their field,' she said bitterly.

232

Now he was on a boat. He could feel the throbbing of great engines. Somehow he knew that they were on the boat, somewhere in warm Pacific waters, probably off the coast of Indonesia and they were there making a movie, under the direction of Mr Gray. Only Mr Gray was not there. He had disappeared. Mysterious Indonesia. Damon had to continue without him.

He descended below decks. A man in a white coat was bent over a radio transmitter. The man had a straggly brownish beard and was young, with a kind face. 'In the absence of Mr Gray,' Damon said to the man, 'I will take over the movie. I appoint you to run the ship.' The man with the beard looked angry. 'I have other things to do,' he said.

A very pretty Eurasian girl with flat features passed through the room. She was wearing blue jeans and a man's shirt hanging outside them, flapping on her. Damon knew she was to be the star of the film. She was supposed to sing in the film, but when she talked her voice was a harsh, unmelodious croak. Damon winced as he heard her. 'You have to do something with that girl's voice,' he said to the man with the beard.

'Leave me alone,' the man said impatiently. 'Can't you see that I'm busy?'

'I called my brother,' Oliver said. It was the next morning. Sheila had slept in the private room, Oliver on the couch in the waiting room. Whenever any of the doctors passed them, they seemed annoyed. 'He asked if they'd put in an arteriogram, to see where the bleeding is coming from. Have they?'

Sheila shook her head numbly.

'Anyway, he said you should suggest it to them. Do you know what it is?' Oliver asked.

'No.'

'Neither do I.'

Sheila nodded. 'I'll try. I don't know if anything'll do any good. The doctors seem to have given him up. They're just going through the motions. Thank God for the nurses. They don't leave him alone for a minute. The night nurse said he's not making any red blood corpuscles, the level is sinking to the

233

critical point. And he's having trouble breathing. They think he has pneumonia now. They keep pumping out his lungs through a tube. His eyes are still open but he doesn't seem to recognize me.'

A little later Zinfandel came in, his eyes red with lack of sleep, his nose twitching nervously. 'I believe, Mrs Damon,' he said, 'that you ought to try to get some rest or we'll be having to work on you too. You're not doing your husband any good by wearing yourself out like this.'

'Is he still bleeding?' Sheila asked, ignoring what he had said.

'I'm afraid he is.'

'Are you going to try an arteriogram?'

Zinfandel looked at her suspiciously. 'What do you know about arteriograms, Mrs Damon?'

'Nothing.'

'You've been talking to other doctors.' The tone was accusing.

'Of course I have. I'll talk to a thousand other doctors if I thought one of them would save my husband's life.'

'As a matter of fact,' Zinfandel said, without grace, 'we've decided to try an arteriogram this morning.' Then he resumed his more cordial pedantic manner, like a kindergarten teacher. 'It's a process in which a needle is put into an artery in the groin and a catheter is inserted through it to the suspected lesion. Then contrasting material, a dye if you will, is introduced. After it has flowed through to the source of the trouble X-rays are taken and with luck we find where the trouble lies. Then small gelatin pellets are blown under pressure through the catheter into the artery, two, three, four, depending on the case. With luck, the pellets block the rupture. There is no guarantee of success. If the hemorrhage is stopped, we must wait for several days to see if it is permanent. Is that all clear, Mrs Damon?'

'Thank you, yes.'

'I am not one of those doctors,' Zinfandel said with pride, 'who likes to mystify either the patient or his loved ones. I believe in presenting things as they are at all times, no matter how drastic it may seem at the time.'

'I appreciate it,' Sheila murmured.

'I will tell you how it comes out as soon as I know. In the meantime, please take my advice and get some rest.'

'Thank you again,' Sheila said.

Zinfandel bustled out of the room. He moved through the hospital at a lope, as though that were the only gait that would keep pace with enveloping death in the impossibly great area he had been appointed to oversee.

'He's a horse's ass, if you ask me,' Oliver said, 'but he seems like one hell of a doctor.'

'Yes,' Sheila agreed. 'If only *he* had operated instead of the other one.'

He was in a vaulted stone room on the top of a building. Now he realized he was in some special place in a hospital. Across from where he was lying there was a large brightly lit room where nurses and their friends seemed to be having a party, eating and drinking and chatting gaily to each other. There was the continual drone of funeral music from several cassette machines. A young doctor said, 'This is a real find. I got it today. The music played at the funeral of Prince Albert of Belgium. It cost two hundred dollars, but it was worth it.'

He said, or thought he said to Sheila, who seemed to float in and out of his consciousness, leaning close over him, 'Tell them to stop that damn music.'

In the same room with him there was an old man. A muscular young black in a skivvy shirt who looked like an ex-boxer was beating ferociously on the old man's chest and abdomen. Damon knew the old man was going to die and he did. Damon knew that he was going to be next, but his hands were tied down one on each side of the bed and there was nothing he could do about it. The corpse of the old man was carted away, and the black turned to him and began to pound him ferociously with the naked muscled arms jutting out of the skivvy shirt. From time to time the black would stop hitting him and shave him with an old-fashioned straight razor. With each stroke he would put a thin piece of adhesive tape on Damon's cheek and write the date and hour on it with a ball-point pen. Then he would resume hitting him again. Damon refused to cry out and resigned himself calmly to being killed by the black man.

But there was a gale of laughter in the brightly lit room across from where he was lying and somebody said, 'We're late for the party. Put him away somewhere until tomorrow.'

He was moved, he couldn't tell where, and everybody left, talking gaily, and he was alone with bright lights shining painfully in his eyes.

Sheila drifted over him again. 'You've got to get me out of this place,' he said, although he knew somehow that no sound came out of his mouth.

'Darling,' Sheila seemed to say, 'people pay a great deal of extra money to die in this room.'

'At least,' he said soundlessly, 'keep the black man away from me. He's going to kill me. They're all going to kill me. You've got to go to the police. Have Oliver call up the *Times*. He knows everybody on the paper. And you have to get away, too. They'll kill you, too.'

Sheila drifted away and he tried to sleep, but the bright light in his eyes kept him awake. There was a big clock on the wall, but it was going backward and moving swiftly, so that the hands on the dial were constantly moving. They want to fool me about time, Damon thought, they don't want me to know day from night. It was an exquisite refinement of torture.

'He can't talk,' Sheila said to Oliver, 'but somehow he let me know he wanted a pen and a piece of paper. At least the arteriogram worked – so far – and he seems a little stronger now. He can hold a pen in his hand and communicate *something*. It's almost impossible to read what he writes, but I could understand that he thinks the black male nurse is trying to kill him. The man is just doing what he's been ordered to do – pounding the chest to dislodge the stuff that's collecting in the lungs so that it can be siphoned up and Roger can breathe. But go explain that to a man who's out of his mind most of the time. Damon's the least racist man I know, but I suppose somewhere inside all of us, irrationally . . .' She shrugged hopelessly. 'Anyway, I told the doctor in charge of the ICU to keep the man away from Roger. He's got enough things to worry about, as it is. Now it turns out that the first day they gave him twenty-six transfusions. Nobody knows what's keeping him alive. His kidneys have shut down. They've ordered a shunt to put him on a dialysis machine, but the doctors who do it won't be able to start till tomorrow morning. And they have to take the tube out of his throat soon and do a tracheotomy so his vocal cords won't be ruined. That's the first hopeful sign –' Her tone was bitterly ironic. 'They think there's a chance that he can live and they want him to be able to talk if it turns out that way. But the specialist who does it won't be in till Monday, that's four days from now, and it may be too late. You'd think that in an enormous place like this they could find someone else to do it immediately. There are all those stories in the newspapers about people doing it with a pen-knife on the floor of a restaurant when somebody is choking on a piece of steak. And they can't even agree on the name of the operation. One doctor calls it a tracheotomy, another says tracheostomy.' Sheila shook her head wonderingly. 'Naming things is important. The addition or subtraction of a single s may change the entire meaning of a word. How do I know? Now I wish I'd gone in for medicine when I was young instead of child psychology. Then maybe I could fight this terrible, hulking hospital machine.'

Oliver sat silently through all this. He had been in to see Damon several times and had spoken to some of the younger doctors and the sympathetic nurses, and while he had been alarmed by Damon's appearance, he was inclined to believe the doctors and the nurses he had talked to who told him that now that Damon had survived the first awful days, he would most probably eventually recover. When he talked to his brother on the phone, which he did daily and as best he could describe the treatments Damon was undergoing, his brother confirmed that the doctors knew what they were doing. Sheila, he felt, was dissolving. Physically, she already seemed to have lost a great deal of weight and her once-gleaming dark hair hung lank and lusterless around her head and her face seemed sharpened to a thin, brittle edge. And she had always been a woman who had spoken briefly and with confidence and her rambling tirades were frightening, as though her character was breaking up into

237

unfamiliar, jagged, uncontrollable fragments. He would like to have the courage to suggest to her that both for her good and Damon's, it might be a good idea if she absented herself from the hospital for two or three days at a time; the atmosphere of the Intensive Care Unit was crushing her as well as Damon. But he knew that he couldn't suggest it. Sheila would think that he was advocating flight, betrayal. As it was, she spent almost the whole day and night in the waiting room, sometimes dozing in a chair, waking with a start and rushing into Damon's room to see if he needed to tell her something. And it was true that she was the only link with the world by which he could communicate anything because she was the only one who could decipher the scrawls he put on paper. He was suffering terribly from thirst now and was continually writing the word *water* on the yellow pad they kept at his bedside. The doctors and nurses said he was getting all the liquid necessary intravenously and through the tube down his throat into his stomach through which he was fed a nutritive powder that was supposed to supply him with fifteen hundred calories a day. He was not allowed to drink because anthing he took orally would slide immediately into his over-worked and cramped lungs. The one time they had tried to feed him some cold Jell-O, it had been pumped up immediately, intact. It was Sheila who got a dozen lemons and squeezed some drops on swabs soaked with glycerine that she ran over his parched lips. He smiled or tried to smile gratefully at the taste, as though the slight sharpness of the fruit gave him, at least momentarily, the illusion of assuaging his thirst.

'He'll forget all this,' Oliver said, searching for words of comfort, 'once he's out of here. All the nurses say the same thing.'

'Torture.' Sheila seemed not to have heard what he had said. 'He keeps writing the one word – torture – before he writes anything else.' She took a folded piece of yellow foolscap out of her bag and read from the wandering, almost illegible script, that looked to Oliver like random bird-tracks on sand. 'Get out of here. Must get out. Call lawyer. O . . . That's you, Oliver. O knows number. Writ. Habeas corpus. Prison.'

'The nurses tell me it's the same with everybody,' Oliver said. 'They even have a name for it. The ICU syndrome.'

'They've taken you in,' Sheila said accusingly. 'They think you're cute. I see you drinking coffee with them, going out with them to the deli for a sandwich. Whose side are you on, anyway?'

'Oh, Christ, Sheila,' Oliver said wearily,

Sheila took a deep breath. 'I'm sorry, Oliver. Forgive me. I don't know what I'm saying these days.'

'Forget it.' He patted her hand.

A doctor passed through the room and Sheila looked at him hopefully. The doctor ignored her and went into the adjoining conference room, where the staff gathered to discuss cases and listen to lectures.

'He's beginning to look like a skeleton,' Sheila said. 'You can see every bone of his face. You wouldn't think that a man's arms – and such strong arms, too – could wither so fast. He seems to be losing five pounds a day. It's as though he's disappearing bit by bit before my eyes.'

CHAPTER
TWENTY

HE WAS being carried into a cave by four masked men. He knew the leader of the four was Zalovsky, although not a word was spoken. The cave was high and spacious, shadowed, hewn out of rock. He could not move but once he was in the cave he saw the carved stone sarcophagus that awaited him. Then he saw that he was not going to be buried alone. Standing against a wall, taller than he had realized, queenly and erect, draped in a flowing rose-colored gown, her hair flowing over her shoulders, her figure bathed in a mauve light, immobile in death, was his wife. Only he couldn't remember her name. Coppelia was the only name he could conjure up and he repeated it to himself over and over again, irritated. Then it changed to Cornelia, but he knew that was wrong, too.

Then he felt a sharp pain in his hand and it awoke or nearly awoke him, and the cave and the tall mauve-lit figure disappeared and he remembered that his wife's name was Sheila and that she was alive, and he was grateful to the clumsy doctor who was trying to draw blood for more tests from his hand because the pain had interrupted his dream. It was the doctor with the straggly beard whom he had tried to appoint master of the vessel on which he still believed he was sailing. Only now he was not free to go up and down between the decks, but was immured below, tied down by both wrists most of the time. The swift backward running clock, false to the hours, was still visible. It was a sly device, he had figured out, to fool him into not sleeping. He had made himself learn to write the word *sleep* almost clearly on the yellow legal pad. Whoever was on duty to torture him made that the first priority – to keep him from sleeping. The bright neon shone in his eyes at all times. He did not remember daylight.

They were constantly jabbing him with needles to give or take blood. His veins had collapsed and most of the doctors never could find a fit target for their needles, and his arms and hands and feet were black and blue from the incessant attempts, and he cursed Dr Zinfandel in his heart because every time he appeared, he ordered either a transfusion or a sample of blood.

Anybody on duty seemed to have the right to draw blood from him or insert an intravenous tube, no matter how maladroit he or she was, and he became piteously grateful to the people with an instinctive touch who could find his depleted buried veins at the first try. Unfortunately he couldn't remember them or their names.

An assorted platoon of doctors seemed to be interested in him, each of them attached to one specialist or another in some obscure medical table of organization. Doctors for his lungs, his kidneys, his throat, with the tube in it at the point where the tracheotomy had been performed, for the bedsores he had developed that went down to the bone and had to be cleansed and bandaged over and over again. He urinated through a catheter and struggled with a bedpan for his bowels, without much success, and had dreams in which he luxuriously pissed normally and sat on a toilet bowl. He was naked and exposed and treated like a piece of meat in a butcher shop and lived, if it could be called living, in a constant state of humiliation.

The nurses took turns at pounding his chest so that he could cough up the silt accumulating in his lungs. The black man stayed away from him but Damon could see him lurking in the corridor waiting for his chance. Damon warned Sheila once more about the man and wrote a pleading sentence to her asking her to get the police before it was too late.

Then one day, or night, he heard the sound of distant sirens coming nearer and felt, triumphantly, that his message to his wife had gotten through. He saw the nurses and doctors scurrying away, leaving only the black man, who came into his room and stood over him and said, 'They think they're going to let me hang in here and take the rap. Well, they're wrong. And if you think you're going to get away, you're wrong, too, Mister.' It was then that Damon knew the black man was Zalovsky's agent, insinuated into the hospital to finish what Zalovsky had begun.

Then the black man sat on his chest and began to rig a wire box with dynamite in it just in front of Damon's mouth. 'When they come through the door,' the black man said, 'this thing goes up. And you with it.'

Damon felt icily calm, pleased that he was going to die so quickly.

Finished with his job, the black jumped off Damon's chest and disappeared and Damon was left alone in a suddenly silent place, with the lights for the first time almost completely extinguished and the sirens getting closer, then starting to fade away until all was absolutely quiet.

Deserted, deserted, Damon thought. Sheila had betrayed him, had not believed him. He lay in the shadows and waited, regretting that the machine had not gone off.

Tied down and unable to call out, he tried over and over again by groans, signals with his eyes, feeble flickers of his fingers, to get the nurses and doctors who constantly passed the open door of his room to give him something to drink. They passed him by as if he were a beggar at a church door and they were in a hurry to go to a wedding or a baptism.

He was on a respirator all the time now because he had developed what some of the doctors diagnosed as viral pneumonia and others merely called congestion or a collapsed lung. He took a remote, cool interest in his condition and their attempts at treatment, and when Dr Rogarth made one of his rare visits, he printed out on the legal pad, 'Am I going to die?'

Dr Rogarth answered, 'We're all going to die,' and Damon tried to turn his head contemptuously away from the sight of the man, but couldn't manage it.

There was one doctor who seemed to Damon to be in charge of depriving him of water. He had a bedraggled wet blondish moustache, very long darkish-blond hair, mad, sly eyes and swept in and out with a loose white open robe floating behind him. He was engaged in a mysterious project that was built around a Persian carpet and involved putting Damon in poses suggested by the figures in the carpet and photographing him in those positions. Damon found himself staked out on burning sands, against looming monuments, the walls of tombs, all in merciless sunlight, hanging from a bare tree on a small island surrounded by a lake from which the noon sun was reflected like bursts of gunfire. He was transported from one place to another as if by magic, in fractions of a second, while the doctor, who by now Damon thought of as the Magician, and who was always accompanied by a wizened nurse in a disheveled uniform, clicked away with his camera while humming merrily to himself. Somehow, Damon managed to communicate with him and the Magician was not loath to talk, often very good-humoredly.

'What, exactly, are you up to?' Damon asked once.

'You will see when I'm finished,' the Magician said. 'If you must know, I am in a contest. A travel magazine is giving a prize for the photo montage that comes closest to the spirit and design of my carpet. You must learn to cooperate without all this complaining about water, like everybody else.'

This was the first inkling that there was anybody else in the Magician's power.

'Everybody would stop complaining,' Damon said, 'if just once you would let them drink as much as they want.'

The Magician laughed. 'All right. I'll let everybody drink their fill from ten in the morning till noon. Then, by two o'clock, mark my words, they'll be wailing for water again.' He untied Damon from his tree and laughed as Damon rushed to the edge of the lake and plunged his face into its cool depths.

At two o'clock, sharp, the Magician tied him again and he was thirstier than ever and from all around him he heard voices wailing, 'Water, water.' Over the wailing he could hear the Magician's laughter.

Suddenly, he did not know how, he could distinguish night from day. He was on a lower deck of the boat at night and during those hours they did not keep shining the lights in his

243

eyes. His night nurse, whom he now recognized, was a fine-featured slender woman, tanned very dark by the sun, with a soft, delightful voice. One of the doctors, a youngish burly man with a bull neck, visited her often while she was on duty at Damon's bedside. He made a joke about the woman's suntan. 'I'd like to be there,' he said, 'the next time you go sunbathing,' and laughed coarsely. He made other lewd remarks to the woman. Lewd remarks, Damon repeated to himself, with distaste. To such a fine and delicate creature. And he was heartbroken when one night, after the bull-necked doctor had slipped into the room to whisper into the nurse's ear, she had leaned over Damon and said softly, 'I'll be gone for a few minutes.' He knew where she was going – to climb into some poor devil's empty bed with the lewd doctor.

The next thing he knew, he was alone with the doctor in an open boat sailing across a lake toward an island. 'I know why you're taking me to the island,' Damon said.

'Why?' the doctor asked.

'You're going to kill me there,' Damon said calmly.

Angrily, the doctor drew a shining metal object from his pocket and slashed Damon with it. The pain was intolerable, but it was over in a second. 'I'm here to save your life,' the doctor said. 'Don't ever forget it.'

He was deep in the hold of the ship. His hands were tied to a wooden bar in front of him. He was kneeling in front of the bar and beside him was another man, whom he had never seen before, also tied and kneeling. Two nurses kept hurrying up and down an open stairway that led to another deck. He recognized the two nurses. They were Julia Larch and what must have been her daughter. Although there had to be a considerable difference in their ages, they looked exactly alike. They paid no attention to Damon's groans and the groans of the other man as they pleaded for a sip of water. Finally, annoyed, Julia Larch came over. She gave no sign of recognition that the man in front of her was the father of her son. 'You will get a drink at noon,' she said. 'Now, keep quiet.'

The eternal clock was there. Now it was running normally.

There was no detecting the movement of its hands on the large dial. It stood at twenty past nine.

With inhuman self-control he kept himself from looking at the clock until he judged that at least an hour had passed. It was twenty-five past nine. The man tied next to him was groaning louder and louder and whenever one or the other of the nurses who were Julia Larch and her daughter appeared on the stairway, he croaked, through puffed lips, 'Water! Water!'

They paid no attention to him, but hurried up and down on their errands.

After a while the man's groans became weaker and weaker, and he began rolling his head from side to side in a demented rhythm. Damon would have liked to do something for him if it was only to choke him and end his torment, but with his hands tied and his tongue swollen in his mouth, he could only make grunting sounds of commiseration. It was the longest period of time in Damon's life, longer than the trip to Europe, longer than any voyage across the North Atlantic during the war. Finally, when he looked up at the clock, it was one minute to twelve. He looked across at the man next to him. There was a last soft groan, like a baby's sigh, and the man's head lolled forward. He was dead.

Damon heard the ship's bells strike noon. Julia Larch appeared with a pitcher of water and two glasses. 'Where's the other one?' Julia demanded.

'He's dead.' Damon watched greedily, licking his lips, as Julia poured one glass of water. He looked for the other man. The cloths which had bound him to the wooden bar were still there but the body was gone. 'They collected him or he turned into powder and blew away,' Damon said stupidly, watching Julia put the full glass of water and the pitcher down so that she could untie his hands. His hands free, he took the glass and drained it, held it out to be refilled. With no expression on her face, Julia poured again and he drained it in one gulp once more. Satisfied for the moment, he said, reproachfully, to Julia, 'If you'd come two minutes earlier, he'd've been alive.'

Julia shrugged, the blank small face impassive. 'Rules are rules,' she said.

From that moment on he could drink all he wanted to. Sheila kept bringing six small cans of cold pineapple juice to him at a time and he never seemed to be able to get enough of them and kept marveling at the glorious tropical flavor of the fruit as it went in an icy torrent down his throat. The Magician and his wizened assistant disappeared and the only doctor of the many who went in and out of the Intensive Care Unit whom Damon had any liking for, a small, owl-faced man with large horn-rimmed glasses, who had performed the tracheotomy, came into the room and told him that he was going to replace the tube in his throat the next day with one that would permit Damon to talk, if he learned the trick of breathing in as he put his finger over a hole in the tube and using the breath to say a few words. The man's name was Dr Levine, and he had promised Damon a long time ago he would eventually be able to talk normally. He was the only one of the doctors who had said a hopeful word to him, which was why Damon liked him.

As he had promised, Dr Levine came in the next morning with the new tube. 'First,' he said, 'we'll take this gadget out.' He took hold of the slender plastic tube that was attached to the bag of nutritive powder on a steel stand above Damon's head that led down through his nose into his stomach. 'Dr Zinfandel says it's about time you started to eat normally.'

Damon watched him fearfully. He was sure he would not be able to eat normally and would run the risk of starving to death. But Dr Levine seemed confident and slid the tube out swiftly and let it dangle from the sack on the steel stand. Then he took up the new metal tube through which he could breathe and occasionally, according to the doctor, be able to make coherent sounds that might be interpreted as speech, to connect him with the rest of the human race. 'This will hurt a little,' he said, 'maybe a lot. But it's over quickly and if I gave you an anesthetic, the needle would hurt more.' Then he reached in unceremoniously and deftly picked out the old, pus-encrusted tube and slid in the new one. The doctor had been right about its hurting, but he tried not to show it on his face because Sheila and Oliver were in the room, watching anxiously.

The new curved metal tube felt peculiar in his throat. 'Now

246

. . .' Dr Levine put his finger over the hole in the tube, like a flute player, 'take a deep breath and then try to talk.'

Damon took a deep breath. He realized he was frightened. Despite what the doctor had said, he was sure he could not speak. But he tried. To his surprise a sound came out. Then he said clearly, although his voice sounded metallic and strange in his ears, 'Get me out of here.'

Oliver and Sheila laughed. Sheila's laugh was hysterically high.

'Now try again,' Dr Levine said.

Damon shook his head. He had said enough for one day.

Sheila was sitting in Dr Zinfandel's outer office. She had had her hair done and put on fresh clothing to replace the rumpled sweater and skirt that she had not bothered to change for days. She wanted to seem composed and firmly in control of herself for the conversation that she knew was to come.

Zinfandel's secretary said, 'You can go in now.'

Sheila stood, brushed the creases from her skirt, strode purposefully into the inner office, where Zinfandel was still bent over the chart on his desk of a patient who had just left the room. He looked harried and depleted. Sheila knew that he arrived at the hospital each morning at five and often was still there at eleven at night. He had mentioned a wife and two children, and Sheila pitied them, although she had never seen any signs of their existence and there were no family photographs on Zinfandel's desk. 'He is a maniac of healing,' Oliver had said, and Sheila agreed that the description fit the emaciated, loping man.

Zinfandel looked up, smiled briefly, his eyes red-rimmed, his brain desperately crowded with a thousand uncured ailments. 'Please sit down,' he said. 'I'm glad we have a moment to talk to each other. You know what I have to say.'

'Yes,' Sheila said. 'And I think you're wrong.'

Zinfandel sighed. 'I can't take him out of Intensive Care, Mrs Damon. Your husband is still a very sick man. His life is hanging in the balance. I do not lie or dissemble with my patients or with their families, as you well know. True, patients who have to endure long periods in the unit have a tendency to fall into a deep mental depression. But in the case of your husband it is his body we must save first. We have our professional principles, our professional experience.'

'I appreciate all that, Doctor,' Sheila said, trying to keep her voice calm, 'but I know some things, too, after living with the man for so many years. He's at the lowest ebb of his life. He's lost so much weight that he's just skin and bones. He's still losing pounds daily. He refuses to eat . . .'

'The formula powder I prescribed, mixed with milk . . .'

'I know all about the formula. You can prescribe it, but he takes one sip and he turns his head to the wall. I bring him delicacies . . . smoked salmon, caviar, soups, fruits . . . All he takes is pineapple juice. How long do you think he can survive on pineapple juice? He's in a state of fatalistic lethargy. He's looking for an excuse to die.'

'You exaggerate, Mrs Damon.'

'I want him moved from that damned Intensive Care Unit, where he's surrounded by dying people, by the machines and paraphernalia of death, put him back in his own room, make any move, any, any change. He's like a wild animal in captivity there, like those animals who refuse to eat behind bars and prefer to lie down and die.'

'It's impossible to move him,' Zinfandel said crisply. 'He needs the machines, the respirator, the oxygen, the monitors . . . his heart, his pulse, his blood pressure . . . his red blood count, which continues to be dangerously low. There may be an emergency at any time. He needs moment-by-moment attention. The ICU is the only place where we can guarantee it. You must understand, Mrs Damon, we are responsible for his life . . .'

'So am I,' Sheila said. 'And he's giving up on it where he is now.'

'I understand your fears,' Zinfandel said gently. 'Yours is a subjective viewpoint. We can't permit ourselves that luxury. We have to make our decisions on an objective basis. Please trust us.'

'I don't,' Sheila said. She stood up and strode from the office.

When Oliver came into the ICU waiting room that evening after work, which he did every evening, he could see that Sheila was much more troubled than when he had left her the night before. 'What is it?' he asked.

'I have to talk to you.' Sheila looked around her. There were two other visitors in the room and the chief doctor in overall direction of the unit was whispering intently to one of them in a corner. 'I don't want to talk here. Let's go out and get a cup of coffee.'

'Is he worse?' Oliver asked anxiously.

'He's worse every day,' Sheila said and didn't say anything more until they were seated at a table in the small cafe near the hospital where they sometimes took their meals and which was frequented by the nurses on their breaks from duty. There was a group of three nurses now near the entrance, and Sheila led Oliver to a table at the rear, where they were alone.

'What's going on?' Oliver asked. His face had been troubled ever since the shooting, but it was intensified now. To Sheila he looked like a small boy who had been lost in a crowd by his mother and was trying to keep from crying while he searched the faces around him for her.

'Something peculiar,' Sheila said. 'And I don't know just what it is.' Then she told him about the conversation with Zinfandel. 'If Roger is losing ground every day,' she said, 'it only makes sense to try to do something else. But the doctors're stonewalling me. They pretend to listen, but they don't. Have *you* any ideas?'

Oliver's face twitched uncomfortably and he made some incomprehensible noises deep in his throat. 'Well,' he said at last, 'I didn't want to worry you, but . . .'

'But what?'

'This is only a guess . . .' He stopped again.

'Go on, Oliver,' Sheila said impatiently. 'Don't beat around the bush.'

'They're spreading the responsibility.'

'Who's spreading the responsibility? *What* responsibility?' Sheila had difficulty keeping her voice down.

'All of them. The doctors. Sheila, I was told this in the deepest confidence.'

'Stop talking in riddles, Oliver, for Christ's sake.'

'Well, you know that pretty blond nurse, Penny?'

'Yes.'

'I've had a meal or two with her.' He was blushing. 'She's highly intelligent, aside from being most attrac –'

'No descriptions,' Sheila said brutally. 'Go on.'

'You remember, Roger wrote you once asking you to get hold of a lawyer?'

'Of course, I remember.'

'Well, somebody read it before they gave it to you. Or one of them – the doctors, I mean – did. He told the others, I guess. They think it's because you and Roger are going to sue Rogarth, the hospital, everybody, for malpractice. Millions of dollars.'

'Roger never would sue anybody in his life. Every time he's read in the papers about one of those suits, he's raged; he's told me again and again it's ruining the practice of medicine in America.'

'You know that,' Oliver said. 'I know that. *They* don't. At least according to Penny they don't. They're scared witless. There's one more thing she told me – Penny.'

'What's that?'

Oliver jerked his head around to make sure nobody had come in quietly behind him. 'When they brought him into the ICU after the operation, one of the doctors on duty said, "Another one of Rogarth's hatchet jobs." '

'Oh, God,' Sheila said. Then accusingly, 'Your own brother told you he was one of the best in the country.'

'I'm sorry,' Oliver said apologetically. 'If he made a mistake, it was an honest one. If my brother said Rogarth was one of the best in the country, that was what he'd heard. Maybe Rogarth was once. Maybe never,' Oliver said, shrugging. 'Reputations. There're writers Roger wouldn't touch with a ten-foot pole who've been getting great reviews for twenty years. As for doctors – it's a closed corporation. To put it mildly, they're not in the habit of rapping each other. And there's one other thing Penny told me. With the log of the operation when he was sent to the ICU, there were three letters on the top page.' He hesitated. 'I don't know if I should tell you this, Sheila.'

'What three letters?' Her tone was fierce.

'CYA,' Oliver said.

Sheila frowned. 'What does that mean?'

'Penny says it means "cover your ass."' Oliver sighed, though he had delivered himself of an enormous burden. 'They knew there'd been a big mistake and everyone was being warned to close ranks, they had to hide it.'

Sheila closed her eyes, then covered them with her hands. When she took her hands down, her face was stony. 'The pigs,' she said quietly. 'The cynical pigs.'

'You won't say anything about this, will you?' Oliver asked anxiously. 'If they trace it to Penny, they'll kick her out in two minutes.'

'Don't worry about Penny. I'll handle it my own way. Roger will be out of that goddamn place tomorrow. Why didn't you tell me this sooner?'

'What good would it have done? They're afraid now. How would it help Roger if they also were furious?'

'Oliver,' Sheila said, 'I can't go back to the hospital tonight. I don't know what I'd do or say. I'd like you to take me out to a nice restaurant, full of healthy people, who're enjoying a good meal and not plotting against anybody and buy me a couple of drinks and a fine bottle of wine. Unless you have a date with the pretty Penny.'

Oliver blushed again. 'We just happened to be going down in the elevator together,' he said, flustered, 'and she was coming off her shift and it was dinnertime and –'

'Don't apologize,' Sheila said. She smiled. 'Just because Roger's in the hospital doesn't mean a man can't look at a pretty girl once in a while. Just go up and if Roger's awake, which isn't likely, tell him you insisted I take a night off with you because the hospital was getting me down. He'll understand. There's a saloon down the block. I'll be waiting at the bar for you. Don't be shocked if I'm drunk by the time you get there.'

When Zinfandel made his usual visit at six the next morning, Sheila was there, sitting grimly in the little easy chair near the window. Zinfandel, as always on his morning rounds, was cheerful and lively. He looked at the nurse's chart at the foot of the bed, touched Damon's bare toes, which were no longer black, and asked the patient how he felt.

Damon, who by now hated the man whose presence at dawn every morning announced the beginning of another endless painful day, said, 'Lousy.'

Zinfandel smiled, as though this show of spirit demonstrated that Damon was on the road to recovery. 'Your toes are still icy,' he said, making it sound that he considered the fact a sign of bad faith on Damon's part.

'Sometimes they freeze,' Damon said. 'Sometimes – like now – they feel as though they're on fire.'

'It may be a touch of gout,' Zinfandel said.

'For Christ's sake, I haven't had a drop of booze for more than a month,' Damon said.

'One thing can have nothing to do with the other. I'll have somebody take some blood this morning and we'll run some tests.'

Damon groaned. 'Do you think you can find someone who actually knows where the veins in the human body can be found? The plumbers you've been sending in here have been stabbing me ten times in a row to get two drops of blood.'

'Your veins –' Zinfandel said sadly. 'I don't have to tell you again about your veins.' He hung the chart back on the foot of the bed after making a notation on it and turned to go out.

Sheila, who had not greeted the doctor or said a word while he was in the room, stood up. 'I'd like a word with you,' she said. 'Outside.' She followed him to the corridor.

'I hope it won't take too long,' Zinfandel said. 'I'm behind schedule as it is.'

'I want Mr Damon moved to a private room,' Sheila said. 'Today.'

'Impossible. I've already explained that –'

'If he isn't moved,' Sheila said flatly, 'I'm going to our lawyer and I'm getting a court writ to get him out of here and I'm putting him in another hospital.' She could see the little flicker in the doctor's pale eyes at the word *lawyer*.

'I'll see what I can do,' Zinfandel said.

'You will not see what you can do. You will have him moved by three o'clock this afternoon.'

'Mrs Damon,' Zinfandel said, 'you keep forcing me to act in a way that runs counter to all my training and principles. You dictate treatment, you listen to nurses' gossip and confront me with impossible demands. Now you threaten a lawsuit . . .'

'Three o'clock this afternoon,' Sheila said, and went back into the room, where Damon was trying to fall back to sleep.

That morning Damon hallucinated for the last time.

For a reason that was not explained to him, he was allowed to wander around the ship at will. The ship itself had changed. It was no longer a dingy cargo vessel, but a white-painted ship crowded with passengers. Everybody was busy packing and saying good-bye, because the ship was due shortly to put into port. Without being told, Damon understood that the port was Seattle. Damon also understood that although everybody else was going ashore, he was not to disembark.

With great blasts of the ship's horn, the ship was tied up. The nurses, whom he had grown to recognize one from the other and for whom he now realized he had developed a hopeless affection, passed him, no longer clad in white but dressed in charming traveling clothes of all colors, their hair newly done, their young faces carefully made up, their high heels clicking on the decks and they waved cordially at him and departed. Only one nurse stopped to say good-bye to him. It was the prettiest of them all, the one they called Penny. Tears streamed from her deep blue, blond-lashed eyes down the angelic face.

'Why are you crying?' he asked sympathetically.

'I'm in love with Oliver Gabrielsen,' she said, 'and he's in love with me and he's married.'

'Ah, Penny,' he said, 'you were born for weeping. You will always weep.'

'I know,' she said, sobbing. She kissed him, her lips damp and soft, and carrying her bag, went down the gangplank.

The bull-necked doctor, now dressed in a zippered windjacket, with 'University of Virginia' lettered on it, stopped in front of Damon. 'Well, good-bye, old son,' the doctor said kindly. 'Is there anything I can bring back for you from ashore?'

253

Damon thought for a moment. 'Bring me a Coca-Cola,' he said. 'With ice.'

'It shall be done,' the doctor said, and shook his head, his grip like steel. Then he, too, went down the gangplank and Damon had the enormous ship all to himself.

That afternoon Damon was removed to the private room. Damon didn't ask Sheila how or why it was done and she did not tell him. The room had a private shower and toilet and using a walker because he could not stand without its support, Damon got to the toilet and sat on it, with a feeling that approached ecstasy. After he had finished on the toilet he heaved himself up, using the walker and looked at himself in the mirror. He had been shaved by the hospital barber before leaving the ICU and the lines of his face were starkly defined. Staring back at him from the mirror was a face he hardly recognized, a face greenish dull white in color, the skin stretched like mottled parchment over sharp bones, the eyes in deep hollows and devoid of all light. They are the eyes of a dead man, Damon thought, then clumsily moving the walker cautiously inches at a time ahead of him, clumped back into the room, where Sheila and the nurse helped him back into the bed, lifting his legs because he didn't have the strength to do it himself.

He was pleased to see that there was no clock in the room.

'I brought the *Times*,' Sheila said. 'Do you want to look at it?'

Damon nodded. He held the paper in front of him. The date was meaningless to him. The headlines made no sense to him. The language might just as well have been Sanskrit. He let the paper fall on the bedcover. He began to cough violently. The nurse attached the tube and put it down into his lungs through the open hole of the tracheotomy tube low on his throat and switched on the compressed air to drain his lungs. He had become accustomed to the treatment, but this was the first time he realized how painful it was.

Sheila had brought him a chocolate milkshake, rich with ice cream and a raw egg. He had had a passion for milkshakes when he was a boy and he drank a few sips, then pushed it away. Sheila looked worried at his refusal and he was sorry about that, but there was no getting any more of the drink down.

The dressings on his chest and stomach had been removed but he refused to look at the scars. The nurses changed the bandages and irrigated and sterilized the one huge remaining bedsore on his buttock four or five times a day and that, too, which he had scarcely noticed until now, proved excruciatingly painful, as did the placing of needles for intravenous doses of antibiotics and the continuing blood transfusions. He remembered very clearly all his hallucinations but was not clear whether they were events through which he had actually lived or merely dreamed, so he spoke of them to no one. From time to time he regretted that he had not been permitted to die before then and was sure that he never would get out of the hospital alive and that the time that lay ahead of him was a needless prolongation of agony.

He resented the prodding of Sheila and the nurses, who tended him in three shifts of eight hours each around the clock, to get him out of bed and walk, first with the walker, then with a cane, a few steps several times a day. He tried to eat, but whatever food he was offered was like dry wool in his mouth, which he chewed with effort then spat out.

His day nurse weighed him every morning. Without interest, he saw that he weighed one hundred and thirty-eight pounds. As the days went by he neither gained nor lost a pound. When he went into the hospital, he had weighed one hundred and seventy-five.

A respirator had been set up in his room, although Dr Zinfandel had told Sheila it was impossible to arrange. But Sheila had gone to the head nurse at the main office on the floor, an old Irish lady with whom she had become friendly and the nurse had snorted when Sheila told her what Zinfandel had said and told Sheila she could put in all the apparatuses necessary in thirty minutes. Damon hated the respirator and the oxygen mask and felt he was being smothered when they clamped it on him and he had to be restrained from pulling the mask off. Oliver was in and out of the room and tried to cheer him up by telling him how well things were going at the office, but Damon shut him up by saying, 'Fuck off, Oliver,' when Oliver began to talk about contracts.

One thing Damon remembered was the pretty nurse Penny crying in his dream as she said good-bye when the ship docked. 'Oliver,' he said, 'are you going to marry Penny?'

Oliver looked stricken. 'I don't know what you're talking about,' he said.

'I must warn you,' Damon said. The dream had hardened into reality. 'Doris is good for you. And she's a winner. Pretty as she is, Penny is one of the world's eternal losers. You would eat the bread of sorrow the rest of your life.' The dying, he thought, have their right to a final honest word.

CHAPTER
TWENTY-ONE

DESPITE HIS loyal attempts to eat the food that Sheila tried to tempt him with and drink the rich milkshakes she prepared for him, he could not regain any of his lost weight and the few steps he managed to make up and down the hall exhausted him for the day. But the tensions and the despair that had nearly overcome him in the Intensive Care Unit had left him. Now he felt calm, resigned to whatever might come.

The idea of death had become so familiar to him that it did not alarm him. He felt that if the doctors and nurses would only leave him alone, he would die peacefully, with a contented smile on his face. Unless, of course, the hallucinations had come *after* he had died and then been reanimated by the wonders of modern medicine. That would make the phrase 'the peace of the grave' a cosmic bad joke, in the worst of taste. Sixty-five was not a bad age for the final passage. 'Time to go,' as he had once said to Sheila when one of his older clients had committed suicide in Hollywood, for good and sufficient reason.

Holding his finger over the hole in the tube in his throat and remembering Dr Levine's instructions about inhaling deeply, he asked Sheila if he had ever really died, then been brought back. 'No,' she said, and she was not one to lie, even for the gravest reasons, 'never.'

Dr Levine, who by this time Damon considered the only doctor in the hospital who knew how to cure anything, breezed in casually and said, 'It's about time you talked like a human being.' Unceremoniously, without preliminaries, he reached over and yanked out the tube. Then, with equal nonchalance, he said, 'Speak up, man.'

Damon looked up at the owlish sharp face in disbelief, thought, What have I got to lose? He took a deep breath. Then in his normal voice he said, 'Four score and seven years ago our forefathers brought forth on this continent a new nation . . .'

'Well, that's that,' Dr Levine said briskly. He shook Damon's hand. 'That's the last you'll see of me. I hope you have something more interesting to say the next time you open your mouth,' and departed.

Taking advantage of his newfound loquacity, Damon said to Sheila and the nurse, who had been watching the operation apprehensively, 'This room is too damn hot. Turn the air-conditioning up, will you please?'

He had been a man who all his life, except for his disastrous years as an aspiring actor, had spent most of his time reading and listening to other people talk, but now he accepted the lie that the gift of speech was what set the human race apart from the rest of the animal world.

The room was full of flowers, the gifts of friends, clients, producers, editors, and assorted well-wishers, and until Damon had insisted that the telephone be taken from the room, there had been at least ten calls a day from people who wanted to visit him and cheer him up. He had refused to pick up the phone and Sheila had blocked everyone, except Oliver and Manfred Weinstein. Weinstein had come to visit him, walking heavily and using a cane, the first day he was released from the hospital, with his leg more or less healed. He had lost quite a bit of weight and his cheeks were not as rosy as they had been, but it was obviously not *his* time to go.

Weinstein was not one to mince words. Looking down at Damon's wasted face, he said, 'Christ, Roger, who shot you?'

'The American Medical Association,' Damon said. 'When're you going to be able to throw away that cane?'

Weinstein grimaced and it reminded Damon of how Weinstein's face had looked when he returned to the bench after he had struck out with the winning run on third when he was seventeen years old. 'I'm not going to steal many bases this season,' Weinstein said. He was going out to California to visit his son, but promised he'd be back as soon as he heard that Damon was getting out of the hospital. He was furious because the New York police department had confiscated his pistol since he only had a license for it in Connecticut. 'Cops,' he said scornfully. 'I'm lucky they didn't put me in jail because I was trying to keep an old friend from being murdered.'

He had talked to Schulter several times, but there was no trace of Zalovsky. The gun had provided no clues. It was Schulter's theory that Zalovsky had been more badly wounded than they had thought and had probably died of his wounds and been quietly buried by the members of whatever family of the Mafia he belonged to. Weinstein thought that he was most likely out of the country, in South America or Sicily or Israel. It was Weinstein's conviction that all organized crime was in the hands of Italians, Cubans or Jews and that Zalovsky, whatever his real name was, had been a mere pawn in a minor extortion racket.

'Get well, old cock,' he said to Damon before he left. 'I want to have something to show for this fucking knee.' But Damon could tell by the expression on his friend's face that Weinstein felt that they would never see each other again.

Oliver pleaded the case of Genevieve Dolger, who twice a week sent huge baskets of flowers to the sick room and who had miraculously given up baking pies and finished a new novel called *Cadenza* while Damon was in the hospital. Her publishers had quadrupled her advance, and Oliver was negotiating with the paperback people and the movies for enormous sums. She insisted, Oliver said, upon seeing Damon at least once to thank him for everything he had done for her. *Before it's too late* – Damon finished the sentence in his head. 'She says she's wildly in love with you,' Oliver said, raising his almost invisible eyebrows incredulously. 'She says you're the only man in her whole life who made her feel really like a woman.'

Damon groaned, but said he'd see her. It was only fair, he thought – he wouldn't be in a private room with day and night nurses caring for him without Genevieve Dolger and there wouldn't be any Dr Zinfandel coming in solicitously every morning at one hundred dollars a visit week after week except for *Threnody* and now *Cadenza*.

'Okay,' he said. 'But tell her only ten minutes. And tell her I'm too frail to hear that she's in love with me.'

But before he had to endure the affection of Genevieve Dolger, Damon had another lady to contend with.

'Your ex-wife, Elaine What's-her-name, called twice yesterday,' Sheila was saying. She had just come from the floor reception desk, where they generously took messages for her and Damon, now that Damon had had the telephone removed from the room. 'She says she just has to see you.'

'Sparman,' Damon said. 'She married a man called Sparman. Divorced a long time ago.'

'What should I tell her?' Sheila had never met Elaine and Damon could tell that she didn't want to meet her now. But he felt that if he was going to die, which seemed like a looming possibility, he owed it to a woman he had once thought he had loved and with whom he had been briefly happy when they both were young, to give her the satisfaction of a last farewell. Besides, with her gambler boy friend and his dubious connections, perhaps she had a clue about who Zalovsky was and what he wanted that she could only tell him in person. And she had always managed to amuse him, in one way or another, sometimes wittingly and sometimes not so wittingly, and he felt he could use a little amusement.

'Tell her I'd love to see her,' Damon said. He could tell that his answer did not please Sheila, but he could not deny his entire past because of a fleeting moment of his wife's displeasure. Sheila started to say something, but at that moment one of the doctors who was on the staff of the specialist for pulmonary diseases came into the room. The doctor was a good-looking young man with an outdoor complexion and beautifully cut and combed long mahogany hair. He came in regularly every day, looked at Damon cursorily from a distance and inevitably said, 'Why don't you get the nurse to wheel you out to the roof terrace where you can get some fresh air?' and left. He, too, charged a hundred dollars a day, although Damon never took his advice, as the benefits of a few gasps of New York smog and gasoline fumes did not seem to him to offer any lasting beneficial effects for his racked lungs.

When Elaine came into the room the following afternoon, he regretted that he had annoyed Sheila by telling her to allow his ex-wife to visit him. She was dressed completely in black and for the first time since they had met, he saw her face absolutely devoid of makeup of any kind. The fact that it improved her appearance was outweighed by the funeral aspect of her widow's weeds and the doleful expression on her face. Sheila had tactfully left the room when the floor nurse came in to announce that a Mrs Sparman was at the desk.

'My poor darling,' Elaine said, and started to bend toward him to kiss his forehead, but he turned his head away roughly. 'I would have come sooner, but I didn't know. We were in Vegas, then down in Nassau, and I just got back to New York two days ago. What a trauma . . .'

'Elaine,' he said, 'you look like a crow in those goddamn clothes. It depresses me. Why don't you go home now and come back some other day in spangles or a bikini or something else a little more cheerful?'

'I didn't want you to think that I was being frivolous,' Elaine said, hurt.

'You *are* frivolous,' he said. 'That's the only thing I still cherish about you.'

'I know about invalids,' Elaine said. 'In their pain they strike out at their nearest and dearest.'

'I am not in pain,' Damon said wearily, 'and you are not my nearest and dearest.'

'I refuse to be offended,' Elaine said with dignity. 'But if this simple little dress displeases you, I left my coat outside and it's not black.'

'Go put it on,' Damon said. Dying would be easy, he thought, if they only left you alone.

'I'll be back in a jiffy.' Elaine stalked out of the room, the well-rounded calves of her legs gleaming, falsely youthful, in her sheer black stockings.

When she came back, she was wearing a bright orange coat with a red fox collar.

There is no end to the indignities a man who is lying in bed must suffer, Damon thought, blinking as a stray beam of sunlight from the one window in the room lit his ex-wife up like a Christmas decoration. 'That better?' she asked.

'Much.'

'You always had a flippant streak in you,' Elaine said. 'I thought maybe, at a moment like this . . .' She left the sentence unfinished.

'Let's not talk about moments like this, if you don't mind, Elaine,' Damon said.

'I prayed for you this morning before coming here,' Elaine said.

'I hope your prayers have mounted to heaven.'

'In St Patrick's,' Elaine said, always one to let people know she understood the importance of a good address.

'You're not even a Catholic,' Damon said.

'I was walking past on Fifth Avenue. Catholics believe in God, too.' Elaine was ecumenical, to say the least. If everybody shared her flexible theocratic opinions, Damon thought, there would be an end to religious wars.

'So they say,' Damon said. 'Now let me ask you a question. In all your travels with your boy friend, did you hear anything about my . . . uh . . . my problem?'

'Freddie asked everywhere. Everyone he could and he knows some big important people on the . . . well . . . on the wrong side of the law, is one way of putting it.' Elaine pursed her wide, fleshy, unrouged lips delicately. 'He got some very funny looks, he told me. It was risky for him, I can tell you, it's not the sort of circles where it's safe to ask too many questions, but Freddie would walk through fire for me . . .'

'Did he hear anything?' Damon said impatiently.

'Nothing,' Elaine said.

'Okay,' Damon lay back and closed his eyes. 'I'm awfully tired, Elaine. It was sweet of you to visit me, but I think I'd like to try to take a nap now.'

'Roger . . .' Elaine hesitated. She was not ordinarily a hesitant woman. 'There's one favor . . .'

'What is it?' He kept his eyes closed. He didn't want to look at the orange coat anymore.

'Remember that photograph I gave you on your birthday, the first year we were married . . . ?'

'The *only* year we were married.' He still didn't open his eyes.

'The one of us together on the beach, that I had blown up and put in that silver frame? You remember?'

'I remember.'

'You were so young and handsome then. It has so many associations. I long to have it. Do you think you can find it?'

'I'll leave it to you in my will.'

Elaine sobbed and he opened his eyes to see if she was faking or not. Tears were rolling down the pale cheeks. She wasn't faking. 'That isn't what I meant,' she said reproachfully, between sobs.

'You'll get it, dear,' he said and reached out gently and patted her hand.

'Please get well, Roger,' she said, her voice tremulous. 'Even if you never want to see me again, I want to know that you're around and happy.'

'I'll try,' Damon said softly. Then he lay back and closed his eyes. When he opened them a few moments later, Elaine was gone.

When the nurse came in the next day to announce that there was a Mrs Dolger who was at the reception desk, he told the nurse to bring her in, but added he wanted the nurse to stay in the room all the time that Mrs Dolger was there.

When the authoress who had made his old age, if he was going to have one, secure came in, he had to suppress a gasp of surprise. The dumpy little suburban housewife had vanished and in her place was a svelte, beautifully dressed lady in carefully coiffed tinted hair. She was wearing a handsome green tweed suit that looked as though it came from Paris and carrying a green alligator handbag to match, and she must have lost twenty pounds since he had seen her last. He wondered what torments she was putting her husband and children through.

Her voice, however, had remained the same, modest and

pleading and grateful. 'Oh, Roger,' she said, 'I kept calling every day and they kept saying you were on the critical list.'

'I'm off it now. You look beautiful, Genevieve.'

'I took hold of myself,' she said firmly. 'I dieted and I went to gym classes and I started reading *Vogue*, and I wouldn't allow myself to go to bed at night until I had written at least ten pages. I can't begin to tell you how grateful I am to you and Oliver. He's been a tower of strength on *Cadenza*. Although,' she added hastily, 'there'll never be anyone like you.'

'I'll go over the proofs when you get them,' Damon said, hoping that they would come in late and the editors would resist any changes because they were weeks behind for their publishing date.

'First,' she said, 'you have to get well. That's the important thing. I brought you a little gift.' Dashing tweed suit and alligator handbag and weighing twenty pounds less than when he'd last seen her, she still spoke shyly. She had put a square baker's box down on a table when she came in, and now she took it up and opened it. 'I know how awful hospital food is,' she said, 'so I baked a pie for you myself. It's apple. Do you like apple?' she asked anxiously.

'I love apple.' He didn't tell her that he hadn't been able to get any solid food down in almost two months.

'Do you think we could get a plate and a knife and fork?' Mrs Dolger asked the nurse. 'I'd like to see him eat a piece with my own eyes.'

The nurse looked over at Damon for a sign and Damon nodded. I'll get it down, he thought, if it kills me.

'We're buying a new house out in Amagansett,' Mrs Dolger said. 'Our old house is right on the street and it's terribly noisy, and there's no place I can really call my own where I can work. And I know I'll write better with a view of the ocean. When I get it fixed up, you must come out and visit us, a nice long visit. With your wife, of course.'

'Isn't Amagansett a long way out? For your husband, I mean. With his office in New York.'

'He's retiring at the end of the month. He won't have to commute anymore. He says there's no sense in having a rich wife if you don't know how to use her money.' She giggled girlishly. 'Who would ever have thought I'd be supporting a man in this lifetime?'

The nurse came back with a plate and a knife and fork and Mrs Dolger cut a vee out of the pie. 'I hope it came out all right,' she said worriedly. 'You never can tell with pies. They have a mind of their own.'

The nurse cranked up the back of the bed, and Damon sat up and accepted the plate from Mrs Dolger. 'It looks delicious,' he said, postponing the moment when he would have to put the first morsel in his mouth.

'Anybody can make a pie *look* good,' Mrs Dolger said. 'But with pies it's beauty is as beauty tastes.' She giggled again, appreciating her own cleverness in changing the hackneyed phrase.

Damon took a deep breath and cut the smallest piece possible from the end of the vee. He put it into his mouth gingerly, as though it were steaming hot. He began to chew methodically. He swallowed. It stayed down. And it *was* delicious. Until now the only taste that he could endure had been that of pineapple juice. He cut himself a much larger piece of the pie and ate it with relish. The look on Mrs Dolger's face as she watched him reminded him of the childlike and blissful expressions on the faces of some of his clients when he had caught them reading a rave review of a book of theirs that had just come out.

He finished the slab of pie.

'Bravo,' said the nurse, who had been trying to stuff all kinds of food down his throat for weeks, without success.

In a sudden rush of affection for Genevieve Dolger he said, 'Now I'll have another piece.' He knew it was the wildest bravado and that he was running the risk of throwing everything up after Mrs Dolger left the room, but he felt that he had to prove his gratitude to this dear and devoted woman and that mere words would not suffice.

Mrs Dolger beamed and blushed at the same time at this tribute to her and cut a larger slab of pie and put it on his plate. He ate it with relish and did not throw up.

'Tomorrow, Miss Medford,' he said to the nurse, 'when you weigh me in the morning, I'll bet you I'll be at least two pounds heavier.'

Miss Medford looked skeptical. When she had weighed him that morning, it was still a skeletal one hundred and thirty-eight pounds.

Mrs Dolger left in a flurry of little uncertain movements that did not go with her new hair-do or the smart green tweed suit and alligator bag. 'If there's anything I can do,' she said at the door, 'anything, my darling Roger, just ask me.'

He could tell that she was not just indicating that she would bake him another pie if he requested it and hoped Miss Medford, who was as sharp-eyed as a forward artillery observer, didn't interpret Mrs Dolger's remark as anything more than a generous offer of her services as a baker.

He was also relieved that Sheila had had to go to Burlington that day, as her mother had recovered sufficiently from her stroke to be taken home and had asked Sheila to help her. Sheila felt that her mother's return to health was a sign that the storm of ill fortune that she, her mother and Damon had suffered in the last months was finally abating. If Sheila thought this, Damon was happy for her. As for him, the fact that an old lady who had always disapproved of him was able to speak and get out of bed in distant Vermont was hardly an event that presaged any quick deliverance for himself.

Being able to eat two pieces of apple pie, one after the other, was far more encouraging to him, even though when Miss Medford weighed him the next morning, he still weighed one hundred and thirty-eight pounds.

CHAPTER
TWENTY-TWO

'DOCTOR,' SHEILA was sitting in Zinfandel's office. Across the desk from her Zinfandel was fiddling nervously with a pencil. 'Doctor,' she said, 'there's no way we can get him to eat while he's in this hospital. He ate two pieces of apple pie that a friend brought him a week ago and that's it, except for that miserable powder we mix with water or milk that you ordered.'

'It is life-sustaining,' Zinfandel said. 'It has all the vitamins, proteins, minerals . . .'

'It isn't sustaining *his* life,' Sheila said. 'He doesn't *want* to sustain his life. We're lucky if we can coax him into taking half a glass of the stuff a day. He wants to go home. *That* will sustain his life.'

'I can't take the responsibility . . .'

'I'll take the responsibility,' Sheila said. Her anger, which she kept in check, but which was evident nonetheless, was working for her. 'If necessary,' she said, using the threat that had worked in getting Damon out of the Intensive Care Unit, 'I shall go to his lawyer tomorrow and get a writ ordering you to release him in my care.'

'You're running the risk of killing your husband,' Zinfandel said, but Sheila knew he was beaten.

'I accept that risk,' she said.

'We will have to make a whole series of tests.'

'I'll give you three days to make them in,' Sheila said, discarding all niceties of civilized speech. All pretense was now gone; they were antagonists and what was victory for one of them was abject defeat for the other.

Damon endured the X-rays, the CAT scan and the taking of blood without complaint or any signs of interest. Sheila had not told him of her conversation with Dr Zinfandel, and he was resigned to the fact that he would never get out of the hospital alive. He still could make no sense of the *New York Times* and the only nourishment that did not make him gag was still iced pineapple juice. His mind wandered and when Sheila said that she had heard from Manfred Weinstein from California, he wept and said, incoherently, 'He made one wrong move in his life,' as though the long throw from shortstop had been his, Damon's, fault. He remembered that a woman in a green suit had come into his room and given him a piece of apple pie, but he couldn't remember the woman's name. Miss Medford forced him to get out of bed from time to time to walk with a cane in the corridor, but once he had looked out of the window at the end of the corridor, the walks no longer interested him, and Miss Medford's assurance that he was walking more and more strongly each day seemed the most trivial of information.

He brightened a little when, after two days of X-rays, tests and examinations, Sheila told him that the doctors had given him a provisional clean bill of health.

Out of superstition, Sheila didn't tell him why he had to undergo the series of examinations. To avoid disappointing him, she wanted to wait until the very last moment possible before his liberation to break the news. So it was Miss Medford who was the bearer of the glad things. 'You're in the paper this morning, Mr Damon,' Miss Medford said, when she came in to relieve the night nurse. She waved a copy of the *Daily News*. 'In a column. It's all about a lady who's written a book and your agency has made a deal for her for billions of dollars or something like that.'

'Don't believe anything you read before eight o'clock in the morning,' Damon said. He was still wondering about Dr Zinfandel's frigid behaviour at six A.M., when he had made his daily visit.

'It says you're getting out of the hospital today after your terrible ordeal, the shootout on Fifth Avenue, they call it. They think you were wounded. They don't mention Dr Rogarth.' Miss Medford laughed sourly. She was not an admirer of the doctor. In the few instances that he had come in to see Damon while she was on duty, she had behaved as though she had only that moment been taken out of the deep-freeze compartment of a refrigerator. 'Do you want to read it?'

'No, thank you,' Damon said. 'I'm not partial to fairy tales. How does nonsense like that get into the papers?'

'In every hospital I've ever worked in,' Miss Medford said, 'there's always somebody, a nurse, a doctor, an orderly, a clerk, who knows somebody on the papers – a cousin, a boy friend, somebody who gets them tickets for an opening night in exchange for information . . . Don't think this place is an exception.'

'Has anybody told *you* that I'm leaving today?'

'No,' Miss Medford admitted. 'Not a word.'

'Let me go back to sleep,' Damon said. 'I was having a nice dream about going to a football game with my father.'

It was only when Sheila arrived in the room with some fresh shirts and underwear and got him out of bed and began to dress him that he realized what was happening to him and broke down and wept.

'Oliver's waiting downstairs,' Sheila said, 'with a car he's rented. We're going out to the house at Old Lyme. We can't have you climbing three flights of stairs up to our apartment and neither Oliver nor I can carry you.'

The nurse insisted on putting him in a wheelchair and pushing him to the emergency entrance of the hospital, although Damon protested, because he wanted to walk out of the place on his own two feet and was sure he was strong enough to do so.

It was a mild, sunny spring day and Damon took a deep breath of air as he was wheeled through the door, then slowly and with effort, stood up. He saw Oliver standing next to the rented car, smiling. Damon waved jauntily with the cane that the hospital had given him. Everything was in sharp focus – Oliver, the buds on the trees bordering the courtyard, the shape of his own hand holding the cane.

He felt neither ill nor well, merely vibrantly observant, the bright colors of the outside world making his eyes squint. He heard Miss Medford's low voice behind him giving last-minute instructions to Sheila about the care of the bedsore that was still a gaping hole on his buttock. He took a step by himself, toward where Oliver was standing. Then he saw a man in a blue wind-jacket step out from behind a car parked next to Oliver's. Damon knew who it was, although why he knew was beyond him. The man took two steps toward him. Damon could see his face. It was flabby and round and the color of wet dough, with eyes that looked as though they had been bored into the man's head by a pneumatic drill. The man took something out of his pocket. It was a pistol and he was pointing it at Damon.

At last, Damon thought, crazily relieved, I am going to find out.

A shot rang out. Damon stopped. Somebody screamed. Then the man crumpled to the pavement two feet from where Oliver was standing with the door to the car open.

Schulter appeared from somewhere with a gun in his hand and two other large men, also holding guns.

Damon walked calmly toward where Schulter and the other two men were converging on the body lying on the pavement. Schulter kneeled down, put his ear to the man's chest, then stood up. 'He's dead,' Schulter said. 'For once the goddamn newspapers printed something useful. I had a hunch he'd show.' He beamed with pleasure, like a hunter who had just brought down a giant stag whose impressive horns would make a marvelous trophy to put over a fireplace. 'Do you know him?'

Damon looked down at the dead man, the jacket gleaming with blood. The face was peaceful. Damon had never seen it before. He shook his head. 'It might be anybody,' he said wonderingly to Sheila, who had her arms around him. 'He never delivered his message.'

He sat in the garden in Old Lyme, looking out at the Sound. It was twilight and lights were beginning to glimmer along the shore and the water had turned to dark steel. Inside the house he could hear Sheila humming to herself as she prepared dinner. He looked forward to it hungrily. Aside from breakfast, lunch and dinner Sheila made eggnogs for him at eleven in the morning and at five in the afternoon and before they went to sleep at night in the rustling old house that creaked like a boat in the wind off the water. He had gained ten pounds in two weeks and he walked around the garden without a cane.

Schulter had been to visit there. 'It's the damnedest thing,' Schulter had said. 'There wasn't a scrap of identification on him. Not a license or a credit card or anything. Nobody claimed the body. The gun was an old German P38 that some GI probably brought back from the war. It could have passed through twenty hands by now. That's all we know. Nothing else.' Schulter shook his head wonderingly. 'He just came from nowhere. Off the pavement. Out of the sewer. Nowhere,' he said.

'Nowhere,' Damon said to himself in the twilight. He remembered that he had wanted to be allowed to die in the hospital and had not been fearful when he saw the man with the gun when he had moved out from behind the parked car.

Sheila came out from the kitchen in an apron, carrying two glasses of whiskey and soda, one for him and one for her. He took the glass as Sheila sat down on the chair beside his and they both looked out at the darkening Sound. He reached out for her hand. 'Healer,' he said. 'Giver of life.'

'Don't get sentimental in your old age,' Sheila said. 'I'm just the lady who brings you your whiskey before dinner.'

'What a nice place to be,' Damon said, as they drank together.